REBEL
ACADEMY
WICKEDLY CHARMED BOOK ONE
CRAVE

Nothing is more deadly than secrets…

…and mine could bring this mysterious academy to its knees.

Many have forgotten my name. Magenta: the wicked witch whose dark magic created the Rebel Academy — a magic paranormal prison for supernatural bad boys. But now I'm back and eager to claim the love and life that was stolen from me, even if first I have to survive the start of term.

My enemies trapped me as a ghost on the very cursed grounds that I helped to create. Yet thanks to three deliciously tempting immortals, I've been awakened. One is a beautiful incubus who hungers for pleasure. The next a gorgeous shifter and mage who always senses the truth but enjoys his lies far more. Oh, and who could ever forget Loki's hot trickster son?

Why choose between these sexy delinquents when having them all is such sinful fun?

The immortals risked everything to free me, and I'll stop at nothing to protect them from the elitist princes who rule the reform school. Will my bond with the magical students and new friendships be enough to battle the dangerous rivalries, as well as the cruel professors' schemes?

Or will I be forced back into the darkness…

…and left to fade away?

REBEL ACADEMY
CASTLE
BIRD TURRET
NORTH WING
CROW HALL
WEST WING
EAST WING
REBEL CAFE
BAILEY
HECATE'S STATUE
CONQUEROR GYM
HECATE'S ALTAR
SOUTH WING
GATEWAY
DRAGON SHIFTER STABLES
GROUNDKEEPER'S COTTAGE
RUINS
HECATE'S TREE
DEAD WOOD

BOOKS IN THE REBEL VERSE

<u>REBEL ANGELS - COMPLETE SERIES</u>

COMPLETE SERIES BOX SET: BOOKS 1-5
VAMPIRE HUNTRESS
VAMPIRE PRINCESS
VAMPIRE DEVIL
VAMPIRE MAGE
VAMPIRE GOD
VAMPIRE SECRET: REBELS AND
RENEGADES

<u>REBEL WEREWOLVES - COMPLETE SERIES</u>
ONLY PERFECT OMEGAS
ONLY PRETTY BETAS
ONLY PROTECTOR ALPHAS

<u>**REBEL VAMPIRES - COMPLETE SERIES**</u>

<u>**COMPLETE SERIES BOX SET BOOKS 1-3**</u>
BLOOD DRAGONS
BLOOD SHACKLES
BLOOD RENEGADES
BLOOD GODS

<u>**REBEL: HOUSE OF FAE - COMPLETE**</u>
<u>**HOUSE OF FAE**</u>

<u>**REBEL ACADEMY - WICKEDLY CHARMED**</u>
<u>**COMPLETE SERIES**</u>
CRAVE
CRUSH
CURSE

<u>**AUDIO BOOKS**</u>
<u>**LISTEN HERE...**</u>

CHAPTER ONE

Rebel Academy, Saturday September 14th 1891

MAGENTA

I knelt before Hecate's Tree in the Dead Wood, ghosting my gloved hand across the trunk that pulsed with magic.

"Sweet Hecate, I crave..." *What didn't I crave?* Safety for every student in Rebel Academy, for Robin to love me with the same fierceness that I loved him and not simply as my best friend, and for father to escape mother's cruelty. I clenched my fists. "...*freedom.*"

I breathed hard, waiting for the lightning crack, earthquake rumble, or at least the frogs to stop hopping over my feet with mocking croaks.

Sunlight speared through the branches of the trees. Lily of the valley wrapped the glade in its intoxicating aroma. Butterflies flitted between violets, which held both the deadly power to kill or cure.

Like me, the entire wood hid both sides within it.

I hissed in frustration, as tears smarted my eyes. It wasn't like the goddess Hecate had helped me before. But tonight, I'd be wed to a fae prince who I'd never met. Mother was only using me to make alliances.

I'd never even been kissed. How could I marry a stranger?

I was the single Blessedly Charmed witch to have been born in the last five hundred years. My magic as a baby had reached with its pink roots through the castle's grounds to bond with Hecate's. It'd created the wards that my mother, Henrietta Crow, had then used to establish the Rebel Academy. Perhaps, I didn't deserve *freedom* myself when my magic had led to the imprisonment of wicked supernatural males as Rebels within the academy. Yet I didn't believe the Rebels wicked but rather rejected, abandoned, and broken.

Since I'd turned twenty-one last week, my magic craved to protect, venerate, and love the Rebels who my magic had trapped.

If I wasn't free, how could I do that?

Mother would've been spitting crows' feathers for a week if she'd known that I loved any of the Rebels.

Please, please Hecate free me…

"Aren't your ancient powers mightier than the House of Crows'?" I goaded the goddess. My heart thudded in my chest at my daring. "I belong to you. Take me!"

A rush of wind howled through the glade that was cool even in the warm afternoon. I gasped, as natural magic thrummed through the yew tree, lighting it up like a firework. I could sense its roots reaching through the estate and underneath the academy itself. Then it burst into me with searing strength, and I howled, falling onto my back amongst the foxgloves.

My black velvet dress with its billowing train, which mother had gifted to me for the Enchanted Ball tonight (where I'd first meet my fiancé, Prince Titus), would no doubt be stained.

It appeared that I'd be closer to Cinders than Cinderella at the altar.

My long blond hair broke free of its clips and tumbled around my shoulders. My own magenta magic glittered around me like fairy dust, just as it had since I'd been in the cradle, which is why I'd been announced *Blessed.*

It was father who'd named me *Magenta*, and I'd always been grateful for that.

Certainly, goading a goddess had been foolish. *But had she just rejected me with a witch slap?*

I pulled myself onto my elbows. "Now see here…"

Then I yelped, as Hecate's Tree wrapped her glowing branches around my middle and dragged me struggling into the air. She yanked me above the canopy, slithering her branches down me, until I was dangling by my ankle. I blushed, lifting my dress away from my face.

My crow familiars who were twins, Flair and Echo, flapped around my head. They'd been another *gift* from my mother for the ball and just as unwelcome. Their midnight feathers *thwapped* across my nose, as they *cawed* like they were snickering.

"*Pretty stockings, petticoats, and drawers*," Flair's mocking London voice broke telepathically into my mind.

"*For a witch*," Echo added with a tilt of his head.

As captured vampires (which were in fact Fallen angels), my mother had only transformed them into familiars on my twenty-first birthday. I didn't blame them for gloating now. After all, they'd been forced into becoming my familiars. Although Echo was too gentle natured to derive satisfaction out of my misfortune. When *their* freedom had been stolen because of me, I almost wished that he could enjoy the reversal.

I flushed, squirming harder.

"Kind of you to notice," I wheezed. "Could you be awfully chivalrous and help me to escape?"

Flair settled with a flourish on my boot like it was

a perch. *"Not a fuckity fuck's chance in feathered hell, boss."*

Black cats, chivalry was dead.

Although, if that meant riding on horses and waving a sword around like a big manly prick, pillaging, and boasting about holding doors open for maidens in between slaughtering dragons, then I imagined that was a good thing.

"Excellent view, this. By my blood, you can see all the way over the river Thames to Oxford." Echo's tone became achingly wistful. I hadn't even asked him where he'd lived before his capture, but had he been snatched from the Oxford vampire court? *"If you don't look down, you don't even have to see your scary academy."*

Of course, I looked down.

Mage's balls on a stick... Too high, too high, too...

My pulse thundered in my ears, and I clenched my fists in my bunched dress. The Gothic gray walls of the ancient Rebel Academy, which hid the truth of what lay inside, bulged alarmingly as my vision blurred.

A witch who doesn't cope with heights is like a werewolf who doesn't cope with howling. That was Number 73 in my mother's **Principal's Motto Book**.

I hated mottos with a witchy passion.

When I glanced up, Echo was peering at me. Was that concern in his beady eyes?

"You look pale. As I have Fallen, are you quite well?" He asked, softly.

"I'm hooked like a worm. It's the perfect answer to all my prayers."

"You're up shit's creek all right, and sarcasm is useless as a paddle. Did no one teach your bouncy bosom to be careful what you pray for?" Flair's voice became steely. *"What's freedom for one, is a prison for another poor bastard. Did you wish freedom from your corset, opera, or…?"*

My eyes widened. "True freedom is death."

That was Number 21 in the **Principal's Motto Book.**

I screamed, as the branch slithered around my ankle, loosening. I jolted down a couple of inches.

Had I risked everything to sneak out today only to ask for my own death by mistake…?

Well, Merlin's prick.

My life flashed before my eyes: *cup of tea — embroidery — cup of tea — piano lesson — cup of tea — reading — cup of tea.*

My goodness, that was boring.

I clenched my jaw and forced myself to look up once again at the academy. Inside there, the men — Immortals, Princes, and their whipping boys like Robin — were allowed a magical education at Oxford's secret college where the most dangerous witches from across the world taught those in most need of reform. An education that'd been denied to *me,* even though I was more powerful than all of them combined.

Today, the Rebels would be studying a class in Shifter and Familiar Training. Flair was lucky that I'd missed that. He wouldn't like the methods, which the covens used to break unruly familiars like him.

But I didn't want to break anyone.

"Go on then," I hissed at Hecate, even though my breath was ragged, "drop me."

Two could bluff like a goddess...

Echo flapped his wings, wildly cawing. *"Ignore the witch, Hecate. She's got too much blood rushing to her head and doesn't know—"*

Hecate's Tree let go of me.

I screamed, bouncing through the branches and wincing at each crack to my ribs, shoulders, or hips. In shock, I could feel the bruises blossoming.

Well, I'd make a battered corpse in a ripped dress. *That'd horrify mother.*

I *almost* smiled.

"Oww, son of a mage..." I snatched at the branches as I fell to slow my descent.

The floor of the glade rose like a flowery grave. The bizarre thing about your last thought before you died, I discovered, was that you have no control over it. Mine was: I shall come back as a ghost to haunt Robin, so that he'll have the satisfaction of saying *I told you so.* He'd always wanted to hold a séance to prove that ghosts were real.

Then I closed my eyes.

Only, I didn't hit the hard earth in an explosion of agony but a soft cushion that caressed me in fizzing waves. I carefully opened my eyes. Then I laughed, and euphoria flooded me.

I wasn't going to die...

My Blessed magic reached out of the earth and the plants to catch me on all sides, before lowering me to the ground.

Had Hecate known that my magic would save me?

I sighed, kissing the earth. *Yuck.* I grimaced, smacking my lips. *Why did people do that?* Oh yes, because I hadn't splattered to my agonizing death from a great height like I'd always feared in my nightmares. But still, every inch of my bruised body ached. I groaned, rolling onto my back. My twin familiars fluttered down, landing on my chest.

Flair cocked his head, staring at me far too intently. I squirmed.

"Well, paint me pink and call me a bitch, that was close." Flair blew out a breath in relief. *"One day I'm a free Fallen just minding my own business, and the next I'm transformed into a bird and saddled with a crazy witch, even if she is beautiful."*

"Don't dare a god," I admitted. "I've learned that they won't blink first."

When Echo rubbed his soft head against my chin in comfort, I stilled in surprise. *"She's still <u>our</u> crazy... beautiful... witch,"* he muttered fondly.

I smiled, rubbing my thumb over his feathers.

"Traitor," Flair hissed.

Unexpectedly, the pink around me glowed, before worming out like roots and tangling above my head into brambles that trapped me beneath my magic... *and safe from Hecate's Tree.*

Yet the goddess' tree had always been my refuge. This wood was forbidden to the Rebels, but that'd never stopped Robin and me sneaking between the trees' hushed darkness whenever we could. I'd spent hours swinging from those branches, which had just swung me upside down and then dropped me.

Hecate's Tree was the traitor... or had she been trying to ignite my magic?

Suddenly, I stilled. Something rustled in the branches of the yew tree. My breath caught, and my pulse pounded. Had I been followed?

Keep calm, Magenta, no punishment could be worse than being forced to marry, could it?

I squinted up at the branches of the tree. Then a bird darted overhead with a silvery burst of song like laughter. The robin circled the web of brambles that protected me, pecking at them like they were worms, as they in turn wiggled away from the bird's sharp beak.

I squirmed myself at the strangeness of the sensation.

"Desist, Robin, you're always hungry." I chuckled.

I should've known that Robin would find me here in his bird shifter form. It was our secret meeting place, after all.

With a sweep of my gloves, the magic parted enough for the small bird to dart inside and settle on my stomach. My familiars swiveled their heads towards Robin with menacing intent.

Wait, did crows eat robins?

"I have a gentleman caller," I tried for mother's haughtiness but I'm certain that I failed, since I'd never admitted a caller in my life before, "so take your feathery backsides hence."

Certainly, my etiquette was perfection. Then again, possibly *not* because Robin let out that silvery laugh again, at the same time as the crows *cawed* their outrage and hopped away to the edge of the glade.

I studied the pretty bird who was (with far too deliberate intent), pecking between my tits and up my neck. I sighed. If I imagined it just right, it could be kisses.

My eyes widened. *Why was Robin's beautiful red breast plucked of feathers?*

Robin was the only mage who'd ever been allowed into the academy. He was also a rare and powerful *shimage*: A mage who could also shift into animals. Yet witches had rules, and they included that mages were their enemy. I'd long wondered if I was a failure of a witch, however, because Robin had been my best friend since I was a child, and for years I'd craved him as something more.

More meaning that I believed our immortal souls were knit together for eternity.

Yet how could you tell your best friend that you'd loved him for years as the one who made your heart and magic thrum with such excitement that flowers would burst awake from the soil? Especially when he was a mage and a Rebel. It'd be a crime for me to choose him.

Why couldn't he be the man who I was marrying tonight?

In a spray of golden glitter, Robin transformed back into his human form. My breath caught, and my skin flushed hot and cold.

I always forgot how handsome Robin was. He caged me with his hands on either side of my head. His muscled chest pressed to mine. I could feel the too rapid thud of his heart through his thin whipping boy uniform: black shirt and trousers with a pink **R** embroidered on the pocket. His tumble of red hair veiled me, and his intense emerald eyes caught me in their gaze.

I never wanted him to look away.

It was the most seductive thing in the world to be seen. If you only saw me, then I was yours.

Was it wrong to crave love?

Then Robin grinned cheekily and pecked at my neck again. His gaze softened. I pinked; my skin tingled at his touch, and warmth curled through me.

Robin drew back. "Well, you looked delicious." Then his eyes widened as if he'd realized what he said. A blush crept up his neck to match my own. "If you're not a worm, then are you a bird?"

I blinked. "Did the Princes hit your head even harder than usual?"

Then I winced when I noticed his swollen eye. I didn't care whether I was forced into marriage or not, I'd still find a way to free Robin.

Robin merely lowered himself closer to me. He smelled like sweet wild blackberries. As children, we'd sneak together into these woods and searched out the berries, feeding them to each other. The fruits burst when we'd bitten into them, then the juices had dribbled down, staining our chins.

Hexes and curses, I could feel Robin's hard-on rubbing against me. I imagined that it was only natural because he was lying so close... Yet he'd never clutched me so tightly before, or allowed me to feel his desire in this way.

Robin's expression, however, had become stormy, and he was shivering. *Was he cold?* "Naturally they hit my head but not so hard that I can't see you're using that as a distraction. Funny, you don't appear to have wings."

"Awfully observant of you."

"Yet you just fell from the sky."

Robin had witnessed my near death. His shaking wasn't cold but fear…for me.

Or possibly anger, *whoops*.

Robin's fingers bit into my shoulders, as if he'd lose me as soon as he let go. When he rested his forehead against mine, I understood.

Because tonight, I'd lose him.

"I just…" *How did I explain that I'd prayed to escape my marriage to Titus at the Enchanted Ball?* "…had a little disagreement with Hecate."

Robin snorted. "You know, there aren't many who'd admit so casually to quarrels with a goddess."

"Ah, but then I *am* Blessedly Charmed."

When Robin drew back to look at me, his gaze was troubled. "I'm aware."

Mage's balls, did he already know about my fiancé?

I gazed at Robin's lush lips, wishing that I could simply pull him to me and kiss him, taking the pleasure that I'd dreamed about since I was young. But what if that changed the only friendship I'd ever had, wrecking it? Did Robin deserve me stealing his own first experiences, when I was destined to wed another?

When Robin's strong finger traced my grazed cheek, I jolted with the electric intimacy of his touch. In turn, I reached to cup his swollen eye, wishing that I could kiss away the bruise. If he'd only allow it, my magic *could* vanish his pain. But he never let me risk my mother discovering that I'd healed him.

How many years had he been protecting me now?

Robin's breath gusted against my lips. I breathed in his blackberry scent like life, joy, and every moment of snatched, forbidden freedom from the Bird Turret that'd been my gilded cage: laughing in the branches of Hecate's Tree, swimming naked in the lake at night, or walking the wards at the edges of the estate like we truly could break them and escape.

Why in Hecate's name hadn't I realized that there wouldn't be a way to take flight, even falling from the air as a bird with no wings?

When Robin tumbled to the side, sprawling on his elbow and studying me, I missed the warmth of his touch and the naughty feel of his prick against me.

What he didn't know wouldn't hurt him. I was awfully certain that was one of the Principal's Mottos.

Robin tucked his finger absentmindedly under my pearl choker. I bit back the gasp at his touch against my sensitive skin. "When I was tiny, mama would tell me tales at bedtime of the ghosts that she'd seen that day."

"Are you certain that the Head Coven didn't

commend her with the Traumatizing Your Child for Life Award?" I crossed my legs.

Robin nudged my shoulder. "Surely, they'd already granted it to *your* mother."

I rolled my eyes. "How amusing. Also, most likely."

"It was mama's power to see the dead." Robin traced his finger along each pearl, slipping his finger beneath to caress the skin. *Black cats, he was barely touching me, and I was aflame.* "I once played a game, where I whispered to my tin soldiers as if I was communing with the dead because I wanted *so much* to be like her. She nearly shrieked the place down because she was terrified that I'd inherited her gift and so become a mage."

I smirked. "Sweet irony." When his fingers stopped stroking my choker to touch my cheek, I struggled not to demand that they *get back to work for the love of Hecate.* Instead, I controlled myself with decidedly impressive restraint and asked, "Did you ever inherit it? Have you been hiding…?"

How could I ask if he was *hiding* anything, when I hadn't admitted to him yet that I'd be wed tonight?

Robin huffed. "When do I hide anything from you? If I have the talent, it hasn't shown itself yet. Do you wish to know what shocks me about ghosts?" I leaned closer. "Mama told me that whatever is keeping them here means that they're always craving. *Eternally craving.*"

My stomach flipped. "I don't understand."

His brow furrowed, as he whispered, "I do."

Then he bit his lip, looking away quickly. My magic pulsed above our heads as if in warning, but when I glanced around, the day was quiet.

"Wait for me," Robin breathed.

"Always," I grinned.

In a burst of glitter, Robin transformed into a red squirrel. Before he could escape, I clutched him by his tail and snuggled him like I always wanted to…or as if he was one of my china dolls. He chattered but still relaxed, allowing himself to be petted. He was soft, and his bushy tail wrapped around my arm like ivy, as if he never wanted to let go either. It was only in this form that he ever truly allowed himself to love me.

He looked up at me, rubbing his tufted ears against my hand with a soft *chuk chuk.*

I snickered. "Mr Tailsy has important business."

Robin twisted, before rubbing his large tail over my face, and I spluttered.

My familiars *cawed,* hopping towards Robin with a malicious glint in their eyes.

"*Time to catch the rat,*" Flair taunted.

Flair wasn't jealous, was he?

Robin squeaked and scampered for Hecate's Tree. My magic drew back on instinct to allow him free, and he skittered up the yew's trunk and into its branches.

I threw myself over the crows, before they could take flight after Robin.

"Are you insane?" I hollered. "You're a little squirrel. What could Hecate do to you if she…?"

Don't let him be hurt because of me.

Robin reappeared dragging a book between his puffy cheeks. I blinked.

What in the ever-witching heavens…?

I sat up, and my familiars shot me aggrieved looks, ruffling their feathers, before jumping onto my shoulders and holding on with their scaly feet like I was a statue. I winced, as their claws sank into my skin through the velvet of my dress.

Were all familiars this possessive?

Robin nudged the book with his nose, and it fell into my lap. Then he took a death leap, and I caught him. I stared down into his cute face in shock.

The adorable…risk obsessed…bastard who I loved.

I shook the squirrel who hung between my shaking hands. "You're lucky that you're in Mr Tailsy form right now. Even so, your fluffy behind deserves a spanking for that stunt. What if I hadn't caught you? What if…"

Breathe…in and out…breathe…

Robin transformed into human form on my lap with his legs straddling me.

My familiars flew away to settle amongst the foxgloves.

"*He's dying for want of a fuck,*" Flair grumbled. "*Put both of yourselves out of your misery.*"

"*He does appear painfully hard in those tight trousers.*" Echo tilted his head.

"A thousand apologies." Robin hunched his shoulders. "You know what I'm like. I didn't think…"

When his lips quirked, I tickled his neck where he'd always been weakest to the attack in retaliation, and he chuckled. "What?"

"When I'm in Mr Tailsy form, I'm rather…impulsive. All I could think about was returning to you." He flushed.

I ached to trace the blush down his cheeks, neck, and then open his shirt and see how far down it went but I didn't know if he returned my love. Not with the hunger, desire, need, and *craving* the same as any ghost.

Robin edged back, lifting the book off my lap. When he traced its spine, I was envious, imagining that his finger was touching *me* with such reverence. "I meant to steal a dance with you at the Enchanted Ball, even if I was beaten for it after. I had this whole scene worked out in my head. It would've been grand and romantic and…" He sighed. "As is tradition, I had a gift for you as well. I have no money. I wish that I could buy you the world but…I made this: It's a Your Heart's Desire Book."

Then he ducked his head.

Your Heart's Desire…?

I stared down at the book that he was holding. I could tell that it'd been created out of sheets, which had been ripped out of other books (possibly his ones for classes).

What kind of risks had he taken to make it?

Orphan whipping boys had no possessions. Was that why he'd hidden it in Hecate's Tree, so that the Princes wouldn't find it?

My pulse sped up, and I swallowed with difficulty. Gifts at the ball were traditionally given to those who you intended to court or marry. Was that what Robin meant?

Had he decided to ask me to…*what*?

I gently took the book from him. "Thank you. I could never wish for anything better."

I studied the red feathers that decorated the front of the book. They were beautiful. Then I blanched.

Hold on a witching minute, Robin had plucked his own feathers to be able to make me this gift…?

Would it be a terrible breach of manners if I vomited?

"How could you…?" I whispered.

Robin grasped my fingers between his. "They'll

grow back. Now whenever we're parted, you'll have me with you still. When you're alone, open the book and you'll understand as well."

All right, that sounded obsessive enough that he *did* feel the same as me…*maybe?*

When he stroked my fingers between his over the feathers, his bittersweet robin's song magically sang out. I laughed. Sometimes, I forgot how powerful a mage Robin was.

"I've been bought the finest gifts since I was a baby," I murmured, "but this is the best one that I've ever received. I shall treasure it."

Robin's eyes crinkled, as he smiled. I lived for those smiles: the times that he lost himself in me, forgetting the dangers of the academy.

Like now.

Then the moment passed, and he frowned. "Don't lie to me."

I crossed my arms. "Don't be a mage's prick."

Robin raised his eyebrow. "That's difficult since I have one."

Now it was my turn to flush.

Why couldn't I have him? Why did I have to deny us both?

There was only one certain way to check that he returned my love. The secret code of *glove flirtation* that mother had taught me for when I was finally taken into balls and witch society.

Robin's face scrunched in confusion, as I drew off both my elbow length gloves, before pressing their tips to my lips with deliberate tenderness, never dropping my gaze from his.

Code: *I love you.*

I didn't expect Robin's bark of laughter.

Instantly, my eyes burned with tears, and I tried to roll away from underneath him, but he was too strong. He held me down, and even though I called for my magic, it only fell in caressing strokes around Robin's shoulders.

"Get off me," I hissed.

Robin clutched my hands, holding me still. "Hush," he murmured, "silly, sweetheart."

I stopped struggling, almost stopped breathing at the *sweetheart*.

"But you don't—"

"I love you." Robin gentled his hold on my hands. His crotch rocked against mine, and I moaned. "For so many years now, I've loved you. But you're my best friend, and even that closeness is more than a mage deserves." When I tried to speak and tell me him that he was *wrong* — the other witches thought he was the enemy, but he must realize that I alone didn't — he licked across the seam of my lips, and I was stunned to silence. "You're to marry another. Yes, I'm aware. And still I crave only you because I'm wicked. I know that it's a crime to want you as I do, and yet I can't stop."

"If you're wicked, then so am I," I insisted. His fingers ghosted against the pulse points on my wrists, and I was desperate to feel them across my aching nubs. "I didn't choose to marry a stranger, and you didn't choose to be born a mage. Why should we sacrifice our love?"

"May I kiss you?" His voice was low and desperate. "If I can't marry you, then let me love you. I wish to hold you forever, but if they steal that from us, then let me at least have one moment to remember."

I shuddered, rubbing my nose against Robin's in a way that was familiar but now so changed, just like everything. "I'm not bound to my husband yet. Even Titus can't hex me for a kiss before we've even been introduced, surely…?"

Robin stiffened. "Fae are insufferably possessive snobs, and I shall hate him on principle. But he'll love *you*, I promise."

I could see how hard it was for Robin to say those words, but it deepened my respect for him that he'd forced himself to reassure me. Even now, he was trying to protect me.

My lips fizzed with magenta magic. I gasped, as it jumped across to Robin's mouth, pulling him into a kiss that was intoxicating in its desperation and savagery.

My first kiss was everything that I'd dreamed, and yet *witching heavens,* so many times better.

I sucked on Robin's lower lip, and he nibbled on mine in retaliation. Then his tongue twined with mine, and I was lost in the sensation of my first kiss, which tasted sweetly of berries and bubbling magic. I arched, as my eyes widened, and all of a sudden, my magic reached out, until I could sense *everything*: the roots of the trees, the birds in the sky, and the pink trails of every student within the academy like their magical signature written behind them.

I'd been awakened.

"Oh, what a delightful discovery." Unexpectedly, mother's voice rang through the glade, and I jolted in shock. Robin didn't pull away from the kiss, however, instead he held onto me more tightly. "I apologize, am I interrupting? I mean, my daughter is only marrying a prince tonight, but if a worthless mage believes that he may touch her, then who am I to tell him that a wretched creature like him has no such right?"

A single tear slipped down my cheek.

Worthless...wretched?

I knew that Robin had been called such words as soon as his magic had come in and his witch family had realized that their son was magical, but after the beauty of what Robin and I had shared, I *hated* that mother would use such words like blades.

My mother, Henrietta, was a dark shadow at the

corner of the glade like Hecate (or my magic) refused to welcome her in. Flair and Echo *cawed* raucously, flapping their wings.

At last, Robin pulled back but continued to peck feather-light kisses onto my lips between each word. "I shall always love you. Please, don't forget me."

"Forget you?" *Hocus Pocus, how could I ever forget him?* "Why would I…?"

"Ah, I know who I am to say that the vile mage has no such right: I'm the principal of Rebel Academy, Head of the House of Crows, and *your bloody mother*," Henrietta snarled. "The mage shall pay for this crime, and Magenta, you'll learn what happens when you choose the path of the wicked over the blessed."

My breathing became ragged, and I clutched Robin. "You're wrong. I'm only choosing the man who I love over a prince who's a stranger."

Then I screamed, as crows' feathers, which flamed like I was trapped inside a blazing black bonfire, veiled the glade in Henrietta's magic, transporting all of us back to the confines of the Rebel Academy and judgment.

CHAPTER TWO

Rebel Academy, Saturday September 14th 1891

MAGENTA

When the fire from the blazing crows' feathers died down, I choked on the stinking smoke, which stung my eyes. My familiars *cawed* like they were also struggling for breath. Robin hadn't made a sound, however, and I focused on him in sudden terror.

Had Henrietta punished him even in the journey back to the Rebel Academy's castle?

Robin was merely studying me with soft sadness, however, like he needed to memorize every detail because he'd never see me again.

What did he know that I didn't?

Cauldrons and cobwebs, did he imagine that after we'd shared our love, I could leave it at one kiss?

I raised my shaky hand to smooth down Robin's hair, as if looking presentable would save him. When I glanced around for my gloves, Echo tossed my right one to me from one side of the portrait gallery, and Flair threw me the left from the other. Golden light flooded through the arched window in the West Wing, heating my cheeks.

My chest ached, as I glanced at the Your Heart's Desire book, which Robin had made for me. I longed to grab it and hold it tight. But I dared not draw attention to his gift, in case mother confiscated it.

Just like she was taking Robin from me.

With deliberate care, I kissed the tips of my gloves — *I love you* — before I dragged them on, imprisoning my fingers again. Robin's troubled look lifted, as he smiled.

When Robin's lips grazed mine, he tasted of blackberries. "Always."

Henrietta stared down at me imperiously. She was already dressed in her ball gown, which was a confection of black lace; feathers fluttered around her with a wide skirt and a high neck like she was part crow. Her blonde hair was pinned in perfect coils on her head that shamed the loose tumble of my own, beneath a hat of woven robin skins.

"*Let's battle this ugly, feathered fuck, boss, and make her regret ever taking on Magenta and her familiars.*" Flair hopped menacingly towards Henrietta.

"*Bones and blood, I shan't let this phony bird harm you,*" Echo added.

"I can hear you," Henrietta said coolly, "since I'm the one who transformed you. I'm no false bird, rather (at the risk of repeating myself), *I'm the Principal.* Clearly, I need to sign you up to Familiar Training. You have the most appalling language and manners, although your loyalty to my daughter is encouraging."

The familiars hesitated.

"*Thank you…?*" Echo ventured.

"Don't forget," Robin whispered, low and urgent.

All of a sudden, Henrietta snatched Robin by his hair, dragging him away from me.

"*Please, no…*" I begged, but Henrietta burst a wall of flame down the corridor, separating Robin from me.

My magic sparkled across the fire, but I hissed at the searing pain that scorched through me to the bone at the touch.

"Hold your peace," Henrietta snapped. "Haven't I always taught you that to be Blessed is to hold responsibility? Do you forget all duty to your House and the Oxford covens?"

How could I forget? I'd been locked in the Bird

Turret and taught nothing else for twenty-one years. All I'd wanted was one moment with Robin, before I was married. But had that been despicably selfish? Had I condemned him through my craving for his love?

Would my weakness lead to his destruction?

When Henrietta's hand tightened in Robin's hair, and he yelped, I winced.

"Then let me take responsibility." I pushed myself to my feet, before straightening my shoulders. "*I* chose to kiss Robin. You make the point with eloquence. *I'm* the Principal's daughter. As a mage, sentenced Rebel, and whipping boy, he had no choice but to…"

"Allow his lips to be forced open…?" Henrietta laughed, but I'd never seen such darkness dancing in her eyes, or perhaps, it'd always been there but simply not directed at *me* before. "You're no liar, daughter, and I'm no fool."

She waved her hand over the gallery's wall, and I gasped. High up, a portrait materialized…*of me.*

It was an identical copy of how I looked right now as if I'd been caught in amber: long hair flowing around my shoulders, velvet dress with tulle like cobwebs, and a black pearl choker necklace.

Instantly, my hand raised to my own neck at the ghost memory of Robin's touch. I hungered to feel

Robin again, even in the innocent way that he'd hold my hand when the summer storms would come. Yet I shivered at the sensation flowing through my magic that I'd never be able to hold his hand again. I swallowed a sob with difficulty. I hated to give in to mother, but there was no way out of the academy. Hecate had been my last hope, and if she'd sided with the covens on my marriage, then I'd be wed to Titus. If I could save Robin first, then any sacrifice was worth it.

I clenched my hands at my sides. "If you don't punish Robin, then I shall marry the prince with good grace tonight."

I couldn't meet Robin's eye. I didn't know how I kept standing, when I was shattered inside.

I didn't expect the way that Henrietta flared the fire higher. "Do you think that after your display in the Dead Wood, I'd give you any other choice?" She yanked Robin closer to the portrait by his hair, and he gritted his teeth. "Now, what do you see?"

"A beautiful, powerful, and kind *woman* who I love," Robin whispered.

I couldn't help the smile, even through the tears that now streaked my cheeks. How long had I been desperate to hear those words? How long had I thought *beautiful, powerful, and kind* about *him*?

Henrietta's nostrils flared like he'd described me

as a *vile and infernal whore* (knowing Flair had done wonders for my vocabulary).

"What you see," Henrietta repeated with the faked patience of the principal of an academy for bad boys, "is my Blessedly Charmed daughter who is too good to have her *feet* kissed by an orphaned mage such as you." I bristled, shooting a glance at Robin and hoping he understood *on all the witching stars that wasn't true*. But he still had his face pressed to my portrait, as his eyes glistened with tears. He gazed at the false me with an adoration that made me shudder because it was like he'd already lost the real...*living*...me. "Tonight, she'll become a princess. Do you think you'll deserve to be in her company then?" *Be silent, be silent, be silent...* "Why, I ask, did you ever imagine that you could compete with the prince who's patron to the entire academy? By his generosity—"

"By Titus' money, the Princes wallow in luxury, whilst the Immortals and whipping boys starve and suffer," Robin growled. My eyes widened. I'd never heard *anyone* talk back to Henrietta before. By the way that she gaped at him, letting out a choked sound, neither had she. *It was magnificent.* "Now, Titus' bribery has even won him your own daughter's hand. Tell me, Principal Crow, how much does a Blessed witch cost nowadays?"

Henrietta shrieked, curling her hand from Robin's

hair to the scruff of his neck and tightening until he yelped. "Shall I teach you what *your* kiss cost?"

I shivered at the resigned melancholy to Robin's voice, even though it was also threaded with a steely determination, "I already know the answer to that, and if the cost was a thousand times higher, then I'd pay it gladly."

My heart hammered in my chest, and all of a sudden, my throat was too tight.

What did he mean?

Henrietta smirked. "Senseless mage, I hardly think a mere caning will be sufficient discipline to train you to be obedient and my daughter to sing small enough for her future husband."

"*Sing small, sing small, sing small,*" Echo mimicked, singing at the top of his tone-deaf lungs.

Henrietta cringed.

"Get on with it." Robin's voice was hard. His eyes blazed. "But do not hide behind the lie of *discipline*. It is you who are wicked, and not your daughter. Horn and hoof, Great Pan, remember what's done today."

For the first time, Henrietta shifted, sniffing. I'd never seen her appear unsettled before. Robin's words had sounded…*almost*…like a curse.

Or a prayer to his god, Pan.

I blanched, filled with the knowledge that if Robin had risked praying to the forbidden god *Pan* in front of Henrietta, then he didn't expect to survive. How long had he known that kissing me would mean his death?

Had he always known?

I couldn't let him die.

I wished that I'd allowed myself to be the same as other young witches, even though I'd only ever met the professors here at the academy. Mother told me that they'd have been dizzy with excitement for their first ball, and twice as excited to be courted by a prince. Only Robin and father had ever understood that I dreamed of actual excitement, relishing adventures in the grounds and learning to fight with my magic. I was my *own* Prince Charming. But mother didn't *see* me, unlike Robin.

Flair and Echo flew to settle on my shoulders. Their weight was reassuring, steadying my magic. I thrust my hands against the flames but then howled as my gloves burned.

My whole body trembled, shutting down. But still, I wouldn't move back from the wall of flames.

"Stop it! Please, for me..." Robin's anguished pleading reached through my agonized haze.

I fell back, landing on my behind. Flair and Echo flapped around me in agitation, and I cradled my scorched hands to my chest. When I looked up, I realized that Robin was silently crying and not for himself...*for me.*

"What in the name of Pan's balls is going on?" My father's voice rang through the corridor, along with the *click clack* of his boots.

When I glanced up through vision that was blurred with tears, I'd never been so glad to see him. Father, Bryon Crow, was handsome in his outfit for the ball: a glossy peacock green dress coat and waistcoat with gold buttons. He looked like he was about to fight a war.

Bryon's ice-blue eyes matched mine, and when he crouched down to catch my hands between his own, before glancing over at Robin, I knew that he understood the situation without me saying a word. He always did. Byron had raised me in the Bird Turret; I'd wondered if he was as trapped there as me.

Byron's gaze caught Robin's for a long moment as if they were sharing a secret code, before Byron paled and looked away. Then he squeezed my hands between his.

"Calm, Magenta," he murmured, although I could tell that he decidedly wasn't by the way that his heel tapped on the floor.

It was his *tell,* just like his fingers would always tighten on my shoulder when mother bothered to inspect my lessons in the Bird Turret. Yet it hadn't been me who'd suffered for my shortcomings. It'd always been father.

"See how calm you are when you're a eunuch and

my beak is decorated with two pretty new baubles." Flair narrowed his eyes.

I winced, and father looked at me questioningly.

I bit my lip. "Papa, I know it's not your place…but if someone's to be punished, at least allow it to be me."

Flair shifted on my shoulder. *"Robin looks like his blood would taste so sweet I'd vomit, but I know you love him boss, so…"*

"Save him," Echo begged.

Byron's mouth tightened, before he leaned closer and whispered into my ear, "Let me deal with this."

When Byron stood and strode to the fire, I hoped that Henrietta would allow it to die down. Then I'd have been able to break through. I trusted Byron, but this was still my problem. Instead, she let it waver, and Byron marched through the flames without them singing him.

I hissed in frustration, before gasping at the crisp *smack*, as Henrietta slapped Byron across the face. He didn't even move his head, as the crimson hand print formed, like he'd been expecting it.

"Deal with?" Henrietta mocked. "I'm sorry, does it hurt? To be reminded of the true *place* of non-magical men? I admit that the fault lies with me as well. I've been so busy with the Academy Project that perhaps, I've been remiss at my Husband Management. In turn, you've spoiled our daughter and her toy."

Byron met Robin's wide eyes, as Henrietta pressed him against the wall by the neck.

Byron's lips quirked. "Perhaps, I have. Yet she's never been anything but good."

Henrietta sniffed. "Your weakness has led to her corruption, where she believes that pleasure and lust are no longer vices."

"Dearest, they're both young." Byron tipped up Henrietta's chin. "Were we not once as they are?"

"Watch what you say, or I'll wash out your mouth with soap," Henrietta hissed. *Yet had her expression gentled?* She glanced at me. "You must put away these childish fancies and face the real world. I should never have allowed you to live in your daydreams and fairy tales for so long. Your father shielded you from witch tradition and law, which I learned from the cradle. He imagined that it'd grant you a freedom of sorts. But it would've been better if I'd taken the whip to him, until he dropped the foolish notion."

I struggled to my feet.

Byron had fought for a childhood with such freedom for me, yet all I'd ever considered was my imprisonment. I'd been jealous of the beautiful boys of the academy.

Yet I'd been so woefully wrong. My guts roiled with guilt.

I shook with fear for Byron, who'd stiffened at the mention of *the whip.*

"I shall not allow you to touch papa." I didn't recognize my voice: it was dangerous and low.

Henrietta's eyes gleamed. "See! Why do you shudder at a simple whipping? Men are eager to be taught how to please their wives. It's how witches have long created happy marriages."

"I'm certain that Prince Titus will be *eager* for such *lessons,*" Robin scoffed. "Do you truly imagine that by marrying him into your House, you'll control him through your daughter?" Robin's gaze shot to mine; it ached with such flayed desperation that I stepped closer to the wavering heat of the flames, as my magic sparked out like it could touch him.

"*Silence,*" Byron commanded with more harshness than I'd ever heard him address Robin, "it's not your *place*, remember?"

"Oh, but don't you find it sweet, husband?" I stiffened at Henrietta's affected amusement, as her thumb brushed over the pulse point on Robin's neck. Was it wicked of me to wish to burn *her* hands for touching him like that? "The infatuated mage wishes to remain with my daughter. Am I right?"

The question was gentle. *Yet it was a trap.* By Byron's indrawn breath, I knew that he'd realized it too.

Yet Robin had already answered, "Always."

Robin's gaze didn't leave mine, and his lips curled into a smile. At the same time, a single tear traced down from the corner of his eye, as if he knew what would come next.

Hexes and curses, he knew what Henrietta was about to do to him.

My scream was like a feral animal's, but it was too late.

"Wish granted," Henrietta whispered with the satisfaction of having caught Robin within her claws.

The wall beneath my portrait opened, and Robin fell into the gaping darkness behind. Bryon grabbed for his arm, but Henrietta slammed Bryon back. My burst of magenta magic sprayed out, touching the tips of Robin's grasping fingers. I wailed, as my gaze locked one last time with his frightened one like just for a moment, he thought that I could save him.

Then the gallery wall sealed.

No, no, no...

There was nothing but silence in the corridor, apart from my sobbing, and Byron's harsh breathing.

"Let him out." I was numb. I couldn't feel my body or even my burned fingers anymore. The way that Robin had fallen, his terrified eyes, and my magic curling around him replayed in my mind. *Was my magic all that he had now in the dark?* I craved to see Robin one more time. "In the name of Hecate, if you don't let him out, then every Blessing that my magic bestows upon this academy, I shall turn into a curse."

"*Your witchy backside is about to get spanked, bitch.*" Flair's eyes glittered.

Henrietta's smug expression fell, breaking into sudden fear. She looked at me like she'd never seen me before. I thought it was perfectly obvious that she hadn't.

"You know the power of both our daughter's magic *and his*. Why would you risk something like this? Free the boy," Byron urged, clutching his wife's sleeve.

Regaining her composure, Henrietta batted him away. "Do I need to cast a Lips Sewn Shut spell to ensure your silence?"

"When did you grow so cold and heartless?" Byron stared at Henrietta, and she shifted uncomfortably.

"Even were I to reconsider…" Henrietta cast a nervous glance at me. My magic was vibrating in a haze; I couldn't control it. "This spell cannot be undone. It's an ancient punishment for prisoners caught in our war with the mages: to be walled up alive in the walls of this castle. Once they're trapped, there's no way to remove them alive."

"Then there's no way to stop my curse." I didn't recognize my own voice, which resonated with an ancient power that was drawn from grief, nature, and my Blessed magic. Only, was if even *Blessed* anymore…?

Robin was gone because I'd dared to love a mage for the sake of pleasure and lust. There was a hollowness in my chest, and the whole world appeared to have slowed. My cheeks were wet, but I didn't notice my tears. What did freedom matter if Robin was lost?

How long would he have to suffer alone in the dark before he…?

Cold flooded through me. My magic sparked to twinkling pink snow-flakes. I'd never be warm again.

Why was the corridor darkening? I stared outside the arched windows at the snow clouds gathering over the summer day.

"In the name of Hecate, stop this madness." Henrietta shivered, vanishing the flames.

But I couldn't. My magic had twisted with loss. Its roots spread throughout the entire academy, and now it *raged.*

When Byron ripped the peacock amulet from his throat, which he'd always worn, dashing it to the floor, I didn't understand his pained gasp or the way that Henrietta cradled him with sudden tenderness.

"What have you done?" She murmured.

"What I should've had the courage to do long before." Byron pressed his hand to the wall where Robin had been walled up, before he chanted the invocation, "By the branches of the tree, save your children, blessed be."

I held my breath, hoping (*please, please, Hecate*),

that Robin would burst free. After a long moment, however, nothing happened. Except, Bryon collapsed, held up only by the circle of Henrietta's arms like whatever he'd tried had taken all his energy.

As a non-magical man, how had he even been able to attempt magic?

Then in a wave of certainty, I knew: Robin would die, and I'd be trapped forever.

I howled, levitating off the floor in a cloud of frozen magic. Flair and Echo flew off my shoulders to flank me. The windows blasted out under the pressure of the snowstorm that now raged outside, *cursing* the Rebel Academy. Shards of glass nicked me, slicing into my skin and destroying what would once have been my wedding dress and now was the dress that I wore to mourn Robin, but I barely felt them or anything but a consuming coldness.

Henrietta's gaze met mine; was she truly terrified of *me*? "I was wrong. All these years, I was fooled by my husband that you were Blessedly Charmed, but instead, you're *Wickedly* Charmed."

It should've hurt. When you're frozen to ice, however, nothing can hurt you any longer.

Even a hollow victory was still a victory. *I'd take it.*

"I wish that I'd known earlier." My smile was sharp enough to slice. "I would've done less embroidery and had far more *fun*."

Then I flew out of the broken window with my familiars at my shoulders, as my soul lay just as shattered as the glass, out into the dark storm. The wind screamed like the grief inside my head, but it also blew at my back. I didn't command it because you don't command nature: you either worked with or against it. Below me, the lake was a frozen teardrop and the Dead Wood was shrouded in white. I dived down, landing in front of Hecate's Tree.

Flair and Echo perched on a fallen log.

I stood, tall and proud, in a glade that was now covered in snow drops, rather than sweet-scented lily of the valley because summer had turned to winter. I'd always felt closest to Robin here, but now I thawed, aching because his absence...*death*...hit me for the first time with all its reality.

He. Would. Never. Be. Here. Again.

I dropped to my knees, hugging the frozen trunk with my arms, resting my forehead against it. I enjoyed the way that it scratched because then I *felt* something. He'd never swing in these branches with me, shift into his squirrel or bird forms when he was at his freest, or...*kiss me.*

Finally, I wept.

"Hecate, hear me!" I pleaded. "I regret that I asked for my own freedom. I pray now for the freedom of *all* the Rebels here in the academy." The tree didn't pulse with magic; the branches didn't shift. In desperation, I remembered my father's invocation, which had sent a shiver through me. "By the branches of the tree, save your children, blessed be."

"You should be praying to save yourself." Henrietta's hard voice struck me like a whip.

Exhausted, I wrapped my hands more tightly around the tree and didn't turn around. The immense magical burst that had brought me here had burned me out like a firework. I could barely move my head.

Flair and Echo *cawed* furiously, flying to rest on my legs like protectors.

"I did once," I rasped, worn out. "It cost me the most precious thing that I craved more than life. Freedom should never be for one person alone."

"A fine sentiment." Henrietta was closer now. I shuddered as I sensed her just behind me; her hand hovered over my head like she was holding herself back from stroking my hair as she would when I was a child. "But awfully naïve for a witch. I've failed you, and for that there are not enough apologies under the heavens. But the House of Crows relied on having a daughter who was Blessed, and you're now *Wickedly* Charmed." When her fingers finally carded through my hair, I flinched. "You shame me and every Oxford Coven. Your crimes are multiple and monstrous: loving a mage, being Wickedly Charmed, and cursing my academy."

"I'm glad that at last I excel at something." I closed my eyes.

"*You shame <u>yourself</u>. I know monsters, and between you and our witch, you're the one who wears robin skins.*" Echo hopped up and down agitatedly.

Henrietta lifted her fingers from my hair one by one like a goodbye. Then she stepped back. I listened to the rustle, as she marched to the side of the glade.

I sighed. *Was she leaving me in peace?*

"Those crimes are punishable by death." Her voice was softer and suffused by sadness. I startled, and my eyes snapped open. *Did she truly mean…?* I struggled to stand, but my knees buckled. Flair dragged on my dress, but I was too weak to escape. "The wicked must burn."

Suddenly, a scorching rope of feathers lashed me to Hecate's Tree, catching my familiars and tying them to my shoulders. A sob caught in the back of my throat. My familiars were innocents. They didn't deserve to die for my crimes as well, simply because they were bound to me.

"If you crave your mage with such devotion, then you shall join him. You're not worthy of my House. Burn!" At Henrietta's command, flames burst around the tree.

My dress caught on fire, and I choked on the stinging smoke that stank of dark magic.

"If becoming like you makes me *good*," I howled,

whilst the flames licked my skin, *"then let me be wicked."*

After that, there was nothing but the embrace of Hecate's Tree, the magenta haze of my magic, and agony, as I was burned alive.

CHAPTER THREE

Rebel Academy, Saturday August 31ˢᵗ
PRESENT DAY

MAGENTA

The worst thing about being a ghost after my own mother had burned me at Hecate's Tree was the *eternal craving*: for touch, taste, love, and a truly decent cup of tea.

The second worst thing apart from being unable to give Robin the satisfaction of telling me *I told you so* or freaking him out at a séance by levitating either the table or the medium…? Even Robin hadn't warned me that you could be trapped with *other* ghosts.

Whether Henrietta's sacrificial burning had been taken as a gift by the goddess or Hecate had finally decided to save me (far too late, if you asked me), she'd caught both my familiars and me between life and death within her branches. Yet Flair and Echo had broken free of her hold to fly across to watch over the Rebels and mimic their strange new way of talking and touching, until over the decades I might've become — *just a little* — crazy as well as wicked.

It'd taken more than a century, but now I might once have been the witch who'd cursed Rebel Academy to perpetual winter, yet I'd been long forgotten by the students. Echo swore that I was still legendary with the descendants of the House of Crows who ran the academy. I'd quite shivered with delight, when I'd heard that they burned black candles at the Enchanted Ball each year to ensure their protection and my banishment.

Ah, family.

I giggled, floating higher through the withered branches of the tree, which had died the same night as I had.

The glade had been turned to bones. It was a black ring in the white of the wood. I could hear no song-birds, only the fizzing of my magic, which had rooted after so long. The moon peeked through the shroud of clouds.

I peered over the snow veiled canopy towards the castle. Then a pink feathery bundle crashed into me in the darkness. I caught Echo, snuggling him as tightly as I once had Mr Tailsy. Echo's magenta feathers were sensitive, and he pushed closer into my hand, rambling a series of *clicks*.

As a ghost, Echo had been reborn with my magic pulsing through him. I'd imagined that he'd be insulted to match my sparkles but I caught him preening more often than Byron had, and Robin had always called my father a *peacock*.

Byron had only smirked at that.

At least, I could touch Echo and Flair; ghosts were connected, even if we were divided from the living. Often, that was the *best* thing about being a ghost.

But then, there were other times…

"By my blood, the elf prince has a spine-tingling voice like ice melting in a spring valley." Echo flapped around in my arms, until he rested both wings on my shoulders. *"Why does he only sing in the shower? I reckon that he's shy or has a dark angsty secret."*

"You're bored again, aren't you?"

"Maybe."

I tapped Echo on the beak. "It wasn't gentlemanly of you to peek into the Princes' showers."

Echo snickered. *"I'm no gentleman; I'm Magenta's familiar."* Then he sighed, dreamily. *"The elf sounded sad. You'd have kissed him better."*

I shuddered at the imagined sensation. Echo was…*mildly*…obsessed with the uptight but ethereally beautiful elf prince who sang to himself when he thought that no one was listening.

I was…*mildly*…obsessed with the idea of showers. *Water that magically attacked your body as if it was a waterfall, whilst you stood beneath it naked…? Why would I not be entranced by such a powerful spell?*

I grinned. "I thought that I'd proved how far I'd go *not* to kiss princes."

Echo wriggled out of my hold, hopping onto a branch, before clearing his throat. "*He sang this strange song, "Would You Like to Build a Snowman?". I told him, by my fangs, I'd love to play with you. But he didn't hear me, of course.*"

When Echo launched into the plaintive song at the top of his off-key voice, I grimaced.

Was that a strange elven song? I hadn't known that they were so desperate to make snowmen.

"*You'd do better to offer to suck him off.*" Flair descended out of the cloudy sky, settling next to Echo. Then he pecked his twin on the wing, until he quietened with a grumbling rattle. "*The stick's so far up his arse that I can see it poking out of his pretty sky-blue hair.*"

Echo nodded. "*He does have pretty hair. Although, it's not as pretty as our witch's.*"

Flair rolled his eyes. "*Magenta is an absolutely perfect young ghost witch.*"

I fluttered my lashes. "Why thank you, my sweet familiar."

"*Now let me tell you what I saw. Here's a clue…*" Flair dropped on his back and writhed like he was dying.

Sadly, I knew better.

"Unless Spells, Hexes, and Potions Class went hideously wrong today, I'm assuming that you've been adding to your Wank Count." I raised my eyebrow.

I knew far more about *wanking* than a Victorian witch burned for wicked pleasures ever should. Hold on, maybe I *should* have known about that…? Either way, the Wank Count was a game played between my familiars for the number of students that they caught indulging in self pleasure, and as this was an academy for the bad boys of the supernatural world, it now ran into the thousands.

"*Fuck me, I always thought that the Dark Fae were kinky.*" Flair stilled. "*But the fae prince—*"

"Don't you dare mention *fae*," I snarled.

Suddenly, I was shaking. My dress billowed out into mist like I was fading, even more ghostly than before.

"*Prince Lysander's not his uncle,*" Echo said softly. "*He's not Titus.*"

"*He's still a prick though,*" Flair muttered.

I turned away from them, staring once again at the academy. I ached to return to it.

Last term, an Immortal had arrived: an incubus. His craving for pleasure had been as great as mine. It'd called to my magic, feeding and strengthening it, until at long last, I too had been able to break free of the tree but only to reach him in the Immortal's West Wing, when he'd summoned me.

I craved him now.

"As the bones fall, I heard the Principal and her daughter talking of something... someone... important." Echo hopped closer. *"A new student has been sent here and he's special."*

With an effort, I solidified. *Hello, ankles, my old friends.*

I blew out a breath, as my heart (or what passed for my ghostly memory of one), slowed. I'd had over a century to understand that I wasn't dead, but also that I still felt alive. The effect was horrifying. Perhaps, I'd been the one *cursed?*

"Special?" I asked, welcoming the distraction.

Flair snapped his bill together with a single sharp *snap* of irritation. *"Just because your witchy bitch of a mum transformed our fuckable Fallen backsides into familiars, doesn't mean that we can't read."*

I blinked. "Thank you, I'm sure that your skill will become invaluable when I ask for my next bedtime story. *Oh wait, I'm trapped in a tree.* Well, do continue to list skills that for some inexplicable reason you think I doubt."

"The new student's file was open on the study desk, and I peeked at the first page, boss. His name's Fox, and he arrives tomorrow morning. By the way, you make me shiver with all that sexy sarcasm." Flair chuckled darkly.

"Special means…different," Echo muttered.

Why did he sound so worried? All students were sent to the academy because they'd committed a crime or were too *different* for their own worlds.

What had this new student, Fox, done that made him such a danger?

All of a sudden, my magic pulsed brighter, tugging on me, until I knew — soul deep — burning and desperate, why Fox was both special and differ- ent. He wasn't a danger to the academy—; He was *in* danger.

Hecate, no…

The new student was a *mage*.

Right now, Fox had crossed the wards and was walking alone down the long path through the Dead Woods, which swept through the estate to the castle's gateway.

I knew because I could sense him.

He had no idea what awaited him.

Not safe, not safe, not…

I could feel his heartbeat in time with my own,

taste the fear on his sweet breath, and in turn feed him my own fizzing magic like candyfloss.

I wouldn't let him be alone.

It took me a moment to register Echo *thwapping* his wing against my face.

"*On my blood, you faded.*" Why did Echo sound like he was weeping? "*Don't leave us, please, don't leave.*"

My voice was far steadier, than my ragged breathing, "Candles and cauldrons, I shan't ever abandon you. The new Rebel doesn't arrive tomorrow but tonight. He's born of a witch family and he has magic."

"*Well, shit.*" Flair blinked.

He always had a way with words.

Fox would be the first mage since my lover to be allowed through the wards into the academy. It'd become a rule: Mages were banned.

Why had it been lifted now?

I clenched my jaw. It didn't matter because this time around, I'd keep the mage safe. I didn't know how but I wouldn't allow him to die, alone and in the dark, like Robin. If it took my second death and fading away for good to protect him, then I'd throw myself on the flames this time, I wouldn't need to be bound.

Rebel Academy was mine and so were the Rebels. I might be wicked, but I protected those whose pleasure I could feel beating through me: a mage, an incubus, and a third Immortal whose godly power was just as fierce.

Then I shuddered, as warm pleasure unfurled through me. I was being summoned to the Immortal's West Wing.

Who was I deny such a sensual call?

The lurch, like my magic was being wound on a thread, rushed to my head. I closed my eyes, only to open them again and find myself stuck in the portrait that mother had created of me on the night of the Enchanted Ball. It chilled me to be staring out of painted eyes.

Please don't let me be hung still in the portrait gallery where Robin was walled up…

When I noticed the torch emblem over the archway that proved I was in the West Wing, however, I calmed. The bedroom was plain with an oak wardrobe and three desks that groaned with books. Then my heart sped up again at the sprawl of naked incubus in the center of the vast bed beneath the portrait.

The incubus had pushed back the sheets, but had nested in the satin pillows like a ruby eyed, alabaster skinned emperor. His silky black hair haloed his face, as if he wasn't every sin that the witches had warned me about.

But what was the point of temptation if you couldn't give in to it? *I hungered to devour him.*

I'd never seen Bask — or *Crave* as he'd been rechristened when he'd entered Rebel Academy — stripped bare before. Although, he still wore long pink gloves as was the law for all incubi. With one touch, they could read your deepest and darkest desires to both feed on your pleasure and to control you. A fed incubus was a dangerous creature, and yet, without your pleasure, they'd starve.

Did he desire touch as much as I did?

For a moment, I was distracted by the music that was playing. A woman sang hauntingly about *craving*, as a man rapped (Echo had explained to me that nowadays *talking* counted as music; I called it *lazy*). Echo was entranced by this *popular* music. It certainly had less dreary warbling than opera, and more the erotic sense that the singers were making love to you, as stripped naked as Bask was right now.

I bit my lip. Echo was right: this twenty-first century was electrifying.

Bask lay on his back, staring up at my portrait with an adoring intensity, which made me shiver. Then he trailed one gloved hand down his chest, circling his nipple, before tugging on it more roughly. He bit his plush lip to hold back his moan.

I breathed in deeply; he smelled delicious. If I leaned forward, could I take his lip between mine and swipe a taste of his coco and almond sweetness? *Just one...?*

Bask arched his back, teasing his hand still lower. He skirted his prick, however, which was straining hard against him, instead touching between his thighs. With a sigh, he opened his legs.

His eyes became half-lidded.

Wait, was I about to gain the first point in the Wank Count...?

Then Bask's heel nudged against a huge crocodile plushie. *Witching heavens, the prehistoric-looking toy was ugly.* Blushing, Bask kicked it by the snout under the pillows.

"Nile, did you have to ruin the mood?" Bask's voice was gentle and Irish.

His crimson eyes were framed with longer lashes than I'd ever seen and gleamed with something so broken that I struggled to escape the portrait.

Inch by fizzing inch, my fingers broke free, glowing magenta.

Let me reach him...

"I don't want to be alone," Bask whispered like a confession. Then he stared up at me, as if he knew that I was there or was desperate for me...*needed* me. "It's already the weekend before the start of term. What if I can't protect Slippy from the Princes, the professors, or *himself?*" He sighed. "But then, Slippy thinks that I'm crazy." He darted a glance up at me. "Here's the thing of it, I *know* that you're there." His voice shook with longing. My temples throbbed, but I forced myself further out of the painting. Bask was in danger, if he gave his love so easily. It shook me to the bones to see the way that he watched me with such veneration. *Who'd protect him from the predators who'd take advantage of such capacity for love?* "I crave you. Let me please and love you."

Bask ran both his hands up his thighs, letting his thighs splay wide open. His prick throbbed. His chest rose and fell rapidly, as one gloved hand cupped his balls, and the other clasped the base of his prick, before slowly running up its length.

My skin felt too tight, and I flushed. I'd never witnessed a man engaged in pleasuring himself before. Especially when I knew that he was imagining that it was *I* touching him in such intimate places. At each throb of his prick, my magic throbbed more powerfully like it was being fed. Yet even more so was the emotion: Bask never dropped his gaze from mine in the portrait like every moan, as he twisted his hand over his prick or slid his thumb lightly over the slit in its head, was in worship of me.

His pleasure was his sacrifice.

In an academy where the delinquents never knew whether it'd be their last day alive, it transformed the Rebels into reckless, passionate thrill seekers.

Could I harness the energy of all that high emotion and sexual need and desire?

I watched with darkening gaze, as Bask's breathing deepened.

He threw back his head, revealing the snow-white line of his throat. "Pet me," he pleaded.

My magic exploded around my hands that flamed like they were being burned once again. I burst from the portrait, hovering over Bask: his spirit lover. Then I pressed my fizzing lips to his. I couldn't touch him, yet my magic still sparked into him. He groaned, jolting like I was magnifying his pleasure and forcing it back into him, until he was sweating and panting.

His eyes flew wide open. His hands grasped the sheets and his knuckles whitened. Then a pearly stream erupted from his prick, marking his stomach, as he shuddered.

"Voyeur Ghost," he screamed in equal submission and ownership.

Excuse me…what? I blinked.

I'd just given him the best orgasm of his incubus life *and he didn't even know my name…?* I had to admit that *Voyeur Ghost* had a brutal truth to it.

Cherished Ghost? Desired Ghost? Bouncy Bosoms Ghost (that was one of Flair's favorites)? Any of those would've been preferable.

Bask grinned sleepily, stretching. Then he glanced at me almost like he *could* see me. He pushed himself to his knees, before starting to pull off one of his gloves.

I paled. He intended to touch my portrait...? Would he be able to read my desires?

Then Bask howled, falling backwards, as freezing water dowsed him in a waterfall stream. He curled into himself, shivering.

"I'm sorry," he gasped.

I shot back into the portrait. *What in the witching heavens was going on?*

At last, the icy water magically shut off, leaving Bask in a puddle on the soaked bed. His skin was blue, and his breathing too rapid.

I'd heard Henrietta talk of Ice Water Punishments, but I hadn't realized how cruel they were until now. What would they feel like to an incubus whose sense of touch was so many times more intense than a humans', especially after the throes of pleasure?

"I take it that would be *sorry* for your attempt to go skin to skin without permission?" The educated American voice wound from the shadows of the archway; it was sultry and promised chaos and darkness.

I pouted. Why couldn't I sound like that? Believe you and me, I'd attempted to sound more wicked witch and less like the sugar force-feeding nanny who couldn't even afford a broomstick and instead, had to fly by umbrella. Echo was always singing about her: *oh yes, Mary bloody Poppins.*

"A-as you w-wish, Professor B-bacchus," Bask chattered, forcing his shaking hand back into his glove.

"Oh, you didn't try anything so dumb, darling, or I'd have to report you, and that would entail far too many dull consequences. Let's say your punishment was for making predictably wasteful use of your free time." The professor stepped further into the room and waved her hand.

Instantly, Bask and the bed was dry again as if they'd never been dowsed in water. Bask scrambled to cover himself with the sheet, and I'd have shielded him apart from the awfully frustrating fact that I was invisible.

List of Reasons that I Hated Being a Ghost: 92

Bacchus arched her brow with a smirk. "Why, so *modest*."

When Bask flushed, I wished that I could touch but this time so I could slap the smirk off the witch's face. All right, her *beautiful* face. Disgruntled, I couldn't help staring at her.

Flair had told me that Professor Bacchus, the Immortal's Tutor in the West Wing, was the most daring and brilliant witch currently in America, who'd been persuaded to travel to Oxford to teach, but that she was more than a witch: she was an *immortal*.

Bacchus glowed with a fervor that sang wild dances even to me but with such a predatory danger in her purple floor length toga, which was pinned at the shoulder with a moth brooch, that my skin prickled. Her amber necklace glinted in the light from the fire, which flared in warning and her midnight black hair tumbled to her waist. Her eyes were large, hazel, and cat-like. In fact, they matched those of the actual black cat who she hugged to her chest.

I snickered. The most daring American witch was also into witchy role play it appeared, complete with black cat familiar. The cat's fur was so sleek that it gleamed. A pentacle collar clinked around the cat's neck, as it turned its head to study me with narrowed eyes. Sometimes, life called for the unladylike. I gave a shrill whistle, and the cat leaped back, puffing up its fur and sinking its claws into the professor's chest.

I grinned, as Bacchus winced.

Familiars could sometimes sense ghosts, as if the trauma of their death and resurrection from Fallen angel into familiar had granted them the skill. I didn't imagine that it was much compensation for becoming a witch's slave.

With remarkable restraint, Bacchus stroked her familiar, until he retracted his claws. "Calm your furry ass, Pet 9, and stop acting like you've seen a ghost."

I paled. Perhaps, this witch was called *brilliant* with good reason. Yet I hated the way that she only called her familiar by a number. It was witch tradi-tion to remove a Fallen's name once they were caught and transformed into a familiar, but I shuddered at the thought of stealing Echo or Flair's name.

"Why'd you force Pocus into cat form again?" Bask asked with far more steel than I'd been expecting. He knelt up on the bed, clutching the sheet to him like it was a shield. So, her familiar could be transformed back into a Fallen? Had that change occurred for all familiars in the time that I'd been trapped in my tree? "He hates it."

Bacchus' eyes sparked. "It wouldn't be much of a punishment if he *loved* it." Yet I didn't miss the way that she slid her hand in comfort down her familiar's back, or how he pressed into her touch. "With my power, Crave, I can transform him…or you…into anything I want." She cocked her head. "You'd be a true cutie pie as a Pomeranian. The new student could carry you around in his satchel."

Bask leaped off the bed like he'd forgotten that he was naked. He wasn't trembling now. He stalked to the professor with such danger in each step that I was amazed she didn't back up. Instead, she smiled *almost* like she was proud of him.

"What new student?" He demanded.

"You pretend to be a tame cub when honestly you're all wild panther." She grinned, stroking Pocus. "I'm the kind of witch who only plays with wild panthers. Well, I'll make an exception for your new whipping boy. I imagine that he'll be an entertaining addition to the fun and games."

Bask's ruby eyes blazed. "Play me with me as you wish, but I won't hurt a *whipping boy*."

Bacchus paused in her stroking of Pocus, instead leaning to cup Bask's cheek as if she meant to pet him.

Hexes and curses, why did that make me want to transform *her* into something slimy? Possibly a slug with a terrible cold and an existential crisis.

Bask flinched, but held himself stiff, as his professor rubbed her thumb along his sharp cheekbone.

"Don't displease me." At Bacchus' softly worded order, Bask grimaced as if even the suggestion of her *displeasure* had punched him in the gut. To an incubus, giving pleasure fed them but it also hurt them physically and emotionally to *displease*. The succubi had established as clever a mechanism to control the men within their harems as us witches ever had with *our* husbands. "I mean, you were sent here because you couldn't satisfy your bonded Duchess. Do you think she abandoned you without reason?" When Bask whimpered, my magic burned, matching his distress. Just for a moment, Bacchus lifted her head like she could sense it, but then she fixed her gaze once again on Bask. She studied him like she hungered to tear him apart and see how he worked. "You're a rare find:

an incubus who's so flawed that they demand pleasure, as well as giving it. Do you believe that you deserve love?"

Bask bit his lip, refusing to answer.

But he was loved. I shook, yearning with the desperation to show him. Did he think that he was alone? Unloved and abandoned?

My magic built, swirling around me. I could sense Bask's need, driving me higher, until I swooped out of the portrait, howling in my joy.

I was free…

At least, I'd escaped into the Rebel Academy, and I celebrated like any lady would. I did a rude gesture at Bacchus, which Flair had taught me. He was right: flicking someone off *was* satisfying.

I circled Bask, wrapping my arms around him. His eyes widened, and he melted into my touch. He wouldn't ever need to be alone again. *He wasn't unloved.*

Now, Bask's smile at Bacchus was sly and knowing. *He knew that I was there.* He shivered, teasing his fingers down his sides.

Bacchus dropped her hand away from his cheek, unsettled. When she stumbled into the archway, Pocus hissed. "Just go to the courtyard bailey to meet the new arrival. Wait in the shadows and watch, until the principal needs you. Don't screw it up. Our Principal, darling Damelza, has been in a darker mood than the darkness within the Dead Wood, ever since the decision was made about the latest admission." *I was darkness...?* Now that was impolite. "We don't need the pressure this term, when we already have the Rebel Cup. The Princes and their tutor are dangerously competitive over it, especially since the prize this year is freedom for one student."

Bask's breath hitched. "*Freedom?* I don't believe you. It's a trick."

Bacchus arched her brow. "I adore tricks. But I promise you, Crave, this isn't one of mine." Then she tossed her hair. In the instant, she became the ancient immortal that she truly was. "Here in the West Wing, you're mine. I'll help your asses survive, but you have as much chance of *dying* as being freed. Now collect this whipping boy, even though I kind of don't think he'll be with us long. After all, he's a mage, and they're hated, feared, and die young."

At Bask's shocked gasp, I tightened my hold around his waist. I'd follow him into the bailey to welcome the mage and protect him. His arrival was my worst nightmare because it felt like Robin's death repeating itself.

Yet was it truly selfish of me that I tingled with joy and pleasure to be free in the academy at last, adored and strengthened by a lover, and seeing a mage once more?

My magic had cursed the academy. There must be a way for me to use it to bless it.

I felt the desperation (rooted all the way through the warded grounds and into Hecate's Tree), not to allow another mage to suffer. But I was only a ghost. How could I save Fox or was Fate already woven that he'd die?

CHAPTER FOUR

Rebel Academy, Saturday August 31st

FOX

I shivered, stumbling through the castle's gateway into its moon shrouded courtyard bailey. My new academy looked more like a shrine to Hecate, the witches' goddess, than a college. I huffed out a breath, and my guts churned.

For a mage, attending Rebel Academy and discovering a shrine was as bad as striding into your enemy's camp and discovering that they were using models of your dick as target practice.

I cringed. *Wait, what if the witch professors were doing that as well…?*

I swung in a circle, staring up at the pink-and-black striped towers at each corner of the courtyard, until I was dizzy. At least there were no huge striped dicks (yeah, I went there…*huge*) with flaming arrows through them.

But *Pan's blue balls*, this academy was vast.

I'd forgotten how it felt to be surrounded by so much space, since I'd been locked up for over a decade. It was overwhelming, and I was caught between the twin sensations of hurling and huddling beneath the altar beside the gatehouse.

Yeah, Fox, that'd give an outstanding first impression.

Why did the witches of the House of Crows need a castle that could withstand siege warfare? Did they expect a horde of orcs to sweep out of the frozen woods? A flock of enraged harpies? *The Incredible Hulk*? Or was it more about who they were imprisoning *inside* their walls…? This was the Rebel Academy, after all, where professors from across the magical arts reformed the most dangerous supernaturals. It was Oxford University's secret college, founded by witches and hidden from the non-magicals' sight on the bank of the river Thames.

Why did it feel like a prison?

I should've been honored that I'd been granted a place as a Rebel student… *Wait, did I mean honored or terrified…?*

I hunched my shoulders, clutching my suitcase

closer to my chest, and that didn't make me feel *at all* like I was hiding from...*whoever*...was watching me from the shadows.

I'd known that it'd be hard to attend the academy as a mage, even though this was the one place where wars were put aside, but I hadn't thought that I'd be in danger on my first night. Although technically, I hadn't been supposed to arrive until tomorrow morning.

Did that count as being *uninvited* and a hexable offense...?

"How original to hold Hell Week before term even starts." I bit my lip to hide its trembling. I'd expected bullying, but it was still disappointing...okay, *devastating*. "You can just skip the hazing because I'm already known as Lucifer in witches' circles: hot, rebellious, and a devil at chess." *So, I admit it, I have a habit of lying.* "You caught me out. I'm actually a devil at Monopoly: The Covens Edition."

I wrinkled my nose against the stink of garlic that wafted from the altar. Did the House of Crows, who ran the academy, believe that it protected them against vampires? They should've known that the whole garlic myth was as false as a witch's promise.

But then, witches had more centuries-old wars and vendettas against other supernaturals (vampires, werewolves, and mages), than ancient rules and they had a cauldron full of those.

So, it sucked to be a mage born to witches...like me.

I grimaced, rubbing at the silver Blood Amulet that hung around my neck beneath my shirt, searing my skin. The blue diamond set in its center matched my eyes, but a guy couldn't find the romance, when it contained his own mum's blood and was used to bind his shifter powers. The Blood Amulet stopped me from being able to do magic. Yet it couldn't contain my ability to read the truth, which was the magical power of *Confess*.

I could always sense the truth, but telling lies myself was much more fun.

My natural shifter powers hissed inside at the cruelty of being trapped by mum's Blood Magic and at the prickling sensation that pressed down from the crenelated but weirdly colorful towers.

The magic here was ancient and dark. The hairs on the back of my nape rose, as my pulse pounded.

I would've guessed that mum had been lying about this castle being the infamous Rebel Academy, if not for the way that she'd stroked my hair from my forehead and then kissed my cheek, before leaving me outside the ground's wards to make my own way through the woods to the House of Crows.

Kisses didn't lie...unlike me.

Plus, I couldn't miss the **RA** crest that sparkled in neon pink and was surrounded in unfurling tree branches. It sizzled in the air above a giant bronze statue of three Hecates, who were standing back-to-back: one held a torch, another a key, and a third a snake.

Had the academy's principal thought that one creepy goddess wasn't enough, so she'd better clone her?

Every few minutes, the statues startled me by slinking to life and smirking as they swung their hips. Their snake slithered between them, as if to prove that a guy's dick would now be redundant.

I blushed, whilst the goddesses sang the school's motto to the tune of "I Put a Spell on You":

Welcome to the Rebel Academy! Live and Die as Rebels.

I arched my brow. "Let's focus on the living, sweet goddess. I'm rebelling against dying."

I blinked snowflakes off my lashes, shaking them from my wavy white blond hair; the snow melted down my cheeks like tears.

Why did Hecate have to remind me about dying? I'd been hiding from that truth all day.

My eyes burned, but I wouldn't let the tears fall. Just like I wouldn't let myself die in this academy like I was a shameful secret just the same as my dad. I'd been dropped off here straight after his funeral. I yanked at the sleeve of my suit, which was too short, gritting my teeth.

Dad would've *hated* the sea of black at his funeral; he'd always shone like the sun. He'd lit my dark world but now he was gone, and I'd been sent to this witches' world that was cursed to perpetual winter.

Wasn't the cursing a little melodramatic...?

Plus, there was all the snow, when there'd been bright sunshine outside the academy's grounds. I was regretting my final act of defiance in not bringing a coat.

Maybe that was how the Rebels died...their balls froze and dropped off.

Suddenly, a bitter wind blew away my misted breath and then puffed across my own mouth, as if a spirit was whispering words across my lips.

I paled, and my eyes widened.

Was there a ghost in the courtyard with me? Was that who'd been watching me from the shadows?

I spun in a circle. "Dad...?"

My chest ached.

Please, please, please...

The sudden cold nipped me again but this time it stroked down my cheek as if in comfort. A faint smell like yew trees wrapped around me. It was rich and dangerously intoxicating.

It wasn't dad... Not dad, not dad, not...

Why did it feel like losing him for a second time? Yet I still relaxed into the touch, needing its tenderness and the way that it zinged through my ensnared magic like it knew what was inside me and *under-stood*. The ghost could be the Wicked Witch, but I'd still take her kindness after I'd lost my dad, family, and home.

A warm sensation far back in my mind tugged at me like *she* was my home.

So, there was some spook with soft breath haunting this castle prison…? So far, she was the best welcoming committee that I'd had.

The Dancing Goddesses and their Performing Snake didn't count.

"Who are you then?" I murmured, straining to make out even an outline. I hurled down my suitcase, wafting my hands through the air in front of me; My fingers tingled with the desperation to *touch*. But I couldn't feel anything.

My eyes pricked with tears again, until that same cool breath whispered across my ear. I jumped and then laughed. My joy echoed through the bailey, and all three of Hecates' statues *tutted*.

Witching heavens, maybe I wouldn't be alone here, even if I was a mage.

I bounced on the balls of my feet in excitement. "I'm Fox of the House of Jewels. You've probably heard of me: lover, legend, and liar." The puff of air against my neck was definitely a laugh. My lips curled into a smile. "Laughing at me already? So, you *have* heard of me?"

When the smell of yew trees faded along with the icy breath, I booted the cobbles, rubbing at my neck.

Why did she have to fade away?

The Rebel Ghost had made me feel safer than I had in a long time, and if she was another student here, then I wanted her back.

I prowled to the altar, which was black with crows' feathers and charred birds' skulls. My suit was too tight and pulled across my chest, as well as rubbing at my dick and balls. Mum still saw me as the boy who she'd locked away for having magic. She didn't realize that I'd turned into a man.

Oh, and a fox, cat, and hedgehog with serious attitude.

My two powers were to shift into animals and to tell the truth behind people's lies. Both were about masks. Although, I'm what dad had always called a *pathological liar* with his secret smile like he understood that it was the only way I could protect myself.

I wished that I'd known to lie when my magic had come in because lies are the only thing more powerful than magic.

My older sister, Hartley, had been begging mum for a kitten, but we didn't have pets in our coven because everything had to be neat, beautiful, and perfect. As the pretty non-magical son, I'd been mum's prize jewel. She'd already had marriage offers for me when I came of age that would further the power of our House.

Animals risked messing up our House's image. Only, it turned out that my magic was natural like the way that I'd shifted into a white Birman kitten with sparkling blue eyes and a crooked tail (because that was how I rolled) to please my sister.

I'd always wanted to make my family happy as a kid. Ironic, right?

My magic had surged through me with a wild warmth and thrilling freedom. My mind had been liberated from lies and the falseness of polite words, leaving behind simply *instinct*.

The instinct in my kitten form for naps, mice, and feathery things to chase.

I'd snuggled on my back, purring and waiting for the strokes to begin. Instead, there'd been screaming, followed by nails digging into the scruff of my neck and hurling me into my room. After that…

Breathe, come on, breathe.

I forced my ragged breathing to steady, counting to a hundred backward in my head. I hated that these memories could still trigger panic but I hated even more that my first shift had stolen everything from me.

After that, I'd never been allowed to talk to anyone but my dad, cousin Aquilo, and the family werewolf again for thirteen years.

It turned out that shimages — or *shit*mages as I'd thought mum had meant until Aquilo had explained it, whilst giggling — who can transform into animals are both rare and the most hated within the witch world.

Wait, maybe I was right with the shitmage.

If dad hadn't died, I'd still be trapped in the attic. It made me numb with guilt that his death had freed me, even if I'd been sent to the one place that I'd been raised to fear. But to a guy who'd spent his teenage years in an attic, a magical education even by witches on cursed grounds was appealing. I was desperate to be allowed to attend classes, meet the other students, and explore *all this space.*

Rebel Ghost had awoken my magic and breathed a life into me that'd been buried since the day I'd revealed my kitteny side. What was a guy to do when he spent his nights dreaming of being stroked and petted, but his days curled shut up alone?

Okay, he wanked... a lot.

"Hey," I called into the darkness, "I know that I'm early and wasn't meant to be here until the morning but..." *...My mum didn't want to hang around because she's ashamed that her son's a mage...* "...I was so excited to shiver my ass off in your charming reception area that I flew by broomstick." *And that, ladies and gentlemen, is how you work sarcasm.* "I tell a lie: it was a magic carpet. No wait, this swirling portal opened and..."

There was only silence.

The full moon hung heavy and fat in the sky. I fiddled with my blue diamond cuff links, which matched my amulet.

"Do I need to summon the witches? Is this the Principal's desk? Would it work with a spook?" I toyed with the bell on the altar, lining it up out of habit with the oak wreath and gagging on the garlic stench. "Hecate, how about helping me out?" The tiny statue of Hecate at the back narrowed her eyes, before flicking me off. I smothered my grin behind my hand. "Oh, you little rebel."

She smirked, blowing a raspberry.

"The gloves are off, bitch." I snatched the bell, ringing it above my head with a sudden buzz that I hadn't experienced in years. At the same time, I sang "Ding, Dong, the Witch is Dead" loudly enough to make even me wince.

Tiny Hecate howled, dropping to her knees and pressing her hands over her ears.

Everyone's a critic.

Then her eyes flashed with a surge of malicious magic that made me break off my enthusiastic song and shrink back, as she wagged her finger at me and pointed behind the altar.

I dropped the bell and crouched down, peering into the shadows at the cage that'd been built there.

Why on a kitten's crooked tail did an academy

(even a reformatory), need a cage? Unless that was one of the more creative punishments for low grades.

I shrugged; I'd been used to an attic. A cage wasn't so much worse.

Then glowing amber eyes glared out at me, and a rumbling growl blew my hair back from my forehead.

This is your best suit...don't wet your pants, don't wet...

When a werewolf, whose white fur glittered under the moonlight, clacked on golden claws to the front of the cage, I clapped my hands. "Hey, gorgeous, why'd they lock you up here?"

The werewolves' growl cut off in shock, and he blinked at me through eyes that had thicker eyelashes than I'd seen on a wolf. Glow would've been sassing up a storm about them. He was my best friend...okay, *only friend*...okay, *werewolf slave*...in the House of Jewels. I'd received more whippings for *encouraging that beast's sass* than for my own backtalk.

If Hecate thought that a werewolf would scare me, then it just showed how little witches bothered to understand mages.

I smiled at the wolf. What did the shifter look like when it wasn't the full moon? I'd bet that he was beautiful. I had the theory that was why witches had forced the Alphas to sacrifice so many of their Omegas into the witches' *not* so loving care, after they'd defeated them in the Wolf Wars.

The wolf's fur bristled. He bared his fangs and snarled.

Lie: I'm a big bad wolf; fear me.

Truth: I'm an Omega slave to the witches who use me as a guard dog for Hecate's altar. I'm lonely. Do you want to play?

My gaze softened. "Have you ever tried the game Two Truths and One Lie?"

When I wriggled my arm through the bars of the cage, my heart thudded against my ribs. If the wolf tore off my fingers, then I took everything back: I *was* a shitmage.

Instead, the wolf nuzzled against my hand like he was as desperate for touch as me. I stroked his ears, and he whined, arching his back and dipping his head to peek up at me.

"One: I'm a pathological liar. Two: I believe that I must count backward from a hundred every day or I'll never be allowed to shift. Three: my mum told me that my own dad died because of my wickedness."

When had my cheeks become wet?

At the Omega's howl — *he'd picked number three* — I shook my head.

"They were all true; that's the trick. Come on, pathological liar here." I gave a smirk but I knew that I hadn't pulled it off by the soft lick of the Omega's tongue across my palm. *Wow, that reminded me of Glow.* Wolves had a charming licking fetish. "I hope that my wolf's okay," I muttered. "He'd hate it if mum's caged him again."

Or if my sister, Hartley, had put him in a dog bed and pinned ribbons in his curly hair like he was her pet. Hartley had always been desperate to play with Glow when we were kids. My breath hitched, as I hit the Erase Button on that image.

The Omega nudged me hard with his nose, and I winced.

Truth: Did you take an insensitive pill? We're *all* caged.

I caressed the Omega's silky ear, before I murmured low enough that I hoped even the Hecate statues couldn't hear me, "Why should you trust someone like me? But even so, I promise that I'll learn the magic lessons from these witches and then I'll free us all."

The Omega's eyes sparked, as he nodded.

Suddenly, Hecate's bronze snake shot out like a lasso, whipping around my neck. I struggled, as the Omega howled and scrabbled at the bars of his cage. Hecate hauled backward, however, jerking me into the air. My heartbeat raced, whilst I flailed. My lungs burned at the lack of air. Hecate dragged me into her embrace, finally loosening the snake just enough for me to take a desperate breath. Then she trailed her hands up and down my chest. Her sisters writhed in excitement that they'd hooked their wizard prize.

I bit on my lip hard not to beg to be put down, as I dangled from the statue's arms.

"Hey, give my *Voted Sexiest Mage's Ass in England* a chance here. Surely you're not going to kill me, before I've even had a chance to become your Star Pupil…or should it be Model Prisoner…?" I demanded.

The high-pitched desperation in my voice was enough to call *bullshit* without needing my powers of Confess.

Mum had always warned me that if she let me free, I'd die. I hated to prove her right on my first night independent from my family.

The snake noosed my neck even tighter, and I choked.

CHAPTER FIVE

Rebel Academy, Saturday August 31st

FOX

There are times that I own the fact I'm a Rebel, shimage, and bad boy. And others when I regret no longer being the obedient son that I'd once been for my family, before what had come to be known as the *Kitten Incident*. This — being lynched by a snake, whilst being snuggled in the arms of Hecate in a castle that looked like a wedding cake — was one of those *regret* moments.

I missed dad. Yet there was nothing like being strangled to make you hunger for life.

Why had mum dropped me off here if I wasn't

good enough to be one of the students? Why hadn't she simply thrown me to the wolves, which was the traditional punishment for mages? Plus, why hadn't I caught her lie that she'd never meant me to enroll in Rebel Academy, only to be murdered?

White lights danced in front of my eyes. I slumped, as my eyelids fluttered. Sluggishly, I began to count backward from a hundred for one final time…

Pink fires blazed across the bailey. Startled, I blinked back to consciousness.

In a flurry of crow feathers that rained down like tears, a witch appeared in front of the statue, and the Omega whimpered. The witch's obsidian dress swept the snowy ground beneath her feathered coat; I bet that *she* wasn't freezing her balls off and not just because she didn't *have* balls. Her silver blonde hair tumbled to her shoulders, and a feather was tucked behind her ear. Her eyes glimmered in sparkling pink.

Her intense gaze spoke of war, death, and vengeance.

She'd have been beautiful if she hadn't also been Damelza Crow, mum's fanatical best friend, who was Head of this coven.

My dick shriveled at the memory of Damelza shoving me into a corner as a kid for daring to ask if she was part crow. I could cope with a time-out now, however, rather than a hanging.

"Stop playing with the new student, even if he is our snared fox," Damelza chided like Hecate was only roughhousing.

Hecate pouted, before her snake released me, and I gasped in desperate lungful's of air. Then Hecate smirked, letting me go. I yelped, cracking my knees on the cobblestones, as I landed.

It looked like the goddess was as much a rebel as the students.

"Cheers, you're a life-saver," I rasped, rubbing at my neck. My shoulders were tight, and I carded my hand through my unruly hair. It'd been a long time since I'd seen a witch and I couldn't help how I shook. "You know, Hecate and I've eloped. All that was merely our passion that got out of hand. I'm meant to be starting my induction here in the morning, however, so if you could tell me where I can find the Principal, then I'll save my kinky fun with my new wife for a more appropriate time."

Bad mouth…stop talking, stop talking, stop…

"Do you know the one thing that I hate more than werewolves?" Damelza clasped her hands behind her back, eying me like I was a fascinating new hex to be countered.

I cocked my head. "Scarecrows?"

Damelza's lips pinched. "*Mages.*" I wrapped my arms around my middle, as Damelza prowled towards me. "A mage has not stepped foot within these blessed walls for centuries, and the first song that you sing is "Ding Dong the Witch is Dead"…?"

I was having another one of those regret moments.

"In my defense," *here came my first Rebel House Points*, "I didn't sing "The Wizard's Vengeance"."

Damelza blinked at me. "Well, I shall simply have to thank Hecate for small mercies." I grinned: *score*. "In her infinite wisdom, Hecate's already Chosen your Wing of our academy with your *kinky* fun and her snake. I'm in full agreement that you suit the Randoms."

"*Woah*, hold on," I pushed myself shakily to my feet, "I'm not saying that I doubt your psycho Sorting Hat…wait, that's exactly what I'm saying…but *Randoms*…? Like the guy who you chat to but you don't even know his name…?"

Damelza's smile was sharp. "Like the *mage* who you don't bother speaking to because his name doesn't matter." I blanched. When Damelza stroked her hand down the thigh of the Hecate who was holding the keys, Hecate simpered. "Had a miracle happened, and Keys here had Chosen you, then you'd have been with the elites of the academy: The Princes in the North Wing." She nodded at the Hecate who was swinging her torch. "Our third goddess represents the powerful Immortals, who shall be your mentors and patrons in the West Wing."

I bounced on the spot. "I wasn't ready before. Let's try this Choosing again. In a former life, I was an immortal prince who was worshiped by—"

"Stop talking," Damelza's cheek twitched, "or you'll have the shortest student record between arrival and visiting the Principal's study."

I stiffened. "Let me guess…"

"*I'm* the Principal, indeed." Damelza fiddled with the feather behind her ear. "What was that special little song you sang again?"

I froze, for once in my life managing to keep silent.

When a chill wind blew down my neck, I jumped. The scent of the woods cocooned me. Rebel Ghost had returned to protect me from Damelza, and I didn't care if I was lying to myself because the sensation of her magic was electric.

No woman had ever touched me…*anywhere*… before, and technically they weren't even now. But who cared about technicalities when my skin goose bumped and my breath quickened?

Then ice-cold lips feathered tentatively against mine, and I pressed back eagerly. This was my first kiss, and it was with death. Yet Rebel Ghost tasted like *life*.

I gasped, and my dick hardened uncomfortably in my tight pants. I took everything back. This was the best welcoming committee *ever*: a bronze goddess, werewolf, and a kissing spook.

Who had this Rebel once been? Why was she still hanging around kissing mages? And more importantly…*please, Great Pan*…don't let her stop.

Even though I now had no home, she made me believe that she could become mine.

Then Damelza rapped on Hecate's ass — *clang, clang, clang*. Hecate hissed in outrage.

"Sorry to break up your sexy times with yourself," Damelza yawned, "but it's late, I'm bored, and you're creeping me out with all the kissy faces." I flushed and could've sworn that the spook snickered against my neck. "Time to be branded."

"Whatever…wait, *what*?" I scrambled backward, but the Hecate with the torch snatched me by the hair, hauling me closer.

She grabbed my wrist, before swinging the torch around. Pink flames leapt out, searing the back of my hand. I howled, and the Omega howled in sympathy along with me. At last, Hecate let go of my hair, and I huddled on my knees, cradling my branded hand, which throbbed with a curling **R**.

"You couldn't just have marked me as a Rebel with a name tag?" I demanded.

"It's **R** for Random," Damelza replied, primly.

I groaned. "Hex me to death now."

"Sadly, that's against Health and Safety." When

Damelza waved her hand, the night sky lit up with an explosion of fireworks that showered us in a showy display of the **RA** crest, followed by:

Rebel Academy — Blessing the Wicked Since 1870

I *oohed* and *aahed*, before politely clapping. Okay, the *wicked* was rude, but I hadn't seen fireworks since I was a kid. So, if Damelza wanted to call me a *worthless son of a spineless hedgehog* in Catherine wheels, then she could.

Oh, but it'd hurt.

Damelza's cheek twitched again. "I always thought that your mum was exaggerating about you. Well, that was a mistake. Let me make something clear: you're here to learn control of your magic, and in turn, you'll help your patrons master their powers. This academy is dedicated to excellence."

My eyes narrowed. *She wasn't telling me something.* I could feel it vibrating through my power of Confess, but she was clever at omitting the truth, which wasn't the same as lying, no matter what parents teach.

What was the Rebel Academy's secret?

Every time that Damelza had mentioned the academy, **SECRET** had flashed up in neon, along with an edgy blast of "Secret" by The Pierces. I didn't always see the truth in words but sensations, smells, or creepy music chilling my bones.

When I prowled towards Damelza, she backed away in surprise. "Hit me with another one of your motivational sayings. I can't get enough of them."

Damelza puffed up. "They're carved onto my study wall, and you'll have a copy of the Rebel's Mottos with your spell books at the start of term. But if you insist: Persevere even if you're cursed—"

"Gateway," I blurted.

Damelza became ashen, before she flew at me far faster than I'd ever seen anyone move. I yelped, as she rammed me across the courtyard, slamming me into the wall. Then she pinned me with her arm across my throat. My pulse pounded too loudly in my ears.

Then I realized that someone was leaning on the wall next to me with half-lidded eyes. I almost forgot that I was being crushed by a witch because if sin had been brought to life, then this student would've found a way to make him wickedly sexier.

Why were my pants so tight again...?

The student smelled like coco and almonds. My tongue swiped across my lips, craving to dart across *his* and see if they tasted as delicious as he smelled. When he winked, I pinked because his gaze was too knowing.

The black haired, alabaster skinned, ruby eyed...way too burningly beautiful incubus.

He lounged in the academy uniform of pink blazer and tie with black pants, as well as long pink gloves like a sexy hook-up, rather than an Immortal. I could only tell that he was one of my new *patrons* by the **I**, which was embroidered on his blazer in a black crest.

How long had he been standing in the shadows? Since I'd had my first kiss? Snuggled a werewolf? Started a feud with an all-powerful goddess?

Wow, this had been a busy night.

Then Damelza lowered her face so close that her nose was touching mine, and even Rebel Ghost and the Immortal naked together in a giant tub of rocky road ice cream couldn't have distracted me from her. And I *loved* rocky road ice cream. "Who's been talking to you of our secret Gateway?"

I took a deep breath. "Oprah Winfrey, Benedict Cumberbatch, Merlin because that wizard is *such* a gossip…"

The Immortal snorted with what sounded suspiciously like laughter, but Damelza's eyes flashed electric pink.

"Silence, Crave," Damelza hissed, before shaking me. "*Who?*"

Truth: Someone dies of a nasty case of boot to the balls tonight.

I fiddled with my cuff links. "I'm *blessed* with the power of Confess, remember? I'm *dedicated to the excellence* of seeing through your lies."

The Immortal — *Crave* — definitely snickered that time.

Damelza took a careful step away from me. Her pale face scrunched in concern. *Well, wasn't that interesting?* "The first rule of the academy is that students aren't allowed to use their powers on witch professors. We'll all be wearing charms against your magic, which your mother has spent years perfecting."

I shoved my hands in my pockets to hide their shaking. Why would mum have bothered with that unless *she'd always meant to send me here?*

I forced myself to smirk. "I hate to tell you that they're not working."

Damelza brushed her hand across the feather at her ear, which must be the Anti-me Charm. "You weren't expected until the morning. Now try to read this with your power of Confess: my academy has been the pride and joy of the House of Crows for generations. I only agreed to accept a mage like you because your mother offered to fund our dragon polo while you're here."

I gaped at her. No one had ever *asked* me to read them before. What a time to discover that I had performance issues. Especially as I'd felt...*nothing*. There'd been no vibrations, sparks, or bursts of song.

So, *had* it been the truth? Did that mean mum had bribed (even I wasn't going to sugar-coat that one with a lie about *donations*), my way into the academy? The House of Jewels was known for buying its way into power. My hand in marriage had been meant to be just such a bribe.

Weirdly, I no longer felt guilty about that.

I rubbed my fingers over the brand like I could erase it. Was this what it felt like for everybody else who was trapped in ignorance and darkness?

Well, that sucked.

"How do the dragons ride the horses?" I asked.

Damelza sighed, before grinning. "Excellent. Now, *decisions, decisions…*"

She raised her arms like a crow's wings, and the bailey lit up with a file that hung from one side of the courtyard to the other, flicking from page to page with a casual *click* of her fingers.

I gawked at my own strengths, weaknesses, and measurements that were written across the entire castle. When pictures of me as a kid appeared, my hands clenched into fists: me curled on my mattress in the attic (when had dad sneaked that one?), wearing a bow tie at one of mum's dinner parties, playing with Hartley and her cat plushie…

"Wait, are those *baby photos*?" I dived for Damelza, but Crave caught me around the waist, holding me back.

The band of Crave's arms was cool. He was strong but gentle, resting his chin on my shoulder. His breath gusted against my skin, calming me.

Damelza paused on a photo of me grinning at the

camera. My eyes were so bright and happy. I'd forgotten that I'd ever looked like that as a kid before…well, the *Kitten Incident.*

Crave turned to press a single kiss to my neck like he understood. I jumped at his touch, and my skin tingled.

Damelza frowned. "Do you have *any* talents that aren't typical of mage criminality?"

I bristled, even as I smiled brightly. "I'm wily as a fox, snuggly as a cat, and prickly as a hedgehog."

"Or just a prick?" Crave whispered in a teasing Irish voice; his breath was warm against my neck, and it flushed me with heat as well.

I stifled a laugh. "It's like you know me already."

Damelza gave a sly grin. "I'm pleased that you two are getting on so well, since Crave is both your mentor and patron. Also, the Immortals have never had a whipping boy, unlike the Princes, but their good grades deserve a reward this upcoming year."

I wrenched myself away from Crave's hold. "*Whipping boy?* Sorry, but can't you hear that…? The non-magicals in Christ Church are screaming for Superman's help because a student's stuck in a tree or it could be a cat… *Whoops*, did I just reveal my secret identity…? Anyway, I'd better go and save the world and not hang around for any of this whipping…"

Damelza snatched my collar, before I could run. "The brand on your hand connects to the wards around the academy. You're imprisoned here. There's no running, even if you're Superman." I paled, tearing at my lip with my teeth. Hecate had truly done a number on me. "And what are we…*barbarians*?"

Don't answer that…

Damelza shoved me back into Crave, who wound around me like *he* was the cat. "The whipping boy is an ancient tradition. It simply means that if the Immortals misbehave, then *you're* the one who's punished. It teaches them responsibility and self-control, which makes the unit stronger. Plus, if there are spells or potions to be tested, they have *you* to try them out on in class."

I wrinkled my nose. "I'm allergic to being the guinea pig."

Damelza arched her brow. "Are you allergic to execution?" I flinched. "The original mage who was the only one to become a Rebel here so many years ago was walled up alive for his crimes. Whipping boy or walled up alive?"

I snatched Crave into my arms. I hadn't realized how much smaller he was than me because he exuded more charisma than should be legal. Then I twirled him, until he was breathless and laughing.

"Whip me, baby." I flashed a wicked grin.

Crave curled his tongue behind his teeth. "If you desire it."

"*Confess*," the bronze Hecate with the keys bellowed like a curse.

I glanced over Crave's shoulder at Hecate. "Okay, I was Jack the Ripper… Wait, I ate the last chocolate chip cookie… Okay, okay, I left the plug in and sank Atlantis. Wow, you're good at this."

"Silence!" Damelza roared. Her coat dissolved in a flurry of feathers, just as the pink fires blazed up again. "Hecate has renamed you as *Confess*, just as she names all students. You've been born again into the academy."

"Original," I muttered.

Damelza's lips thinned. "But truly fitting, Confess."

In a flurry of black feathers, she disappeared.

I shivered, before disentangling myself from Crave and marching to snatch up my suitcase. I wiped off the snow in furious swipes. Branded, trapped, and reduced to whipping boy without the ability to use my power on professors.

I was starting to understand why this was viewed as the deadliest of the academies.

All of a sudden, the Blood Amulet that trapped my magic weighed heavily around my neck, searing me.

I measured everything in **BM** and **AM**: Before Magic and After Magic.

BM, I'd lived in the main house with my sister, dad, and mum.

AM, I'd been trapped in the attic.

When I'd first been moved from my rooms and realized that all my toys and books were being left behind, I'd sobbed. Until Hartley had struck me.

"Mages don't cry," she'd hissed, even though she was crying as much as me.

Who was the liar now?

When I'd been thrown into the warded attic like I was a dangerous criminal, I'd curled up on the floor with my arms around my knees.

I'd always been terrified of the attic because when I'd been tiny, I'd heard noises from it like someone was living up there. Hartley had taunted that it'd been *monsters*.

I'd fearfully peered around the dark. "P-please can I s-stay with you?"

Hartley had shaken her head.

Tears had blurred my vision. "Why's m-mum locking me up h-here?"

Hartley's smile had been twisted. "Because this is where the monsters live, remember?"

I'd wailed, and dad had dropped to his knees to pull me into his arms and stroke over my shaking shoulders. I'd already noticed the chains shackled to the wall.

Maybe somebody...*more than one person*...had already lived here before me? *Was this where the mages of the House of Jewels lived?*

I'd quaked that I'd be shut up and hidden away forever.

"I won't let your mum do this…not again. I'll save you, no matter what I have to promise or suffer. I'll keep you safe, cub," dad had whispered in desperate pants.

Truth: I'll save you, just like I couldn't save your older brother from being thrown to the wolves.

I'd screamed at the shock of my new power and the revelation that I *had* heard my secret older brother trapped in the attic all those years before *and that he'd been sacrificed to the werewolves.*

Dad's gaze had been sadder than I'd ever seen it, as he'd slipped a Blood Amulet over my neck. "I'm sorry, but mum insists that you wear this if you're to continue to live with us."

I'd choked. Instantly, I'd felt ensnared, as if my new powers and true self were being forced behind an invisible wall. I'd clutched onto dad's shoulders like he could make the sensation stop, yet he'd been the one to put the amulet on me.

It'd always hurt to imagine what dad had sacrificed to get permission from mum to take the Blood Amulet off so that I could learn to shift or to earn small comforts like my mattress, a TV, or a text from Aquilo. Yet every time that dad visited me with a joyful grin, he brought something new for me.

But the strain of it had killed him.

I'd killed him.

Crave's hand clasped mine, warming it, and my ragged breathing steadied. I blinked, brought back to the cold reality of the academy.

When had I started to tear at the Blood Amulet, bruising my neck?

Hurriedly, I dropped the amulet.

Crave's gaze was shrewd almost like *he* could see the truth, before he dragged me to the corner of the bailey, where a dragon gargoyle perched with its wings outstretched, as if it'd been caught in the moment of fleeing.

Crave's eyes glittered crimson in the dark, before his lips ghosted against mine. My pulse fluttered in my neck, and I leaned forward.

Just a little more…come on…

Two kisses in one night would mean…touch, love, and someone both desired and *wanted* me.

It'd mean two more kisses than I'd ever had before.

Incubi were experienced, right? Crave wouldn't be able to tell that I hadn't popped my cherry…?

I clasped Crave's hips more firmly, but he only giggled against my lips.

Then he whispered, "Your sexy self doesn't get travel sick…?"

Pulled out of my haze (could incubi mesmerize?), I mumbled, "*Hmm*…? Is that the lead into a dodgy pickup line about riding your spaceship because if so, I applaud your traditional approach."

Then my eyes widened, as the gargoyle winked at me and its mouth opened impossibly wide, sucking Crave and me into the darkness.

CHAPTER SIX

Rebel Academy, Saturday August 31st

BASK

The gargoyle dragon sucked Fox and me through into the West Wing for the mage's first night as my new whipping boy. Strange, but as his hold on my hips tightened, his touch didn't hurt but only burned deliciously.

All the pleasure without the pain was brilliant. *I could get used to that.*

I treated myself to a sniff of his curly hair. He smelled like sweet wild raspberries tangled beneath a yew tree…or like my sexy Voyeur Ghost had claimed him first.

My ma once told me that non-magical scientists

believe the center of the galaxy smells like raspberries. Fox already smelled like he was *my* center.

I should've just told him the dick chat-up line about the spaceship.

I shivered at the memory of Voyeur Ghost and how I'd sensed her returning my love tonight, just before I'd come so hard my dick almost exploded. I'd never loved a ghost before, maybe Exploding Pleasure Dick was her curse.

It was worth it.

This new Rebel looked like he'd faint if I turned on too much of the incubi charisma (away with you, it's a *thing*), and also like he didn't have a clue how hot he was. At least he'd been accepted by my *angel... queen...goddess...*

I sighed. What was above *goddess* because Voyeur Ghost didn't feel like any of those pet names? I'd never had to choose something to whisper to a lover before but I thought that my other attempts of *Spooky Snookums* or *Witchy Pants* would lead to less Exploding Pleasure Dick and more blue balls. Yet I felt as green as Fox looked from the sudden trip through the gargoyle to only imagine her as just another wicked witch.

The pink fires blazed in the braziers, warming me after the freezing chill of the bailey. Snow trickled down the back of my neck in melting trails. An aroma like bonfires sparking with rich magic wrapped around me.

I let go of my whipping boy's hand (**Rule 7 of the Incubi Night Code** states: You can never be too possessive), and his legs buckled, before he collapsed onto the polished stone. His suitcase lay crushed next to him with its contents vomited over the floor. He looked like he'd copy it and puke too. I didn't know why he appeared so embarrassed. After all, I'd already seen him in a diaper.

And he'd made almost as adorable a baby as I had.

Humming Madonna's "Crave" because multi-tasking was *winning*, I shot a cheeky glance over my shoulder at my arse.

Yep, still pettable.

I grinned at the sound of Sleipnir's guitar music (my gorgeous god would love this new magical student who I'd brought home for him...or he wouldn't, he was hard to read), I patted the mage on the shoulder. "Poor wee Fox. Transportation around the castle is tough on humans."

"There's nothing *wee* about me," Fox attempted to snarl, whilst actually whimpering and clutching his guts. *Cute.* "Can't you see how tight my pants are? My third arm is busting out."

I snickered, patting him on the head this time. "*Wee.*"

His eyes widened, before he staggered to his feet. He spun around, staring at the room in shock. My guts roiled because I understood. I'd only been dropped off (*abandoned* made me sound too much like a dog), last term, once the Duchess had broken her bond with me. Should I point out to him that there was also no TV or wi-fi or would that spark a full-blown panic attack?

Had I looked just as terrified?

Wait, the way that Fox was eying *my* nest of blankets and satin pillows (had I hidden Nile well enough because no one was snuggling my plushie but me), made him look like more of a cat than Pocus, at the same time as if he also had the urge to piss all over them.

There would be no pissing on my bed, me, or Nile, even in kinky fun, and that was non-negotiable.

I needed Nile for the times that I was desperate for soft touch, and Sleipnir was meanly studying, playing his guitar, or eating. Even Voyeur the goddess Ghost couldn't sway me…maybe…oh, who was my slinky self kidding, *everything* was negotiable to her.

Except, was it Sleipinir, *my* Rebel god (I covered the never being *too possessive…?*), who Fox was eying like he wanted to piss on him…?

When I whacked my own forehead to clear *that* image, Fox shot me a wary glance. Then he ran his hand through his damp hair, turning to scrutinize

Sleipnir, who lounged on the bed in a sprawl of long limbs and guitar.

As always, Sleipnir looked like insolence had been invented for him alone. His cotton candy pink hair fell in gentle spikes, which matched his eyes. He wasn't wearing the uniform's blazer and had wrapped his tie around his neck like a bandanna. I wished that I could pull off that look. Note to self: try to pull off more daring looks. His shirtsleeves were rolled up to reveal shimmering sea serpent tattoos that coiled like they were alive. He strummed the haunting melody of "Mad World" by Gary Jules, which crept through me, as if it was infused with magic. He didn't even look up at Fox or me, which was the downside of living with dominant Immortals who acted like, well, *gods*.

This incubus didn't *do* ignored. It must be in the Night Code somewhere. Probably towards the back.

I shot Sleipnir a coy look, before snuggling against Fox's chest. Then I shook at how much I needed...*craved*...the touch like a fever heating my skin. "I wished for another student, and now we have our own whipping boy."

Sleipnir still didn't look up as he drawled with a cultured New York accent, "I'm delighted that you're excited."

You know, Sleipnir should've taught lessons on How to Slay with Sarcasm.

Fox's expression became haughty. "You should be,

after all, I'm secretly King of the Supernaturals. I'm only in hiding here from my wicked stepmother, and it's your job to serve me until I ascend to rule you all."

The mage truly was my little bundle of lies. He was going to be fun.

I rolled my eyes. "Get on with you, I saw your file, remember?"

Fox deflated. "*Whoops...?*"

Then he stiffened. His breathing became too fast and ragged, but he dropped his gaze to try and hide it.

I froze myself because I knew what it was like to wait in fear of punishment. In the Duchess' Court, I'd known little else. How could I've let him think that I'd ever *whip* him? I was descended from the ancient lineage of Night, and just as I knew that I could never have shiny enough hair, so I knew that I'd do anything to protect and look after those who belonged to me.

And this mage belonged to me. If he let me, I'd love him.

I touched Fox's cheek with my glove, which to an incubus is a more intimate greeting than a kiss and means safety, reassurance, and love. Fox's breath stuttered, and he flushed.

The thing of it was, here in the Rebel Academy we were all the *abandoned*, but it didn't mean that we couldn't make it our home.

My brow furrowed, when I noticed Fox's shivering. Humans weren't as naturally hot as incubi (*of course, snicker*). I bustled around Fox, pulling off his damp suit jacket and gathering his possessions from his suitcase to place at the bottom of the wardrobe. After all, it was now *his* wardrobe as well, and that made me glow with joy. It'd shattered me to have to clear out Hector's belongings at the end of the summer term after his death. The room had seemed so empty.

But now we had Fox.

I slunk back to Fox, winding his hair around my finger. "I can care for you, protect you, love—"

"I don't care what the freaky statue or the psycho principal said: I don't belong to you." Fox disentangled himself from me, backing away and wincing as his arse was scorched by the fire, which shot up like the room itself was insulted. My eyes flashed with hurt, before I carefully masked it. "Even if my name's fox, I'm not a pet."

"But I *am*." I prowled towards him. My eyes glittered. Did he think that I wasn't a predator? *Silly human.* "Don't you want to pet me?"

When he reached out his hand, stroking my silky black hair, I sighed and bowed my head.

At last, Sleipnir looked up. "Incubi require touch because they kind of feed through the giving of pleasure, and in the case of our Lord of the Cuddles here, the taking of it too, which makes him seriously demanding—"

"Does it please you to be cursed only to be able to sing Brittany Spears songs?" I raised my head, narrowing my eyes.

Fox snatched his hand away from my hair like he'd just realized that he'd been stroking a grizzly that'd disguised itself as a plushie.

I smirked. Pettable arse, shiny hair, and predator vibes all working. *I was on fire.*

Sleipnir *almost* stopped playing, before he masked his alarm. "Did I say *demanding*? I meant pettable, trust me."

I snuggled back onto Fox's shoulder with a sigh like I'd just won a war.

Fox tilted his head as he studied Sleipnir, who sprawled across the bed, as if he owned it as well as the academy. "Are you a jinni?"

Sleipnir broke off his tune with a twang of broken notes that set my teeth on edge. Then he gaped at Fox. I tightened my hold on Fox just in case Sleipnir decided that he was in a spanking mood and not the fun kind.

My arse was made for spanking, stroking, and kissing. Well, it was versatile. Fox's arse belonged to Voyeur Ghost; it was why he was anointed with her scent.

And why I loved him.

Sleipnir frowned. "I'm a rock god."

I spun towards the bed, launching myself onto it

and crawling towards Sleipnir, who smelled like the sun on hot mountain pebbles. "Can we be groupies, please?"

Fox crossed his arms. "I'm no one's groupie. I'm a shimage."

For the first time, Sleipnir's expression softened, and his eyes flashed with something close to pity. "Odin's spear, stop kicking your own ass. I'm certain that you're not a shit mage. I can be a bit of a prick but I'll still help you discover your talents…"

Fox gritted his teeth. "Are all immortals this…?"

"Alluring?" I waggled my eyebrows.

"Awesome?" Sleipnir suggested.

I bounced to my knees. "Adorable, angelic, and assalicious."

Fox spluttered with laughter. *That was a fine sound.*

Sleipnir shrugged. "Only Bask here," he tucked a strand of hair behind my ear, and I preened, "and me." He held out his hand like suddenly *he'd* remembered his manners and was the one doing Fox a favor. "I'm Sleipnir, the son of Loki."

Fox shrugged, before strolling to the bed and shaking the hand of the god like it was only polite.

I rolled my eyes. "Why don't you just say *Loki's son?*"

I'd never doubted that his da was Loki, the Norse

god of mischief and mayhem. I still didn't know who his ma was though.

Sleipnir's fingers squeezed Fox's, as his candy pink eyes danced with laughter like he was sharing a secret joke with him. Fox shook with the shock of the new connection like he'd never had anyone offer him friendship before.

Had he been as lonely as me?

When Fox wrenched back his hand hurriedly, Sleipnir raised his eyebrow in surprise.

Then Sleipnir flicked my forehead. "You have no style."

Oh, he so didn't just insult my honor...

Rule 18 of the Incubi Night Code: If someone attacks your sense of style, attack them where it hurts.

My lips curled in a way that would make even a god's balls shrink back inside them and wave the white flag, before I straddled Sleipnir's lap. "I have plenty of style, Slippy."

Yet when I ground down on Sleipnir's lap, it was *Fox* who groaned.

Perhaps, he *had* been as lonely as I'd been, when I'd been trapped with no one but the Duchess and the other bonded incubi, because the way that I conquered Sleipnir with just my arse (an incubus must use whatever weapons they have handy), made him cross his arms in a poor attempt to hide how his hands shook.

Sleipnir gripped my hips, stilling me, before he

assessed Fox. "Hey, talking of style, I take it that you're a Goth?"

Fox blinked at him and then glanced down at his black suit. "Did my copy of The Satanic Bible give it away? Or did the porters bring up my coffin? I mean, tomorrow I have plans to slaughter someone…or myself, I haven't decided yet, but it's in my diary for between 9 and 9:30."

"Whatever," Sleipnir scoffed. "So, you want to lie that today was your mom's funeral as well?"

"Why would I do that when it was my dad's?" Fox replied, softly.

My breath hitched, and I tumbled to sit cross-legged next to Sleipnir on the bed. My eyes smarted with tears, but I didn't let them fall because crying was ugly, and it'd been beaten into me enough that I had no right to make myself ugly.

No one loved an ugly incubus.

I missed ma. It'd been three years since I'd last been allowed to see her. Now that I'd been shamed (so, the truth of it was that I'd shamed myself by failing to please the Duchess, and even thinking that felt like a boot to the balls), and sent away to the academy, I had no right to see my family ever again.

My hands fisted in my lap.

Sleipnir's expression became stricken. He laid down his guitar, before tugging Fox to perch on the bed next to him. I curled my hand around the back of Fox's neck again.

"I'm sorry," Sleipnir whispered.

Fox blinked away tears.

Then Sleipnir grinned. "The asshole witches are going to hate you. You've more of a silver tongue than my dad, and hey, I'm only here because they're trying to capture his ass."

"You're bait?" Fox questioned.

Sleipnir's gaze turned frosty. "How about we at least give it the title of *hostage*?"

Over the summer, I'd asked Sleipnir why his da hadn't ransomed him or brought down some Norse god wrath on the academy for taking him prisoner. It was the only time that I'd seen Sleipnir look so shaken that he hadn't been in control. Sometimes, even I could be an idiot (*startling discovery*). Of course, my brilliantly versatile arse had saved me that night.

When Fox clasped Sleipnir's hand, Sleipnir's gaze shot to his, as his expression became warm again. Yet Fox still cast an uneasy glance at the bed, and I didn't miss the way that he made love to the pillows with his eyes…

Yuck. I shuddered, officially withdrawing that image on behalf of my poor pillows.

Fox still looked set to snuggle into them like they were his heaven, even if there was something unsettled about the way that he shifted.

"I didn't expect to get this cozy on my first night." Fox nodded at the bed. "I may be Don Juan wrapped up in Romeo, with a touch of Lancelot and the charisma of Mr. Darcy," *I didn't even attempt to smother my snicker*, "but I still don't share a bed with strangers."

"We're not strangers; we're the Rebels." Sleipnir raised their joined hands to show the brands on the back of them. I clasped my own over the top. It felt like discovering family, and my breath caught. "We share a bed because Bask needs the touch, right? But it's your call. Whipping boys are traditionally meant to sleep on the floor anyway. If you'd rather not share with us…"

Fox yelped, as Sleipnir grasped his waist with a dangerous glint in his eye, attempting to tip him off the bed.

Oh no, he didn't… This mage was *my* toy, and he slept with me. Just not with my pillows or Nile. All right, it wouldn't kill me to spare *one* pillow.

I gasped in outrage, falling off Sleipnir's lap and grabbing onto Fox's arms to haul him further onto the bed, so that he was caught in a tug-of-war between us.

At last, Sleipnir gave up with a huff, and I smirked: an incubus always wins his prize. Then I wound my arms around Fox's shoulders in victory, pushing him down (with great generosity), amongst the pillows. He sighed, wriggling around in their softness.

Yep, he definitely had a pillow fetish or maybe a satin one. I wouldn't know until I checked out his underwear to see if it included panties.

Where there was an imagination, there was hope…and wanking.

All of a sudden, something glinted in the light. My brows furrowed. An amulet had worked its way out of Fox's shirt in the struggle. When Sleipnir yanked at the amulet, Fox gagged.

"What in the Nine Worlds is *this*?" Sleipnir's eyes blazed with a godly fury that had my toes curling.

Sleipnir's eyes transformed from pink to glowing cinnamon red, just like his hair. The muscled arm that gripped Fox's locket no longer glimmered with a sea serpent but snarled with a werewolf baring its fangs.

The mage was screwed because Sleipnir was *pissed*. And when he was pissed, he was a bad bastard, even for a god.

Fox cringed back. "Don't…you're not allowed to touch that. It'll explode if you—"

"Drama queen." Sleipnir's hand tightened, and Fox panted. "By the runes, my dad told me that some asshole once bound him like this with a Blood Amulet, and it was the worst *violation* of his magic. But then, he always uses pompous words like that."

Fox grabbed a pillow, clutching it to his chest like

it could shield him from whatever haunted his past. Were they the same nightmares as haunted my own?

Why had I ever thought that I'd mind sharing my pillows?

I pinched my inner thigh, furious at my own incubus nature (curse my need for touch), but when Fox swayed, lightheaded, I wrapped my arms around him.

I wished that Voyeur Ghost was here. *We needed her. I didn't want to remember the other sort of touch, and how I'd begged for pain.*

Sleipnir's lips feathered up Fox's jawline and then mine in sweet kisses, pulling us both back to a present that was joyful with casual magic and love.

"See, I'm a rebel, and you deserve to be wild and free." Sleipnir yanked at the amulet, and it snapped.

Fox hollered, as his magic flooded through him. My eyes widened, and I was forced backward by the burst of power. Fox's back arched. Then in a blue shower of sparkles, he shifted into an Arctic fox.

I brushed my hand through my hair because when shocked, there's still always time to look your best. But no matter how beautiful I looked, it'd never be as beautiful as the Arctic Fox, which was bouncing up and down on its stubby legs and thrumming with magic and excitement.

And if that didn't set off my incubus Envy-o-Meter, then it must be love.

Fox twirled in a circle to catch glimpses of his creamy fur and bushy tail. I'd have laughed if his admiring his own fur hadn't made me glow with pride. There definitely weren't enough mirrors in here. I'd have to send another petition to Professor Bacchus.

When Sleipnir hurled the Blood Amulet across the West Wing with scary accuracy into the brazier, the fire surged up to consume it. Then Sleipnir settled back onto the bed with a smug smile.

That was such a god thing.

I stroked behind Fox's ear, and he cuddled into a tight ball on my lap. He was better than a plushie. This new student was the gift that just kept on giving.

Wait, did I just coo at him?

Sleipnir exchanged a glance with me, and I knew that there was another Rebel who I loved that Fox needed to know about, even if she'd already claimed him. "How about we introduce the ball of fluff to the final Immortal?" Fox's ears twitched in interest and sleepy outrage. "I take it that since you arrived, you've felt like you were being watched since you've arrived?"

Fox barked, licking my hand.

I knew that my brilliant lover would've watched over and chosen Fox, in the same way that I was protecting him. I'd felt her ever since I'd arrived, devastated and hurting last term. But she'd been there, allowing my worship.

Without her, I'd still feel worthless.

"That's fox for: of course I've met the Voyeur Ghost or the Sexy Spirit. Either name is good." I winked. "How about some specter loving?"

I gasped, as the scent of yew trees wound around me.

She was here.

A wintry breeze ruffled the fur down Fox's back. Then icy kisses trailed down my neck. I arched, moaning. Hot and cold flushed through me, and the tips of my fingers tingled. I ached to trail them down *her* skin. She hadn't been able to stroke her frozen fingers down my sexy little body before. Was she growing stronger or was it because the mage had arrived?

I twisted, rubbing my thumb tenderly over the wall behind the bed.

Fox blinked his blue eyes with their long lashes, as Voyeur Ghost's portrait (that I'd hidden by magic), materialized back onto the wall. Then he bounced off my knee and raised his tail, furiously *gekkering*.

It looked like a certain mage hadn't yet worked out how to conceal or control his emotions in animal form. Instead, he worked on instinct.

That must've been freeing...and also made him look like a dick.

I sighed dreamily, studying my love's portrait. The woman Mona Lisa smiled like she was watching me. She was *beautiful*.

How was it possible for the same person to look both innocent and wicked at the same time?

Her long blond hair flowed around her shoulders, and she wore a velvet dress with tulle like cobwebs. Her swan-like neck was adorned with a pearl choker necklace. Gloves covered every glimpse of skin up to her elbows. I loved that she must understand how I felt being forced to wear them.

Fox shifted back into his human form in a spray of overexcited sparkles. Then he humped my thigh, whining. His eyes gleamed with an intense *need, need, need* that had washed through me when I'd first seen the portrait. Was it *her* desire for me or only *his* amplified that made him reach for me as a lover?

I snickered, lying back. Fox could put on a decent show. Sleipnir shot me a judgey look (I considered reminding him of the incubus saying *never look a gift hump in the mouth,* but then decided that it sounded vaguely too kinky), before nudging Fox with my elbow.

The tips of Fox's ears flushed red, as he scrambled away from me. "*Woah,* sorry. What the….?"

"Behold the mighty Dick Power of the Ghost Immortal." I smirked. "Although, if it pleases you, my sexy behind is at your service."

Fox glanced away, even as his breath quickened. "I already have enough sexy behinds begging to serve me, cheers," he muttered. "I had to turn down Selena Gomez just yesterday."

Sleipnir cocked his head. "Huh, do you ever start to believe your own lies?"

Fox shrugged. "Sometimes, if I'm lucky."

I crawled to the portrait with a sinful slink of my hips (on purpose to outdo his memory of Selena), before kissing the painting on the cheek. For a moment, I smelled the wild forest.

"Night, Ghost Immortal," I whispered. Then I glanced over my shoulder at Fox. "It's like this, see, she has no one else to care for her, and somehow, she's trapped here the same as us. I've felt her more strongly since *you* arrived." I scrutinized Fox, and he squirmed. "At least I can kiss her each night. I'm a romantic."

I threw myself back on the pillows dramatically.

Sleipnir arched his brow. "Obsessive."

I nodded. "Obsessive romantic."

Why did the Immortals have such a connection with death?

My lover in the portrait needed us now. I'd do anything to set her free.

"Who was she?" Fox asked.

Suddenly, I doubled over in agony, as the **I** brand on my hand heated. It hurt worse, however, to hear Fox's howl, as his brand heated as well. He waved his hand frantically like that would cool it. Wide-eyed, he stared at Sleipnir and me like we could make the pain stop, before realizing that we were also clutching our hands and grimacing.

It'd been brilliant to pretend that the whipping boy was truly mine to keep safe. But outside the walls of this room, there were the Princes, the professors, and the Rebel Cup. It didn't matter how hard I worked to keep my arse pettable, I couldn't save even myself from them.

"Did we break one of the witch rules like 'no talking about spooks or your brands will torture you'? Because that's the sort of thing I should've been told in my induction," Fox rasped.

"You're kind of a tightass, you know that?" Sleipnir gritted out, leaping off the bed. "Induction'll cover Orientation, Control of Powers, How Best to Avoid Dying—"

"*What*?" Fox stumbled after Sleipnir with far less enthusiasm after his casually thrown in *dying*.

"The burning is a summons meaning *battle* or *danger*." Sleipnir's grin was all teeth. "Trust me, this'll be exciting."

Sleipnir's hair bristled into sharp spikes. He looked more dangerous and wilder than any creature I'd seen or imagined, as the werewolf tattoos on his arms threw back their heads and howled.

I forced myself to smile, even though my knees felt like buckling with pain. Yet I knew that look on

Sleipnir: it meant he'd set a reckless plan in motion. After all, where had he sneaked off to earlier, whilst I'd enjoyed the best wank of my life?

Sleipnir had been threatening all summer to bring *the chaos moment*. Did he even know how risky it was for him to fly his da's *freedom and rebellion* flag in an academy like this? Now on my new whipping boy's first night, we were being summoned to face an unknown danger.

Rebel Academy, Saturday August 31ˢᵗ

FOX

When the dragon swooped overhead with a *screech* that made my ears ring, I dived for a snowbank. Then I spluttered, as I swallowed a mouthful of freezing snow. The brand on my hand throbbed like a pulse.

When I'd arrived only a couple of hours earlier in the bailey, I'd been frightened that the witch professors could've been using my dick for target practice. Yet all along I should've been worried that the *dragons* hungered for my cock and balls and not in the kinky *Witches Who Swing* party way, which Aquilo had whispered to me he'd overheard was his sister's style.

It'd turned out that Damelza had been telling the truth about mum's donation...*truth:* Bribe to the dragon polo team. Unfortunately, that meant dragons existed. Then it meant that *candles and bells*, I'd be forced to ride one.

Wasn't it enough that I'd had to travel through the dragon gargoyle perched outside the West Wing, who'd licked me with his stone tongue? The only licking I wanted was from Rebel Ghost.

This time, when I'd stumbled to my knees outside the castle's walls, I *had* puked in the snow. Pan knows, I'd snuggled on Bask's lap as a fox, which meant that I'd already broken too much of the House of Jewels' etiquette to stand a chance at that good first impression.

Then Sleipnir had yanked me up, bouncing with excitement like we were on our way to a punk concert, rather than heading into danger, and pulled me past a host of mysterious buildings that I'd barely been able to make out by the light of the moon.

What other secrets did the Rebel Academy hold?

From the outside, the academy had looked rugged with gray walls. The witches hid the truth of their colorful inside just as well as they hid their lies with their charms.

The closer that I'd walked over the crunching

snow towards a huge building, which appeared with its barred stalls and smoky scent to be a cross between a prison and the gateway to hell, the more tender the brand became.

Voldemort in panties, was the brand like a screwed-up Bat-Signal?

"The stables," Sleipnir had muttered, whilst something dark had flashed in his eyes.

Truth: I know the danger that we'll discover there.

My powers of Confess had blasted me with the nu metal roar of Adema's "Immortal". Either Sleipnir had missed his Mortal Kombat sessions with his dad (and I'd have given anything to be a fly on the wall to those), or he'd been certain that we were going into battle.

How did he know? Why hadn't he told me?

It'd been a godly kick in the balls that Sleipnir had promised I wasn't a *stranger*, but he'd kept me in the dark like one. I'd been treated like that by my own family. After Sleipnir had gifted me a coat and scarf, before I'd followed him to the gargoyle, I'd allowed myself to think of him as better than my mum and sister because only dad had ever risked giving a shimage gifts.

Bask had told me that whipping boys weren't handed out their own coats because in witch tradition they *didn't feel the cold*. I figured that Damelza had a catchy bullshit motto about it.

I'd shivered, pushing my hands into the pockets of my black woolen overcoat that was embroidered with a pink **RA** crest. I'd loved the way that it'd been too long for me and smelled like Sleipnir. I'd sniffed the collar, burrowing further into its warmth.

Bask had brushed his hand across the hollow of my back. "The funding always goes to polo because it's the Princes' favorite class." Bask had sighed. "Don't you want to please the Principal and start the term as the golden boy?"

As I lay cowering from the dragon who'd attacked us Immortals, before we'd even been able to reach the stables, I'd say *fat wizarding chance.*

When a sizzling spray of golden fire scorched the snow above my head, I hollered, only for both Sleipnir and Bask to throw themselves over me like a shield. I stiffened in shock.

Wait, were they protecting me…?

The dragon roared and circled again. If the dragon *was* able to escape, then the academy had some serious breaches of risk assessments and safety precautions. I'd be writing a strong letter to the *nobody cares Fox; be thankful that you weren't thrown to the wolves.*

Yeah, that ought to do it.

I peeked up into the night time sky at the sharp stars.

Then Sleipnir grunted as the back of his collar was

snatched and he was hauled to his feet. He struggled, twisting around in the snow, whilst he was shaken. He stilled, however, as he looked up into the blazing eyes of a delicate fae who was more beautiful than I thought it was possible for a guy to be but who was also wearing an expression that could flay Sleipnir alive.

The fae's eyes were emerald and bright against the alabaster of his skin. They were the same shade as his steam punk style military officer uniform. A leather whip coiled around his waist like a snake.

I shuddered at the sight of the whip but even that couldn't stop me from gaping in fascination at the fae's wings, which were golden like his hair and beating violently, gusting wind across my cheeks.

I'd never seen a Seelie fae before. Especially not one who was shaking with anger. I'd take a wild guess that he was the Dragon Trainer who was guilty of failing to control the dragon and setting it loose to flambé me.

Unless, he wasn't the one who was guilty of setting free the dragon?

Yet why was a fae shivering in these cursed grounds? Dragon Wrangler at a witch led academy wasn't top of a Seelie's career path. The fae tribes and their Courts were fiercely independent and had so many civil wars between themselves that I didn't know how they remembered whose wings they were meant to be kissing or hacking off.

I wrinkled my nose. How could anyone hack off something so awe-inspiring (and also so soft that I wanted to kneed it with my paws?).

"Do you see what your daft slackness has caused, boy?" The Sexy Fae (sometimes I lied to myself and sometimes I called it as I saw it), snarled with a Scottish accent that thrummed with dominance. Plus, how big were his cojones to call a god *boy*? "I should never have allowed your refusal to use spurs, bridles, or even a saddle. Now Marcus is free. Your ridiculous insistence on treating these dragons as if they're—"

"Shifters, Prince Ambrose?" Sleipnir shot back with the practice of a familiar argument.

"Professor," Ambrose hissed.

I stiffened. My pleasing Damelza before term started just went up in flames. *Plus, Marcus...?* Shouldn't he have a dragony name like Smaug, Drogon, or Puff, the Magic Dragon?

"*Professor*," Sleipnir drawled as insolently as if he'd just called Ambrose *asshole*. Ambrose's wings stretched out in an alpha display. Sleipnir cocked his head, although the look in his eyes was dangerous. "*Hmm*, I wonder why I'd treat them as if they're shifters kind of like me? *Could it be because they are?*"

Wait, Sleipnir was a shifter?

Was that how he could change his hair and eyes like other people changed their shoes? It'd been startling to watch in the West Wing, as his tattoos had morphed like they were connected to his emotions. I'd never met anyone who was like me before, and it made my chest ache because I didn't think that Sleipnir was a *monster*.

Did that mean that I wasn't?

If the dragons like this Marcus were shifters as well, then neither were they. They didn't deserve to be shut away in that barred building and rode by posh boys with spiked spurs.

Whatever sabotage Sleipnir had set up tonight, he could count me in.

Ambrose glanced around like he thought he was being spied on, which for all I knew he was. Finally, his expression softened, "Aye, you're right. Don't you think that I understand?"

I jolted at Ambrose's troubled intensity. He couldn't have been more sincere if he'd scrawled the words on his own balls in blood. The princely fae hated how the dragon shifters were treated as much as Sleipnir did. So, why was he helping to enslave them? I mean, I understood being competitive, but no sports trophy could be worth trapping a supernatural to ride as if they were a horse.

There were kinky parties for that type of thing, but consent had to be given in writing first.

Sleipnir grinned; it was wickeder than anything I'd ever seen before. "Then hey, what's your problem, *professor?*"

Ambrose's wings beat furiously, as he gripped Sleipnir's elbow and yanked him closer.

Bask and I launched ourselves up. The urge to protect Sleipnir rushed through me, even as the scent of yew trees enveloped me. I shuddered, as Rebel Ghost's kisses nipped down my neck. Despite the danger of both the dragon and its fae trainer, I felt safe now that the final Immortal was here.

Did she feel safe now that I'd arrived in the academy?

I knew that I'd save her. I hadn't been able to save my dad or older brother from my witch family *and I hadn't been able to save myself.* The craving for plea-sure...*and love*...that had trapped me beneath her portrait, despite the cringe factor of humping my patron's thigh, had been the most outstanding sensa-tion of my life. I'd die to set her free, just like Sleipnir had finally freed me. *Okay, it'd been thirteen years too late.* But then, how long had this ghost been waiting around for someone who'd rescue her?

Ambrose's gaze darted to me. "A new Rebel?"

Bask's fingers curled possessively around the back of my neck, and I leaned into his touch.

I shook my head. "I'm an inspector from the Ministry for Training and Enslavement of Shifters, and *you've* just failed. If you'd open the stables, so I can look around and take any remaining dragons into my care…"

Bask cupped his hand over his mouth to hide his grin, and Ambrose blinked at me in confusion.

"Are you mocking me?" Ambrose demanded, as pink flushed his translucent cheeks.

Shut up mouth…please…I promise, chocolate tasty treats, if you just…

"Great Pan, of course not," *saved by the power of pathological lying,* "I'd never mock one of my esteemed professors."

Ambrose growled. "Right, like you rascals weren't sent here to drive the gold from my wings." I grimaced. Wow, my lying had never been accused of *that* before. "As long as the shifters wear the House of Crows' collars, then they're trapped in their dragon form, and your daft arses will treat them like beasts."

"Just our asses?" Sleipnir asked coolly, even though his gaze darkened. "What about our ears or our dicks…?"

When Ambrose gripped Sleipnir hard by the chin, I realized that I was shaking with rage in a way that I never had before because this fury wasn't for my own mistreatment but for Sleipnir's and for the dragon shifters'.

Prickles jabbed beneath my skin, and I rocked

from foot-to-foot. Bask tightened his hold on my neck.

Any moment, Mr Fierce the hedgehog would burst out, and I wouldn't be held responsible for any bloodshed, smackdowns, or even (no matter how much my kittenish side mewled in protest), pricked wings.

I was going Hedgehog on the pretty fae because that was how I rolled.

"If you don't, then I'll sling *all* of you…asses, ears, *and* dicks…into detention with Professor Bacchus again." When Ambrose's lips curled back, I recoiled.

Ambrose's teeth were pearly white and as sharp as fangs.

Why had no one told me that fae were part vampire?

I didn't miss Sleipnir's shudder or the way that he bit his lip. He still rolled his eyes. "Huh, threatening me with the witch who kidnapped me. That's the type of messed-up dickishness that I'd expect from a jerk ex-Prince turned professor."

Ambrose snarled, tossing Sleipnir backward into a snow drift, where he landed with an *oomph*. My eyes widened. Sleipnir was taller than Ambrose — *and a god* — but Ambrose was one badass fairy.

I often became confused between the tales that dad had told me of the real supernaturals and the ones that

I'd read in my novels written by non-magical authors and the Disney films that I loved.

Aquilo had sniffed in disdain when he'd caught me watching *Peter Pan*, but he'd still settled down to watch it avidly with me because most witch Houses didn't allow TVs in their homes. Witches protected non-magical humans but had no interest in their true lives.

Dad must've bargained…*sacrificed*…something major to ensure I had that entertainment.

Yet now all I could imagine was Ambrose's emerald military uniform transforming into a short green dress and slippers with white puffs. Maybe I had a secret cross-dressing fetish hidden so deeply that I'd never realized it until now because okay, who hadn't wanked over that naughty but seductive Tinker Bell?

What, just me then…?

Even the vision of Ambrose with pixie dust erupting from a wand that was definitely *not* Disney approved, couldn't stop the flush on my cheeks being from anger at Ambrose's attack on my new student friend, rather than arousal.

Truth: it was a heady mix of both. Sue me.

With a *pop* of glitter, I transformed into an albino hedgehog. Hex my balls and call me a witch, Mr Fierce was on the rampage.

Berserker rage flooded my mind. *Kill, kill, kill…*

My ghost white bristles stood out like spears, as my red eyes blazed. I let out my warrior high pitched squeal, before tucking my head down and rolling through the snow to hit Ambrose's foot.

Feel the hedgehogy wrath...

I emitted a furious clicking sound as I jumped up and down because if the professor didn't fear me after this display, then maybe I'd pull out the big guns and start with the biting.

Ambrose gawked down at me. "Would one of you care to explain why the new student is making sweet love to my boot?"

Worms and prickles, he'd done it now.

I hissed, uncurling and biting Ambrose's toes through the leather. *Any minute, he'd be screaming... Any minute...just a little longer...*

My little black nose whiffled in disgust. *Yuck*, how long would I have to lick Ambrose's boots, before he broke?

Bask giggled. "He's a shimage."

Ambrose shot Bask a censorious look, hooking his hands on his waist around the whip in a way that should've been intimidating but *hello, Tinker Bell wank bank fantasies.* "I know that he's nothing but a ball of prickles," *hey, I resented that anti-hedgehog prejudice,* "but will you leave off insulting your fellow Rebels."

"A *shimage*," Bask repeated more slowly. "Who

right now looks like his inner *shifter* has a problem with you."

Ambrose shook his boot, and I fell backward with a grunt. "Respect my position. You swagger around forgetting that once I was a Rebel just the same as you. I was one of the few to survive, however, and I earned this professorship." His gaze slid to Sleipnir's who suddenly pinked. "How long do you imagine that I'll survive if my dragons keep escaping?"

Was that a flash of guilt in Sleipnir's eyes? Was this freeing of the dragons one of his campaigns and would Ambrose pay the price?

My fury died down to a bubbling simmer.

I knew what it was like to suffer in fear of witches. How long had Ambrose been imprisoned here, under the control of the House of Crows, even if he was a professor?

And *survive*...? I knew that this academy was dangerous, but the Seelie was simply being dramatic, right?

Sleipnir tilted his chin up defiantly; the wolf tattoos snarled. "Whatever. I can only count one escaping right now. Are you certain that you graduated if you can't count, professor?"

Ambrose's wings arced out in golden glory, before he dropped over Sleipnir, caging him with his arms. "If I can prove that *you* broke Marcus' collar to free him...?" Then he took a shuddering breath, calming himself. When he continued, his voice was quiet but even deadlier, "The principal in her infinite kindness hasn't granted me permission to fly until term begins. But then, wasn't that part of your plan?" *And there went the flash of guilt in Sleipnir's eyes again.* "Maybe you want me to suffer or perhaps, all you care about is mayhem and mischief like your dad."

Sleipnir became ashen. "Don't talk about my dad."

Ambrose huffed with laugher; it blew across Sleipnir's cheeks like dragon mist. "Aye, right because he'll appear any moment and spank me. Oh, wait, he *won't* because he's abandoned you." Bask hissed in fury at the same time as me. Ambrose glanced around at all of us; the moonlight shone on his fangs. "Recapture Marcus or you'll be punished. Then this term, you'll have more to fear than the Princes. You'll discover why the fae are the cruelest warriors." His eyes flashed dangerously. "If you make me your enemy, I swear that it's a battle I shall win."

Truth: You're leaving me no choice. Obey me or suffer.

When Marcus roared above us, swooping towards the stables, Ambrose didn't even flinch. My nose twitched, however, and I curled into a ball. Rebel Ghost's cool breeze cocooned around me.

What kind of ever-witching choice was that for a hedgehog?

I either captured an enraged dragon or turned my

fae professor into an enemy who'd make it his mission over the next term to see me suffer.

As a fox shifter trapped in an attic for over a decade, I'd dreamed of hunting many things: crows, reality show contestants, and Jiminy Cricket. But even I hadn't been able to trick myself that I'd get the chance to stalk a dragon.

Rebel Academy — offering new hunting opportunities since 1870.

I'd have to drop that in the Suggestion Box for Damelza. Maybe she'd give me a gold star.

I lowered my head in my Arctic fox form, slinking through the snow around the stables. My cream coat camouflaged me. I hesitated in the stables' shadows. My eyes stung in the smoky mists.

For the first time, my powers were a *strength*. I'd only just arrived in the academy, but it was my magic that would help recapture a dragon and save my friends from the professor. I wasn't simply the mage who didn't deserve to live in a witch's House (and embarrassed myself all over the floorboards because Mr Fierce was a pooping rebel), I was the fox whose fur *fitted* with these wintry grounds like I'd always meant to be sent here.

I usually knew if I was tricking myself with a lie but somehow, that felt deep in my bones like the *truth*.

Was it because of Rebel Ghost who hadn't left my side from the moment that I'd shifted? Her icy fingers brushed my tail, and I shivered at its sensitivity. I was certain that the gust of air across my fluffy ear was a chuckle. In fox form, everything was heightened: my sight, hearing, smell, and touch.

It should've felt like an assault, but instead, it was like coming alive.

I eyed a snowbank. Hartley and I had built snowmen and laughed, whilst chasing each other through the formal gardens behind our mansion in the final winter **BM.** We'd checked that mum had been out visiting the House of Seasons first, which was the coven in charge of Oxford. Otherwise, Hartley would've been chided for setting a bad example:

How will your brother ever find a good wife, if you don't show him his place?

Was being a mage truly worse than becoming some rich witch's trophy husband?

I wriggled my ass, desperate to jump in the snow and play. But Sleipnir had chosen me for this mission to sneak closer to Marcus, and no one had *ever* picked me because of my talents before. Except, my power of Confess sucked because I knew Sleipnir was lying that he wished to recapture Marcus.

Had he broken the collar?

Sleipnir's lie had blasted me with The Animal's haunting "Don't Let Me Be Misunderstood", which had made me shiver. Sleipnir was one complex, troubled, and way too hot to be fair god. I figured that he schemed as much as I lied and Bask desired sexy times. The problem with *Confess* was that it didn't explain the *why* behind the lie.

Sometimes a lie was kinder than a truth, and a liar was braver than an honest man…or woman. On the other hand, sometimes lies were cowardly, cruel, or cunning.

Which type was Sleipnir's?

My ears flicked around as Marcus circled overhead again. Why hadn't he flown away and escaped? Why would he risk remaining so close to his prison? I'd have been halfway to my mountain cave, treasure hoard, Pokémon trainer…or however it worked. Dad had been sketchy on that part.

Air *whooshed* against my fur. I flattened myself to the ground and then risked peeking up.

Marcus was like a streak of sun flying across the moon. His smooth skin was golden, and his long neck and tail were sinuous, as he coiled above me. Yellow magic fluttered out of his bat-like wings, as if he was wearing a decadent outfit. He was more ethereal than the fae prince.

He was *nothing* like the monster that I'd always imagined dragons to be.

How could I hunt another shifter, when inside he was the same as me? I mean, I could be a prick, but I wasn't a dick. And that there was an important distinction.

I whined, lowering my ears, before I stepped out of the shadows and padded through the snow in front of the stables and under the dragon, no longer attempting to hide from him.

If a dragon shifter didn't deserve to be imprisoned, then did that mean that I didn't deserve to be either?

Truth: I'd *never* deserved to be shut away.

I whimpered as that truth ripped through me, tearing down the lies, which I'd built to protect myself. I didn't need them now. I could be my true self, and I *would* be free.

Behind me, I could hear the other Immortals and the professor wildly hollering.

I quivered, as my heart pounded in my chest. I whimpered, glancing up from underneath my eyelashes at Marcus. He'd flown lower, and his molten gold gaze fixed on mine. Then Marcus' magic whipped out: furious rays of the sun that were heading directly for me. I crouched in the snow. Any moment, Mr Fierce wouldn't be the only one to embarrass himself with an accident.

I covered my head with my paws, as fire streaked from Marcus' jaws, and his magic prickled across me.

Closer, closer, and...

Suddenly, I was lifted by the scruff of my neck. I yelped, as I found myself staring into the golden gaze of the dragon transformed into man. He was just as beautiful as he'd been in his dragon form.

Wait, did that mean that I was…let's settle on as *handsome* because I wouldn't admit to *adorable* unless sugary treats changed hands…as I was as a fox?

In a spray of blue glitter, I transformed back into a mage. Marcus was still holding me by the neck, but his lips twitched as if trying not to smile.

Marcus' hair hung in soft blond waves to his waist, but his stance was that of a warrior. His cheekbones were high and sharp, and his yellow jacket and trousers, which were embroidered with orchids, were cut like a military uniform.

"Nice moves." Should I tag on a *sir*, *master*, or maybe a bow…? I shrugged: *screw that.* "I'm scoring you full marks. Now, how about you fly away home, before you're collared again?"

I darted an anxious glance over Marcus' shoulder at Ambrose who was sprinting towards Marcus and me. Ambrose's wings beat in frustration at being unable to take flight. My breath caught, and I clutched Marcus' shoulders, trying to urge him back into the air.

Marcus' eyes narrowed. "Are you not a spy, little fox?" He asked in a deep, rich voice.

I froze. "Why would the King of the Fox People be a spy?"

So, who doesn't exaggerate on their resume…?

Marcus snorted. "Uh-huh. Well, Your Majesty," (I shivered: I could get used to hearing that), "I happen to be an *archduke*." My shoulders slumped. *Why hadn't I gone big on the lie and made myself Emperor of the Fox Universe?* "And my dear brothers are still *collared* in the stables." He let go of my neck to stroke his fingers through my hair. I hated the anguished expression in his eyes. "It's simply that I belong to Prince Lysander, and I fear being ridden by him again. The Princes believe in nothing but subduing and conquering. They don't understand shifters. This academy holds the most terrifying of secrets. But if I leave my brothers behind, it'll be dishonorable—"

"Wouldn't your brothers want you to be safe?" I whispered.

It'd been all I'd ever wished for Glow. I hoped that it was how he felt about me being sent away from the House of Jewels and leaving him by himself. And I knew that, despite the fact that he'd died, dad had given *everything* to keep me safe because he hadn't been able to protect my brother.

Marcus scrutinized me in a way that made me squirm. "I wish that I saw the truth as clearly as you."

"Believe me, you don't," I muttered.

Ambrose was just the other side of the snowbank now. When he slipped the leather whip from around his waist, I gasped.

All of a sudden, Marcus clasped me to his chest. He was hot, despite the cold, and his magic coiled around me like he was cocooning me in the sun.

"I'll take warning to my people," his grip was harsh in my hair, as if he never wanted to let go, "but you shouldn't be trapped here either, King of the Foxes. Let me free you as well."

I flushed. "I'm sort of collared myself. I was branded by this dancing Hecate, which means that I can't escape the wards."

When Marcus drew back, I was shocked by the gleam of tears in his golden eyes.

Nobody had ever cried for me before. Not even dad. Glow and I had cried for each other, but that wasn't the same thing.

Marcus smiled, tracing down my cheek. "It's kind of you to urge me to go, when you shall be the one to pay for it."

So, he hadn't been conned by my royal ploy...

I shrugged. "Someone did the same for me." My throat was thick with tears; I struggled to swallow. "Drive safe."

Marcus huffed with laughter. "You're a funny little fox. But I like you."

Then he kissed the corner of my mouth, before darting into the dark. Ambrose bellowed at him, but Marcus shifted into his dragon form, beating his wings and winding towards the stars and away, over the ancient woods.

My eyes blurred with tears, but I'd never thrilled with such joy, until Ambrose cracked his whip into the snow at my feet. I jumped, wrapping my arms around my middle. Ambrose panted, out of breath from his dash to catch Marcus.

Bask and Sleipnir were still sauntering after him. *Had Sleipnir plotted Marcus' escape?* Why had he wanted me to be the one to witness it?

Ambrose stalked towards me, raising my chin with the butt of his whip. The hardness of his emerald gaze made me realize just how gentle Marcus' had been.

If the Seelie were so tough, maybe the Princes should be saddling *them* up and riding *their* asses…?

"You let him go," Ambrose hissed.

I licked my dry lips. "I *lost* him. Dragon beats fox. Sorry."

Ambrose eased back, glancing between me and the other two Immortals. "You're not yet. But you will be tomorrow morning."

When I flinched, Bask dived for me, slinging his arms around my shoulders and fussing, whilst he checked me for injuries. Sleipnir stood between Ambrose and me, crossing his arms like he was my bodyguard — and I wasn't the whipping boy.

Yet it didn't matter how much they pretended that

they could protect me because that was just another lie. In Rebel Academy, I sensed the truth that the professors held the power, and even though Prince Ambrose was male and an ex-Rebel, he was still a professor.

In my first morning in the academy, what punishment would I suffer?

CHAPTER EIGHT

Rebel Academy, Sunday September 1st

SLEIPNIR

When you were the son of Loki, you had a duty to create the *chaos moment*. I'd spent my life by my dad's side being hunted, and yet he'd still taught me that freedom was worth every sacrifice.

It sucked that my fellow Rebels, however, would be punished alongside me because I'd broken Marcus' collar.

I was indeed the awesome warrior who'd freed the dragon. Omens and runes, I swore I'd find a way to free all of us who were trapped in this dick academy.

Who did they think they were, taking a god

hostage…? *Oh yeah, the most powerful witches alive…*

When Damelza's crow *cawed* and battered at the bedroom window in the West Wing, I awoke with a start at the punishment time of 5 a.m., after only a couple of hours sleep. It was still dark, and I winced at the House of Crows' feathery alarm clock.

Bask's arms were slung around the new whipping boy's neck. They both wore pink and black striped silk pajamas like me, which had ridden up revealing pale glimpses of skin. Black hair mingled with white blond. I missed the way that Bask normally hugged me, searching out touch, as his sweet breath would gust across my neck, until I'd shiver.

I sprawled across the bed, pretending to sleep, even though I was cold with the sheets pulled off me. I slyly watched Bask and Fox wake up in each other's arms as naturally as if they were family. I didn't understand Bask's easy offers of friendship and love like it was no different to choosing whether to press his hand to Fox's cheek.

I didn't need friends, but I couldn't survive here without allies. Weirdly, I knew that I'd die for Bask, but was that love?

I'd never had a friend before, so how would I know?

When something soft tickled my cheek, I turned my head and realized that in the night I'd ended up snuggling on top of Bask's crocodile plushie, whose reptilian eyes now stared predatory into mine. I stifled my grin; I might've been hunted all my life, but that'd honed me into one badass hunter.

I watched the way in which Fox stiffened like he suspected we'd kick him out of bed. Did he believe that we'd treat him as a true whipping boy? On fear of the Valkyries, I'd never hurt anyone under my protection, unless it was Bacchus and even then, I'd kick her ass in a fair fight.

I wished that Bacchus would take the cursed charms off my powers that dampened them, but *fair fight* was as much a banned phrase here as *Loki Rules*.

That's why I'd pissed <u>*Loki Rules*</u> *into the snow last term. My dick had almost frozen off, as I'd carefully looped each letter, but some sacrifices were worth it.*

Last night, I'd watched amused, as Fox had built a wall of pillows between himself and us. Fox had ducked his head, struggling to ignore Bask's pout. Yet at some point during the night, Bask had shoved the pillows onto the floor and snuggled into Fox's side to spoon him.

This morning, Fox stroked Bask's cheek. Bask's almond scent wrapped around me. Then Bask's eyes fluttered open, and his gaze settled on Fox. When Bask smiled softly, my breath hitched. I'd never seen him smile at anyone but me like that before, even Hector before he'd...died.

I clenched my fists but forced myself not to move.

Valhalla! For his part in Hector's death last term, the fae prince would suffer torments worse than any… Okay, let's just say that Prince Lysander was an asshole, and I was going to *wreck* him.

"Welcome to the Rebel Academy." Bask's hand tightened around the back of Fox's neck. "Here's the thing of it, you're ours now. You belong here. And I want to wake up every morning like this."

Bask hovered his lips over Fox's. The whipping boy shook like he'd never been desired before.

I'd bet that he hadn't.

"Pet me," Bask demanded.

Huh, it appeared Bask needed feeding before the Discipline Run. Most incubi were fed by *taking* orders. If he was in the mood, Bask loved it when I became all commanding, but he was considered broken because he could feed on *giving* orders as well.

In his culture, being different truly *was* a crime.

Fox snorted. "Don't worry, gorgeous, you're in the hands of a professional. I won the Mage's Pet an Incubus in a Wet T-shirt contest three years running."

He cracked his knuckles, and Bask snickered.

I forced myself to remain still with a self-control that would've made Loki proud. Even my tattoos faded without a growl. My hair this morning was aquamarine like my eyes, and my lip was pierced.

I always liked it best this way. I loved my brothers

(hey, you couldn't get closer than being born a triplet), but when they appeared magically within me, their personalities flooded through with such dominance in their shifter identities that I wasn't *myself.*

I was always a monster though.

Why did I have to be a monster…?

My nails bit crescent shaped moons into my palms, as I forced myself not to break and dirty the picture of love in front of me.

How could I resist it?

Dragons and dwarfs, I'd brought down punishment on them. I didn't deserve their comfort.

Fox crawled over Bask, caging him between his arms. Bask's eyes glittered, and his chest rose and fell rapidly. Fox trailed his fingers up and down Bask's ribs, bunching the silk of his top and revealing his taut stomach and the light trail of hair down to where his pants were slipping off his hips. Fox pressed harder with his fingers, until Bask squirmed. His breath started to hitch, and Fox's sped up.

To my surprise, Fox launched a tickle attack on Bask, and he giggled, thrashing underneath him. Then Bask accidentally caught my balls with a flailing kick.

Odin's cock…

I hissed, rolling onto my side and cradling my poor balls. My eyes shot wide open like I'd drunk a triple espresso. *That was one way to put an end to my playing Sleeping Beauty.*

Nile's toothy mouth appeared to be laughing.

Asshole.

My gaze darted between Bask and Fox, who glanced back sheepishly. "Would you call down Ragnarök with your flirting? Screw, suck each other off, or get up because this Liberator of Dragons has earned us a Discipline Run."

When I dragged Fox into the grounds, as Bask bounced around like a hyperactive bunny (hyped on the yummy combination of pleasing Fox and pleasing himself), I broke yet another rule by bundling him into my coat again. Whipping boys were forbidden from wearing anything more than their uniform of black shirt and trousers with an embroidered letter of their patron: **I**.

I wrinkled my nose. It was kind of like a mark of ownership. Only, Fox was a human mage, and as much as the sexy image of licking him like a Popsicle made me flush, I wasn't letting him freeze on his first day under my protection.

Was it wrong that I loved the way Fox burrowed into my long woolen coat, sniffing the collar kind of like my scent made him feel safe? I brushed a stray curl behind his ear, and he shot me a cocky grin, before setting off at a sprint like that'd impress me.

I gave him ten minutes before he was a gasping mess on the snowy floor…okay five minutes…wait, it looked like more like *one* minute.

Bask shook his head in fond exasperation, before darting after the wheezing mage, and I jogged to join them. The morning's breeze was like life across my cheeks. I took deep breaths; its freeze forced new clarity on me. I was imprisoned in these grounds, but right now, I *chose* to be free.

Discipline Runs were always around the frozen lake. Bask wound his arm around Fox who was rubbing his numb hands together. Next time, I'd better bring him gloves…and a scarf and…

Hey, when had I become his nanny?

With a growl, I put on a burst of speed, passing Bask and Fox. My blood pumped with sudden adrenaline at being in the grounds; the fresh air burned my lungs. Pink fireflies hung in glowing mists over the lake, lighting my way with an eerie beauty.

In the distance, the spires of non-magical Oxford hung like a mirage.

I could almost make myself believe that I could just keep running and reach it without the wards stopping me, but that dream wasn't real. There didn't need to be bars, locks, or walls to trap me.

Trust me, I'd been raised to fear witches because they were skilled in their cruelties. It kind of made me wonder what magic the Ghost Immortal had cast that I hungered for her the same as Bask did. I couldn't help smirking as I glanced over my shoulder at the sexy incubus.

I didn't love her in the same romantically obsessive way as Bask. I craved to *consume* her...

Loki had always told me that I had to stay away from witches and perhaps, I wanted to taste the forbidden.

When the forest glowed with a sudden burst of magenta magic, I took a step towards it like I'd been drawn that way. My breath stuttered. The magic from the forest was dark and ancient like Ghost Immortal was reaching out to me. My magic feathered within me, straining to join her.

She was seriously powerful.

I clenched my jaw. I could sense her pain and loneliness. *I had to free her.*

Except, it was *our* Ghost Immortal that I was feeling, right?

Without thinking, I took another step towards the throbbing magic, which pulsed in time to my own heartbeat. I could feel it behind my eyes, pressing on my skull, and in the twitching of my hard dick. I hadn't come in my pants yet, and I wasn't breaking that record, even for some sexy spook who had me by the balls in more ways than one.

Then there was a *crack* underneath me, and I froze.

I'd stepped onto the thin ice at the edge of the lake without even realizing it, which now spiderwebbed out. I drew in my breath, carefully lifting my foot off the lake, before it could plunge through.

Shove Mjolnir up my ass, that'd been close.

Why had I forgotten that this place was cursed? It wasn't like a witch could love me back. If she wanted to play games, then I'd learned from the god of mischief.

You didn't screw with a god raised on mayhem.

I touched the silver plectrum at my neck, which Loki had gifted to me; it was cool and sleek. *Just like dad.*

I grinned. I loved the academy's grounds, but Loki would've hated them. He'd have moaned about the quiet, the cold, and the lack of prank opportunities. Honestly, he'd have been bouncing off the walls for something to fight against. Yet when my brothers and I had been young, we'd spent years camping in America in places as wild as this because it was the best way that Loki could keep us safe and he'd borne it…for us. Although, he'd still moaned, of course. He'd also shown my brothers and me how to fish on the Great Lakes buried in the forests of Michigan. We'd never known when we'd had to forage for our own food or make a run for it.

If Ambrose thought that he'd break me with early mornings and two-hour runs in the cold, then he had no idea what I'd endured. He'd need to get a hell of a lot more creative. Wait, maybe hold off on the whole *more creative* part.

When I caught sight of the way that Fox swayed, and his legs buckled, my guts squirmed. Was I hungry already? Wait, it felt more like…*guilt.*

I blinked. Screw the runes, how long had it been since I'd felt…*that?* I shuffled my feet almost like this *guilt* wanted to burst out of my ass. The messed-up thing was that the two-hour run in the early morning cold was nothing but an invigorating start to my day, but it was *hell* for my whipping boy, and hadn't that been the point? To punish me through the one who could be hurt…?

Fae were fiendish, and when magic was banned on these runs, so that Fox hadn't even been able to transform and run it in animal form, watching him struggle was the true punishment.

This was why I didn't have friends: *I broke them.*

The only human who'd ever played with me when I'd been younger…well, he hadn't played, he'd sat with his hands tied with rope. I'd found him hiking through the woods. I'd tried to talk to him, but when he'd screamed like I'd been a monster, I'd pulled off my top and stuffed it in his mouth.

Then I'd sat clutching my arms over my cold chest and rocked, until all of a sudden, Loki had been there, waving his hand with his magic in front of the human's eyes to make him sleep, before cradling me in his arms. I'd laid my head on Loki's shoulder, and he'd rubbed my nape in the way that'd always calmed me.

"So, you're kidnapping non-magicals now, huh? Since when did that overtake your guitar obsession? Honestly, you can never keep up with your kids." I'd been able to hear the smirk in his voice, and I'd bristled.

"It's not a kidnap; he's my friend."

Loki had pulled back, raising an unimpressed eyebrow. He'd gripped my chin, turning me to look at the snoring human. "Usually — as a general point — friends don't need to be tied up to stop them running away."

How should I know? I'd never been able to take one for a test drive before.

I wouldn't have kept him anyway. He'd been far more boring than my brothers, Fenrir and Jormungand. *We were each other's worlds.*

Yet, just once, I'd wanted to see if there was something outside our tiny universe of four.

I'd stubbornly jutted out my lip, but Loki had run his thumb over it like he had ever since I'd been little to smooth out the pout. "But you said that those witches were friends who tied *you* up…"

Loki had paled; he'd become suddenly serious in a way that made my heart thunder. "I was wrong. Witches can *never* be your friend." He wiped his elegant finger through the kid's tears to show me the wet shimmering on the tip. "Why would you want someone to be sad, little stallion?"

I'd pushed away from Loki, as anger flooded me. I'd clenched my fists. "*You* cry and try to hide it. I've heard you at night. Plus, Fenrir once saw, and you said—"

"*Simply to imagine that I was smiling on the inside.*" Loki had smiled then as well, but it'd been brittle and fake. *I'd wished that he'd been crying instead.* When he'd reached to stroke my hair, I'd pulled back from him. His smile had fallen. "You know that I have to take the non-magical back, right? If you have to force someone to belong to you, then they were never yours. Everybody deserves to be free."

"I hate you," I'd whispered.

I didn't mean it... Don't let dad think that I meant it...

I'd fought not to let my own tears fall because I was too old to cry, even if Loki did.

"I'd imagine that you would." Loki had sounded weary, before he'd pressed his hand to his face. "Screw the Norns, I'm a terrible dad."

My eyes had widened. *What on earth had I done?*

I'd launched myself onto Loki so hard that I'd knocked him backward into a laughing heap.

"I love you." I'd kissed his nose, even as he'd

chuckled, playfully wriggling to get away. "I love you, dad."

"I know, little stallion. Although from now on, you swear to me that you never imprison another. If you wish someone's love or friendship, then you make certain that they're free to make that choice."

I'd swallowed and then given my oath.

Nothing would make me break it.

I shook my head, as my heart ached at the memory. Then out of the corner of my eye, I glimpsed a flash of long blond hair, ice-blue eyes, and wisps of black.

When I grinned, it was all teeth. Ghost Immortal was watching me with an amused expression, *and she didn't know that I could see her.*

My dick was back to twitching, pulsing and heavy in the tightness of my pants. I sped up. My breath created spooks in the cold air, as I closed in on a real one. Just because I'd spent my life being hunted, didn't mean that Loki hadn't taught me how to hunt.

Loki lived close to death; he straddled the line between the worlds, and so did I. Since last night outside the stables, I'd seen the glowing outline of Ghost Immortal. She'd been beautiful in a way that'd made me want to pull her into a snowbank (in a far sexier way than Ambrose had thrown me into one), and show her every trick that I'd learned over the decades. Hey, I had godly skills, and just then, I'd hungered to strip off those

Victorian clothes and lick over every curve, until I'd worked my way down to between her thighs.

Then I'd have made her scream.

I have a talented tongue, and everybody needs a talent.

I forced myself to smother my grin as I called over my shoulder, "Is this a Discipline Run or a Pamper-Yourself Walk?"

"It's the tortoise who wins the race." Fox bent over with his hands on his knees. "The hare ends up in the stew."

Trust a fox to imagine the hare eaten.

"Not this hare, shell boy." I pulled further ahead.

Almost there... Don't let her vanish like she did last night... Almost...

I pushed myself to run faster around the curve of the lake; the muscles in my thighs burned.

She was laughing at all of us, just like she had last night. Except, outside the stables she'd watched me with a too knowing smile, as if she'd *seen* me breaking the collar.

Little...gorgeous...spy.

I snarled and just for a moment, my hair spiked to cinnamon red, before calming back to aquamarine.

I slowed, pretending to clutch my side like I had a stitch.

Only three steps away...

Ghost Immortal was stroking a pink crow on her shoulder. *What in the nine worlds was that creature, and why was it singing "Beauty and the Beast"?*

I grimaced. I might be a monster, but I was no beast. Just like that feathered asshole was no singer.

Two steps...

Ghost Immortal waltzed around to the tone-deaf serenading of the crow.

One step...

When I caught the witch around the waist and waltzed with her, her mouth fell open in a silent 'o'.

Valhalla! I could touch as well as see and hear her.

My pupils dilated, and I flushed, at the same time as her breath hitched. Her crow stopped singing with a strangled *caw*. At least I'd surprised him to silence. When I drew Ghost Immortal to me, her blazing gaze met mine with such shocked fierceness that my throat became tight. She was terrifying and sexy in equal measure.

This was the *chaos moment*: the spark of mischief when everything changed. She now knew that the veil had been torn between her world and mine, although only for me. I clung to the sense that I alone had this connection, and until I knew more about her, I wouldn't risk Bask or Fox knowing that I could see her.

I could delude myself as thoroughly as Fox, who knew?

When I leaned closer, until Ghost Immortal's breath gusted across my cheek, I wondered whether mine was as hot to her, as hers was cold to me. My pulse fluttered in my neck.

Ghost Immortal's yearning wound around me as thickly as the scent of yew trees.

"Are you stalking us?" I pushed her hair back from her ear; it was like silk. "Because that would be awesome."

Her laugh was low and musical. It thrilled me.

"May I kiss you?" I murmured.

She pressed her thigh between mine, and I moaned, as she rubbed it against my dick. "Charming god, I must demand that you kiss me or I shall take matters into my own hands."

I chuckled. *It looked like I'd met my match.*

"As long as I'm yours, and you're mine…?" I hated the pang of insecurity, but even in my lust fueled haze, I couldn't hide it. "I promise, we're all working on freeing you."

She stiffened, and her eyes sparked. "Why would you free me?"

"Because no one should be caged." I swept her around in an even faster waltz.

Then she *did* take matters into her own hands, hauling me closer and kissing me with a passion that took away my breath. Her lips were cool and like life where I'd expected death. With a savage intensity, I pressed my tongue across the seam of her lips, and when her mouth opened, our tongues twined in a dance that equaled our waltz.

She lowered one hand from my waist to my ass and squeezed, whilst her other edged up into my hair, pulling hard. I groaned at the twin sensations like a claiming. Then her black dress wafted into mist, curling around my dick and between my legs, until my balls were rubbed as well.

My eyes widened. I shook, as she edged me higher.

I broke the kiss, caressing up and down the hollow of her back. "Who are you?"

Finally, Ghost Immortal's expression became shuttered, and the mist between my legs squeezed my balls in a way that would've been painful if I hadn't been so turned on.

I bit my lip, panting hard.

Seriously, she had to be kidding... I couldn't hold back... I was going to...

I tasted tangy blood as I tore the skin of my lip to keep in the keen, as I came in my pants.

There went my record.

Damn it all to Hel, it wasn't like the other Rebels would miss the wet spot on my trousers. I'd intended to make Ghost Immortal scream.

Perhaps, I should've listened to Loki about witches.

I drew back from Ghost Immortal, glaring. She looked way too smug, and the crow hopped up and down with the bird equivalent of a smirk. But then she kissed my cheek gently, and I couldn't feel cross anymore.

"I'm the original wicked witch who cursed this academy," she whispered.

She looked at me with a gaze that was so broken yet hopeful that it tore me up inside.

I froze because honestly, that was worse than I'd been imagining. It was no wonder that her magic tasted so powerful, ancient, and dark. I'd just promised to unleash the original wicked witch.

And that's why a guy shouldn't be led by his dick. But was she truly *wicked* or just a Rebel like the rest of us?

When I stepped back, Ghost Immortal floated away across the icy lake, and I was flooded with an immense wave of loss.

Then Bask clutched his arms around my neck, and Fox collapsed in a panting pile at my feet.

Fox's breath came in pained gasps; he looked like he was about to puke. "Y-you weren't k-kidding when you s-said that gods loved r-running."

I blinked. Had the punishment driven him mad? That squirming *guilt* was back roiling in my guts. I'd have to get him into a serious training regime or the Princes would wreck us in the Rebel Cup. After all, it was kind of my fault...okay, no need to be a hardass...*entirely* my fault that we were on this run.

When Bask sniffed and swiped at the wet patch on my trousers, however, I understood what Fox meant. I raised an imperious eyebrow.

On Bor's beard, I wouldn't blush.

"Dancing, kissing himself, and coming...is that a god thing?" Bask nipped at my neck on each word. "Are you practicing for later with us, Slippy?"

"Apricots are brilliant for practicing kissing, I mean, that's what I heard." Fox couldn't hide *his* blush, although he tried to by nestling down into my coat, which was too big for him.

There was something else squirming inside me, as I watched Fox with his adorably innocent pink cheeks looking to *my* coat to protect him.

I shifted, uncomfortable. How could I love him already, in the same way that I loved Bask? Why did I desire Ghost Immortal so intensely? I'd been taught not to have friends or love witches. Yet now I'd broken every survival instinct taught to me over the centuries. I'd brought the *chaos moment*, but it could destroy me.

CHAPTER NINE

Rebel Academy, Sunday September 1st

FOX

I stumbled through the narrow portrait gallery in the West Wing. My lungs burned like they were on fire. Only Bask's arm around my waist and Sleipnir's cocky gaze that screamed that he *dared me* not fall on my face stopped me from collapsing.

I'd begged Sleipnir not to take the gargoyle route back to our room because with the panting mess that was left of me at the end of my first punishment, I'd have puked on the floor. And I might be a shifter, but I wasn't an animal.

Dawn's cold light was finally edging through the

arched windows, yet I and the Immortals had been up for hours. I sneezed, snuffling into the sleeve of Sleipnir's overcoat that he'd wrapped around me. How had Ambrose been expecting me to survive if Sleipnir hadn't broken the rules by giving me his coat? Or had the professor wanted me to become an ice sculpture?

Merlin's balls, the muscles in my thighs ached, and my knees wobbled dangerously.

Maybe Ambrose had cast a Jelly Charm on them as part of his punishment?

Truth: I'd been locked in an attic for over a decade. I was one unfit foxy.

At least, I wasn't fit enough to keep up with a wired god and well-fed incubus on a Sunday Discipline Run. It had sounded like a Fun Run, which is something that I'd watched on TV and always craved to take part in, although less with the *fun* and more with the pain.

What had I expected from an academy run by witches?

Thank Pan, I'd followed a strict gym routine and workout regime, even if I'd only been able to watch Hartley jogging around the formal gardens each evening.

Liar, liar, prickly pants on fire...

Okay, more like I'd danced like a kitten on fire to James Brown every night because this cat had *soul*.

Now, I stumbled in the portrait gallery, dizzy. Lights danced in front of my eyes. Bask's and Sleipnir's anxious voices sounded far away as if through sheets of ice. Gentle hands helped me down to the floor, resting my head against the stone wall. Fingers carded through my curls, and I leaned into the touch.

Maybe I'd better start a training routine that was more than shaking my furry ass to James Brown...? Not that I was going to give that up because that was how my whiskery self got down.

You haven't seen true dancing, until you've watched a cat with a crooked tail getting funky to "Super Bad".

I blinked, and through my blurry vision I made out the Immortals' concerned faces, as they crouched in front of me. Only dad had ever looked at me like that.

My throat was tight, and I swallowed with difficulty. "I'm f-fine. I'm just...taking a b-break to look at the pictures," I slurred.

"Uh-huh." Bask raised an unimpressed eyebrow, even if he continued to pet my hair. "Does it usually please you to faint, fall to the floor, and then look at paintings resting on your arse?"

"It's better than looking at them out of my ass." I shrugged.

Wow, had that been a bad idea. I blinked back the wooziness.

Sleipnir slouched to his feet, crossing his arms, as

he leaned against the wall. His hair this morning was aquamarine like his eyes. Had his lip been pierced with that glittering stud before?

Was he pierced anywhere else…?

"He's okay, aren't you, *champ*?" Sleipnir drawled. "Seriously, why don't we run another lap?"

I'd rather tie my dick in a black bow and deliver it to Damelza as an early Halloween gift.

"Why not make it a race? The winner chooses the forfeit." *By my weight in jewels, stop talking mouth, stop talking…* "I know, who's up for a marathon?"

When Sleipnir burst into laughter, I stared at him. "Valhalla! I'm a god, and you're hot but kind of out of shape. Remind me to never let your lying ass get into a bet with the Princes because they'd wreck you."

Bask tapped the end of my nose in reprimand. "Didn't anyone teach you that fibbing will get you in trouble?"

"Well, Pinocchio had it coming for being such a dumbass…literally." I rubbed my nose. "It's the truth that's dangerous."

When Bask pulled away from me, wandering across to the portraits, I peered at them. Then my eyes widened.

"Wait, what is my gorgeous self doing in that portrait, and why's it moving like a GIF?" I demanded.

Bask grinned, running his hand over the gilt frame

of a portrait of me dangling in Hecate's embrace, as if he was caressing me. I found that I wouldn't mind that, especially if Rebel Ghost got in on the action. "They're like the school photo of every Immortal. You must've been added here because you belong to us."

Sleipnir licked across his lip piercing as he tapped my shoulder. "Hey, wicked entrance to the academy."

I pinked. I hadn't had my photo taken since I was a kid and now, I was immortalized in the arms of Hecate...? That was a wizarding world of wrong.

"Oh, the best," I gritted out. "Who's that kid next to me?"

Both Bask and Sleipnir stiffened.

Inside the portrait, a dark-haired guy who looked younger than me stuck two fingers up as he snarled with a rage and despair that vibrated through me. Yeah, he was more the type of rebel that I'd expected to meet in the academy.

And by expected, I meant *feared*...

Bask's eyes glinted with tears, before he swiftly turned away. His voice was small and echoed with the same loss that I recognized, "He was ours, and now he's gone."

Truth: My friend died, and I couldn't save him. *Please, not again, not again, not again...*

The intensity of Bask's grief hit me through Confess, but worse was his despair that he wouldn't be able to save *me*. I'd expected to see tears trailing down Bask's cheeks, but he was dry-eyed, which was as much a lie as my marathon bluff.

Yet what was the danger? The professors? These Princes that I hadn't even seen yet?

Rebel Ghost…?

My eyes narrowed. "Term starts tomorrow, and I know that this is a castle, but even so, where's everybody hiding?"

Sleipnir exchanged a troubled glance with Bask. *Well, that wasn't good.*

Sleipnir slipped his hands underneath my shoulders and helped me to my feet. Then he rested his cheek against mine in a way that was more tender than anything he'd yet done. But it made me tremble because when he drew back, he had the same look in his eyes that dad always had just before he delivered the news that mum had demanded I be whipped.

Whipping boy was just a name, wasn't it…?

"My dad would call this the *chaos moment* but then, look where that's got me: taken hostage by a cursed academy." Sleipnir's gaze darted to Bask who nodded, before it settled back on mine with a steely determination. "There's only you, me, and Bask. Then there's the Princes and their whipping boy." He tilted his head and his bright hair fell into my eyes. "Huh, I sort of think we should add our Ghost Immortal to the head count, even if we can't see her."

All of a sudden, I was hit with a yearning that

made me shiver and a burst of Heart's rock ballad "Secret" that was so schmaltzy, I almost longed to scoff chocolate ice-cream in front of a weepie.

Almost.

My powers of Confess told me that Sleipnir was hiding something, and with his change from nu metal to ballad, I'd say that it was to do with *love*.

Aquilo had always refused to watch weepies or any type of romantic movie with me. He'd told me that he didn't believe in any of that *nonsense* because men were *property to be bred*, and one day, his family would choose who he married, so why pretend that he lived outside the covens?

Mage's balls, I hoped that Aquilo was okay. I'd been the one stuck in an attic, but I'd made it my mission to keep Aquilo happy.

Back in the House of Jewels, when Aquilo had been allowed to visit me, I'd discovered that he had two weaknesses: he'd never hug and he was seriously ticklish. Dad had once asked why Aquilo squealed with laughter every time that he entered the attic. I'd told dad that I was perfecting my Harry Potter comedy routine. After all, that'd been Aquilo's favorite book.

Dad had scrutinized me; his lips had twitched. "You always try every trick in the *spell* book, cub. What's your room…the Chamber of Secrets?"

I'd gaped at him and then snorted with laughter

myself. Dad had always surprised me like that because ironically within witch Houses Harry Potter (who was a wizard success story), was as feared as Voldemort.

Yet Dad had read the books as well…? Maybe he'd been trying to convince himself that I wasn't a monster, even if the books were all lies. I understood because I'd done the same.

Now, I was surrounded by both love and lies.

"*You'll* be the one sleeping on the floor if you don't include our Sexy Spirit," Bask huffed.

I rubbed my nose against Sleipnir's. I couldn't help the kitteny urge because despite what he was hiding, I was one sunbeam away from shifting and snuggling into his arms. "Hey, interesting fact: Damelza's also clever at omitting the truth because I can't sense that, only lies. Does it suck to discover you're as sly as a witch?" I winced. "*Ow*, I'll admit that was below the belt. Okay, does it suck to learn that you're helping to cover up the academy's secrets, as well as the spook's?"

Sleipnir sighed, before snatching my arm and dragging me staggering after him down the corridor. He pointed at each portrait in turn. "*This one…this one…this…*"

Bask clutched at my sleeve, trying to pull me to him, but Sleipnir was too powerful. After all, he was *the son of Loki.*

"Please, I want... not like this... please let me," Bask begged.

"All of these are the students...*prisoners*...of the Rebel Academy." Sleipnir hauled me to a stop at the end of the corridor in front of a mirror.

I stared at the three of us, panting and flustered but united in the reflection: *Rebels*.

"So, they've each cast Invisibility Spells?" I scoffed.

Sleipnir's lips pinched at Bask's stifled sob.

My shoulders hunched. *What had I said?*

Sleipnir clenched his jaw. "That's kind of hard to do since they're *dead*."

By the witching heavens, what had killed so many students?

I'd known that this academy was dangerous but not that mum had been sending me here as a death sentence. But what if that was exactly why she'd gained me an invitation?

After all, she blamed me for dad dying.

In a blur of dark hair and alabaster skin, Bask clung to me, warm and as close to breaking down as I was. Had he loved the boy in the portrait? When had he died?

I shook my head. "But I was sent here to study spells, potions, and the arcane."

"Son of a witch, you truly do believe your own

lies." Sleipnir's intent stare made me squirm. "You'll take classes taught by the most powerful witches in Britain and you'll also be taught to survive." Then he clung to me just as tightly as Bask, so that I was caught as the mage filling in an Immortal sandwich. "I won't lose anybody else."

"Yeah, that's touching." I stilled because *hello, inappropriate hard-on that I couldn't will away...* I blamed the way that Bask was nuzzling against my neck, slinking up and down me, as well as remaining untouched by anyone for all those horny years... *I'd be milking that one for a good while yet.* I bit my lip. "But why…?"

Then I gasped. Rebel Ghost was kissing down my neck, and I arched into her touch, as she trailed her hand around and over my aching dick. My breath hitched, but then Bask shivered, hugging me tighter, before Sleipnir widened his stance and groaned.

When I glanced into the mirror, I was shocked… Oh sweet mage, I'd never even imagined that I could look so *bewitching* caught between the alluring beauty of an incubus and the commanding hotness of a god.

It was only an ego trip lie though that our sexy image in the mirror had summoned Rebel Ghost; I thought that it was our *pleasure* that had called to her.

"You do this often then?" I rested my head against Sleipnir's shoulder, as he held me. "Did you position this mirror so that you could watch, whilst the spook fondled you?"

Bask snickered. "Away with you, she was never strong enough to touch until you arrived." I jolted. *Why was the ghost becoming more powerful through her connection to me?* "I've spelled this mirror to look like a portrait to any non-Immortals."

I blinked. "It's a magic mirror?"

Bask nodded.

"That's a thing?"

Sleipnir snorted with laughter.

"But why…?"

Bask smiled against my neck. "I might be a wee thief."

This was where Rebel Ghost's portrait had hung.

"You wanted her to be safe, so you hid her above our bed…?" I questioned.

If there was one thing that I understood, it was the drive to protect even something like a portrait because Rebel Ghost hadn't felt dead…*she wasn't*. Even if she was hanging in this gallery. And if she wasn't, then it meant that we all had a chance at life as well.

When Bask drew back and touched his gloved thumb to my cheek, I quivered at the joy in his gaze, as well as the *need*. "*Our* bed…?"

On the oath of a liar, it'd just slipped out. It hadn't meant anything, right?

The tips of my ears became hot. *Distract, distract,*

distract... "Why's she hanging amongst all these rebels anyway, when she's a witch and—"

"Do you want to hear a ghost story?" Sleipnir grasped my curls, wrenching back my head. His breath was hot in my ear.

"Shouldn't we get the campfire and marshmallows going, before we move onto the scary?" *Mage's balls, why had my voice cracked on the last word?*

"Chill out," Sleipnir ordered, "you've been in the *scary* since you arrived. I suspect that the ghost of this magical castle is more dangerous than anything else, however, and that includes me."

He flashed a grin that wasn't at all reassuring.

My brow furrowed. "Why though, when she's trapped just like me? All I was ever desperate for was someone to free me."

Truth: But they never had.

Bask's arms tightened around me like he'd heard the unspoken truth anyway.

Sleipnir bristled. "For someone who was locked away by his asshole witch family, you're kind of slow at seeing the dark side of the House of Crows. Think about this: what did our ghost do that was so unforgivable that she became the only ever witch Rebel?" His lips pressed to my ear with each word. "She's the original *wicked witch* who cursed the academy."

A bitter wind blasted in protest down the gallery, knocking us to our knees. Bask sheltered me against the wind's howl, and Sleipnir battled onto his feet. Sleipnir's eyes flashed with furious fire.

Suddenly, the mirror frosted as if with panted breaths and then froze with pink icicles from its corners inward. My eyes widened at its spiderweb beauty.

My mum and sister had thought that I was a monster because I could shift. Had this witch been trapped for centuries by the House of Crows, just because her type of magic hadn't been what they'd been expecting from a daughter?

After all, witch rules were dickish rules.

I had to save Rebel Ghost. Yet what if that meant unleashing a wicked witch who could be crueler than even Damelza?

My breath became ragged, as my heart pounded too rapidly.

Then ice-blue eyes flashed in the middle of the mirror, before it could frost over. A black gloved hand reached towards me, tracing on the other side of the mirror, and in neon pink a word appeared:

MAGENTA

I gasped, soaring with joy, despite the roar of my pulse that deafened me.

Rebel Ghost was called Magenta.

A name had power, and *Magenta* had just given that power to me. Her need to touch thrummed through me. It ached as much as *my* need to touch *her*.

But if I did, would it trap me forever or free her?

This was my first morning in the Rebel Academy, and I was risking my life to save a witch, which was like a mage coating his dick in honey and then dipping it in a colony of starving red ants.

Bask hissed, trying to pull me back, but I stretched out my fingers towards the first woman to kiss me, the wicked witch, and the original Rebel...*Magenta*.

Magenta's magic hung in the air. It was scented with the intoxicating aroma of the woods and prickled across *my* magic.

Time for the ghost story to begin.

I gasped, as my fingers touched the mirror...

But then, Sleipnir yanked me back by my hair, and Bask's hand clasped around mine, as I struggled.

"Does it please you to have your foxy arse pulled through into some *Alice Through the Looking Glass* world?" Bask's fingers were shaking, even as he squeezed mine. "This academy is death."

"But *she* isn't." The truth of Magenta's *life* prickled beneath my skin. "Anyway, I laugh in the face of death. It really pisses him off."

Sleipnir traced over the brand on the back of his hand. I was surprised to see that his hair had softened to candy pink waves. "I respect death, but son of a troll, I respect every Rebel's life more. I've kind of grown fond of you, so here's a tip. No touching magic mirrors."

He let go of my hair with a shove.

I flushed. *Okay, as tips went, that didn't suck.*

"Especially ones that send cryptic messages." Sleipnir's jaw clenched, as he nodded at the mirror.

Words had appeared as if traced through the ice:

I'm the Wickedly Charmed Crow.

Why did this feel like a first date? I mean, I'd never *been* out with anyone before, but if I based it on the movies that I'd forced Aquilo to watch with me, then we'd introduced ourselves and now Magenta was sharing more intimate details.

Yeah, I didn't understand those details, we were talking via a magic mirror with two other guys listening in, along with enough creepy vibes for this to be a horror movie. But still, *romantic*.

When had I ever gone for the conventional?

Truth: Please let somebody love me.

I watched in fascination as a tree spread around the words in crackling pink-tinged icicles.

"Beautiful." Bask's breath ghosted across the glass. "What do you want? Are you a sphinx?"

Sleipnir snorted. "Not unless they also used to run the academy." He vibrated with pain and disappointment. My feline side longed to rub against him in comfort. He waved his hand with a languid disinterest at the mirror that I no longer believed. "It means that Magenta's from the House of Crows, just like Damelza. This is what comes of trusting a witch."

A blast of wind howled in outrage down the corridor. I clutched Bask, staggering under the freezing onslaught. Then the mirror shattered in a thousand shards, flying like ice crows from the frame to slice me bloody.

Rebel Academy, Sunday September 1st

BASK

I tweezed the last shard out of Fox's palm; I winced, even though *he* didn't. He'd only saved his gorgeous face by throwing up his hands in time. He hadn't flinched or even cursed me out, during the whole time that it'd taken to rid his palms of glass. Maybe he'd been trained to take pain as well?

Beg me to let you burn yourself...

I shuddered, clinging to Fox and forcing back the memory of the Duchess. She didn't have a right to haunt my sexy self any longer; now I had Magenta. But then, my Spooky Snookums had hurt Fox (who was studying me like he could *see* even the ugly parts of me that I usually hid behind my beauty), and my own love for her frightened me.

Could you die from the aching *beat — beat — beat* of your own heart?

I preened. Incubi could do romantic gestures better than anyone: I could die of a broken heart...or the curse of the Exploding Pleasure Dick.

I snuggled with Fox on a suede sofa in the center of the Rebel Café, which was outside the castle in the grounds. Holograms of the ocean washed across the walls, along with the soothing crash of waves. The café had been built to relieve the stress of students in their free time. Professors used it as a privilege that could be taken away or granted as a reward. Serenity, who'd been magically created to run the café, had a wee crush on my Sleipnir, which meant that we could sneak in here like now, rather than risk the professors discovering our secrets.

I shuddered at the thought of letting Bacchus know why Fox was injured. It didn't matter who Magenta truly was, she was still *mine*, and I'd save her. Witches were *never* imprisoned as Rebels, so why had they placed Magenta's portrait in that gallery?

Once an incubus loved, they were loyal until death. It was a *thing*.

Fox was still watching me like I'd been the one to be sliced as if with the death by a thousand cuts. I frowned (and no one loved a frowning incubus), before carrying out a quick check: arse pettable, hair shiny, and lips kissable.

This incubus was sizzling.

Then I flushed, uncomfortable. Was my whipping boy distressed because I didn't protect him or because Magenta had turned out to be a Crow? I'd seen his file, and along with the cute-as-a-button baby photos, I hadn't been able to miss the cruelty by his family.

It looked like it was time for a certain ruby-eyed Immortal to show him that pleasure could heal pain.

Fox's eyes widened in cute surprise, as I clasped his wrists, slamming them against the sofa. Then I straddled him, pushing him down amongst the sofa's cushions that softened in response. As if Serenity sensed the change in mood, the lights dimmed. I sighed; this was the cuddliness that I needed. When Fox's hard-on pressed against mine, my eyelids fluttered at the sensation. Inside, my powers built like champagne bubbles: sparkling and fresh. I panted, licking across Fox's jaw and tasting his tangy blood, at the same time as I breathed in his delicious scent of raspberries.

If I could build my powers, then I could heal Fox. Here's the thing, incubi have the talent of healing but only if they charged themselves first by giving plea-sure (*such a hardship, snicker*). If I healed Fox, then Bacchus wouldn't discover about Magenta.

I could protect both my new lovers.

"By Tyr's ass, stop wriggling against each other like eels and help me plot how to summon a ghost who doesn't seem to know her own dickish strength," Sleipnir snarled.

Mood. Officially. Killed.

Sleipnir paced from one side of the café to the other. His hair cycled between pink, red, and aquamarine so fast that it hurt my eyes. Even *I* didn't mood swing that badly, and I'd been told that I could be one changeable hottie (*unbelievable, right?*).

I treated myself to a final stroke of Fox's curls, whilst he treated himself to a cheeky squeeze of my ass, then I settled myself in his lap with a satisfied *wriggle*.

If Sleipnir wanted an eel, then I'd give him one.

Sleipnir appeared torn apart by his thoughts on Magenta. He already had hang ups about witches, and it looked like it was down to my pettable arse to help him over it. My deliciously divine Magenta might not know her own strength, but every one of the Rebels had faulty powers. It was why we'd been sent here. Why would she be different? I could convince him.

See, I could be resolute. Ma called it *stubborn*, but it was a trait of the Night lineage. Definitely *resolute*.

All of a sudden, the room pulsed to a calming green, and a steaming bath with petals floating on top appeared in front of Sleipnir. The cloying scent of roses suffused the café. Sleipnir grunted with shock as he tumbled forward, splashing into the oily water headfirst. He spluttered to the surface, kneeling back on the floor with his hair plastered across his face in the brilliant impression of a wet dog.

I snickered, and Fox hid his chuckle against my neck. *Woah, that tickled.*

"A hot bath is just right to ease your stress, godling," Serenity's Welsh voice crooned from the walls, as if her aim was to make Sleipnir come from her voice alone. *Everybody had to have a goal in life.* "It's usual to take your clothes off first, mind."

Serenity was a minx.

Sleipnir wiped his wet hair out of his eyes, as water dripped down his neck. It was such a waste that I didn't get to lick it off. "I'm a *god*, and it's usual to ask if a guy wants to bathe first."

"That's right: assert yourself! But remember, I'm here to reduce your stress, so I'm only responding to your own needs. So, how about a quick wank to relieve the tension?"

Fox shook underneath me with silent laughter.

Sleipnir blinked. "Did you just say…?"

"Smile," Serenity continued with pretend innocence, "I said: a quick *smile*. Come on, it'll help. Scientists have proved that if your face thinks you're happy, then your brain will be as well."

"Awesome," Sleipnir muttered (*my sarcastic godling*), "now she's getting all scientific on my ass."

When the bath vanished with a *pop*, Sleipnir's shoulders slumped in relief. He pushed himself up, growling at the way that water slipped down the front of his shirt. I always forgot how hot he looked when wet like Darcy in *Pride and Prejudice* emerging dripping out of the lake if he'd somehow discovered punk rock.

"Does someone need a hug?" Serenity offered.

Sleipnir stiffened. "I'm just wrecked that you don't have arms."

"When you're this stressed—"

"I'm not stressed," Sleipnir hollered.

"I rest my case," Serenity commented, smugly. "You need to let it out. Don't snarl at me like that. How about a good cry or a swear?" I'd been taught that either of those only led to ugly incubi…and pain. When I stiffened, Fox stroked his hand down my thigh in comfort. "Come on, try it with me: *fuck, fuck, fuck…*"

"Serenity, it'd relax me to eat an apple, if it pleases you to feed me." I cut across Serenity's cheerful cursing with my sweetest pout.

My gaze became half-lidded, as I held out my hand in supplication.

I could do *sweet* when I tried.

Sleipnir shot me a grateful glance, as Serenity concentrated on producing peeled slices of apple on my palm. When Fox grinned, before opening his mouth, I fed him one, but not before he'd tongued my finger in thanks. I shivered, pecking a kiss to the tip of his nose. Then I munched thoughtfully on my own slice, sucking on the sweet juices between my own fingers.

We'd finished the Discipline Run and could hide out here for a couple of hours before Bacchus became suspicious, if we were lucky, but what about after that? Term started tomorrow, and we had to win the Rebel Cup. We couldn't have this Mystery of Magenta, which sounded like we'd fallen into a paranormal mystery, distracting us from the dangers *because then we'd die*. I could tell that Sleipnir was as troubled as me.

Into the silence, Serenity burst out, "I know — orgasms!"

Fox grinned. "The Shout Out Inappropriate Words Game: I was the champion at this three times running. Diarrhea! Bomb! Daddy!"

I slammed my palm across his mouth. "Was the champion spanked?"

Fox hesitated, before shaking his head emphatically.

Sleipnir slumped against the wall with a sigh. "The weird thing is that I can't fight it because she's honestly not wrong."

Rule 6 of the Incubi Night Code states: You can never have too many orgasms.

Except, I'd once been forced to have seven in one night with the Duchess, so I knew that rule sucked.

Yet I needed more pleasure to heal Fox's hands. Plus, it appeared to be the only way that we were connected with Magenta.

I winked at Sleipnir, blowing him a kiss. "As you wish."

When a green mist formed in the center of the room where the bath had been, I drew in my breath. In a sinuous dance of limbs, a fae appeared with a gust of his golden wings. The mist bled into emerald hair that hung to the fae's waist and matched his large eyes because he was an Unseelie, unlike Ambrose. Then he dropped to his hands and knees with a sexy wiggle of his ass and crawled teasingly towards me.

"I didn't request a fae sex doll." Fox stared trans-fixed at the fae, as the fae rested his hands on my thighs and then nuzzled at my crotch. "I think you've mixed up Ambrose's fantasy with ours."

Sleipnir snorted. "It'd be more like Ambrose's *nightmare*. Meet Prince Lysander."

I shot Sleipnir my best *you're a naughty god but I love you* look, at the same time as the *prince* laid his head in my lap and held out his hand shyly to Fox.

In a daze, Fox shook it. "Delighted to meet... Wait, no I'm *not* because you're the rival here, cruel to the dragons, and even if you're prettier than Tinker Bell, the *lie* that I can feel is dressing you more like Hook, which isn't a a turn-on."

The fae snatched back his hand, snuggling closer to me.

I slid my hand through his hair. "He's a clone of Lysander: My Andro."

Prince Lysander didn't know about the existence of Andro, who was precisely alike in all ways apart from his personality. Lysander's eyes were hard as jade, but Andro always looked at me, as he was now, with the same softness as a loyal dog. I'd have made an outstanding owner, and now I had a dog, cat, fox, and hedgehog…

Maybe I wouldn't mention that line of thought to Fox.

Serenity created him whenever I needed someone who was happy and willing to submit. Prince Lysander would kick my arse and then hex me into a eunuch if I even dared to kiss him. Andro, on the other hand, loved to take commands, and I'd never been allowed to show my dominant side before I'd arrived at the academy. It was a strange thing to feel so grateful to a clone.

Sleipnir had insisted that I couldn't love Andro because a clone couldn't feel love back, but I wasn't so sure.

"Take me out, if it pleases you," I whispered.

Andro shivered, wrapping his wings around me

and kissing my inner thigh, before nodding. It only fed me, if it brought pleasure to Andro, and I'd never *take* from the unwilling. Plus, did he feel lonely stuck in this café, or did he only spring to life just for me? Either way, I had to give him something to remember each time.

I loved the way that his eyes darkened with desire, as he undid my pants and reverentially slid out my dick, pumping me a few times, although incubus here: I was already hard and aching. When he licked around the head of my dick, swirling over the slit, I gasped.

Fox's hand closed over my mine, even though it had to smart against his bleeding palm. I met his gaze, which was as glassy as my own. He thrummed with magic like it was *his* dick that was being sucked.

At last, Andro stopped teasing me and swallowed, at the same time as playing with my balls. I arched but didn't break gazes with Fox. When Andro hummed, and his vibrations shuddered through me, as he pressed harder on my balls, I spiraled higher. Then he relaxed his throat, and I pushed deeper — *once* — *twice...*

"Andro," I gasped in warning, but it was too late.

I'd just broken **Rule 89 of the Incubi Night Code**: You can never have too many orgasms but always give your lover the option of swallowing or spitting.

Yet Andro looked smugly like the cat who'd got

the cream as he drew back, giving my dick little kitten licks to clean it. I squirmed at the oversensitivity.

Silly incubus, post orgasm torture was his revenge.

Andro looked up at me from underneath his eyelashes with pretend innocence but it didn't work because I'd patented that look.

I pulled my hand out of Fox's, hurriedly tucking my dick back into my pants and away from Andro's sneaky tongue. Although, I did *love* that tongue.

I vibrated with the new power, which had had been boosted by the pleasure. It sparkled through me.

"You pleased me, Andro," I murmured.

Suddenly, Sleipnir marched to Andro, wrenching back his head by his long hair. I stiffened at his yelp.

"You're done with this *thing* now, so you can send him away." Sleipnir shook Andro.

When Andro's eyes flashed with hurt, I knew that it wasn't about the hair pulling because that was one of his kinks.

My gaze became steely. Sleipnir should know better than to hurt one of my lovers. "Does it please you to be cursed with tangled earbuds every time that you listen to music?"

Fear the curse of the incubus...

Sleipnir blanched, letting go of Andro and stepping back. Andro smiled at me like I was his hero.

"By the runes, have you forgotten that asshole Prince Titus sent us on the mission last term or that your asshole Lysander *beat* us, which is why we were chosen to be sent on it. If not for that...*asshole*, Hector wouldn't have been killed."

Andro whimpered, huddling closer to me.

Fox glanced between us. "Wow, that's a lot of assholes."

"Andro isn't Lysander, and Lysander isn't his uncle." It was only with Andro's soft wings cocooned around me that I finally understood that truth.

I no longer blamed the prince for the mission through the Gateway, which had gone wrong and killed my friend, or the fact that his uncle, Titus, ran the academy from the shadows. After all, Lysander was stuck here the same as us and he fought to protect Willoughby and his whipping boy.

It wasn't any of the Princes' fault that we were forced to compete against each other.

"Imagine what the Princes do to *your* clones." Fox cocked his head.

Sleipnir's eyes opened wide with panic. "They don't... I mean, you don't think... They wouldn't...?"

"Prince Willoughby pets Bask's behind and then spanks it until Bask comes," Andro supplied helpfully. Well, I *do* have a spankable arse. "And Prince Lysander banned Serenity from ever producing a clone of Sleipnir."

Sleipnir's expression became shuttered, before he

stalked to the far side of the café. "Just get rid of him and fix our whipping boy."

Sleipnir hadn't had the same revelation as me. But then, he didn't have the same advantages. Maybe I should advise him about the shiny hair?

"Someone's sounding stressed," Serenity chirped, "would you like to dance it out?"

When the joyful "Love Shack" by the B-52's burst out like the café's anthem, Sleipnir growled in defeat, turning to bang his head against the wall in time to the rhythm. I grasped Andro's chin, tipping up his head. His eyes widened, before crinkling at the edges with happiness.

I kissed him, tenderly. "See you soon."

When Andro faded in a twist of green mist, the loss speared through me. I turned to Fox, clutching his shoulders to be certain that he was still with me...and real. Yet wasn't Andro real to himself, at least?

Fox's smile was sad like he understood the way that I shook, as I kissed him with the same tenderness as I had Andro. His lips were warmer than the fae's had been and plusher. I sighed, running my tongue across the seam of his lips to encourage them to open, and then I drew back, hovering just above the lush mouth that I'd already become addicted to kissing.

I could taste that he belonged to Ghost Immortal, just like I knew that we should all be together.

My magic bubbled up in a ruby stream, glittering

out of my mouth and into Fox's to heal him. He moaned at the sensation. The cuts on his hand closed up, until his skin was as perfect as before.

Then I sat back on my heels, shooting Sleipnir a smug grin. "Healed as good as new. Pet me."

Sleipnir slouched with an indolent elegance to run his hand through my hair. *The petting tribute was acceptable.* "Now your pleasure's sated, it's time we all used the power of our dicks."

"I knew all the Alpha posturing was just horniness." Fox bounced up, snatching Sleipnir and swinging him around to "Love Shack" with wild abandon in the face of his outrage. "Feel the power of my dick, baby."

"Valhalla! Did you just call me...?"

"*Baby*," Serenity crowed. "Although, I prefer *godling.*"

"Co-co," Sleipnir hollered.

I dived up from the sofa, catching Sleipnir around the waist, as Fox spun him to me tango style.

Fox's eyes gleamed. "Is this another round of the Shout Out Inappropriate Words Game? Okay, my go: Cockmuppet!"

"Stop," Sleipnir gritted out, twisting in my arms, "this is a round of Find the Witch."

I sobered, letting go of him. He straightened his blazer, before holding out his hand, and a crystal goblet appeared, which sizzled. I peered at the brown liquid that could've been hot chocolate but it also smelled of sweet vanilla, hot ginger, and ancient magic.

"I'm allergic to drinking magic potions." Fox grimaced. *Ah, my cute little liar.* "I come out in hives, my throat closes up, and then I turn into Ivan the Terrible. It's truly an affliction."

"It's called Co-co because it makes you co-co-come." Sleipnir smirked. "I assure you, I've never stopped thinking about the times that Magenta has appeared to us or become stronger. I take it you've noticed as well that she's connected to us all: our pleasure and emotions." Sleipnir hesitated. *Why did he look shifty all of a sudden?* "Hey, I felt her out on the Discipline run, didn't you?"

Fox and I both nodded. There'd been a pulsing ancient magic in the Dead Wood. It'd called to me, and I'd battled not to dive between the trees.

Sleipnir examined his nails. "Honestly, I have the feeling that Magenta's power once fed from nature, but now she also feeds from *us*."

Fox edged closer, until we stood around the goblet like it was a witch's brew. I guessed that it was. I'd never willingly drunk one of those before.

"Why now? Why us?" Fox asked; his expression was brittle.

"You're special to her," I tilted my head, "you're the reason that everything's changed."

Fox hugged his arms across his chest. His voice was small, "I don't want to be special. I just want to be *me.*"

"You could ask why *any* of us." Sleipnir's eyes narrowed, as he studied me.

Fox stroked across the back of my hand. "You're the one who makes me —"

"Hard? Wild with lust? Desperate to pet?" I bounced up and down on my toes.

I'd bet that it was one of those.

Fox smiled, fondly. I wasn't used to that. "Feel safe and loved."

My breath hitched, and my vision became dangerously blurry.

Sleipnir ducked his head. "Of course, the powerful son of Loki has nothing to do with this magic."

Fox rolled his eyes. "My power's screaming that you *know* you're connected to the dead."

Sleipnir raised his head. "My dad's the one with that power. I can just see the places that the living and dead walk the line. It's kind of obvious that Magenta needs all three of us, and that we all care about her. So, let's enhance the pleasure."

He raised the goblet and took a deep swig, before raising it to my lips.

I'd been taught about this by my ma: *peer pressure.* I was an incubus, which meant that I was already a walking aphrodisiac. I pressed my lips tightly together.

Sleipnir raised an imperious eyebrow. "Think how intense this will make the experience. Aren't you a romantic, Bask? Don't you want to rescue your lover?"

I only took a sip of the thick liquid, however, because an incubus didn't truly need aphrodisiacs like a non-incubus, otherwise we'd end up with **R.I.P Drowned in Cum** carved on our headstones. The liquid tasted sweet like chocolate but then burned with the aftertaste of fiery ginger. As Fox downed it like it was beer, I choked at the searing hotness.

Instantly, my soft worn out dick twitched in my pants, before springing to attention. I groaned, scrambling to drop my pants and let my dick jump free like an angry throbbing pole.

I stared at Sleipnir and Fox who'd done the same next to me, but were bent over groaning in pain. *Whoops*…this looked less like pleasure and far more like the pain that the Duchess would train me with, and the others were less used to it than me.

Maybe Serenity had overdone the co-co?

"Orgasm coming up!" Serenity purred.

To our collective horror, the door to the Rebel Café crashed open, and Juni Crow, who was Damelza's daughter, our professor, and the Prince's tutor, stalked into the room. She was a slenderer version of Damelza with short sculptured hair that was bound underneath a woven cap of feathers, and sharp pointy features that would've been impish, if her eyes had danced with less malice.

Right now, however, her eyes danced with astonishment.

With our pants around our ankles, us Rebels backed against the wall like we were before a firing squad. I didn't know of any execution where you had a dick so enlarged that you couldn't even hide it behind your hands.

I shuddered, and my balls drew up. I needed to come.

Not now…not now…not now…

I could tell by their strained expression and shaking legs that Sleipnir and Fox were waging the same battle.

"When you didn't return after the Discipline Run, my mother sent me to find you." Juni's gaze ran dispassionately over us. "Does Professor Bacchus know that her precious Immortals behave like whores? I'd cast a Shaming Hex on my Princes if they hid in corners with their cocks out."

I'd been jealous of the pampered Princes wing (Sleipnir told me that they had silk sheets to make nests out of and at least three times as many pillows), but their tutor made me twinge with sympathy for them, and that was a weird new sensation.

"We had a bet," Fox bluffed.

Pathological lying was a definite turn-on.

Don't think about his cuteness… *The Duchess in suspenders kissing Damelza…*

I shuddered, just managing to push myself back from the edge.

"A Dick Bet," I shrugged my shoulder. "It's the sort of thing that guys do, you know: my dick is longer than your dick."

"More girth," Sleipnir panted.

"Prettier," Fox added.

Juni stared at us unblinkingly. "Who won?"

"I did," we all chorused together.

Juni's cheek twitched, then she marched closer, batting at our hands. I protested weakly but I didn't dare move because if she even breathed on me…

Dick, are you listening? This is my stern voice. You do not have permission to come…

"I wonder if the Princes play these games?" I didn't like the gleam in her eye. The Princes were our rivals in the academy, but I was sure that Juni only played the role of the indulgent tutor, whilst being as cruel as her ma. The Duchess had pulled the same trick. Juni scrutinized our dicks. "The incubus wins."

Of course. I grinned, but it faded at the way that her eyes lit up. She tapped my chest. "What's the forfeit for losing the bet?"

"The losers have to ask a witch for a kiss," I smirked.

Sleipnir gasped in outraged horror.

To my surprise, Juni smiled. "Well, pucker up." She leaned closer to Fox as if to claim his lips, and he *eeped*. "My mother's in her study. Why don't you see what happens when you go and ask her? I'd love to see the Immortals start term transformed into frogs. Damelza has been planning such delightfully agonizing hexes."

I was about to co-co-come…

A pearly arc burst from my pulsing dick like a gleaming fountain, before falling onto Juni's shoe. I screamed more in pain than pleasure, collapsing against the wall. My release started off a chain reaction: Fox came longer and harder even than I had (that'd teach the whipping boy about downing potions), and Sleipnir shook, bent over, through his orgasm.

At last, when I was able to look up through my eyelashes, Juni appeared frozen in shock.

Uh-oh…

"Next time you do that, you'll be licking it off. Clean yourself up and get back to the West Wing." Juni turned, sweeping out of the café like three Immortals hadn't just come on her shoes.

To be fair, the witch had class.

Sleipnir bumped my shoulder. "Kiss a witch…?

That's the volley in what I promise will be an epic dick war."

"Get on with you, we *all* want to kiss Magenta." I glanced around. "*Are you here Magenta?*"

Surely, three super-powered orgasms at once was enough? If we were batteries, we'd be shining bright to summon a ghost.

But I couldn't sense Magenta. There was no smell of yew trees, icy tickle of wind, or feeling of protection and yearning.

"It didn't work," Fox whispered.

I wiped my tacky hand on my stomach, biting my lip.

"Why would I let some *ghost* in here?" Serenity's voice was sly. "I only allow authorized Rebels. This has to be a safe space or how can you relax? As your Stress Counselor, I'd also like to point out that what you just experienced registered as pain, rather than pleasure."

Sleipnir yanked up his trousers so quickly that I winced on his behalf. "Trolls balls, why didn't you tell us?"

Serenity replied smugly, "You didn't ask."

"She's jealous." Fox fumbled to cover himself. "Can magically intelligent cafes get jealous? Okay, I'm having an *AI* moment here."

"Of course, she's jealous." I ran a hand over my arse just to check that it was in perfectly pettable condition. "That's the curse of being so slinky. But how do we summon Magenta now?"

"Who feels like a walk at midnight into the forbidden Dead Wood and then a picnic at Hecate's Tree?" Sleipnir asked coolly.

"Honestly, you're not selling it to me." Fox met my gaze. "But I remember the freaky tree that appeared in the mirror. If she's trapped in it, then I'm down with the plan. But no potions. Let's make the pleasure real."

I nodded.

Hecate's Tree was sacred to the witches. Tonight, we'd break a serious rule in Rebel Academy: *never go into the Dead Wood.*

CHAPTER ELEVEN

Rebel Academy, Sunday September 1st

MAGENTA

If there was one thing that consoled me about my ghostly existence, it was that it proved life could always be rewritten. I'd never guessed that I'd discover a second chance at love after my death.

After all, I'd gone a little crazy but I wasn't so conceited that I'd have dreamed the Immortals would offer me their hearts, calling me with a bond that screamed *home, home home…* I too craved each of them with a brutal desperation, longing to show them the love that had slumbered inside me for over a century, as I'd been trapped between the veil of life and death.

Now, as I watched in shock as the incubus, god, and my sweet mage traipsed into the glade that was silent apart from my fizzing magic, laughing and joking like it was a field trip to Hecate's Tree, I realized one thing: *they* were just as crazy as *me*.

Had they no idea how many rules they were breaking or how harsh the punishment would be if they were caught? Didn't they understand how much they should be shielding Fox from the dangers of the academy? Then I stiffened.

Cauldrons and candles, had even Robin's death been forgotten?

I swung on a high branch of Hecate's tree above the Immortals heads. Echo and Flair flapped through the night sky, moving as shadows across the pale moon, before landing either side of me.

Flair smoothed his ruffled feathers with his beak. Then he peered down at the Immortals, who were laying out their coats, before settling uncomfortably on the charred earth.

Flair whistled. *"Well, fuck me."*

I wish that I had such a way with words.

"They came for you," Echo said, wistfully.

My breath hitched, and my nails bit into the withered branch. I'd been desperate for anyone to remember me, but I didn't want them to endanger themselves.

I was already lost, wasn't I?

When Sleipnir peered upwards, catching my eye, I almost fell off the branch. He winked, before pretending that he couldn't see me again. I grinned at the charming god's antics.

"*Stop thinking with your cock lane,*" Flair grumbled. "*These idiots are about to get their bollocks hexed off.*"

"Would you awfully mind not referring to my flower as my *cock lane*?" I arched my brow.

Flair's pink eyes glittered. "*I apologize for the vulgar term, boss. Stop thinking with your quim, muff, cu—*"

"Hold your peace and listen," I hissed, flushing.

Down below in the glade, the Immortals sat in a circle on a nest of woolen coats, shivering. A single tied tea towel rested between them. Sleipnir set a crimson candle at the base of Hecate's tree, before lighting it. The flame flared a sizzling magenta, before dying down into a wavering specter in the dark.

Sleipnir watched the flame with an odd intensity, before glancing back at Bask.

Bask rested his hand on Fox's neck in a casual gesture of protection. "We're at the heart of the academy. Can't you sense...?"

"Hecate cursing the bravest but dumbest mage of his generation?" Fox looked up and down the tree like he was weighing up an opponent. *Bright boy.* "Forbidden. Dead. Sacred to witches." He counted off each point on his fingers. "Do you have any idea how much trauma you're creating in my mage psyche, unless this ritual that we're about to do involves slicing my neck as the sacrifice?" His eyes widened. "Okay, I take that back. This neck is steel; the knife would just bounce off…"

My familiars *cawed* raucously in unison. I swooped lower. There'd be no sacrificing of mages in *my* glade.

Bask snorted. "Get on with you, just feel it. Magenta doesn't wish blood, only love."

I hovered above their heads, suddenly breathless. How did Bask seem to know me? Why did they all feel as familiar to me as family?

"Strip." Sleipnir sat back on his heels, rifling in the pockets of one of the coats.

He pulled out a charm bag, which glittered with stars.

I shivered, as the hair raised on my nape. I ached to touch and be touched by Sleipnir again, and it'd be awfully nice to see my mage naked for the first time.

I admit, they were possibly as familiar as *lovers*, rather than family.

"You know that I adore your commanding voice," Bask gazed at Sleipnir through half-lidded eyes that had warmth curling through me, "but it's freezing, Slippy, and there are no blankets to snuggle."

Sleipnir's expression gentled. He was even more

handsome when his eyes became soft like that. "Omens and runes, I swear that it won't be for long, and I'll find a way to keep you warm. It's for the ritual. Hey, I know that this is a long shot, but we have to give this the best chance of freeing her."

Freeing me…?

Sleipnir had made that promise beside the frozen lake, but that'd been before the Rebels had discovered who I truly was. I hadn't wanted to deceive them. For once, I'd wanted the truth to be seen. Unfortunately, I'd never attempted to communicate as a ghost before, and the mirror hadn't withstood my power. I winced at the thought of injuring Fox.

So, were they attempting to free me back into life or free me from my ghostly existence and finally, allow me to die in peace?

My breathing became too rapid, and I sank lower and lower.

I wasn't ready. After all this time…not ready. I collapsed with my arms over my head. If I died, how could I protect the mage?

"*Breathe,*" Flair sounded panicked and very far away. "*Why does an infernal ghost have to fucking breathe or else she does this fading trick?*"

"*I don't care, mate. I just need my Magenta.*" Echo's wings curled around my back.

All of a sudden, I could smell the sweet woodsy

scent of white sage smudge sticks burning: the start of the ritual.

I raised my head, cautiously.

Sleipnir had lit a red candle, which channeled passion.

Sweet Hecate, let them be sacrificing their pleasure to free and then love me because all I desired was to love *them*.

Moonlight drifted through the canopy of the trees, draping like delicate veils across the beautiful limbs of the naked Rebels, as they sprawled in the center of the glade. Sleipnir glanced over his muscled shoulder at me; his hair was candy pink tonight, and sea serpent tattoos wound around his arms. As I watched, the coils of the tattoo wound higher and tighter. Sleipnir's smile was shy and concerned.

I blinked. *Ah, the huddled and shaking thing.*

I straightened onto my knees like I'd simply been studying some fascinating fauna on the (scorched) woodland floor. Echo sighed in relief, before perching on my shoulder, and Flair *thwacked* me around the head with his wing.

It was a delight to have such faithful familiars.

I watched with genuine fascination, as Bask bounced up and down (it wouldn't be ladylike to say how much I enjoyed the sight of his bouncing prick), as Fox started to untie the tea towel.

"The feast before the sacrifice is the only decent part of this plan." Bask bit his lip. "Feed me."

At last, Fox undid the knot, and the flanneled towel fell open to reveal the food inside. "Ta da!"

They'd planned a picnic...? My Rebels had sneaked out at night from the castle, broken the rule to enter the Dead Wood, before violating the sanctity of Hecate's Tree, and now they were going to merrily scoff a picnic?

I grinned. *Robin would've loved them.*

Sleipnir scanned the pile of squished sandwiches. "Well, that was underwhelming."

Bask petted Fox in comfort.

Fox shrugged. "Do these hands look like they were trained in petty thievery? This was all I could steal from the kitchen that you shoved me into."

"If it pleases you, did you see the Princes' salmon, cupcakes, and special chocolates...?" Bask asked, hopefully.

Fox huffed. "All the luxury stuff was locked and warded in this separate larder with the sign: **KEEP OUT, PRINCES ONLY. THAT MEANS YOU, IMMORTALS.**"

"What kind of jerk would put their name on food?" Sleipnir sneered.

"Well, my first guess would be the *Princes*." Fox grinned with sudden glee. "But look: I made crisp sandwiches."

He picked up a sandwich, biting in with a sharp *crunch*. Then he munched on the crisps with an orgasmic sigh, which made me cross my legs.

Sleipnir stared at him. "My life is complete."

Fox took another large bite. "This is salt and vinegar in buttery white bread. It's the food of kings, my Norse friend."

Grudgingly, both Sleipnir and Bask munched on a sandwich.

I shook my head. Forget the danger of Damelza, the witches, and the academy, the Rebels were in dire need of my picnic etiquette skills. On that alone, I had to find my way back to them. Where was the basket, napkins, and cutlery? I remembered my own picnics in these grounds with delicious roast beef, cucumber, or banana and sugar sandwiches, meat pies, and cakes with cream fillings.

Oh, and never forget the tea...

"*You're drooling, boss,*" Flair muttered.

Echo hopped onto my head and then bent to stare me in the eye. "*Are you having another flashback to your life again because it was boring the first time, and I know that you don't want to relive it.*"

Blushing, I shook him off my head, and he flew to a low branch with a series of rattling *clicks*.

When Fox wiped his hands on the tea towel, a hush fell on the glade. The candle was a bright point in the dark, focusing the magical energy, until it pulsed at the base of the tree. The intoxicating scent of white sage wound around all of us, binding us together.

"Should we pray?" Fox's tongue darted out, wetting his dry lips. "Except, I'm a mage, and there's a risk that if I pray to Hecate, my balls will be struck by lightning."

"We can't have that." Sleipnir appeared to be struggling to hide his smile. "There are different ways to complete the ritual and sacrifice."

Sleipnir pulled out some of the *technology* that Echo loved so much from the tangle of coats, before a modern song burst out, filling the glade with more lust and longing than I thought was possible in music alone. Gently, each of the Rebels kissed each other in turn, before Bask pulled Fox to his feet and swayed to the music like his soul was part of it. Fox wrapped his arms around Bask's neck, whilst Bask laid his head on Fox's chest. Their pleasure and love fed me, winding me higher, until sparkles lit the glade, brighter than any candle. As Bask rubbed his hips against Fox's, I swallowed thickly. Shaky, I skimmed my hand along my jawline, before pressing it to my throat; my pulse fluttered underneath my fingertips.

I sighed. *Please, please, let me be brought to life...*

I found that I didn't want to die.

Sleipnir studied Bask and Fox tenderly for a

moment, before he shuffled to kneel at the base of Hecate's Tree in front of the candle.

My brow furrowed. He was so close to me now that I could've reached over to smooth the dip of his tense shoulders. It took vast restraint not to press kisses down the exposed back of his neck. His naked submission for my sake was the most exquisite thing that I'd seen since my death. At least it was, until he slipped the pendant off from around his neck, which held a silver plectrum, and placed it before the candle: his sacrifice.

Then I realized that he was shaking.

Whatever Sleipnir had just sacrificed was of great value to him, and *that* made this moment the most exquisite thing that I'd witnessed since my death.

Sleipnir rested his hand over the plectrum like a goodbye. "Honestly, I know that this may seem like a poor offering, Hecate, but trust me, it's everything to me. Dad could never give my brothers and me much. He knew that I loved my guitar, however, and when I turned eighteen, he gifted me this." He tightened his hands around the plectrum. "I've never taken it off. It's all I have of dad, since the witches kidnapped me." My eyes burned. I wanted to scream at him to *take it back*, but he hadn't even glanced at me. His head hung down, and his hair covered his eyes. "But dad would want me to give it up to free you. He'd be proud."

"I'm proud too," I whispered.

Sleipnir's head jerked up, and our gazes met. His eyes gleamed brightly with unshed tears. "What do you want from us?"

Well, this god certainly didn't pull his punches.

I shot a look at Flair, who was still perched on my shoulder but more like a devil than a guardian angel. With a reluctant sigh, he flapped to join Echo.

Then I inched closer, before resting my hands on either side of Sleipnir's head, pulling him towards me, until my lips grazed his on each word, "I want you to hold me, need me, *love me.*"

When Sleipnir claimed my mouth with a moan that echoed the yearning that had swirled for long decades inside me, his lips were hot and his tongue warmed me. He smelled of raspberries, almonds, and co-co; his bonding with Fox and Bask lingered in his kiss. I could touch all of them at once.

Bask stopped dancing with a gasp. "Either it pleases you to kiss thin air *or you can see my Magenta.*" He dragged Fox with him to crouch either side of Sleipnir. "What does she desire?"

When Sleipnir cocked his eyebrow at me, I became quite giddy with the power of such decisions.

Fox snickered. "Shouldn't we be shagging over a pottery wheel?"

First, I learned that elves wanted to play with

snowmen, and now that mages were intimate over clay. The world was strange indeed.

"I'd imagine that we should start with a kiss," I tried for casual, but Sleipnir's gaze was too knowing.

"She wants a kiss," Sleipnir stated.

Fox's eyes lit up, and a slow smile spread across his face. Then he wrapped himself around me with intense concentration and sucked on my earlobe. *Wow, that tickled and wasn't unpleasant.*

Sleipnir chuckled.

"Would you mind terribly informing him that he's missed my mouth?" I squirmed away. When Fox sat back, looking shyly happy though, I quickly added, "Wait. Don't tell him that. Just… Pass on my thanks."

"She says that you're an awesome kisser, although not as good as me," Sleipnir informed Fox.

Perhaps, I should fire Sleipnir as my interpreter.

Fox's face fell, before he frowned. "You do remember that I'm literally able to tell when you're lying?"

Sleipnir only patted Fox on the head, before Bask slunk lower, bending down like he was prostrating himself. "Hey, her mouth isn't down there."

"She didn't say *where* she wanted to be kissed." Bask glanced up at me teasingly from underneath his eyelashes.

On the witching heavens, I could almost believe

that I wasn't invisible. Even though the tips of my ears suddenly became red with embarrassment, I still nodded at Sleipnir who sat back.

Bask licked, as if testing for the coldness of the air, before nipping kisses up my thighs. I knelt up, allowing my dress to fade to mist, before widening my legs. Bask's lips pressed to my inner thighs in worshipful lines. I struggled not to shield the most intimate part of myself, which I'd been taught no one but my husband had a right to touch. Yet that had been whilst I'd lived, and before my own mother had tried to marry me off to a fae prince.

Dying had truly changed my whole perspective on virginity. Also, the game of Wank Count. I'm certain that I knew far more about the Rebels' fantasies than any witch before me.

When Bask's soft lips kissed across the cotton of my drawers, licking and sucking at them, I arched my back, clasping my hands to my neck and my choker necklace like that could stop the coiling inside me. I'd never experienced such a sensation, even with Robin. When I pushed closer, riding Bask's face in rhythmic waves, he gasped; Sleipnir's eyes were dark, as he watched me.

Sweet Hecate, please, please, please...

My magic prickled and sparked inside me, until it burst out at the same time as the wave of spasmed pleasure that screamed through me. I fell back against Hecate's Tree in shock, as my heart beat wildly.

The candle blew itself out.

"I think you've killed her," Sleipnir breathed.

"Actually, it could be the opposite." Fox pushed himself to his feet, before reaching down to pull up Bask and Sleipnir.

My magic pulsed through the roots of the tree, before exploding upwards, lighting the branches that swayed in a dance of their own. Finally, magic sparkled like blossoms in the midst of winter down onto the Rebels in blessing.

Bask let out a delighted laugh, catching the sparkles in his palm. "Never underestimate the power of an incubus kiss."

"*Boss*," Flair's voice was softer than I'd ever heard it, "look by your hand *right. Fucking. Now.*"

When I forced my hazy brain to focus, I saw a snowdrop had pushed its head through the dead earth for the first time since I'd been burned to death here. I gasped. Then I glanced up and realized that the Rebels were also staring in amazement at the tiny white flowers that'd been brought to life by our love and magic.

By the ritual.

Snap my broomstick, had it worked?

For the first time in over a century, the ghost like paleness of a barn owl swooped across the glade, before frogs croaked out their song. Then tears did streak my cheeks because maybe I wasn't lost, if the glade that I'd loved with Robin (and that had been murdered by my mother), could be reborn.

"I never thought that a mage could help create something so beautiful." Fox shook, ducking his head. "But understatement of the century: something bad happened here. It screams through my magic that it murdered these trees and Magenta too. Okay, I know that I'm a brilliant kisser." I tried to smother my laughter, especially as he lifted his finger and pointed it above my head, "And no denials, future Mrs Fox." *Well, that shut me up.* Was that how men proposed nowadays? "But Hecate's Tree should be trying to burn me, whacking me in the face, or spanking me. The Hecate statues in the bailey had a lot of fun playing Hurt the Fox."

"What if the House of Crows are controlling the ones in the academy or this is the true Hecate?" Bask offered.

"Then what if the goddess saved Magenta and trapped her? Maybe we should touch—"

"You're suggesting we become tree huggers?" Sleipnir's gaze met mine with a dancing amusement.

Fox strode to the tree, encircling it with his arms. "Who's a gorgeous hunk of wood, *hmm*?"

Bask sidled next to him, resting his cheek on the trunk. "You can spank him now, Hecate."

When Sleipnir strode to join them, resting his hand against the blackened wood, I concentrated on pulsing my magic through it. He jerked, panting. Then he wrapped himself more fully around the trunk.

I shuddered like a thread was winding too tightly around me. My eyelids fluttered.

Was it working? Would I finally be saved?

Candles and broomsticks...

The glade lit with an eerie light, and my breath caught.

"I guessed that you'd have the shortest student record before being sent to my study, mage," Damelza's enraged voice boomed out of the shadows, "but even I didn't imagine that it would be for violating such a sacred place."

I shook, staring at the academy's Principal, as she swept towards my Rebels who were still hugging the tree. Her feather coat was ruffled up in her outrage. She trampled on the newly born snowdrops. I hated both the way that she glared only at Fox like he must've been the corrupting influence (my mother had always thought the same about Robin), and that I felt too weak to stand.

Echo and Flair hopped in front of me protectively.

"*Awkward,*" Bask mock whispered.

"Why do we always get into these situations?" Sleipnir groaned.

Fox tilted his head. "Perhaps because we keep hanging around with our dicks out…?"

"Silence, Confess," Damelza snarled. "Didn't you think that your brands would've alerted me that you were outside the castle without permission? Tomorrow you'll come to my study for punishment. I knew that the shimage criminality ran too deeply within you. I wonder if the taint can be cut out."

"Sorry, but I'm bad to the bone," Fox smirked.

"Let's test that, shall we?" Damelza's eyes glittered with malice.

She plucked a feather from her hair and shot it flying at Fox. When the feather sliced Fox's cheek, he gasped, hugging the tree tighter. He rested his bloody cheek against it, squeezing shut his eyes in pain. His blood trickled down the grooves of the dead tree.

Bask gasped, snatching Fox to his chest and backing away, as Sleipnir stepped in front of them. Damelza stalked closer.

My eyes widened, as that winding sensation began in my middle again but more intensely this time. The tree pulsed brighter and brighter. I was fading.

Would I be freed or die?

It turned out that Hecate *had* demanded both love and blood. She was an ancient deity, after all, and Fox had been the lamb.

Ah, irony.

"You promised not to leave me," Echo wept. *"Promised."*

All of a sudden, my vision grayed. My stomach lurched. I faded to nothingness, and then…

The trunk of Hecate's tree cracked open like a womb, and I slithered from its insides at Damelza's feet.

At long last, I was reborn as a living witch.

CHAPTER TWELVE

Rebel Academy, Monday September 2nd

MAGENTA

In all the excitement of being freed from Hecate's
Tree and reborn again as a human (well, more of a
witch and ghost hybrid, but it'd been the Rebel's first
ritual, these things happened), I'd forgotten how it'd
felt to be alive.

How had I ever survived? My stomach growled
like I'd already eaten a bear cub, a twinge of pain
lanced through my lower back, and my nose itched.
Plus, had my bosoms *always* been this big…? I
jiggled them in my corset.

I would *not* be defeated by my own bosoms.

But then, I glanced up and caught Fox watching

me with an amused expression. With a tilt of my head (because a lady must always act with grace and elegance), I gave a final wriggle, before focusing back on Damelza, who sat behind her study desk. Fox and I stood on the other side because there were no comfortable seats for chastised students, of course.

Fox and I had been called at the punishment hour of 5 a.m. to present ourselves to the Principal. I'd heard my mother summon plenty of Rebels to her like this, but it'd never happened to *me* before. Being a witch of the House of Crows had some perks.

Last night, I'd been assaulted by such a sudden burst of sound, smell, and touch that I'd been lost in a haze. I hadn't even been able to talk, as someone had bundled me in warm coats and then carried me as carefully as a new-born back into the castle. I'd woken up in the morning in the middle of a tangle of Immortals, to the *cawing* of crows who weren't mine and a summons to the study like I no longer deserved the protection of belonging to the House of Crows.

My nose wrinkled at the powerful aroma of garlic from the shrine to Hecate, which had been built under the narrow window. Dawn struggled to light the shadowy study. I studied my descendant, who reclined with such authority in the blood-red leather chair that would've been mine, if I'd married Titus. But even for a chair as spectacularly special as that, nothing was worth marrying a fae.

Damelza's mouth turned up in a sly self-satisfied curve, although the skin underneath her eyes was purpled like she hadn't slept at all last night.

My heart clenched at the sight of the obsidian desk that glittered like Damelza's dress. Its top was cobbled with crow skulls. I remembered running my hands over them as a child on the few occasions that Byron had been ill, meaning that Henrietta had grudgingly allowed me to play in here as she'd worked, rather than in the Bird Turret nursery.

It hit me then, stronger even than the stink of garlic that pervaded the dark room that was stacked with books and potions, *that the people I'd once loved were dead.*

Of course, after a hundred years I'd known that they had to be but…being back here…it didn't matter that I'd been granted life again.

Robin and Byron were still dead.

When my knees buckled, Fox caught my elbow. The shock of his touch tingled through me. My skin was aflame. How incredible it was that such simple contact, after so long being denied to me, could now send tears tumbling down my cheeks.

I was truly alive and I was back in the Rebel Academy.

When Fox's gaze met mine, it was soft and understanding. *Yet why didn't he understand the danger that he was in?*

All of a sudden, my heart beat so hard in my chest that I thought it'd break my ribcage. How did anyone breathe with such a wild creature inside them?

"I've only just found you," Fox whispered, drawing me closer. "I won't let anyone hurt you. I'm actually Lancelot in disguise. This **R** on my hand doesn't stand for *Random* but *Renowned*."

"Renowned liar?" I teased.

Fox winked. "Renowned and unreformed liar."

I couldn't help the snort.

"If you've quite finished flirting on my time with the wickedest witch to ever live..." Damelza coiled her silver blond hair around her finger. She didn't look up from the thick file that lay open in front of her.

I pushed myself away from Fox and onto my tiptoes to squint at the file.

Hmm, maybe if I cast a Reading Upside Down Spell...?

Fox shrugged. "How do you know that she was the wickedest? There must be some stiff competition. Is there like a Wicked Witch Contest each year with rosettes awarded and...?"

"You truly have no understanding of the term *thin ice*, do you?" Damelza still hadn't looked up from my file or acknowledged that I was in the room, as if I was still an invisible ghost.

I'd take great delight in teaching her that I'd no longer be treated in such a way.

"I really don't." Fox bit his lip like he was trying to force himself not to say anything else.

This mage could talk himself into trouble with a coven under a Peace Spell, and they were even compelled to be kind to vampires, spiders, and mime artists.

Damelza fiddled with the feather behind her ear, which she'd used to slice Fox's cheek. "This academy has a reputation to uphold." She pointed at the far war, which sparkled beneath the **RA** crest with alternating pink and black motivational slogans, which were carved underneath the scrolling:

Rebel Academy — Blessing the Wicked Since 1870

I cocked my head. "Am I not wicked enough then?"

At last, Damelza's sharp gaze snapped to mine. "That depends if even half the stories my grandmother told about you were true."

I narrowed my eyes. "It's rude to listen to gossip."

In turn, Damelza narrowed *her* eyes, which was weirdly like seeing myself in an evil mirror. "And it's rude to become a rogue witch, be burned alive, and then be born again just before term starts. Do you have any idea how much paperwork is involved in running this place?"

"My apologies, next time I'll choose a more convenient stage in the university year," I drawled.

"Although, if it's any consolation, I appear to be still part ghost. It's perfectly exciting that I get to name a new species: what do you think to *Ghost Witch*?"

"Do you suppose that I shall let there be a next time?"

"Don't kill her." When Fox slammed his palms down on the desk, I jumped in shock. Fox appeared to have surprised himself as well, quailing under Damelza's cool look. He wet his lips, before carefully removing his hands from the desk, whilst pretending to give the skulls a polish. "Or me. Okay, I have strong feelings about killing us both."

Damelza glanced between us. "Then what does my snared fox suggest? I know that it'll be a struggle for your small brain, mage, but don't let it be said that I don't encourage all my students."

I winced, but Fox didn't even react like he was too used to being seen as *less*. My hands curled into fists; *that was going to change.*

Fox sneaked a glance at me. "Make her the third Immortal. She's this *rogue* witch, right? You'll have to make her a Rebel because I get that you're not keen on her showing up to take over the family again." When Damelza blanched, Fox smiled. "Yeah, I'm a P.I in disguise, and your dead relative is back for her claim to the castle."

"You're a pain in my witchy behind," Damelza muttered, "and *this* isn't Magenta who was declared

Blessedly Charmed. It's..." She paused, thoughtfully, "...*Crow*, who's decidedly Wickedly Charmed."

"How about a DNA test?" Fox demanded.

Damelza's smile was dangerous. "How about a fox hunt?"

I snatched Fox's hand, dragging him closer to me. His heart was thudding too rapidly in his chest, but he still squeezed my hand like he understood that I needed to *feel* that I wasn't alone in this battle.

I shook at the thought of Robin walled up in the dark. How long had he been alone before he'd died?

When Fox's thumb rubbed circles on the back of my hand, I wished that I wasn't wearing my gloves, so that I could feel the deliciousness of his touch. I loved that in this age there was such intimacy and that it could mean love in so many ways: comfort, understanding, and connection.

I craved to feel alive.

When my stomach rumbled again, I pinked. Fox's scent of raspberries was driving me mad. I couldn't touch him with my hands, but I wasn't living in the Victorian age any longer, and I had other body parts that were unclothed. It hadn't been possible to live with Flair and his vivid descriptions of the Rebels' passion and not learn a trick or two. When I nuzzled my cheek against Fox's, he flushed. Then he relaxed against me with a soft smile. Encouraged, I nosed along his jawline. Then I had the sudden impulse to lick down his neck.

"Mages aren't lollipops," Damelza chided.

I froze. "I'm simply hungry."

For the first time in over a century, *I could eat.* For all these years, I'd been tormented by the memory of food that I'd never taste again but now… *Oysters, roast duck, cranberry tart with cream, and a cup of tea…*

Fox sighed. "Only the Princes get treats like *lollipops.*"

My dream feast shattered.

On Hecate's tit, hadn't Fox said something in the glade about the luxury food being locked away in a special larder? I clenched my jaw. No matter how much I desired those treats, I'd never *ask* the fae prince for a favor. Although, there was also Prince Willoughby, and if Flair's crush was based on more than the elf's pretty hair and prettier voice, then perhaps there was a way to persuade the Princes to share their food.

I wouldn't let my Immortals be starved any longer.

I delighted, however, in the chance to try Fox's specialty and the food of kings: a crisp sandwich.

"I'm about to say something that breaks every one of my beliefs." *What in the name of Hecate was Damelza about to tell us?* Had she changed her entire outlook on mages? Had the bravery of my men broken her prejudiced view that the Rebels were broken? "The mage is right: you should become an Immortal."

Well, baby steps.

Fox ducked his head, but I didn't miss the way that he was struggling to smother his smile.

The *small brained mage* had just outfoxed the Principal.

"This is your sentence and punishment. I hope that you're overwhelmed with the *shame* of becoming the first witch (and one of our prestigious House), to become a student here," Damelza scolded.

"Oh yes, I'm quite ruined...*the shame...*" I gasped, holding my hand against my forehead as if I was about to faint.

Fox held me up around my waist and hid his snicker against my neck.

"Don't think to escape." Damelza held up her finger warningly. *As if I would without my lovers.* "It's against protocol to ask Hecate to brand a witch, but if you decide to go for walkies, I'll simply punish the whipping boy who you like to lick."

I straightened, stiffening. I'd seen the shrewd look, which Damelza was using to assess me, before on mother, as she'd studied Robin and me.

Damelza would exploit my attachment, and it'd *destroy* me.

I pushed away from Fox, despite his hurt expression. "He's not *my* whipping boy."

"Since I'm appointing you *Prefect* of the Immortals, you'll find that you're in fact responsible and in charge of both the Immortals *and* the whipping boy who they're patron to." Damelza's lips pinched. "Crown is the academy's only other Prefect, so you'll have to work closely with him."

"Crown…?" I asked.

"Prince Lysander."

"No," I barked, before I could stop myself.

"*No*, you didn't curse the academy so that I spent my childhood shivering, the boys here freeze in their Wings, and we all wade through nothing but snow and ice because of you…?"

I shrank against the wall. *She was right.* My power in its loss and grief had done that.

I'd condemned every Rebel and witch to suffer alongside me.

Damelza's fingers tapped on the armrests. "Just one more thing. Crave is special. The Duchess who was once bonded with him is my guest this week and will be inspecting him to see if the sharp shock of his time with us has helped him see the errors of his rebellious nature, which means that he must remain unbonded and pure."

The breath caught in my throat. Who was this Duchess? If she'd once been bonded to Bask, she certainly wasn't now. Yet she wanted to *inspect* him like he was still her property?

Was she attempting to claim him back?

Fox stared at Damelza. "*Pure*, as in: we can't touch him?"

Damelza's expression hardened. "We must respect incubi culture."

"Why?" I hadn't seen Fox's gaze so steely before. "I don't respect some bitch who thinks that she owns Bask. Loving someone won't make him *dirty*."

Damelza yawned. "Your self-righteousness is tiring, Confess, I'm bored, and your brands have already been set so that you can't touch him."

Fox gasped. "But he's an incubus. It's *torture* for him not to be touched."

"The Princes have offered to massage him so that he can still function." She waved her hand. "A separate bed has been added into the West Wing."

I eyed her. "How charmingly naïve that you're prepared to simply trust me."

Damelza snorted. "I wouldn't trust you, if you shaved your head and became a devout acolyte to Hecate."

Damelza clicked her fingers, and I shrieked, as an electric charge hit me, vibrating across my skin. My legs buckled, and I fell to my knees on the thick carpet.

Vaguely, I heard shouting (Fox defending me just as if he was Lancelot, although without the sword), and at last the hex stopped. I shuddered, and even my gums tingled.

"Just a little something that I developed last night to keep you at least three inches apart from Crave at all times, otherwise you'll be given an electric shock. *Look but don't touch*; you should be used to that," Damelza crowed. Dazedly, I realized why she had shadows under her eyes. She must've stayed up last night working on the spell, which had already seeped through my skin and into my bones. It felt heavy and wrong. "Now onto the whipping boy's punishment because I don't want you to miss your first classes."

"*Woah*, I thought that I was the one with the bright idea…? Why don't we say this has all worked out and give that student a reward?" Fox flashed Damelza a winning smile.

Damelza pushed herself up, pressing on the wall behind her, which slid open to reveal a trophy: The Rebel Cup. I'd watched from the window of the Bird Turret, as it'd been presented below in the grounds at the end of the first week each term. It was a huge obsidian trophy, which was in the shape of a dragon. The dragon's tail wound around the cup and back into its flaming mouth.

Fox whistled. "I was only expecting a gold star."

Damelza caressed the snout of the dragon. "The Rebel Cup is a cherished tradition. To the parents of the Princes, it's a cause of great pride if they win.

Every day, either the Immortals or the Princes will win a contest, and at the end of the week, the overall winner will be awarded the Rebel Cup at the Dragon Polo Tournament."

How many times had I wished to be allowed to be part of this tradition? But now, dread pooled in me at the creepy satisfaction in Damelza's smile.

Ah, the advantages of thinking like a witch.

"So, I'm banned from taking part?" Fox rocked on his heels. "Yeah, I'm heartbroken. How about I take my sobbing self back to the West Wing?"

"On the contrary, yours is the most essential role." Damelza's fingers closed like claws around the Rebel Cup. "Curse and you, the whipping boys, have just become the stakes." Her glance at me was triumphant. "As punishment for resurrecting Crow, whichever team loses the contest, shall have their whipping boy executed."

Lightheaded, my vision dimmed. I staggered, as I forgot that I needed to breathe.

I couldn't have been brought to life, simply for the mage to die. *I couldn't cause another's death again.*

My legs melted into mists and then my hands. This time, however, the fading was my choice. A cold wind blasted through the study, tossing my file like paper crows furiously across the room and pecking against Damelza's face in retaliation. Fox watched in awe. Damelza waved her hand, and the wall closed with a *snap*, shielding the Rebel Cup.

"I'm terribly sorry," my eyes glowed with raging flames, "but you shan't hurt either whipping boy."

I thrust my black mists to crush Damelza, but she shrugged them off like they were nothing but a summer breeze. I stared at her in shock. My strength coursed through my ghost form. Was she truly so much stronger than me?

My word, that was frightening.

"The professors wear charms, so that we can't use our powers against them," Fox muttered. "Her Anti-Me one is the feather in her hair."

Deflated, I drew back my mists.

Damelza chuckled. "The Anti-*You* one I also invented last night and cast on all the professors. I've always been especially talented at charms. Is your tantrum over now?"

"I won't permit you to kill him," I growled.

"Hecate above, are you as dim as the mage?" Damelza sighed. "If you wish him to live, then win the Rebel Cup."

Fox sidled closer to Damelza. "Look, this is my punishment. I've been a bad fox, I get it. But why drag this other poor bastard into it? Couldn't he just be put into Time Out or something if the Princes lose?"

For the first time, Damelza's smile was genuine.

"See, you're learning already. Curse is a pathetic excuse for a Fallen, but the Princes appear to take pleasure in the games that they play with him." I shuddered at the same time as Fox. "I'm in a generous mood. If they lose, I'll only break his wings."

Why, my family were truly the spirit of generosity.

"Cheers, you're a saint," Fox gritted out.

"Now, I have private business with Confess." When the study door clicked open, Damelza's chuckle was dark and low. "It's time for you to *fade out*."

I yelled in shock, as I was blown out of the room into the stone gallery beyond, before the door slammed in my face. I caught a final glimpse of Fox's pale face, before he was shut in alone with the Principal.

Outraged, I banged on the study door, but I had a feeling that even that had been muted.

I'd been turned invisible yet again.

Then there was a sudden hoarse *cawing* at the open windowsill, and joy hit me so hard that I struggled not to cry.

"I thought that I'd lost you." I rushed to sit next to Flair and Echo who hopped onto my lap. Echo rubbed his head against me with as much desperation as I stroked through his feathers. "How can I still see and touch you?"

"Now isn't that the question, boss. But I'm happy as a pig in shit that you can." When Flair pecked my

finger, I knew that it was as close to a kiss as he could get.

I cuddled Echo tighter, and he wrapped his wings around me.

"Would you've forgotten us like everybody else?" Echo asked, softly.

I bit my lip. "Never. Who'd forget your superb singing voice?"

When Echo preened, Flair snorted.

"So, are you human now?" Flair asked.

"I'm something that's caught between the living and dead, only this time I'm closer to the living side." I scrunched up my nose. "The Rebels weren't dreadfully experienced with magic, and resurrection is a tricky business."

Flair's scaly claws bit into me, as he circled in my lap looking for a comfortable spot to settle down. *"Does that make you a zombie?"*

"Do you want to eat brains?" Echo offered, helpfully.

"Mother once had pigs brains served for supper." I shivered. "It was most unpleasant."

"If you have no craving for brains, why aren't you riding those Rebels and letting your bouncy bosoms out to have some fun for the first time in...forever?" Flair demanded.

"Firstly, I'm magically unable to even touch Bask. Secondly, Fox is trapped in there with the Principal, and thirdly," *surely, I deserved a little boast*, "a *Prefect* does have duties, you know."

"*Hark at her, la di da!*" Flair fell onto his feathery back, kicking his legs in a way that was disconcertingly close to his wanking impression. "*Just give her a Prefect badge and suddenly it's all: where do you want me to bend over, ma'am?*"

"There wasn't a badge," I muttered. "In fact, I don't even get a uniform."

Echo stroked his wing along my cheek, and I leaned into the touch. "*My Magenta hasn't changed. I trust her.*"

I glanced back at the closed door. Damelza thought that she could tame me with a couple of spells and charms. Yet my magic ran through the entire academy. From my birth, it'd woven these grounds, creating the wards and spells. I'd *cursed* it for decades.

I was choosing to play their tamed Prefect for the sake of my lovers, but only until I could find a way to free them. When I'd lived here before, it'd been on the other side, as the part of the coven in charge. Now I was here as one of the students. Yet, I was still *me*.

Even if I couldn't protect Fox from whatever was happening within the study, I could watch over him.

I nudged my familiars off my knee as I stood up. "Witches aren't meant to care for their familiars, but I love you both deeply, you do know that?"

Echo fluttered his wings, which pulsed pink. He rubbed his head against my ankle.

Flair cawed. *"And you're all right for a witch, boss."*

"He means that we love you too," Echo whispered.

I grinned, focusing on fading entirely. The sensation was odd like unraveling myself thread by thread. Then I floated to the study door. I took a deep breath.

Please let this work...

I *whooshed* through the thick door, exploding through the other side. I expected a howl of outrage from Damelza, but she only continued to talk with a quiet intensity to Fox.

I was invisible again. My pulse pounded at the thought that I wouldn't be able to reverse it. *Bubbling cauldrons, what if I was stuck like this?* I forced the thought away, wrapping myself around Fox. He stiffened, as if he could sense me, before relaxing into my touch in the delicious way that he had.

His frown became a smile. He knew that I was there, and he was no longer alone.

If I couldn't save him yet, then I could at least grant him that.

"...even I hadn't imagined that your criminality extended to corrupting your own family to demand your release against the wishes of your House," Damelza finished with a flourish.

Fox's face lit up with painful hope; it was beautiful but as fragile as the snowdrops in my glade. "My sister's trying to free me?" He impatiently brushed a stray curl behind his ear. "Hartley's come for me?"

"Why would the only heir to the House of Jewels, and your mother's darling," when Fox winced, I stroked across his cheek, "ever release her mage brother? Have you no sense of honor? The witch outside the wards, who's giving me yet another headache at the start of term, is your cousin. Do you wish to enlighten me on *why*?"

"L-lux?" Fox stuttered, paling. Whoever his cousin was, who'd been unusually flooded with kindness towards Fox, he still feared her. He'd also tried to hide the way that disappointment had ripped through him on hearing that his would-be rescuer wasn't his sister, yet he shook with it. "Cheers for the laugh, but the only thing that Lux would want with me would be as a punch bag, subject for experimentation, or as someone to play with her broken Omegas."

Damelza prowled around the desk, and I backed against the wall, just in case she could sense me. "I don't care if she wants you to play Romeo in a jazz version of *Romeo and Juliet*, I don't simply release students unreformed. No one leaves here who hasn't graduated, unless they win a special contest, Tournament, or at my great benevolence. Most who do graduate are offered teaching positions because usually nobody wants them back. You're here because you're too dangerous to allow out into society."

"I don't need my power to know that's a *lie*. Why'd you let this Duchess into the castle to paw at Bask then? Why's she different to my family?"

"Because she's the one who signed Crave into the academy with a special understanding *that is none of your business*," Damelza snapped. "But your *cousins* appear to believe that if they pressure the House of Crows, where no one but Hecate has held sway for centuries, then I'll let you go. Your mother is the one who registered your place here, and not your cousins. I don't have to bow down to Lux, simply because she's now Head of the Oxford covens. The House of Crows is *above* witch law and tradition."

"Cousins?" Fox's voice was tentatively hopeful again. My guts roiled, and this time I knew that it was neither guilt nor hunger making it churn. I was confused by the desperate desire to hold onto Fox, and at the same time, the need to let him go. This could be his best chance to escape. He had to take it. *Please, let these cousins help him.* "As in, Lux and her twin, Aquilo?"

"Huh, you imagine that I'd count her *mage* brother?" When Fox stilled, Damelza pressed closer, until their noses were almost touching. She scrutinized his deliberately blank face. "Lux even allowed him to try and break through our wards. He's powerful, isn't he?

Are you hiding his level of magic behind that *mouth* of yours?"

Fox's smile was strained. "More like, behind my balls. And haven't I introduced myself? I'm Merlin."

Damelza only leaned closer. "Then it's a good thing that I have both you and Aquilo *by* the balls. No one's getting through the wards, even if they're *Merlin*…or a god. And your cousins have one of those tamed. The angelic god rants and flaps his glittery wings, which I can't wait to pluck." I flinched at the same time as Fox. "If they don't take the hint and leave, then I'll have to decide that they're all Rebels. I'll lower the wards, allow them to arrogantly waltz in here and then…" When she *clapped* her hands together, Fox and I both jumped. Damelza's eyes glittered maliciously. "I'll raise the wards again, and they'll be trapped the same as any Rebel."

"Please, don't," Fox gasped, before promising in a rush, "I didn't ask them to save me. What do you want me to do?"

Damelza's smile widened. "Write them a letter. Tell them how *happy* you are to be here and how much you don't want to leave. If you're lucky, they'll respect that. You love your family, don't you? I thought that the one talent you at least excelled in was *lying*."

Fox's eyes were bright with tears. I quivered,

glaring at Damelza. How dare she use Fox's power against him to tear him apart from his family.

How many families had tried to take back their children or changed their minds only to discover that it was too late? I'd always thought that the Rebels were abandoned here but perhaps, the House of Crows had tricked just as many people to make it look like that?

My eyes became flinty, as I studied the way that Fox lowered his head before Damelza. Discovering the academy's secrets had shot right up my To-Do list, just beneath surviving the start of term.

"They'll work it out," Fox said, quietly. "Aquilo knows me too well."

With a flourish, Damelza snatched a peacock feather off her desk, before grabbing Fox's hand and rubbing the feather over it. "The effect only lasts a few minutes, but now you can only tell the truth."

"With my hand?" Fox ventured.

Damelza clutched him by the wrist, wiggling his fingers in the air in front of him. "Whatever you write here, they'll see in front of them and know that it's the truth. So, be creative."

Fox swallowed, before glancing to where I leaned against the wall. *He could sense me.* I curled out strands of mist to wrap around his ankles, although it did look weirdly like he'd walked into a hag's cave, but it appeared to anchor him. Then even though his face was etched in grief, he wrote in curling script:

My Principal's allowing me to write. It's magical, I'm sure you can tell, so I can't lie. It's odd like a tugging on my brain when I try. Normally, it's frowned upon, okay, seriously forbidden, to have outside contact, except with the person who registered you for the academy. The Principal doesn't like you being here because I'm settling in.

Today, I start my classes. Warrior Training is the first lesson, but I can't take part in that, so my first real lesson is Spells, Hexes, and Potions. And yeah, I know that's a mouthful. Apparently, the students call it SHP, but I just sound like a robin when I say it. I've made some friends already who truly look out for me. I've even met a witch who's sexier and kinder than any witch I've met before.

Aquilo, I'm free from the attic. We never thought that would happen, right? I'm not kept in a cell and I haven't been whipped even once. I went on a picnic, and I never thought that would happen again.

Please, don't try and break me out because it's dangerous. I need to learn to be independent after so long locked away.

I love and miss you...

Fox's finger wavered, shaking so hard that he could no longer write. His face was wet with tears, and when I reached up to touch my cheeks, so was mine.

Locked in the attic? Happy that he hadn't been whipped? I shuddered at the thought of the life that Fox must've led before, if the academy in truth meant *freedom* to the mage.

I flew across the room, ignoring Damelza, who slunk back around her desk, sinking into her chair with a satisfied nod.

Fox hugged his arms around his middle like he was hugging me.

"Is that everything? Would you like to cut out my heart as well?" Fox muttered.

"Not just now; hearts are always harvested at the full moon." Damelza rifled through the papers on her desk like she hadn't just torn Fox apart. "Well, go and wait for your classmates to be finished in Warrior Training. Remember, you're the whipping boy. If I were you, I'd make sure that I won every lesson because if the Immortals lose the Rebel Cup, you'll die."

CHAPTER THIRTEEN

Rebel Academy, Monday September 2nd

BASK

Warrior Training was deadly for an incubus whose arse was slinky, sexy, and *not* for kicking. I'd been trained in diplomacy. Ma had never intended that I wield a sword, but rather that I use both my body and words as weapons. But then, she hadn't intended that the Duchess would choose me to bond with either.

Good intentions made pettable arses out of all of us (*snicker*).

When Bacchus pulled me aside before class, with a sweep of her toga that trapped me against the side of the building, I drew in my breath. The rough stone of the Conqueror Gym bit into my back, and I squirmed. The breeze cut across the frozen river and my cheeks. The spires of Oxford always looked so close from here.

Was the tutor going to punish me for sneaking out of the Wing, my part in stealing the food, entering the Dead Wood or… I cocked my head.

Yep, I was *bad*.

When I smirked, Bacchus narrowed her eyes. The aroma of spicy red wine coiled around me, as she casually leaned closer. Pocus wound over her shoulders like a scarf, blinking at me sleepily.

"I made a mistake to forget that a panther lurked beneath your cutie pie mask." She stroked the back of her hand down my cheek, and I fought not to flinch. "I concentrated on the *mage*, when it was the *witch* that I should've feared."

"Don't hurt Magenta," I hissed.

Bacchus' eyes widened in surprise. "Why would I do that? And why would *you* defend a witch? She's the Prefect, and we have a whipping boy now to play with."

I gritted my teeth. "If it pleases you, just punish me now, so that I'm not late to class."

Bacchus blinked. "But you haven't displeased me, Crave." I couldn't fight the way that warmth flooded me at pleasing her. It was simple biology like waking up with a boner. *Never turn down a pleasure feeding.* I was certain ma used to say that, or I could've made it up. Either way, it was good advice. "You've *surprised* me, and that's always thrilling. The Immortals now outnumber the Princes, which tips the balance in our favor, but the stakes are much higher. Trust me, there's a joy in the dark, and Magenta overflows with it."

I frowned. "Stakes?"

Pocus yawned, and Bacchus patted him on the head. "Whichever side loses, will have their whipping boy executed."

No, no, no…

My legs buckled, and I fell to my knees. I wrapped my hands over my head like I could block out…*everything.*

It was Hector all over again.

I'd promised to keep Fox safe, but Bacchus had warned that the Princes were fiercely competitive over the Rebel Cup.

I couldn't watch Fox die.

As if she understood, Bacchus crouched down, firmly pulling my arms away from my head. "Did hiding ever help you before?"

Rule 65 of the Incubi Night Code: Never hide because punishment is always worse once you're found.

I shook my head.

"Then let me see your *claws*, panther, and ensure

that you win the Rebel Cup. You may not even be here at the end of the week to see the punishments carried out." My pulse pounded in my temples at the way that her expression gentled into pity. *Wow, that was a disturbing look on her.* "Darling, you fight me like I'm not on your side, but believe me, I am. I'm not meant to warn you but then, the Duchess is Damelza's guest this week. I have a feeling that if you *win* the Rebel Cup, you'll be the student who's freed into *her* custody."

Don't cry... Tears make you ugly... Nobody loves an ugly incubus...

I took desperate gasps, struggling to hold back my tears. All of a sudden, Bacchus' hands were on my shoulders, steadying me. Pocus leaped into my lap, rubbing his head against my legs in comfort. But their touch felt muted and far away because I was back in the Duchess' palace, as she'd trained me.

As she'd broken me.

I'd been made to lie down but lever myself up onto my fingertips and toes, so that I didn't touch the marble floor, which the Duchess had then lit with a magical fire. For an hour, I'd managed to hold myself up, but my shoulders had quivered with the strain, and my thighs had ached.

The Duchess had watched me calmly from the bed.

All the Duchess' other incubi (she'd bonded with

four, and I was the youngest, *lucky me*), had swooned at her beauty: her flowing red hair and peachy skin. But she'd treated me differently to the rest because I'd been the *weird* kid. She'd only chosen me because she'd been excited by the *challenge* of the Night son who'd been known to be *different*.

Ma had tried to keep me in the shadows and away from the Succubi Court, but the Duchess had still selected me.

You could never hide.

"Stand up, if it hurts," the Duchess' words had been quiet, yet they'd rung inside my mind, "but then you won't please me. It's your choice."

I'd despaired because I hadn't understood. Where was the choice, when you were hardwired to please? Instead, I'd collapsed onto the fire.

The next day, she'd repeated *the training*.

Except, she hadn't said a word.

"Please," I'd gasped, as my arms had shaken.

"Please, what?" The Duchess had been reading a book and hadn't even glanced up.

"Please tell me what you wish. What do you desire? I want to be yours." I'd ached to be hers because that was what a bond was like. I'd been young and hopeful still

I'd just craved to be loved.

"I want…" The Duchess had slipped in a book-mark, before placing down her book. She'd folded her hands in her lap. My heart had clenched, and I'd been flooded with joy that I could at last please her. "…you to hurt yourself."

I'd shuddered, willing the tears that were matting my eyelashes not to fall.

Please, don't let her see them.

I'd bitten my lip to hide my disappointment, before I'd let myself fall onto the fire.

The following day, I'd been back in the same position, but this time the Duchess had towered over me, watching me with a hungry intensity. She'd been taller than me, and I'd never felt it as much as in that moment.

"*Beg me,*" she'd whispered, "beg me to let you burn yourself."

At last, Bacchus' quiet words reached me again like I was rising up from the bottom of a dark river, along with Pocus' purr, "It takes a cruel trauma to break a bond. Taming a guy is one thing but… If I had my choice, she wouldn't get a second chance."

It was a struggle to remember Rule 3 of the **Incubus Night Code**: An incubus must mask their true feelings.

I kept my gaze lowered as I asked with difficulty, "She wishes to take me back?"

Maybe I could get Bacchus to transform me into a Pomeranian before then…? Fox would love to carry my fluffy cuteness around in a satchel.

Bacchus' lips thinned. "She's here to inspect your progress."

I knew what *inspect* meant.

I needed to hurl. But whatever happened, I had to hide it from the other Rebels because their love was real, and if the Duchess did take me away again, then I wanted something to hold onto that was untarnished by fear or sadness. I craved just one week of love to keep me warm for the rest of my life.

Don't let them learn the truth…not like this…

I could be brave if it gave them the illusion that we were safe in our love for one week.

"That means no *touching* any of the Immortals for the next week. Damelza even struck Magenta, whose new name is Crow, with a powerful Incubus Repellent hex." Wow, that was *rude*. "She'll be hit with an electric shock if she goes within three inches of you, which would be admittedly amusing."

I paled. *No touch…?* I'd go crazy, and worse, my hair would go lank.

"I can't survive a week without—"

"Sorry, didn't I say?" Bacchus' grin was wicked, as Pocus jumped back onto her shoulder. "The Princes will take turns massaging you."

I choked on my own tongue.

So much for not being punished.

Although, the thought of the Princes being forced

to serve my sexy self, made it worth it (especially the coldly regal elf).

Could I choose what they wore? I sighed. Juni seemed the type who'd go for it.

Yep, Willoughby in a maid's outfit: fantasy role-play Number 49. And Sleipnir had told me it'd been a waste of an evening to make that role-play list.

Bacchus dragged me to my feet, before shoving me towards the Conqueror Gym. "I take it that you're clear about not touching the Immortals? You'll just have to love yourself, darling. At least you've had plenty of experience, and so has your hand."

I blushed. But who was I kidding? She was right. I wiggled my fingers: *you're not out of a job, boys.*

I trotted into the gym, which streamed with sunshine from the wide windows out over the river, only to be faced with the frowning angelic Professor of Dueling, Ezekiel, as the class waited on my slinky arse. I ran a hand through my hair in case a morning without snuggling had already forced me to lose my edge and brought on Ezekiel's *I'm five seconds from spanking you* face (which was admittedly scorching hot).

Nope, I still had it.

I ducked my head: time for the innocent face. Away with you, I was better than *Puss in Boots* at it. "Sorry."

Ezekiel's expression gentled. He tucked his beautiful violet wings behind him, whilst studying me with his equally violet eyes. As an Addict Angel — angels who became obsessed with the human world, which was forbidden by the dick angels who considered themselves purer in Angel World — he wore only ash harem trousers.

Be warned: incubus envy was a dangerous thing, and I *envied* Ezekiel's bronzed six-pack. His abs, obviously, rather than his beer. When I met Magenta's shy smile across the gym, as she rested with her head on Sleipnir's shoulder, however, I could've done with a quick drink. Maybe it would've settled the crawling underneath my skin that demanded I *please* someone or they *please me*.

The Duchess had called those whom she'd punished through removal of touch: The *Not There*. Everyone in the palace would be ordered to ignore them like they'd been turned into a ghost. It'd only happened to me once, and *that* had been what'd broken my bond.

I shivered at the thought of Magenta's hands caressing me, plucking at my nipples, or cupping my balls. Then the thought of Willoughby dressed in a maid's outfit and massaging my arse intruded, and I sighed because that was all I was getting from now on.

Last night, I'd been filled with nothing but a happy tingling across my skin. Magenta had been free and alive in my arms.

The woman from the portrait had been made flesh.

All right, she'd been unconscious. But I liked to look on the bright side. I'd even allowed Magenta to snuggle in my nest with *all* my pillows as a special concession (even Nile).

If that wasn't love, I didn't know what was.

But now, she was spelled so that we couldn't even get close to each other. I squared my shoulders. If the Duchess wanted to turn me into a *Not There* even within the academy, she could kiss my pettable arse. I wouldn't break for her twice.

"Glad you could join us." Ezekiel tried for commanding but he couldn't help the smile. *Cute... and hot.* Away with you, I had a thing for angels, even if they were professors with more muscles than was decent. "I've been warned about your special needs, so I'm afraid that we'll have to mix things up for this session. You need to be partnered with someone different."

Why did he look apologetic?

Then Ezekiel's wings were wrapped around me, as he led me to the far corner, which was painted in murals of grand battles that had been fought by previous Rebels. I took a moment to cuddle into the feathery softness. They smelled tangy but sweet like citrus cream.

Resist the urge to suck as well as to snuggle.

I knew that Ezekiel was offering me this short

treat of gentle touch. He was the kindest of the professors, even if he was physically the strongest. Then I noticed who was lounged against the wall, waiting to be my *partner. Wait, I retracted that part about the kindest.*

Ezekiel twisted me, until I was forced to look at him. "Whipping boys aren't allowed in my lesson, although I've fought for their inclusion, and you can't touch Crow. She declined with certain choice words the offer to be partnered with a fae."

"Choice words like: It would cause the slow death of my soul?" I cocked my head.

Lysander straightened. His eyes narrowed dangerously. He'd neatly folded his black blazer with the **P** crest embroidered in silk to one side, and his pink silk shirt hung open at the neck, revealing a glimpse of his translucent collar bone. His tight black trousers left less to the imagination than mine. He looked as much like a dashing but arrogant warrior *as I didn't.*

Ezekiel crossed his arms. "Crown wasn't exactly overjoyed to be paired with you either."

I took a cautious step towards Lysander. "Did I spoil his play date with the wee elf?"

Lysander's eyes narrowed even further.

Ezekiel stalked back to the center of the gym. "When he heard that Willoughby was to be replaced today by you, he gagged."

Well, didn't that just help a guy's ego?

Lysander smirked, tossing his emerald hair with a beat of his golden wings, and I couldn't help seeing… just for a moment…*my Andro*. I flushed with the memory of that little swirl Andro did with his tongue on my dick (it should be a superpower), as well as his delicious cuddles. But then, I saw the harshness in *this* fae's eyes, rather than the softness, and there was no doubt that it was Prince Lysander.

Andro might've been a clone but he was his own fae.

"Why are you looking at me like that?" Lysander arched his brow. "I demand that you stop looking at me like you wish to eat me."

"Since I'm not one of your subjects," I scanned him from head-to-toe with a sexy leer that walked the line of insulting (okay, I *might've* fallen over the line), "you don't get to demand. And that means an incubus may look at a prince."

Lysander slunk closer. "And a prince may gouge out an incubus' eyes."

My wee break down over the Duchess might've made me forget just how dangerous the Princes were.

Oh, well…

I tilted my chin. "May both sides of your pillow be forever warm."

Lysander blinked. "I tremble before you."

Odd, but he didn't appear to be frightened of my curse.

I still smiled smugly, patting his cheek. "Of course you do. I'm a mighty incubus."

Lysander slapped away my hand. "Don't touch my royal personage."

I ached at his mention of touch. I yearned for Magenta with an urgent desperation. When I glanced at her, however, I wished that I hadn't because Lysander then studied her with a contemptuous hatred.

"So, the witch is back," he breathed, bitterly.

I flapped my hands, trying to claw his eyeballs off her. I didn't mean that. *Yuck*.

At last, Lysander turned back to me. "Is your fit over?"

"Keep you bastard...*everything*...away from my Magenta."

Lysander barked with dark laughter. "I assure you that I've never had less interest in having my *anything* near that woman. Not even if she begged me."

"Less flirting, more fighting," Ezekiel commanded. He stood with his hands smartly behind his back, eying both pairs warily.

Magenta grinned. "I bet you say that to all the girls."

Sleipnir laughed, but dropped into a crouch. Magenta's legs swirled in a black mist that coiled around him.

I spluttered, blushing. "This...us...not flirting."

Ezekiel raised his eyebrow. "*Hmm*. Then concentrate. You all know now about the Rebel Cup…?" Next to me, Lysander stiffened. "The Punish and Reward Game is daily this term. In each lesson, either the Immortals or Princes will win and be allowed to choose either a punishment or reward for the other Wing." My breath hitched, at the same time as I heard Sleipnir's curse. They should've simply called it the Punish Game because the chances of the Princes *rewarding* us was the same as me climbing Hecate's statue in the bailey and declaring my undying love for Lysander. *Big fat zero.* "The number of wins a day is added up, until Thursday. Then the overall winner becomes the Champion of the Rebel Cup. Of course, the student who's behaved the worst must submit to the Memory Theater if a professor orders it." There was something in the way that Ezekiel shifted from foot to foot and stared hard at the ground, which told me *that* would be less fun than fighting Lysander. "So, work hard."

I stared at him. *That* was the pep talk?

Well, I was one motivated Immortal.

"I know that I'm new here," Magenta sparkled with magic, which thrummed through me; she was more dangerous than any of us, even if she sounded as polite as if she was asking for directions, "but why are we training as warriors in the first place?"

Ezekiel finally looked up. "This isn't simply an academy. You're an army and you're *assassins*. The supernatural world send their undesirables here, and we train them to take on the dirty missions that they can then deny all knowledge of. It's how we're funded and have such independence from witch law."

Put like that, it sounded even worse than in my own head.

I glanced underneath my eyelashes at Magenta. She looked pale and stunned, as if she hadn't known. But her family had established this entire operation with its Gateway to the missions. *How hadn't she known?* And if she hadn't, then that made her the most innocent, rather than the most wicked, witch in the academy's history.

I couldn't help the grin that she wasn't truly like the other witches, and then realized how creepy it must look considering that she'd just been told that we were assassins.

When Lysander shot me a funny look; I shot him one back.

"I'm awfully sorry but I need to fight now." Magenta's eyes blazed. "I suddenly have a terrible amount of rage to express."

Sleipnir nodded. "By the Valkyries, I'm right there with you."

Ezekiel held up his hand. "We're not here to simply beat each other up."

"Pity," Lysander muttered.

I rolled my eyes.

"It's about the discipline in the kill. Today's lesson is to knock your opponent to the ground in two moves. Creativity is awarded extra points or…" He marched towards Lysander and me. "…disarm your opponent within two moves. But no drawing blood; there are enough others who'd hurt you. Rebels should stick together."

Ezekiel should've been a camp counselor.

When Ezekiel stretched out his wing, it flamed so brightly that I covered my eyes. Lysander stepped forward eagerly, however, thrusting his hand into the flames.

My eyes widened. The fae was a bastard but he had balls (*big ones as his trousers showed, snicker*).

When Lysander pulled back his hand, he was holding a glowing scimitar with runes down one side. He looked different. *What was it…?* Then I realized: *he was happy*.

Lysander cradled the scimitar, kissing the metal. "Welcome back, baby."

I looked away because his joy made me uncomfortable and I wasn't even sure why. "Whatever gets you off."

Ezekiel's wing flamed again, and Ezekiel shook it at me encouragingly. I bounced up and down on my toes because the angel had never allowed me near a weapon before, saying something about me being at risk of *cutting off your own fingers or something even more important* (maybe he had a point).

I took a breath, before I thrust my hand into the flames and pulled out…

A wee fencing sword.

A wee *blunt* fencing sword.

The gym echoed with the grunts and hollers of Magenta and Sleipnir as they practiced moves on each other, but all I heard at that moment was Lysander's mocking laugh.

"To be honest," Lysander drawled, "I was expecting him to get a dagger." He held up his long, curved scimitar next to my short, thin sword. My sword almost wilted. "He probably measured our dicks and—"

"Decided that I didn't need to overcompensate," I snarled.

"You're fast, graceful, and cunning," Ezekiel interjected, gently. "You haven't the strength to swing a scimitar." At Lysander's smirk, he added, "And Crown hasn't the speed for your sword. This lesson is about working out your strengths." All of a sudden, Ezekiel swept closer to Lysander. He looked as ancient as I knew he was and a truly righteous angel. "Oh, and it's tipped with iron. It'll hurt like a bitch if it even grazes a fae."

Lysander shrank back. "You can't do that."

Ezekiel's lips curled into smile. "And yet look, I

have. I'm only making things *fair*. Surely *your royal personage* isn't frightened?"

Lysander's face smoothed into a haughty mask, as he strolled closer to the windows and into fighting stance. "One is *never* frightened."

I snorted. *Royal liar.*

I slunk after him, holding up the sword like a snake. What happened when you struck a fae with iron? I was hoping that he'd start singing and dancing the "Chirpy Chirpy Cheep Cheep" song.

Lysander eyed me. "Don't slow me down today. I'm aware that you Immortals don't take training seriously but I do. It's the only time that I'm allowed a sword in my hand and to feel like…" His face was strained as he looked down. "From the time that I was a boy, I was never parted from my weapon."

I bit my tongue from the obvious joke because Lysander had never spoken so many words to me that weren't insults, and I knew that it pained him now to speak to a lowly incubus. This must be important, so I didn't want to be a dick.

I nodded.

Lysander finally let out a breath of relief. "I'm glad that we can work together on this. My guardian, Prince Titus, expects me to train hard and a prince doesn't let down their elders."

"I know, just everybody else." My palms were sweaty on the hilt of the sword; I circled Lysander.

Lysander was so rigid that he could've been a puppet. "My uncle—"

"Got Hector killed."

"My uncle got *me* locked up," Lysander growled.

He lunged, and I dived to the side, escaping his blow, but then he twirled around cracking my back with his open palm. When I stumbled, he locked his arm around my throat, forcing me to drop my sword.

"In two moves." Lysander shoved me away, grinning. "Pick up your weapon."

Incubi had an old adage, and it went like this: *owww…*

I rubbed my sore back. Then I snatched up my sword and held onto it more tightly.

How was I supposed to beat somebody who'd been fighting like this since he was a kid?

"No need to be rough," I grumbled.

"I thought that your kind liked it rough," Lysander sneered, prowling around me in a way that made the hairs on my nape rise. "You only have yourself to blame for bringing out my bad side. Your stunt at Hecate's Tree has risked my whipping boy in the Rebel Cup. Do you believe that I wish his wings to be broken?"

I'd once watched Lysander make Midnight, the Princes' whipping boy, crawl at his heels for the length of the castle. It was a tough call on which way to answer. But there was something about the way that

Lysander's hand tightened, until his knuckles were white around his scimitar, which meant that he *didn't* want Midnight to be hurt.

I pouted. "Aw, how sweet that you care."

Lysander tilted up his snooty nose. "I don't. Yet one such as me doesn't have the time to care for a sniveling whipping boy who can no longer fly. Damaged goods are beneath royalty." I flinched: *he meant like me.* "That's why I intend to do anything necessary to win."

"Do as you wish." My gaze was steely "But I love *my* whipping boy, and no one's killing him."

Lysander studied me with a look of regret. "*Love…?* Then I'm sorry…"

He punched me in the nose with the hilt of his sword.

I hollered, falling backward onto my arse (and that'd bruise). I cradled my nose, dropping my sword, as my eyes watered.

"One," Lysander said, quietly.

Why wasn't he grinning smugly this time?

"Enough," Ezekiel bellowed; his wings pulsed a deeper violet in his fury. "And you two, don't you dare move."

"I rather thought that I'd punch a fae in the nose." Magenta's eyes were ice-cold.

"By Odin's cock, make it *two* punches," Sleipnir snarled, as his hair darkened to an ominous red.

Ezekiel stretched out his wings; his flaming gaze never left Lysander's. "You were told not to draw blood. Do I need to write to Prince Titus and inform him that you no longer obey orders?"

Lysander flinched.

I stared at the blood, which had dripped from my nose onto my shirt. I didn't know why I hadn't expected Lysander to break Ezekiel's rule. Except, Lysander was usually a suck up. He didn't like to be in trouble, and by the look on Ezekiel's face, there wasn't enough sucking up in the world that Lysander could do to get out of it.

"Not the face," I moaned. "Does it please you to pretend to be sorry and then disfigure me?"

Hurt an incubus but never damage their face. Punishments must never mar the visible beauty.

Lysander only chuckled, before reaching down to hold out his hand to help me up. Perhaps, he hoped that it'd get him out of punishment.

Rage surged through me. He thought that I was nothing but a *weak* incubus with the *wee* sword who could be knocked about by the regal fae, did he?

Never underestimate the power of a member of the Night Lineage when he'd been made to bleed.

Vibrating with adrenaline and fury, I snatched up my own sword and jabbed its blunt tip across Lysander's cheek. I would've taken the time to carve a **B,** but the moment that the iron tip touched

Lysander's skin, it seared him. Lysander howled. I watched in horror, as he staggered, clutching his cheek.

I'd wanted to hurt him, just like he'd hurt my throbbing nose, but now I only wanted to take it back. I wasn't a warrior. I hated making anyone, (even as big a bastard as Lysander), look at me with eyes that gleamed with tears, which he was struggling as hard as I ever did to not let fall.

"I-I d-didn't know that it'd..." I chucked the sword as far from me as I could. It clattered against the wall. "I'm s-sorry..."

"You hate me." Lysander's agonized gaze darted between all of us Immortals, even Magenta. "But it's not my fault who I am. And you're not sorry yet but you will be."

"I said *enough*." Ezekiel grabbed my arm, yanking me to my feet next to Lysander. *Should I tell him that he'd officially lost control of this lesson?* "The only way for you to survive is to put the past behind you but you can't do that if you're too busy fighting each other. Except, the Crows like to keep you distracted because they delight in your rivalries." When he wrapped his wings around himself, I wished that I was safely snuggled in their tangy warmth again. "If you learn anything today, it should be that that there are enough enemies outside the academy. Don't make them inside as well."

His look at Lysander and me was so painfully hopeful that we both plastered on fake smiles.

The moment that the prince discovered me alone, I was officially dead.

Lysander rubbed at his tender cheek. "I understand that I'm pushing my luck, but who won the lesson?"

Ezekiel huffed. "After that display…? *None of you*. It was a draw. I should punish you all."

I stilled, glancing at Magenta. Sleipnir's arms were slipped protectively around Magenta's waist, and I wished that I could be in their arms, instead of on the other side of the gym with a sullen fae.

Ezekiel rubbed his wing across my nose and to my shock, the pain vanished. "Now stop looking like a kicked puppy." He glanced at Lysander, before repeating the trick across his cheek as well. I was so relieved when the burn vanished that I even grinned at the prince. Weird, I felt dirty. Maybe I had a fae kink. "Both of you stop looking like kicked puppies. As you drew, *I* get to choose the outcome of the Punish and Reward Game."

My grin faded. The only consolation to my sexy self was that Lysander looked about as stricken as me.

When Ezekiel burst into laughter, I startled. "You'd think I was about to send you to the firing squad."

"Aren't you?" Sleipnir queried.

"I'm *rewarding* you by canceling today's session

in the Memory Theater. No other professor can order it, even if they wish to punish you." Ezekiel's expression darkened, as he scrutinized Magenta. "The original spell was cast by your mother, and even Damelza can't break it. We all have our secrets that we wish to keep buried." *Beg me to let you burn yourself...* When I swayed, struggling to breathe, it was Lysander who steadied me. Just for a moment, as our gazes met, it was if he understood. Then he shoved me away from him like he feared that he'd catch fleas. "Tonight at least, you'll remain in the present. Both Immortals and Princes shall share an evening in the Rebel Café and live for once."

"Living it up with the Princes... Hey, are you certain that this isn't a punishment?" Sleipnir demanded.

Lysander marched to the door; his shoulders were tight. "If you wish to discuss punishment, then set your godly imagination to what I have awaiting *you*. Because Professor Bacchus is not renowned for her mercy, and I shall win the next lesson."

"Bring it on, Oberon." Sleipnir stalked after him.

"I'm a prince," Lysander replied stiffly, "and not—"

"King of the fairies, yeah, yeah." Sleipnir winked at me over his shoulder.

I tried to smile, but the crawling sensation was back under my skin, and I struggled not to scratch.

Once I started, I'd draw my own blood and that was forbidden. I tucked my treacherous hands underneath my armpits, and stared at Magenta, who drifted as close to me as she dared, skimming her hand through the air over my nose, as if to check that it truly was fixed.

I fought not to lean into her touch (because electro shocking your lover was not sexy unless negotiated beforehand).

"We shall get through this together," she murmured. "You're mine, and even though they think to keep us apart, there's nothing they can do that shall ever separate us again."

My guts squirmed with guilt because she was wrong. Even if the Principal had told her about the Duchess' visit, she didn't *know* about the Duchess. Ma had thought that she could keep me from her and look where those intentions had got me: bonded to a psychopath who loved to burn rebellious incubi.

I forced those thoughts away because I already had to face another psychopath in my Spells, Hexes, and Potions class. This morning, Fox had sounded like a cute robin when he'd repeated *SHP*, which meant that I'd innocently pretended I couldn't hear him, just so that he'd had to say it again a couple of times. *Adorable*. Bacchus was Sleipnir's most feared teacher, however, and I might not be able to protect my own pettable arse, but I'd sworn that I'd protect Fox's pretty one.

Yet Lysander had shown just how far he'd go to win the Rebel Cup. What was he planning? I had a feeling that Ezekiel hadn't taught the lesson that he'd been intending.

After today, Lysander would be even more dangerous.

Rebel Academy, Monday September 2nd

SLEIPNIR

My connection to my brothers was the one thing that the witches hadn't been able to strip away from me. They were my heart. But they were also dicks because sometimes, when I needed to feel most in control of myself, they surged to the surface to defend me.

Just like every time that I was forced to enter Professor Bacchus' classroom.

My hair bristled to red, and the tattooed wolves on my arms growled warnings, as I steeled myself for a new term of lessons in SHP. As the son of Loki,

Bacchus had hunted me, but she'd no idea what she'd caught. It sucked that she didn't care.

At least she hadn't arrived yet.

You weren't late for Bacchus' class unless you wished to be transformed into a chair that was pillowed with pink blossoms for her to sit on. Trust me, I still had the sensation of her ass on my lap.

Bor's beard, that'd been enough to scare me into behaving for life.

Bacchus' magic prickled across my skin; my own magic feathered in fear inside me. I willed it to still, as I glanced around the room that was set out like a lab, if science took place inside a tree. Roots burst out of the floor, curling up and around the walls that were thick with moss. It was kind of like Hecate was possessively cradling Bacchus, and it gave me a sick feeling that the goddess was as close to Bacchus as she was to *my* Magenta.

I wrinkled my nose at the earthy scent, tightening my hold on Magenta's waist. I adored that our ritual had freed her, but not that she was now trapped as an Immortal. Weirdly, Magenta didn't appear concerned. I imagined that it was because she both had some sort of plan and had awesome power herself. After all, she'd kicked my ass in the Warrior Dueling.

Valhalla! It'd been hot to go hand-to-hand with someone who wasn't my family, and see such strength, as well as love reflected back in her eyes. Honestly, I'd had to fight the urge to tear off her clothes and thrust my achingly hard dick into her, until she'd screamed out her surrender because that'd would've been both a creative way to win *and* what she'd desired just as much as me. The way that she'd caressed my dick, every time that Ezekiel had turned his back, meant that she'd been the reason for my blue ball predicament now.

I stealthily adjusted myself in my pants.

Then I steered Magenta to the lab table next to the window, which looked out over the bailey. The bronze Hecate statues were dancing to themselves in the snow like they were at a rave.

Huh, that was freaky even for them.

Magenta dropped gracefully onto her stool. "My gracious, I love what Bacchus has done with the place."

I chuckled. "Hey, she's just living the American dream. Woodland retreat, university career, and even a cat…"

I pointed at Pocus, who was curled up in the far corner in the shadows. Of course, he'd transformed back into a Halfling because his punishment must've been completed, which is why Magenta gasped.

"Unless animals have changed since I died, I'm pretty certain *that* is not a cat." She pointed at Pocus who raised his head to glare at us.

I closed my hand over Magenta's because pissing

off Pocus was more dangerous than magically rewriting the school motto to glow:

Rebel Academy — Screwing the Innocent Since 1870

Yeah, that'd been me.

Interesting that it'd taken the professors over a week to notice that it'd been changed.

"Pocus is Professor Bacchus' familiar," I explained.

Magenta cocked her head, studying the lithe Korean vampire who was naked apart from a pentacle collar. He had striking black eyes but soft features that made him look like he'd burst into a K-pop dance routine at any moment. I winced at the memory of pointing that out to him, and the way that his fangs had latched onto my ass.

"Don't lie to me." Magenta's magic sparked across my skin, but it drew me closer, rather than repelling me like Bacchus' did. "I spent over a lifetime in dreadfully close quarters with twin familiars. That creature has the *ears* and *tail* of a cat, but retains the cock, balls, and fangs of a Fallen."

By the Norns, I'd forgotten just how strange it'd been to see Pocus for the first time with his cute black ears poking out of his mop of black hair and his swishing tail. Familiars in the Victorian age hadn't been freed into this form. How hard was it for Magenta to wake into such a changed age?

"He's different," I said, gently, "because someone brave broke the rules and freed the familiars from total enslavement. He's a Halfling now — half vampire and half familiar. Adorable, right?"

Pocus preened.

Magenta nodded. "Who's the equally naked gentleman that he's trying to hide?"

I stiffened, and Pocus hissed, winding closer around the vampire who was kneeling in the corner.

"The Princes' whipping boy," I muttered. "If they'd got here yet, then I'd tell Willoughby and Lysander just what I thought about making him kneel like that. Here's hoping that they're late, and we get to watch Bacchus transform them into a couch." I arched my brow at Pocus. "We get that you're a fierce warrior and bow down before you in fear." Pocus smiled with a hint of fang, satisfied. "You don't have to guard your friend from Magenta."

I stared at the pale beauty of Midnight's back. Midnight's dark hair fell to his waist in waves. His ash wings were neatly folded. He held his hands behind his head and didn't move, as if he was a statue.

He waited as he always did, like he was a not yet in use Bunsen burner, for his masters to need him.

I scowled. Had I promised to wreck the Princes? I was wrong: I'd *doubly* wreck them.

I glanced up as my own whipping boy bounced into the classroom in a ball of hyperactivity that was the opposite of Midnight. Did Fox have any idea how lucky he was not to have been assigned to the Princes? The first time that he'd been told to kneel still in a corner, he'd have been punished within five minutes…wait, two minutes…*more like ten seconds…*

Huh, at least Fox appeared to be distracting Bask from the *no touching* rule that I could already see was sending tremors through Bask. Since Bask had been sent…*abandoned*…here last term, I'd constantly had an incubus plushie swinging from my neck, grinding on my lap, or spooning me in bed. Now it felt like I'd lost a limb.

Dwarf's breath, what did it feel like to him?

Now, Fox was trying to make Bask laugh with a scarily accurate impression of Damelza, at the same time as herding him (without touching him), to the table at the front. As they settled onto stools, Fox turned to wink at Magenta.

"What's this I hear about you becoming our Prefect? I mean, of course I was Head Boy at Mage College and…" I watched, amused, as Fox lost himself in the lie. Yet there was a flicker of sadness in his eyes, which made me wonder if like me, he'd never actually been to College. *Was he excited because this was his first taste of education and freedom?* "…you know, a good boy."

"And if you were a bad boy, I'm certain that you

took your thrashings with great courage," Magenta smiled, encouragingly.

Fox blushed and made a choking sound. Bask patted him on the back.

I glanced between them. "I take it you're aware that Magenta becoming a Prefect to rival Lysander makes us all a target?"

Fox paled. "Still… #TeamImmortal!"

Magenta blinked. "What is this *hashtag*? My Greek is not what it should be."

Bask snickered. "It means *love*."

"Ah," Magenta smiled, and her icy eyes warmed, "then let me say what has been in my heart but unable to be on my lips: I most deeply and madly *hashtag* you, my Rebels."

I smothered my laugh, but both Fox and Bask couldn't hide theirs.

Magenta glanced at us uncertainly, until we chorused together, "We *hashtag* you too."

I couldn't hold back the laugh, and on all the omens, it was awesome to feel surrounded by joy, mischief, and love.

Loki would've been in his prankster element.

Magenta grinned. "I never heard laughter in this castle as a child. I hope that we shall laugh together often."

Suddenly, the door slammed open, and Lysander barged in with a furious glower. He dragged Prince Willoughby after him by the arm, who managed as always to appear entirely unruffled. Honestly, I'd always thought that it was kind of weird the way that Lysander pulled the elf around like he was his guard or Willoughby was dangerous.

Prince Willoughby always looked dangerous, of course, even though he was smaller than Lysander. It was the way that his sky-blue eyes were predatory with the same struggle for control that I knew lurked in my own. Yet at other times, like now, he'd appear dazed, as if something was keeping him pressed deep inside, crushing him.

Did he even know that he was in the Rebel Academy, rather than free?

Willoughby's hair was as sky-blue as his eyes; it was snatched back by ribbons that curled like snakes. A royal blue silk wound around him in a military style, binding him. In the light, it glimmered: it was both gossamer light and as constricting as whatever held him inside his mind.

I narrowed my eyes at how hard Lysander's fingers were biting into Willoughby's arm. Why was he manhandling the elf, and why did Willoughby not react?

As if he sensed Magenta (and hey, the elf had a dick, I could see the bulge outlined though the thin silk), Willoughby's gaze sharpened like he was rising from sleep, before he glanced at her and then quickly away.

He'd have to be made from ice not to desire my witch.

Lysander yanked Willoughby after him to the table at the back, shoving him onto a seat hard enough to make *me* wince, even though Willoughby didn't.

Fox spun on his stool to stare at Willoughby. "Why don't you have to wear the uniform?"

"Why's your whipping boy talking to me?" Willoughby's voice was regal and ethereal, but it hadn't sounded like an insult, rather honest curiosity.

Lucky for him, or I'd have been adding it to my Wreck the Princes Fund.

Fox pulled himself up with a shrug. "Because I'm actually the Light Elves' High Emperor in a *very good* disguise and you, pointy ears, have just insulted me."

"I beg your forgiveness." Willoughby bowed his head. I gaped at him. Was he truly playing along with one of Fox's lies? The Ice Prince had melted for *my* mage? "A High Emperor no less? Of course, calling a *prince* pointy ears is also a serious crime..."

I detected banter. Immortals and Princes fought: we didn't *tease*. Maybe I needed to explain that to Fox?

Next to me, Magenta lent on her elbow, cradling her chin on her palm. "Oh, do tell. What's the penalty?"

Now even our Prefect was in on it? Had they forgotten the Rebel Cup? The generations of rivalry? They hadn't been here: they hadn't lost Hector.

"*Oi*, traitor," Fox grumbled.

Lysander slammed his fist onto the desk, but Willoughby only arched his perfect eyebrow at the *bang*. "Why are you conversing with a *whipping boy*? On my wings, don't encourage him *or them*."

Bask snorted. "Get on with you, he doesn't need encouragement." Then his tongue curled behind his teeth. "And you should know that I never do."

Lysander threw his hands up in exasperation. "Now they *all* think that they can talk to our royal personages whenever they like."

Willoughby's lips twitched, at the same time as Magenta giggled. I didn't miss the way that he sneaked another glance at her.

"Why are you wearing those bindings?" Magenta leaned across from our desk to point at the silk wrapped around Willoughby, and her stool wobbled. Willoughby drew back like she'd been about to launch an attack. "There's no need to be bashful. I wear a corset; I know all about clothes that don't let you breathe." Then she mock whispered, "Plus, you don't know how lucky you are not to have to worry about freeing your bosoms."

Could any of us truly be blamed for the way that our gazes dropped to her gorgeous tits? When I raised my gaze again to meet hers, my dick gave an appreciative twitch, and she smirked like she *knew*.

"I shall call myself a lucky elf not to have bosoms." Willoughby's lips thinned. "But I need this special suit to control—"

"Silence your tongue. You have no need to explain anything to Immortals," Lysander spat, before glaring at Midnight who'd turned to glance at Magenta over his shoulder. Midnight's charcoal eyes were suffused with pain from kneeling for so long; his eyelashes were sinfully long. "And you'd better not be picking up bad habits from their whipping boy like moving out of position, as you are now. You've earned a punishment tonight."

Instantly, Midnight turned back to the wall, but he couldn't still the way that he vibrated with fear. Pocus shot a venomous look at the Princes, before rubbing his soft cat ear against Midnight's shoulder.

Magenta's eyes flashed dangerously. "I very much think that he has *not*."

Lysander's smile was sharp. "You have your whipping boy to treat as you wish, fellow Prefect, and I have mine. The other witches expect it to be this way, why are you different?"

"The other witches are bitches," Magenta snarled, leaping up.

All of a sudden, the room shook, and the roots curled up into a bone-white throne. When I swallowed, and my pulse quickened at the sudden scent of mulled wine, I noticed that Fox looked close to a panic attack. The mage had crouched down as if he was only just stopping himself from transforming into his cat form and hiding underneath the desk.

Honestly, Bacchus made *me* want to join him.

Branches of purple ivy coiled like sinuous vipers over the edges of the root throne, tangling into the professor, who smoothed down her dress like she hadn't just transformed out of the foliage.

Instantly, Lysander and Willoughby sat straighter like good little princes.

Bacchus adjusted her moth brooch, and met Magenta's steady gaze. "An all-powerful immortal follower of Bacchus, actually. But you're right, I'm just as much a *bitch* as the others. Please, take your seat."

Magenta's mouth hung open. Stunned was a good look on Magenta. Perhaps, I could use *my* talents to make her look like that in much more fun ways?

I entwined my fingers with hers, gently pulling her back onto her stool.

Bacchus studied the way that our hands were joined. "So, the new witch that I've heard so much about has already tamed the monster."

"He's not a monster: he's the mighty son of Loki." Bask announced, proudly, whilst shooting me a *see, I can learn* grin.

Bacchus ignored him, tapping her thigh instead. Pocus looked up at her signal, kissing the hollow of Midnight's back, before crawling with a sexy wiggle of his hips to Bacchus. Her expression softened, as she carded her fingers though his hair, scratching the back of his ear. Pocus purred, nuzzling against her hand.

It didn't take Heimdall's sight to see that they loved each other in the same way that I loved the other Immortals. Yet how long had Pocus been her familiar? Had they loved each other for centuries?

If Bacchus could love a Halfling, why did she hate dad and me? Why had she destroyed my brothers' childhoods along with my own?

"So, what's the lesson today?" I growled. "One hundred ways to hex a god? Potions that force someone to play air guitar? Castration Spells?"

Fox winced. "Okay, you're kidding right? I mean, tell me that Castration Spells aren't a thing."

When I simply arched my brow, he paled.

Playing with mages was so much fun. I ignored Bask's censorious *tutting*. For once, the *no touching* rule worked in my favor.

"Well," Fox sighed, "I guess that I now know my least favorite lesson plan."

Bacchus rapped the root throne with her nails in a way that was too casual to mean anything good. "What an inventive imagination you have, monster, it's only transfiguration."

My magic feathered inside me, and I gritted my teeth.

Magenta didn't see me like a monster, nor did the other Rebels. They didn't need to know the truth. It'd dirty them. Perhaps, I'd been stupid to relax and think that I could have friends as well as allies.

Don't let Bacchus spoil it. Not again, not again, not again...

Lysander stood up like he was on army parade. "Pick me. I'm certain that I shall excel at—"

"Sit down. Not you," Bacchus snapped.

Lysander's wings drooped, and he sat down, as if his strings had been cut. Willoughby patted his shoulder in comfort, but it was awkward like he didn't know if he was doing it right. Lysander didn't even acknowledge him.

Bacchus pointed her long finger at me. "*You.*"

I rolled my eyes. Consider my ass surprised. Not the rest of me. Just my ass.

I hated this class because as Bacchus' hostage, she always used it to humiliate me. But as long as she did that, she wouldn't focus on the whipping boys...I hoped.

Yet when Magenta's hand tightened around mine, I realized that suddenly I wasn't alone. I had a witch by my side for the first time, and it didn't feel forbidden but *right*.

Bacchus might be the most powerful witch in

America, but Magenta had told me this morning that she was the only Blessedly…or Wickedly…Charmed witch in existence. Even with her powers dampened or controlled, Bacchus had better watch her ass. This academy couldn't hold us forever.

Bacchus raised her arm, and a short iron spear appeared in her hand that was covered in ivy and topped with a pine cone.

Magenta clapped her hands in delight. "How perfectly delightful! I've never seen a real wand before."

When Bask snickered, Bacchus' knuckles tightened around the *wand*.

Bacchus cocked a haughty eyebrow. "This is my bacchal thyrsus, and more dangerous than a mere *girl* can understand."

Magenta huffed. "My mother was fond of fancy words for things as well. Your *wand's* pretty, but I remember a time when the ritual of *tea* meant something," *huh, she was passionate about that*, "and *you're* not old enough to call me *girl*."

Bacchus smile was beautiful but so deadly that my balls attempted an escape back into my body. "I'm so much older than any of you. Mine is *true* immortality, darlings. The ancient kind." When her gaze flickered to mine, I froze. "Loki and I are like snakes biting each other's tails. I'm chaos as well: neither good nor bad but that which delights in the storm and the fire."

"Dad's not like that," I whispered. "He only seeks—"

"The *chaos moment*." Bacchus sprang up, and Pocus drew back, startled. "Let me tell you a story." She prowled closer, and my heart thudded in my chest. I blanked my expression, however, because I didn't want her to have the satisfaction of knowing that she was getting to me. "Once upon a time, a certain God of Mischief did a great wrong to *my* god, Bacchus. Luckily for Bacchus, the God of Ecstasy, he had his cult and could choose his most dedicated followers to transform into immortals. He named each one *Bacchus*, giving them a single task: *hunt and hurt Loki*."

Bacchus prowled around me, leaning down to stroke my hair. I flinched. "And I *love* to hurt him. How much do you think it hurts him every day to be separated from you?" I bit my lip hard. "To know that you're trapped in here with me, and that I could be doing *anything* to you? Don't you think that he must be in agony?" My eyes burned. *I wouldn't cry...* Then she tightened her hand in my hair as she whispered, "It's weird though that he hasn't tried to save you yet. Do you think it's because he doesn't truly love his monster kids?"

Finally, a tear tumbled down my cheek. I hated the wet sensation as it trailed down my skin, its coldness, and the way that I was helpless to stop it. I hated…*everything.*

Bacchus wiped the tear onto the tip of her finger like she was collecting a payment. "Every tear is one more drop of justice for Bacchus. *Cry*, son of Loki."

"Remove your hands from him, *now*." Magenta's voice was low and dangerous.

To my shock, her mists were wrapped around Bacchus' neck, and her magic lit the entire classroom like fireworks. The room vibrated; a single spark could send us all sky high.

It was kind of hot to have someone defend me with such intensity.

"This is why a wicked witch like her should never have been admitted," Lysander spluttered.

Yet Bacchus only grinned. "Such frenzy! I wear a charm against your powers, or had you forgotten? But it's far more interesting for me to see them for real. Lesson Number One: Transfiguration works best through emotion. That's why you're *both* my subjects this class." She glanced down at our hands, which were still clasped together. "Your fierce angst is perfect for transfiguration." Then she tapped her thyrsus on the desk sharply. "Just chill out on the strangulation."

Magenta hesitated, until I nodded. Then her mists faded, and the dancing pink lights dimmed. Yet they didn't disappear.

Bacchus rubbed her neck. "Seriously, you'd think that I was all bad. But look, I even brought you a gift."

When Bacchus drew back her thyrsus and waved it over my head, I flinched, expecting to be turned into a chair again or a pumpkin, but instead, something cool settled around my neck. I reached up to touch the silver, and my eyes widened.

I stroked over the plectrum with shaking fingers. *Just one moment longer, before I had to part once again with the final link to my dad...*

"Take it back." I couldn't help the way that my other hand broke away from Magenta's to clench around the plectrum. "This was a sacrifice to..."

"Hecate appreciated the gesture, but do you truly think that she needs trinkets?" Bacchus asked.

"It was my blood that raised Magenta," Fox murmured. He raised his fingers to his cheek, where the feather had sliced him. "I'm officially hating that it's always about blood."

Bacchus waltzed back to her bone-white throne, throwing herself into it. When Pocus crawled around her, settling between her spread thighs, I held my breath. If the second part of this lesson included Pocus' tongue, then I was noting this as a war crime against hostages.

"Lesson Number Two: transfiguration is stronger if you create or change the item, whilst thinking of the person with whom you have a strong emotional connection." She stroked Pocus' hair, settling his head against her thigh. I let out my breath in relief, and Bacchus studied me slyly. I flushed. "The spell is even stronger if you enchant something that belongs to them."

Why was she staring at me?

"You're her pair of dim-witted favorites," Lysander shot at me under his breath. *Favorites?* I blinked. "Get on with it and fail this class already."

I bristled. Every class counted towards the Rebel Cup. I refused to fail Fox. "I'm a hostage; the witches stole everything of mine. Unlike you, Prince of the Assholes, I don't have my vintage porn collection, golden fairy statuettes, and secret pantie collection, hidden away in my luxury wing of the castle."

Willoughby cocked his head like he'd been daydreaming, but had just caught my last sentence "How do you know about the panties?"

Lysander reddened, gripping Willoughby's chin hard. "You shall not talk about the Prince's illustrious self."

"Am I not a prince too?" Willoughby asked with the iciness of a winter breeze.

"You own *one* thing." Bacchus met my gaze.

So, that was what it was like to be punched in the dick.

The thought of taking off the plectrum and sacrificing it for a *second* time was paralyzing. But then, I met Fox's concerned gaze from across the room, and I remembered the feel of his curls, the surging power of his freed magic, and the beauty as he hunted as an Arctic fox under the moonlight. And it was the easiest thing in the world to rip the cord necklace and hand the plectrum to Magenta.

Magenta took it with a wink. "How much I desire to kiss you now. The angry way in which you tore this from around your neck has made me quite hot and bothered." I smirked. "So, I simply imagine something and this silver changes form…?"

Bacchus shook her head. "I've cast an enchantment on it already." My skin prickled at the thought of that: *her magic* on *my* plectrum. "It'll work alongside your own magic. All you have to do is channel your emotion about the person who it belongs to. Love or hate: it doesn't matter. But the more powerful the emotion, the better the transfiguration. Indifference won't spark magic."

The look that Magenta cast me, as her fist closed around the plectrum was anything but indifferent, but I guessed that this enchantment would test the theory.

I understood why Bacchus had chosen us, as well as riled us up, even if I wished that I didn't.

Magenta lay her hand on the desk, allowing her mist to coil out of her and around her closed fist. Her brow was furrowed with concentration. Then she opened her hand, and her palm was veiled in black mist that coiled as if alive. I drew in my breath, as it took shape and changed color into a tiny red horse. When he snorted, smoke coiled out of his nose like fire.

No way... On the World Tree... Don't let it be...

The Mist Horse neighed, stamping his hooves, as he circled on her palm. Except, he wasn't truly a horse. My heart sank. Of course, if the creature had sprung from me, he couldn't be.

I'd been dumb to think that I could hide it forever.

Magenta laughed with delight, as the horse wound around her hand. "He's so soft." Perhaps, she would love him, after all? But then, she jerked back, and the Mist Horse tumbled onto the desk with a pained *grunt*. I winced. "Ah, I did it wrong. It was my first attempt, after all. Poor little thing; he's all misshapen like he was born wrong. I believe that he has eight legs. Let me try again, and I shan't create a monster this time."

The Mist Horse *squealed* in distress, floating as much as galloping to the back of the desk.

Monster...

I kept up the mask that I'd worn since I was a kid, and Loki had taught me why I could never have friends, but I couldn't help the way that my shoulders stiffened. At least I now knew that I should allow the others to have their love, but that I had no part in it.

Bask gasped. "Slippy, she's wrong, see, he's beautiful."

I jumped at the scrape of a stool being shoved back, before Willoughby stalked out of the room without a word. The door banged shut after him, and Lysander paled.

Magenta stared between us all and then back at Bacchus, who was smiling smugly. "Was it something I said?"

Bacchus leaned forward. "All Loki's children are monsters. Don't you recognize his son in his shifter form? I'm impressed with your magic. Your transfiguration was perfect."

Mist Horse's ears flicked back and forth in distress. His long tail was tucked in his hindquarters like he was showing the emotion that I was desperate to hide. When Magenta ghosted her fingers across his back that was stiff with tension, I swore that I could feel them as well. Mist Horse relaxed, and the same calming sensation flowed through me.

Magenta's eyes widened with understanding and a crushing compassion, before they sparked with rage. Her sparkles blazed to full brightness around the room again. "These Rebels belong to me. If you ever hurt them through me again with such calculated cruelty, then I shall *impress* you with a demonstration of how my magic is powerful enough to curse an entire coven."

Bacchus' eyes flashed an answering amber. "And

if *you* ever threaten *me* again, I'll show you that my power can curse *worlds*."

Fox slapped his hands together. "If you're done with the I'm the Most Badass Witch Contest, then can we get to the deciding who won the lesson because it's *us*, isn't it?"

Lysander fluttered his wings in agitation.

Bask twirled a strand of hair around his finger. "Prince Willoughby did break academy rules by leaving…"

"And I made the beautiful horse!" Magenta held up her palm with the Mist Horse like a kindergarten with their first wonky clay pot. Then she shot me an apologetic glance. "He *is* beautiful, you know. I'll name him Mist."

I couldn't help the shy smile, as Mist shook his flowing mane, transforming to aquamarine. I reached up to pat at my hair that had softened to match the same shade as well.

Mist flew up, settling himself in the pocket of my blazer.

"More like My Little Monster," Lysander sneered.

Bacchus shot Lysander an inscrutable look. "The Immortals won. The new witch has style." Bacchus' lips quirked. "Go ahead: play the Punish or Reward Game."

Fox bounced up, rushing over to Magenta and slinging his arms around her shoulders. "Let's huddle." *Like I didn't know that it was any excuse for Fox to sneak a kiss onto Magenta's cheek.* "Ever since Lysander hit Bask, I've been thinking up devilish ideas. Number One: the fae prince stands on a desk in only his underpants, singing "It's Raining Men"."

Lysander bit his lip hard enough to break the skin, clutching the edge of the desk like it was a raft in a stormy ocean.

Bask slunk across the room, eying Lysander as he passed him. It hurt that he didn't drop onto my lap or kiss down Magenta's neck like I knew he craved to. "As much as it'd please me to see that," he cocked his head in thought for a moment like he was imagining the scene, "*truly* please me, I already hurt Lysander." Bask's gaze was anguished as it met the fae's. "Here's the thing of it, I didn't know what the iron would do to you and so I shouldn't have even been fighting with it. Ezekiel used me to hurt you in the same way as Bacchus used Magenta. You're still a bastard, but I'm sorry."

Lysander barely looked like he was breathing; he was mesmerized by Bask. Had anyone ever apologized to Lysander before, who hadn't been motivated by fear alone?

"Reward," I stated, glancing around at the other Immortals. "Giants and dwarves, I can't believe that I'm choosing this, but let's give the Princes a reward."

Lysander wrapped his wings around himself, studying us in confusion.

The other Rebels nodded.

"The Princes' whipping boy," Magenta said, softly. Pocus lifted his head to stare at her, but the only sign that Midnight had heard was a twitch of his shoulders. "He's knelt in the corner all this time. Such treatment is barbaric. Yet positive change is better than negative destruction. I wish to reward him with the rest of the day off."

Bacchus rapped the thyrsus on the floor. "Done."

"You can turn around now," Magenta urged.

Cautiously, Midnight straightened and twisted, glancing at her from underneath his eyelashes. She flushed, and I couldn't blame her. Midnight was hot in a smoldering vampiric way, with charcoal eyes that begged *save me* at the same time as his fangs and muscles screamed *before I bite your throat.*

Who could resist that combo?

Yet Midnight appeared as flustered as her. Had he been included in any reward since he'd arrived here? Huh, I didn't even know how long ago that'd been. He'd already been the Princes' whipping boy when I'd arrived.

Fox *whooped.* "Whipping boys on vacation go wild…"

"When we say that he gets the day off," I wagged my finger at Lysander, and Mist snorted aquamarine flames at him as if to punctuate the point, "that means no crawling, answering to your bullshit orders, or any other whipping boy asshole duties."

Lysander shoved himself away from the desk, marching to the door. "If you insist."

"Hey, look at that, I do."

"Gloating is unbecoming," Lysander's voice was dangerously low. "Shifter Training is this afternoon with Prince Ambrose. Us fae are formidable enemies, and you made a mistake to turn him against you. The torments of Seelie Fae can be creative and excruciating." Lysander shuddered. *Was he speaking from experience?* "One was shocked to hear about the escape of *my* dragon, and how you Immortal delinquents were involved. Perhaps, now that I no longer have a steed, Ambrose will allow me to saddle *you* up…? It's clear you need a good dose of my riding whip to break you. Are you capable of being *trained*, monster?"

When he laughed, slamming out of the room, I stormed after him. Magenta snatched for my sleeve, but I shook her off.

Mist retreated to the back of my pocket, trembling. But my own eight-legged horse reared inside me in distress at the thought of being ridden by the prince. Loki had taught me that shifting was a sacred power that mustn't be forced but only ever be willing, but the professors treated it as something that should be controlled.

Just like me.

What if Ambrose forced me to shift?

I trembled as violently as Mist. The horse was small and no more dangerous than a toy. It was no wonder that the Rebels had accepted him so easily. But this afternoon, if I became Lysander's replacement dragon, they'd discover that *I* was truly monstrous.

CHAPTER FIFTEEN

Rebel Academy, Monday September 2nd

SLEIPNIR

I stormed ahead of the other Rebels, avoiding them like I had between classes since the nightmare that'd been SHP. I huffed a breath into the freezing afternoon air. Storm clouds fled across the gray skies. I shoved my hands deeper into the pockets of my black woolen overcoat. Then I sniffed its collar, calming at the sweet scent that still lingered from when I'd bundled Fox into it for the Discipline Run.

Valhalla! I wished that whipping boys were allowed to train at Dragon Polo because if anyone could understand the struggles and shame of a shifter, then it was a shimage.

When I breathed in the faint aroma of raspberries, it was kind of like Fox was as invisible as Magenta had once been but he was holding me as tightly as I needed him to right now.

Was that friendship?

I stared up at the towering barred stalls of the stables. *This lesson was going to suck dwarf balls.*

Honestly, after Bacchus' fun and games, the last thing that I needed was to face an irate fae who wanted my dick on a spike. Oh yeah, and this fae was a *professor.*

My breath sped up, and my hands curled into fists. *Misshapen...born wrong...monster...*

Stop thinking. Stop thinking. Stop...

I punched my fist into the stable wall.

Crack — in the fight between stone and bone, my knuckles lost.

I grimaced, shaking out my fist. On the runes, my brothers were right: I could be a dumbass sometimes.

Mist poked his head out of my coat pocket with a squeal, stamping his eight hooves in pain.

"Sorry," I stroked my finger over the flowing wisps of Mist's mane, which curled around me like smoke.

Mist allowed himself to be petted, before nudging me with his head.

I rolled my eyes. "Don't you start."

My own eight-legged horse inside pawed at me to

run. But on the Norns, it wasn't truly Prince Ambrose that I was scared of but my own darkness. Every academy had its secrets, but so did I.

Prince Ambrose wouldn't miss me for one lesson, would he?

I twisted on my heel, but before I could take a single step, Magenta materialized out of a cloud of pink and black mist that burst towards me, pinning me against the wall with my hands held above my head.

Woah, she could do that…?

Perhaps, I'd better save the impressed questions for after she'd flayed me because she looked *pissed.*

"I'd considered that gods may be arrogant, but do you not care that your behavior has the incubus believing that he's displeased you, until he shakes like he's been most soundly beaten, and the tender mage is close to tears?" Her eyes flashed, as she leaned closer. I didn't struggle because how hadn't I noticed the distress of the other Rebels? I'd been wrapped in Fox's scent, but I'd allowed him to suffer. "Our emotions and our actions affect others. I've learned this in the harshest way. I wish yours to be gentler."

My cheeks burned, and I couldn't meet her gaze. "I wasn't punishing them. I was…" *Punishing myself.* I bit my tongue hard to stop myself finishing the sentence, but Magenta appeared to have understood anyway because her expression gentled.

"I wish that you could see your merits as I do.

Why should you require punishment?" When Magenta rested her forehead against mine, the intimacy of her touch suddenly meant that I trusted her with my shame.

It gutted me that I'd never had such a close connection with anyone outside my family before, and yet once she'd heard the truth, I was certain that it'd be shattered.

My breath hitched, and Mist trembled, sinking down into my pocket like he could hide from the words. "Dad's Loki, this powerful shifter god. And mom…well, she's even *more* powerful or that's what dad said. She was a Seraphim, which are kind of the angels' gods. It's me who came out wrong." My voice dropped to a whisper; forcing out the words was like birthing snakes. "Loki refused to abandon me, which was another black mark against him." My gaze flicked to Magenta's and then away. Her breath gusted against my cheeks, and the feel of her fingers encircling my wrists was real and anchoring in a way that I never wanted to lose. Only, I knew that I had to, and that *wrecked* me. "You don't really want me. No one does. You should run from me like everybody else."

Magenta's fingers tightened hard enough to make me hiss. "I'll never run from you." She kissed me with a passion that shook me. I was lost in the aroma of yew trees, her ancient magic, and the twin points of her hands around my wrists and her lips on mine.

When she finally drew back, I was panting. "Are you now clear on the *I'm not running*?"

I grinned. "*Hmm*, I'm pretty dumb. You may need to teach me that lesson again."

"Ah, but I'm a *good* teacher." When Magenta leaned closer to kiss me again, slamming my wrists once against the wall, I couldn't hide the wince or the way that Mist squealed in sympathetic pain from my pocket.

This sharing of emotion thing was kind of freaky.

Magenta drew back, gently drawing my arms down and examining my hands in shock. "My word, who did you fight?"

I tried for nonchalant, "A wall, and I kicked its ass."

Magenta chuckled, before raising my hand to her lips and kissing each bruised knuckle with the tenderness of a promise. She never took her burning gaze from mine, and I drew in my breath.

On the World Tree, I was hers.

She knelt crunching in the snow. "Let me make you feel how *beautiful* you are."

"How about we start calling it *handsome…*? Plus, you know that I'm more than willing, but you'll freeze down there."

I grabbed her arm to pull her up, but she shook her head.

My dick had already hardened at the sight of

Magenta at my feet because I'd learned to move amongst humans to satisfy my urges, and so who could blame the Pavlovian response of a hopeful dick...? But Loki had also taught me to be a generous lover and never cruel to humans. How would he expect me to treat a witch lover?

I was pretty certain that he wouldn't expect her to kneel on snow to suck me off. Plus, we needed a rubber.

"Trust me, I want this more than anything. I've been fantasizing about it since Bask put up your portrait. He's not the only one who had dreams about you. But can we park this until tonight, when I have a rubber?" I wanted to bite my own tongue to stop the words, but hey, I'd played with orgasm denial before, and it'd be even more mind blowing when I eventually got to come.

My blue balls didn't believe me.

Magenta blinked at me. "You wish to...erase me?"

I would've laughed, if I didn't now have to hold a sex education class with a Victorian witch.

"Condom, raincoat, sheath, prophylactic..."

At last, Magenta's confusion cleared, but she pulled a face. "You wish to wear animal guts on your dick? It's no matter anyway because I died once, and if I know one thing it's that I don't need to fear protection against procreation or natural diseases. I'm not human." For a moment, sadness flickered across her face. Then she cocked her head. "And I'm a virgin. Aren't you?"

Valhalla give me strength to deal with Victorians.

"We've kind of advanced past the animal guts variety of rubber." I wet my lips. Did she expect me to be a virgin like Fox? Did she want us to be exploring all these sexual *firsts* together? "Look, I'm not as ancient as Bacchus but I've been alone and unloved for a long time. Sex was an easy and fun distraction."

Magenta studied me; her brow furrowed. "It wasn't about love…?"

I shook my head. "Pretty the Hel far from it."

Magenta ran her hands up my inner thighs, until I let them fall open with a shiver. "Then this will be. You're a virgin in love, my god."

My breath stuttered, and our gazes met. When I noticed the insecurity and need for reassurance in hers, it calmed me. I smiled, and her lips curled into something devilish.

"The snow will soak through your dress," I whispered; the thudding *beat* in my temples felt like it was pulsing through my dick as well. "Don't you mind the cold?"

"I *am* the cold." Magenta shoved back my coat, yanking open the buttons on my pants. I hissed, as her soft gloves slipped inside my pants and freed my dick and balls to the chilly air. My dick sprang hard against my stomach, as she gave it a couple of strokes. "You warm me."

Magenta's cool mouth enveloped my dick, as her hand wanked its base. My knees buckled at the intensity of the sensation. I pressed myself against the wall to keep myself standing, thudding my head rhythmically to hold myself back from thrusting my hips because this was Magenta's first time, and I wanted her to be in charge. But it was the way that she looked up at me, as she licked and sucked, as if eager to taste every inch of me, that blew my mind because she was right: this was love wrapped up in each touch. I'd never experienced that with a woman before, and I was close to coming already.

She sucked with greater intensity, until pain mixed with pleasure. I gasped, as her fingers tugged, exploring my balls. It struck me then that she'd never been so intimate with a guy before.

How could she trust me enough to be her first? Did that mean she truly didn't think I was monstrous, even when she knew the truth of my birth?

Then Magenta pulled back, before her tongue darted across the head of my dick, and (Valhalla!), my mind blanked of all thoughts apart from the white-hot throbbing between my legs. My balls ached.

Please, please, please...

"Look at me," Magenta murmured.

I hadn't even realized that I'd closed my eyes.

When I opened them, I met Magenta's ice-cold gaze. She licked her tongue in a circle over the head of my dick and then into the slit.

I howled as I came, surprising myself by the pulsing rush. Magenta continued to suck, pulling my…*everything*…from me like a Claiming and a victory.

At last, she sat back with a triumphant grin; I panted, as tremors ran through me. "Do you *feel* now that you're beautiful? Is there no more need for lessons?"

When Magenta reached for my oversensitive and bravely twitching cock, my eyes widened in alarm. "On the runes, I swear, I've learned my lesson."

Her grin widened. "Good boy. I shall enjoy repeating the lesson at a later date because I'm a firm believer in frequent reminders."

"Frequent sounds good."

When I heard the sound of footsteps in the snow, I glanced up in panic. Magenta's nimble hands tucked my dick back into my pants, buttoning me up.

Prince Ambrose marched around the corner, stopping to stare at us, before Magenta could stand.

Ambrose shivered as always from the cold because Seelie Fae were never meant to live in snowy conditions. *What in Hel's name had he done to be sent to the academy? I'd have admired his strength on surviving to become a professor, which he was so proud about, as well as his tight ass in those steam punk trousers, if he wasn't oppressing shifters*

Ambrose's emerald eyes studied us with a contempt that was reflected back in Magenta's gaze.

Huh, she truly hated fae.

"Are you praying to Hecate that I'll forget the escaped dragon?" Ambrose's voice vibrated with a dominant rage that made the werewolf tattoos rise onto my own arms and growl.

He *knew* that I'd just been sucked off. Why wasn't he calling us out on it?

Magenta rose gracefully to her feet, before brushing down her dress. "Why would I pray to a goddess who doesn't answer my prayers about fae princes?"

I'd never seen Ambrose taken aback before. It was awesome.

Ambrose glanced away, before dropping his hand to the hilt of his whip like it was a security blanket. Then his wings drooped, *clanking*.

When I startled at the sound, Ambrose's lips thinned. "You've clipped my wings, boy. You can't mean to tell me that you didn't know it'd be the consequence of me failing to guard the beasts?"

"Do you see me smiling?" I snarled. "And how about you stop calling them *beasts* and me *boy*, Prince Ambrose."

Ambrose's lips curled. "Aye, right. About the time

that you remember to call me *professor* and bring back a dragon for Lysander's missing one."

"That'll be *never* then."

Ambrose huffed out a frustrated breath. "It's time for training."

He snapped his boots together and turned on the spot, before marching around the stables.

I cringed, however, when I finally saw the punishment to Ambrose's wings because of my rescue effort. Iron chains had been looped from their delicate golden tips to the base of his shoulders. At their ends, they were clamped into the sensitive skin. At each step, the chains moved, searing his wings.

I'd seen in the Conqueror Gym how even a small touch from iron hurt a fae. Why wasn't Ambrose hollering in pain? Yet his shoulders were stiff with it; I guessed that his pride stopped him revealing the truth…or was he protecting *me* from it, after all?

I stroked my thumb over Mist's back, pushing him deeper into my pocket. "Stay down, Junior. This is familiar training as well, and I'd rather feed my dick to a troll than let you get pulled into that."

Magenta clasped my hand, pulling me after Ambrose. Her eyes twinkled. "Flair and Echo mysteriously developed headaches this morning, poor things. They needed nest rest. Such a shame that they'll also have to miss this."

Dad would love Magenta.

When Magenta and I strolled after Ambrose into the yard in front of the stables that curled with smoke, which stung my nostrils, my eyes narrowed at the Princes' corner. On their side of the yard, bridles, saddles, spurs, and every other tool to dominate another creature lay spread out. Willoughby knelt crouched over them, carefully checking and polishing each one. Lysander stood watching him, tapping a leather riding crop against his thigh impatiently.

Bask stood — alone — in the Immortals' corner, which was opposite the Princes, below the stable block. I rushed to him because I knew now that it didn't matter what I had inside me or how bad *I* felt. Bask was my friend and he loved me.

Omens and runes, I swore that I wouldn't hurt him.

I swept my arms as close to Bask as I could without touching him, and he drew in such a deep breath that it was like he was trying to inhale *me*. He was pale, and his forehead was beaded with sweat. Magenta had been right: it looked like I'd been kicking him in the balls since SHP.

I grinned, kissing the air over Bask's cheeks and nose. "Have I told you that you please me, even when I'm acting like an asshole?"

Instantly, the pained look cleared from Bask's face.

"Have I told you that you that to please me, you

don't have to *stop* being an asshole, you just have to not *ignore* me?"

"Someone taught me a firm lesson."

Bask's face lit up. "That must've been a fine sight."

"If you rascals are finished flirting on my time," Ambrose snapped his whip on the ground between us, and we jumped apart, "let's get started. Lessons will be ground based to start with, until I can work out—"

"How we manage without my dragon?" Lysander drawled.

Ambrose's brow furrowed, as he stalked towards Lysander. I expected Lysander to back away, but instead, he haughtily stared down the professor. It was strange to see the two fae together. Golden hair mixed with emerald in a sparkling waterfall. Yet in other ways, they were so alike. The Seelie and Unseelie were enemies outside the academy, and the princes weren't BFFs inside, either.

"Something to say, boy? I'm giving you this one chance only, and then your Unseelie arse will show me the proper respect owed to my position." Ambrose pressed the hilt of the whip underneath Lysander's chin, and Lysander's jaw clenched. With the way that his hand tightened around the riding crop, I thought for a moment that he'd slash it across Ambrose's cheek in retaliation. "We both know that I can punish creatively."

Willoughby had paused in his polishing. His hand clawed the saddle like he dared not let go.

"One is more than aware of your *creativity*, just like all Seelie." Lysander's voice shook, but he held himself with the same poise as if he and Ambrose were dancing. "Are your wings sore? It must smart."

Next to me, Magenta stiffened, as Ambrose drew back his hand as if to slap Lysander but then, he stopped himself.

"Aye, it smarts. We must all suffer if we fail." Ambrose pushed away from Lysander, glancing between us. "You should remember that. This isn't a game. Your decisions will lead to rewards or punishments."

"Your decision," Lysander accused, "led to *my* personal dragon escaping."

Ambrose's expression softened. "Ask yourself why he ran from you. If you'd treated him with even a wee bit of kindness—"

"Are we talking about a dragon or my boyfriend?" Lysander arched his brow.

Ambrose snorted. "I pity both. Now I have to get all of your daft arses ready for the Dragon Polo Tournament on Saturday, when the Rebel Cup will be presented. Have you even ridden on a dragon before, lass?"

Magenta shook her head.

Ambrose fluttered his wings in agitation, and then

couldn't hide the gasp of pain. When I glanced at Willoughby, he'd paled.

Ambrose kicked a snowbank. "A non-rider and only four dragons, which is why the whipping boys aren't riding. Drain the gold from my wings now, Damelza will have my hide."

"And my dragon…?" Lysander asked with fake sweetness.

"You'll have Hector's dragon: Rayn." Ambrose strode to the stall to unlatch it, but Bask darted to him, scrabbling at his hands.

"If it pleases you, *no, no, no…*" Bask begged.

Ambrose froze, staring at Bask in shock. His voice was softer than I'd expected, "Enough of that. Hector's gone, lad, and that's just the way of it in this place. You can't hold onto his ghost, and I can't keep Rayn in retirement any longer like a memorial to him. Do you know how many *I* lost? *All of my friends.* But I'm still here, right? You have to become stronger; I know you can."

Huh, that'd almost been inspiring. Plus, fae needed touch and love like incubi. If Ambrose was alone, how did he cope? I'd never considered how hard it must be for Lysander before. Weirdly, I was glad that he had Willoughby, however twisted the Princes were.

"My royal personage doesn't need Rayn." *Wait,*

why was Lysander studying me like that? "One is inclined to saddle up a far more interesting beast."

And I'd just been feeling sorry for the bastard.

"You'd better not complete that sentence, twinkle wings," I growled.

Lysander swaggered towards me, swinging the crop loosely in his hand. "You son of a bitch…"

I blinked at him. He hadn't even sounded like he'd meant that.

Ambrose was watching us in confusion. "Apologize, so your daft selves can start this lesson."

Lysander swept me a mocking bow. "My deepest apologies. Of course, what I should've said was: *You son of a mare.*"

Silence.

I froze, reddening with humiliation. My hands curled into fists. My heart beat too rapidly in my chest. Lightheaded, it was only Magenta's hand on my shoulder that brought everything back into focus.

Then my hair spiked to red, before I roared out my fury and launched myself on top of Lysander. I knocked him into the snowbank, tumbling him over. I vibrated with hate, but I didn't know if it was for Lysander or myself. Weirdly, Lysander wasn't fighting back, but I was way past the point of caring. When I raised my fist to punch him in the nose as he had Bask, however, a whip curled around my wrist, yanking me off him.

I yelped at the whip's burning *snap*, tumbling onto my ass. Then both Lysander and me jumped as the whip snapped with a sharp *crack* like a furious snake three times between us.

Ambrose towered above us, thrumming with rage. I tensed, waiting for the next strike to be laid across my shoulders.

All of a sudden, however, a young Scottish voice called from the top window of the stables above us, "Da, I drew the p-picture of you and me, but then, I heard bad s-sounds and I got s-scared... Are they fighting m-monsters?"

In shock, I stared up at the tiny fae boy who was hanging precariously out of the window, waving his drawing at Ambrose. He wore a plain green tunic and leggings. His golden hair curled behind his ears, and his eyes were startlingly jade. There was no doubt that he was Ambrose's son: he was like a kid Prince Charming if he'd been dipped in sparkling fairy dust. Except, unlike a full fae, the boy didn't have wings.

I paled.

They were admitting *kids* to the academy? And Ambrose had a *son* who was only part fae? In his culture, that meant his kid was seen as a 'mongrel' and as much a monster as me.

I shuddered. I bet Ambrose was a hardass as a dad.

Ambrose's eyes widened. "Ty, get inside *now*. You know that you're not allowed out."

"But the m-monsters…" Ty's lip trembled.

Lysander smiled maliciously as he looked between Ambrose and Ty. "Do tell your son, *father*, about those wicked monsters."

Ty leaned further out of the window to stare with terrified eyes at Lysander. "You're a *bad* Dark Fae. Da says…"

All of a sudden, Ty overbalanced with a shriek, tipping out of the window. My heart raced, as I threw myself under him.

By the Valkyries, no…

I couldn't reach him, and nor could Bask, even though we both leaped to catch him. The Immortals were on the opposite corner of the yard.

Out of the corner of my eye, I saw Ambrose's wings attempt to beat and take flight, but the chains only *clanked*. He moaned in agony.

In shock, I watched as Magenta materialized in the air out of a cloud of mist, catching the falling boy, before he could hit the ground. Calmly, she hovered down to the snow bank, cradling Ty to her chest. She stroked his hair, murmuring to him in comfort as he trembled, before passing him with a final stroke to his dad, who was trembling more than his son.

"Never do that again, you hear me?" Ambrose tried for stern, but as soon as Ty wrapped his arms and legs around him like a limpet and wept into his shoulder, his expression softened. "What would your da do without his daft wee man, right? You gave me a scare. You must…" He took a deep breath; his hands shook. "Be careful."

"S-sorry," Ty forced out between sobs.

"No need for that. You've had a scare too." Ambrose raised his gaze to Magenta. "Thank you. A Seelie fae always honors their debts, and I'll never be able to repay you for saving something so precious to me."

Was this the same Ambrose who whipped dragons, threw me into snowbanks, and was a typical fae prince?

Loki had told me that it was having kids that'd brought out the best in him. I'd thought he'd said that to make my brothers and me feel better about the fact that he'd been burdened with us. But seeing the softer side to Ambrose with his son made me wonder if dad had been telling the truth.

Could guys get broody because seeing Magenta carrying Ty and now Ambrose getting in the cuddles was kind of making me regret that Magenta couldn't have kids with me. And that wasn't something that I'd ever wanted before.

"Allow me." Willoughby gracefully stood, stepping towards Ty.

Ambrose took a step backward, twisting to shield his still crying son from Willoughby.

Did Ambrose know something about Willoughby and how dangerous he was that I didn't?

Willoughby froze, unable to hide the hurt. Then his expression became shuttered. He swallowed, before offering, "It's only an elven lullaby to help him sleep."

Grudgingly, Ambrose turned back, allowing Willoughby to step closer and place his hand on his son's shoulder.

"Is that your father and you?" Willoughby asked with the same hint of mild curiosity that he usually showed, pointing at the drawing that Ty had managed to keep holding, despite the tumble from the window.

"A-ye," Ty whispered. "I'm the o-one in g-green. You can t-tell it's da because he has m-metal on his wings." I winced at the same time as Ambrose. It was screwed-up that a kid had to witness his dad's punishments. I bet that Ambrose had tried to hide them, as much as my dad had tried to hide when he was in trouble. The problem was that we'd still known when Loki had cried. "C-can you take it off? It h-hurts him."

Willoughby's gaze slipped to Ambrose's. "I'm a mighty elf prince; I can help your father stop hurting. You rest now and forget the fear. Would you like that?"

Ty nodded.

In wonder, I watched as Willoughby placed his

hand on Ambrose's wing, as well as pressed harder on Ty's back. When Willoughby started to sing, it was so hauntingly beautiful that the hairs on the back of my neck rose, my toes curled, and my eyes fluttered shut. I was caught in a flow of winter waters, drawn into their depths. Honestly, I hadn't truly understood the Other World that the elves had been ripped from, until Willoughby had offered up his song out of kindness.

Why had he?

When it ended, it felt like being kicked out of Valhalla.

My eyes snapped open, and as I glanced around, everyone wore the same dazed expressions as me. Ty was cradled, sleeping in Ambrose's arms.

When Ambrose smiled with genuine happiness, it shocked me how truly *hot* he could be. "How long will…whatever you did…stop my wings hurting?"

Willoughby's face clouded. "Only an hour or so, I'm afraid."

"That's more respite than I've had." Ambrose wrapped his wings around Ty. "Right, this lesson is ended. I have a certain wee lad to get to bed."

Lysander watched Ambrose with his son like he couldn't understand the tender way that he was holding him. "You intend to reward the child for his misbehavior? How can you teach us, when you've no conception of how to discipline your own son?"

Ambrose's smile faded. "If you fail to teach us our lesson, there shall be consequences."

Ambrose straightened his shoulders. "Aye, right. Your concern is touching. Your daft arses will learn that there *are* always consequences, no matter what you decide. But right now, my son is what matters." He glanced at Magenta. "You saved Ty, which means that you win the Punish and Reward Game." Then he glowered at Lysander. "Punish *his* arse for me. As he's so interested in discipline, a beating sounds good."

As Lysander gaped in outrage, Ambrose marched into the stable block, carrying his sleeping kid.

In the silence, the Princes glanced at us Immortals, waiting for the ax to fall. Bask bounced to my side, smiling.

"If it pleases you," Bask wrapped his arms around himself in anticipation as he whispered, "I've been thinking all day of the perfect punishment. It's a punishment to Prince Lysander, but it'll reward Midnight. Tonight, in the Rebel Café, Lysander has to serve him."

"I don't like taking part in this game at all," Magenta sighed, "but if we must, then that appears the best compromise."

"Come on, get on with it," Lysander spat. "Lay hands like the brutes you are on my royal person."

Bask snickered.

"Hey, there aren't enough chocolates in your

private larder to bribe me into touching your *person*." I lifted my brow. "The punishment is for Prince Lysander. Tonight, you have to serve your whipping boy."

He blinked. "How?"

I grinned wickedly. "That depends on the café and your whipping boy, but since you've had this whole *master and servant* thing going on, I have a feeling that you're in for a long night of humiliation, *slave*."

Always hit them where it hurts, and for Prince Lysander, that was right in his *pride*.

Lysander's cheeks pinked, before his eyes darkened with a deadly rage. "Have your fun. But tomorrow, I'll be certain to win the Game, and you'll regret making me suffer. Roles can be reversed for a single night, but the whipping boys shall be whipping boys still and princes shall always be princes. I'll be certain that *yours* remembers that as much as mine."

My eyes narrowed at Lysander's threat to Fox. Didn't he get that we could seriously hurt him with the Game, but instead, were trying to teach him to treat his own whipping boy with some respect?

Even though Magenta had manged to make a friend of one fae prince, another had become a deadlier enemy. Lysander looked set to wreck us, before we could wreck him.

CHAPTER SIXTEEN

Rebel Academy, Monday September 2nd

BASK

I sat cross-legged on the floor in front of the suede sofa in the Rebel Café. The rest of the Immortals and Princes sprawled in a circle, eying each other warily. You could bring rival bad boys (and girls) to water, but you couldn't make us magic it into cocktails and drink. If Ezekiel had wanted tonight to be a team bonding session, I didn't think that he'd imagined it to go like *this*.

Snowflake patterns swirled across the walls, until I was dizzy. I tossed my blazer and tie to the side; my skin itched and crawled with need. I was burning up. My hair was limp, and my arse was barely pettable.

Shoot me now.

I perked up when Serenity dropped from the ceiling an even more deliciously snuggly pile of pillows than my West Wing stash. I narrowed my eyes at Fox, who gazed at the pillows with as much longing as me.

"Sorry," Magenta pulled Fox against her, stroking a curl behind his ear, "but they're for my crow familiars to nest in. They're ghosts, you know, but they need pampering too."

"Finally, someone who understands about my importance in the healing that is *relaxation,*" Serenity gushed like she was about to come from being appreciated alone. "Familiars suffer stress too."

"Why the snowflakes?" Magenta gestured at the walls. "Wouldn't a tropical island be a rather pleasant break for us?"

"Scientists have proved that repeated patterns like *snowflakes* reduce distress. Aren't you soothed already? Come on, what's with the tension in here? How about a group wank?"

"A group…what?" Magenta demanded.

"*Laugh,*" Serenity answered with pretend innocence. "It's perfect therapy. How about I start…? *Hahahaha…*"

I winced as Serenity's shrill laugh echoed throughout the café.

"Wow, I'm all relaxed now," Fox gritted out,

before twisting in Magenta's arms. "Okay, that's a lie, I'm sitting in this freaky circle with the Princes and the female version of *Hal*. Do you know what'd help…?"

He glanced significantly at the fluffy pillows.

I drew in my breath. Fox was trying to steal *my* snuggle patch. *Yep, I was claiming it.*

Magenta cocked her head like she was listening. "Flair says: *How about his beak biting into your cock like a worm? You're never getting our nest, you foxy fuck.*"

Rude.

When Fox paled, I snickered. Although, what would the invisible crow do to *my* dick…? I covered my crotch. **Rule 11 of the Incubi Night Code** stated: Guard your dick and balls like they're truly as precious as the royal jewels.

Magenta even managed to resist the power of Fox's puppy dog eyes. She had some talent. I'd have at least shared…*one*…of my pillows by now. Away with you, I could be generous.

I glanced across the circle at Sleipnir who sprawled in only his rolled-up shirtsleeves; his cotton candy pink hair fell in gentle spikes. He wore his tie around his neck like a bandanna again. Note to self: when not dying for lack of touch, take more clothing risks. Sea serpent tattoos coiled up and down his arms like they were dancing to his gentle strumming, as he played Depeche Mode's "Master and Servant". Serenity even supplied the whip and chain sound effects for the song.

I grinned, but Lysander grimaced, flinching at each whip effect. Sleipnir had a wicked sense of humor. Watching Lysander next to me was almost amusing enough to forget the buzzing wrongness that edged through me, the fear of the Duchess' return, and the weirdness of sharing a night out with the Princes.

A *double* weirdness because when Midnight had ordered Lysander to kneel with surprising firmness (payback was a *bitch*), and told Serenity that Lysander was there to serve for the evening, she'd magicked him into a French maid's frilly black uniform.

I'd told Sleipnir that my role play list was anything but a waste of time: *Willoughby in a maid's outfit had been fantasy role-play Number 49, but Lysander in one had been Number 48.*

There were few things that I treasured: Nile, holding my brothers after their births, and Magenta's first kiss. Now added to those was Lysander's yelp and expression of mortified horror when he'd realized that he'd been dressed in nothing but a maid's outfit, which had barely covered his arse.

Sweet (scorching hot) memories...

To be fair, Lysander had pouted but hadn't moaned

as much as I'd been expecting. Perhaps, he secretly enjoyed a taste of taking orders for once, rather than giving them. Midnight was kind with his power, like I'd known that he would be, and it was only in play. The thing of it was, that it *wasn't* play for Midnight… he was a true slave to the Princes.

I smiled softly, as I studied Fox who was cuddled in Magenta's arms, kissing down her neck. It didn't matter that I was his Patron; he'd never be my slave.

That didn't mean I wasn't owed a twinge of envy that it wasn't *me* kissing Magenta's long neck.

Lysander spooned chocolate dessert on a golden spoon into Midnight's mouth, as Midnight lay on his back with a blissed-out expression. I sighed. Why couldn't I just snatch Midnight and make him *my* whipping boy as well?

Yep, it'd be *kidnap*. Why was that wrong again?

I shivered, as a wave of pain swept through me. I clawed my nails into my palms to stop myself scratching my shoulders. I'd even take Lysander's touch right now. Buzzing jangled my nerves. My eyes screwed shut.

Too much, too much, too much…

Cool hands gripped my hips, sliding me onto a narrow lap that was all hard muscle. My eyes snapped open. When soft hair swept my cheek, and the scent of herbal green tea, like a wintry breeze across wild grasses, shivered through me, I knew that it was *Willoughby's* lap.

I squirmed but even as I tried to pull away because my sexy wee self was sitting on an elf's lap in front of everybody (at least there was no hard dick poking against me as there would've been, if I'd wiggled around like this on top of Sleipnir), I pressed more firmly against Willoughby and *moaned*. Could I help it if my cute body knew what it needed more than my brain, and if Willoughby found me pettable, even at my least pettable level for years?

Witness the mesmerizing power of an incubus' arse.

Willoughby only tightened his arms in silence, calmly running his fingers up and down my arms, before turning my hands over and tracing patterns across my gloved palm. I ached to go skin to skin with him. His touch was nothing like the rough massage that I'd been dreading from the Princes. I arched, panting at the excruciating but perfect *touch*. I could've kissed him that he hadn't made me *ask* for this. The Duchess had loved how I'd begged. How had Willoughby known that to speak would've been too much for me?

Willoughby's lips brushed my ear, as if he'd sensed my darkening thoughts. Then he hummed like a tinkling waterfall…promising to show me Aladdin's "A Whole New World."

I had the sudden image of Lysander playing Disney songs to the regal elf, as they cuddled.

Away with you, it could happen.

I giggled, and Willoughby danced his fingers down my chest. Everywhere he touched hummed in joy along with him, rather than pain. When I caught Willoughby's hand between mine, tracing his palm back in turn (because never let it be said that an incubus of the Night lineage was selfish with pleasure), he broke off his humming, smothering a groan.

I preened. *This incubus still had it.*

Serenity's voice crooned, "That's a fine sight. Massage his earlobes. It's a pressure point. Science can't be wrong, *hmm*? Perhaps, the witch can massage *your* earlobes next, godling…"

Sleipnir stopped playing with a *twang* of wrong notes. "No one's getting near my ears. Just call me the God of Relaxation." He sprawled on his side, pillowing his head on Magenta's lap, as Fox carded his fingers through his hair. "See?"

In the silence, I was certain that Serenity was pouting.

Willoughby's low chuckle tickled *my* ear, and his fingers massaged my earlobes. Wow, he'd discovered a secret line straight to my dick that tented my pants like an eager puppy.

Yep, that was the massaging goodness. Come to the stressed-out incubus…

"If you *desire* to keep massaging them..." I sighed.

Willoughby chuckled again.

Lysander slammed down the bowl, and the spoon clattered with a spray of chocolate dessert onto the floor. I frowned. Ma always taught me to lick every trace of pudding clean, which hadn't appeared sinister at the time. Now I'd discovered more about my role as a bonded, licking didn't feel so innocent.

"Are you satisfied, *master*?" Lysander arched his brow.

Midnight stretched out his wings with a smile. "You always satisfy me, my prince." His voice had a soft Welsh lilt; it was gentle, teasing, and didn't tremor with its usual fear.

I wished that us Immortals had been able to reward Midnight with more than one night of freedom.

Lysander blinked like he'd expected a slap, rather than the tender response. But then, Midnight's gorgeous ass wasn't the same as his bastard one. "Well, be that as it may, my noble personage most certainly am not."

Lysander smoothed down the front of his apron to ensure his modesty. I smirked; I'd bet my slinky cuteness that he was hard under there. His pale thighs already peeked out of the silky fabric. It'd be a fine thing if the apron rode a wee bit higher... *Objectifica-*

tion was allowed if it was of a fae prince who made his own whipping boy crawl around naked. That had to be in the rule book. Probably in small writing. Seriously, look it up.

Magenta studied Lysander. "If it's any consolation, you make as fair a maid as a man."

Lysander reddened, starting to rise, but Midnight laid his hand lightly on his knee.

"Don't start and make trouble." *Wow, who'd known that Midnight could sound so commanding?*

Willoughby paused in his massaging. I squirmed around to encourage him to start again, but he'd frozen, watching the role reversal between the whipping boy and prince.

Lysander stared at Midnight and then he swallowed. "One cares not about the insult. What shall not stand is that we drew in the Rebel Cup today, which means that only three days remains to settle who wins overall. We all know how high the stakes are." His gaze flicked to Fox, whose hold had tightened around Magenta, before settling once more on Midnight. Then he stroked his fingers, just once, along Midnight's wingtip. "I would've thought you more than most, *master*."

"By my fangs, I never asked you to call me *master*," Midnight murmured. Lysander flushed. "Look you, the Rebel Cup is rigged by the House of

Crows. You can battle all you like, but one side has to lose."

"I shan't let it be *us*," Lysander hissed.

"And I shan't allow the Immortals to lose either." Magenta clasped her arms around Fox; her eyes flashed.

"Then we're at an impasse." Lysander knelt straighter, as something malevolent glimmered in his eyes. "So, let's act like the royalty and immortals that we are and take back the control. Every Friday, one Wing of the academy has to complete a mission. It's why we train, after all. Why don't we settle who that is between us now like gentlemen…and women, of course?"

Not another mission.

I growled, wrenching away from Willoughby and wrapping my arms around myself.

Missions: I hated them. Simply because each of our supernatural societies had decided to imprison us, we'd become expendable. Damelza sent either the Princes or the Immortals on missions that the patrons of the school paid for (and they weren't to bring presents to kids in orphanages).

Last term, I'd refused to go on my first mission because I'd said that it was against my code to be an *assassin*. Damelza had hung Hector from Hecate's statue, and threatened that if I didn't fight in her army, then she'd kill him.

I'd chosen Hector over my code. But then, I'd already been a broken incubus. Did it matter if I broke myself?

"Of course," Magenta replied, coolly. "What do you suggest?"

Lysander's wings beat eagerly. "A game: the losing side goes on the mission."

Sleipnir sat up. "How can we trust you to play it honestly?"

Lysander's eyes narrowed. "How can I trust you?"

Fox untangled himself from Magenta, thrumming with sudden energy. "Just call me Grandmaster Wizard of Games. It's my secret title, handed down for generations to those who have the magic touch at Pictionary, Cluedo, and Scrabble. Okay, which of you bitches wants to test a Grandmaster Wizard's skills?"

Lysander pulled at a thread on the carpet, unraveling it. "One believes that strip poker would be more appropriate."

Instantly, Midnight sat up, wrapping his wing around Lysander as if he was protecting his slave's modesty. *Interesting.*

An incubus, however, doesn't have any modesty. Come on now, just look at my sexy self. How could I be so cruel as to deprive others of this view?

"Fine with me," I smirked.

Magenta raised her eyebrow. "Echo says that these contests are *modern duels*. Although, he's also excitedly chattering about adding to his *Wank Count*, so I find myself fascinated to witness how a duel can end in…self pleasure."

I flushed, as Magenta's tongue darted across her lips. She never broke her gaze from mine, as her black mists spread across the circle, surrounding me. I was drowning in her, and yet she hadn't even touched me. *Did she know?* Her eyes sparked with love, and I smiled, willing her to understand how much I longed for her.

The Duchess had made me hurt for her, but I'd die for Magenta.

Fox edged closer to the center of the circle (*don't think you're sneaking a pillow, foxy*), before casually offering, "Okay, I've never played strip poker before, but I'm sure that I'll get the hang of it. The loser has to take off a piece of clothing, right? Wow, it'll be fun to find out if Serenity magicked you silk panties."

Lysander's expression darkened, as he shifted uncomfortably on his knees (*he was enjoying the sensation of silk on his dick for definite*). "*Hmm*, am I temped to play poker with the mage whose magical talent can tell if I'm bluffing…?" He cocked his head as if in thought. "Shockingly, I'll pass."

"Godling," Serenity cooed, "as your stress adviser, I suggest that it'd be a fine way for you to relax if you took off all your clothes, so that I could take a closer look at your muscles… I mean, if you played strip poker."

Sleipnir crossed his arms. "Like an Unseelie wouldn't cheat at cards."

Lysander pressed his hand to his chest in mock outrage; I smothered my grin. "Like a prince would ever be *caught* cheating."

Sometimes, I thought Lysander was as much an incubus as me.

Magenta glanced between us. "As Prefect, I insist that the game should be fair and mustn't risk any of my Rebels."

"Are you pulling Prefect rank already?" Lysander sneered. "The same responsibility rests on *my* shoulders. Then how about magical Russian roulette?"

"Bullets have a tendency to risk death." Magenta commented with a deadly coolness. Sparks lit the dim room, and Lysander quailed. "I died once, and I'm not quite ready to repeat the experience."

"*Magical*," Lysander repeated, clasping his hands tightly on his knees. "One is excellent at potions, remember? Each Wing chooses a challenger who takes two attempts to drink. So, four turns in total. Three shall be harmless and the fourth…"

"Please say: Turns you into a parrot, which can only be taught to squawk "Help! I've been turned into a parrot!"" Fox bounced up and down with excitement but stopped when we all looked at him. He shrugged, awkwardly. "What? That's been a lifelong dream of mine."

"It wouldn't be fun if you knew what the potion did now, would it? But I swear that it shan't cause death or any lasting harm." Lysander's smile grew.

Willoughby shuffled backward. "I don't want to play. None of us should."

"Honor dictates that we're all part of this." Lysander gripped Willoughby by the ankle, dragging him to the circle. "For your refusal, I think we have the volunteer from the *Princes*."

I gasped, and my gaze shot to Willoughby's frightened expression, although he masked it hurriedly with his usual haughtiness. But he knew Lysander better than us, and I'd learned at the Duchess' hands that there was a brutal amount you could still do to someone that didn't leave *lasting harm*.

What if the potion made me less pettable…?

Magenta's expression hardened. "If you had any honor, fae, as Prefect you'd be playing yourself. I'd be delighted to try this game."

I froze, horrified. There was not a chance that I'd let Magenta play against the Princes. I hadn't saved Hector, and I might not be able to save Fox. If the Duchess took me away, then I wouldn't be able to protect any of the Immortals like I'd sworn that I would. But I could now, even if it was only playing magical Russian roulette.

I wondered if this was how the ancient incubi had thought their warrior descendants would turn out? I'd say *not*...at a wild guess.

When I grasped Willoughby's hand, his confused gaze met mine. "If it pleases you, let me fight for the Immortals' honor."

At the chorus of *noes*, I bristled.

"I'm not weak." I shuffled, until my knees touched Willoughby's, and we faced each other: opponents but not rivals. "I can't touch you," I glanced at Magenta, and she bit her lip, "but let me show you that I love you."

Sleipnir shook his head.

I tilted up my chin. "I'm doing this. Let me *feel* something."

Willoughby's smile softened from his usual icy-cold. "You're a worthy and brave adversary."

Then I spluttered, as Lysander thrust his wing *thwapping* across my face.

"Let's play this the traditional fae way," Lysander said. "Serenity, infuse my feathers with Potion One."

I blinked. I was meant to lick the first *bullet* from his feathers...? *Yuck.* I didn't know where he'd been.

I wrinkled my nose, as my pulse pounded. Was this the harmless potion or the one that'd magically kick me in the balls and lose me the game? I took a deep breath, before licking.

Lysander wasn't able to hide his shiver at the

touch because a fae's wings were as sensitive as an angel's. *He'd use any excuse to get my tongue on his privates.*

Then I choked on the intense taste of sweet cherry blossoms. Somehow, I'd expected Lysander to taste sour.

The Immortals crowded closer in alarm, but I held my hand up to keep them back. After a long moment, I did a thumbs up.

Lysander thrust his wing to Willoughby's lips. "Potion Two."

Willoughby clenched his jaw, before licking. When he also nibbled, hard enough for Lysander to yelp, I grinned. Except, my heart beat too rapidly in my chest, as I watched Willoughby's shuttered expression desperately for signs of pain, transformation, or...*something.*

Was I hoping that he took the bullet or that I did? I had to win or my lovers would be forced on the mission at the end of the week. But I didn't want Willoughby to be hurt either. I'd barely thought about the elf before, but being massaged and touched by someone held importance to an incubus. He'd treated me like I was precious, and no son of Night could ignore the debt owed. It was this whole *thing.*

After a moment, the tension in Willoughby's shoulders relaxed, but he gripped my hand tighter.

Lysander's wing raised to my lips again. "Potion Three."

I couldn't look up at the other Immortals. The silence was poisoning. My pulse pounded, and I couldn't swallow. There were fifty: fifty odds of this being the dangerous potion. I'd had experience of deliberately harming myself before for my love; the uncertainty was always worse than the pain.

I didn't hesitate. I licked Lysander's wingtip, but this time, a bitter taste like cabbage with just a hint of ginger, invaded my mouth. I gagged, sitting back on my heels. Instantly, I knew that I'd been shot with the bullet.

Helplessly, I curled around my aching guts. "I'm sorry," I whispered.

I'd lost...forced us to go on the mission... I'd failed to protect my lovers...

I'd have cried if it wouldn't only have made me weaker and uglier.

The itching ballooned out, until I was nothing but a buzzing ball of needy incubus. My mind was hazy, as I fell on my side.

Where was I? What did I...? *Was the Duchess punishing me again?*

There were voices, but I didn't recognize them. They were lost in the pulsing *need, need, need*, which was centered on the hard-on pulsing between my legs.

May I come, please, please, please...?

I didn't even know if I was begging out loud. *Wow, I hoped not.*

"What did you do?" Magenta howled, floating in a black cloud towards me. "You swore that you'd not harm him."

"He's not harmed," Lysander insisted. "It's just a lust potion: Love Me Quick."

"Witless fae." Magenta curled her magic around Lysander. "Have you no idea how dangerous it is to give an aphrodisiac to an incubus who's already…"

"Suffering from touch deprivation," Sleipnir gritted out. "You know that I'm going to kick your ass, right?"

"Don't you think that there's enough danger in this academy without the rivalries, which are fostered by the coven to divide us? Why must you make it worse?" Magenta demanded.

"Says the *witch* from the *House of Crows*." Lysander struggled in her magic's hold.

I rolled onto my back, scrabbling at my clothes. The fabrics grated my sensitive skin. I needed them *off, off, off…* I tore and ripped, hauling off my shirt, before shoving down my pants and kicking them away with a sigh of relief. Then I wrapped my hand around my throbbing dick, which hurt so much. *But it wasn't enough.*

Why wasn't anybody helping me?

"Please," I whimpered.

Magenta leaned over me. Her hand hovered over my dick.

Just a wee bit closer...

"Don't touch him," Fox warned. "Unless you want a shock that could fry his dick as well."

Magenta snatched away her hand, backing up.

No, no, no...come back, witchy...

I arched, moaning. My own hand wasn't enough, as I stroked and tugged. I needed...*touch*. I was aflame again, back with the Duchess. She was burning me, and I was begging for it.

"It was just an experiment," Lysander said, shakily. "Stop your fussing; it'll wear off. What's an hour's humiliation for him, when you wished a *night's humiliation* on me?"

Midnight rose up, towering over Lysander. Midnight's charcoal eyes darkened to black. "When did I take advantage of that power over you, my prince? How long will you allow your guardian's twisted hate to rule your life?"

Willoughby leaned closer, stroking the back of his hand down my cheek. The touch settled me, clearing my mind for a moment, but it still wasn't enough. I squirmed, trying to encourage his hand lower, but he shook his head.

"You're drugged and can't tell me to stop. I shan't touch you like this. I'm sorry." When his sky-blue hair froze to ice, I shuddered at the sudden danger. The room became as chilly as the grounds. There was fleeting fear in Lysander's eyes now. "Was your revenge worth causing such pain?"

Lysander's lips curled. "Who are you, *killer*, to act pious over causing pain?"

Killer?

Even through the haze of need, I paled, pulling away from Willoughby. I knew why all the Immortals had been sent to the academy, but not the Princes. Their crimes had to be greater for an entire kingdom to depose and abandon them. *But killer...?*

Willoughby paled, and his eyes flashed with raw pain at the way that I'd recoiled from him. Then his expression became blank again, and he looked down, avoiding everyone's intent stares.

I closed my eyes, sensually tracing my fingers over my aching nubs, twisting and pulling. Why wouldn't someone suck on them? *Just one?* I'd take even a foot rub...

All of a sudden, Sleipnir gave a small smile, "You knew that we wouldn't be able to touch Bask to help him. But what your loser ass doesn't realize is that Serenity knows a fae who'd *love* to help him through this." *He couldn't mean...?* "Andro, get your ass out here."

I tried to sit up, covering my dick with my hands...*anything* to stop what was about to happen. I whined, as unshed tears burned my eyes. I was desperate for Andro to touch me, but devastated for Lysander to see his clone.

Don't let Andro appear, please…

I'd agreed to the bet. I'd known that if I lost, it'd suck. I didn't blame Lysander because by incubi standards, he'd only schemed and won. I respected that. But I didn't want him to witness the version of him that I both used and loved. Even if I knew that Willoughby had a clone of me that he spanked. I was sexy, after all. Who could blame him?

I didn't think that Lysander, however, would be flattered in the same way.

Andro appeared in all his beautiful, naked, and submissive glory, kneeling fluidly at my side. His hair veiled his face, but he gasped at my distress, leaning to feather kisses across my eyelids, as I screwed shut my eyes like that could save me from Lysander. I'd never known that such a simple gesture could make me feel cherished.

Instantly, the buzzing settled, and I sighed with pleasure.

When I peeked at Willoughby and Midnight, they appeared shocked and mesmerized. Midnight was checking out Andro's arse; it *was* a fine sight.

When I dared to look at Lysander, however, my stomach twisted even worse than it was with the potion. He was close to tears. His eyes were wide, as he studied the way that Andro rubbed my shoulder with tender love.

"Tricks don't always play out the way that we intend," Sleipnir said, quietly, "I should know."

Andro's soft gaze met mine; and I nodded my permission. Unlike with Willoughby, there was no question of consent because weird as it might be, Andro *was* my lover, and he knew how to meet my needs, as much as I'd ever been molded to suit the Duchess'. Except, I'd failed with the Duchess, whereas Andro never had with me because he'd been created *for* me.

I wished that I could free him too.

Then Andro kissed down my neck, and I lost all coherent thought, apart from *make me feel*...

Kisses, sucking, touching. I was ablaze, but this time with pleasure. Andro licked across my nipples, and I moaned, before he trailed a path with his fingers and tongue to my dick. I gritted my teeth because I was beyond the point of teasing. When Andro lowered his lips over my dick, sucking on the head, I lifted my gaze to lock it with Lysander's.

"But I *won*," Lysander's whisper was tear-tinged.

Magenta's voice vibrated with power, "I'll lead my Rebels on the mission, and I'll be damned if they won't all survive. But do you truly believe that *you* won?"

When Andro sucked harder, I howled, consumed

by pleasure that was agonizing even in its release. *How many times would the potion force me through it?* I panted and clenched my fists, coming for a second time.

Yet I'd always been a slave to pleasure, whether it was forced on me or taken from my body. Pleasure was dangerous, and the mission could be deadly.

CHAPTER SEVENTEEN

Rebel Academy, Tuesday September 3rd

FOX

Divination Class that included enchantments, as well as the art of telling the future, was a lot less fun than I'd been hoping. I blamed J. K. Rowling. Okay, witch families already blamed her for everything from showing non-segregated witch and wizard learning to creating a patriarchal world with men in robes. But this was different: *it was personal now, bitch.*

Nowhere had J.K. (as I'd liked to imagine in daydreams in my attic, she'd allow me to call her), written about her mage hero (yeah, I was casting myself as the *hero*), hanging upside down by his ankles in Divination as the whipping boy test subject next to a naked vampire.

Although, Aquilo had whispered to me about some kinky fanfiction that he'd read about Draco all tied up. Maybe Divination Class was meant to include bondage as well, after all?

How would I know? This was my first week of school in a decade, and I had to be honest, *so far it'd sucked.*

Yet freeing Magenta hadn't, nor had sleeping in a real bed. The friendship of the Immortals was like being wrapped in a warmth that I'd never realized I'd been missing. I'd spent most of my time alone in the House of Jewels, but here, I hadn't even been able to brush my teeth, without Sleipnir jostling my elbow to style his hair in the mirror.

There were only three more days to win the Rebel Cup, and if we lost, then I died.

Yeah, *no pressure.*

I didn't want to kiss goodbye to my furry tail but at the same time, I knew now that I'd been slowly dying, locked away in the attic. If I only had this week of life, then I'd take it.

I could lie to myself, but I couldn't lie about that.

The rope burned my ankles, as it dug in. My shoulders ached. My temples throbbed from the blood rushing to my head. I flailed, swinging around. Then I spluttered, as my shirt rode up to cover my face, revealing my stomach and chest.

Cocooned in the dark, I still heard Lysander's snicker.

The smug... wish I didn't keep thinking about how hot Andro and him together would be... bastard.

I shoved away the shirt from my face, flushing. Then I yelled in a *manly* way... Okay, shrieked... Okay, squealed like Mr Fierce when he'd been a hoglet. Midnight had twisted to me, and his fanged face was so close, that his nose touched mine; his dick that was hanging free pressed against my thigh.

Wait, this wasn't actually the Rebel Academy version of pinata with the best prizes if you hit our cock and balls?

I winced, wishing that I could cross my legs.

Floating silver candles lit Juni Crow's classroom, which was next to Bacchus' in the East Wing, in a glimmering glow because there were no windows. I'd guess that it was Juni's way of making it easier to *use* the vampire because although they could go into direct sunlight, it gave them a crippling migraine. Who was feeding Midnight? Dad had told me that the Fallen liked to bond with the willing, taking Blood Lovers. Somehow, I couldn't imagine either of the Princes becoming bonded to a whipping boy.

The walls, ceiling, and floor of the classroom were obsidian, but the pentacle shaped table that Midnight and I swung in the center of was royal blue lapis lazuli. The other Rebels hunched over it — Princes on one side and Immortals on the other — one with an icy alertness, and the other with the slacker attitude of *The Breakfast Club*.

Lucky for Sleipnir, who'd lifted Magenta onto the table and hiked her skirts up so that she could wrap her legs around his waist, whilst he busied himself studying up on her neck. Mist galloped around the table excitedly like it was his personal racecourse. Juni hadn't arrived yet. Otherwise, both Sleipnir and Mist would've been strung up next to me.

Bask lay on the table gently snoring. But then, he'd barely slept last night.

Nightmares, I reckoned.

Why was there a cage in the corner? Just for a moment, I grinned with excitement, hoping that I'd see the Omega werewolf again. But the cage was empty. Did the wolf belong to Juni?

Midnight rubbed his nose against mine and smiled like this was a relaxed day at the office for him. "Thank you for the freedom you granted me in the café. It was a fine thing that you did to reward me like that."

"Don't mention it…I mean, really *don't*. The last thing I want to think about is Lysander in that outfit right now." *I didn't have to admit that it was because I'd added it to my Wank Bank, right?* I tried to pull off casual, but I'd obviously had less experience of Bondage Small Talk because it came out as a squeak.

Midnight's lips curved onto mine; his fang caught on my lip, and I tasted tangy blood. "Do you want to know how long it's been since anyone's shown me such kindness? Us whipping boys must look out for each other, see?"

Truth: Finally, I'm not alone. Maybe somebody will save me now?

Breathe, come on, breathe…

I yanked back from Midnight sharply. I counted back from hundred in my head, desperate to calm my thoughts.

How many years had I thought exactly the same as him? But I couldn't let him know. I'd never allowed anyone to discover my desperate hope because no one had *ever* come to save me.

"If I've offended…?" Midnight said, tentatively.

I clenched my jaw, forcing myself to close my eyes and spin myself away from him. I felt him stiffen next to me.

Don't look at him… don't look…

My power of Confess washed Midnight's despairing pain through me in haunting waves of piano that crested in Twenty One Pilot's "Goner". He was calling out to me through my magic without even knowing it. I shivered at his pain and need. Yet also, his strength that was drummed in every screamed syllable. He was holding on, desperately waiting for that single connection that could save his life.

How could I turn my back on that? Pan's balls, I didn't care that Midnight was meant to be my rival, I *wouldn't*.

I twisted back to Midnight, catching his surprised gaze with mine. Then I kissed him, so that I could whisper against his lips, "I promised the Omega that I'd free him. I helped break Magenta through the veils, but I know that she's still trapped. On Merlin's breath, I've no idea how I'll manage it, but I *will* free us for real from this academy. Hold on for me, okay? Swear it on your fangs or your gorgeous wings."

Midnight shook. He raised his wings to wrap them around me, hiding us from sight. The feathers were soft, and my feline side urged me to snuggle into them, claiming them as mine.

"Mind you don't make promises that you can't keep." Midnight licked across my lips just once. He was as cool as moonlight. "On blood and bones, keep yourself safe. You're only a whipping boy like me."

"Hey, foxy, the vampire's only touching you in all the good places, right?" Sleipnir called.

"Swear to me," I urged Midnight, "or I'll start screaming that your fangs are getting bitey with my delicious throat. My blood's food to the gods. It resurrected a ghost witch."

I swallowed nervously. Was it a good idea to use your blood as both a boast and threat to a vampire?

I mentally slapped myself. *Oww, that smarted.*

Midnight's eyes widened in alarm, but I didn't know if it was at my threat or fear of being unable to control himself around my throat. *I would taste epic.* "You have my oath."

"Desist kissing *my* vampire," Lysander snarled. "If there's anyone assaulting another around here, it's *your* common wretch of a whipping boy. One warned you what would happen if you didn't discipline him."

"Listen to that," Magenta said, coolly. "Why, Midnight is quite screaming the classroom down with his pleas to be saved from our ruffian of a mage."

When Midnight laughed, I startled. Well, wasn't that a nice sound? Just like the sound of Magenta's quiet sarcasm in my defense.

"Shall we go out and brave the world again?" I asked. "You have your knight, Sir Fierce, now to protect you. My prickles are at your service."

Midnight rested his forehead against mine. "My fangs are at yours. And I'm *your* knight, see, you're my *king,* and Magenta will be my queen."

My skin tingled, and my heartbeat raced. *What had I done?* In vampire culture, had I more or less made Midnight my slave, warrior, or asked for his hand in marriage?

I had a sense that it was a combination of all three.

100, 99, 98, 97...

I closed my eyes and I continued to count, as Midnight dropped his wings away from me.

Magenta scooted around on the table to check me over with an assessing eye and a comforting smile. I pinked at the thought of how I must look strung up. Sleipnir's hair was aquamarine today and styled punky (he'd taken long enough messing around with it), whilst mine hung in messy curls...upside down. I should've transformed into a fox and just gone with the whole *waiting to be skinned* look.

Yet even though Magenta was in Sleipnir's arms, it was *me* that she was gazing at like she craved to devour me.

"*Finally,*" Lysander huffed. "Now we're ready for our lesson. My uncle mustn't have bad report of my whipping boy management."

My skin prickled. If I hadn't been tied up, Lysander would be seriously close to Mr Fierce's first attack on behalf of Midnight.

Fear the hedgehogy wrath...

"Wow, that'd be devastating like everyone discovering that you love wearing French maid's outfits. Wait, that already happened. So, what'll he do? Take away your shiny Prefect's badge?" I smirked.

Yeah, I managed a smirk even upside down. It was a skill.

I didn't expect the way that Willoughby gently rested his hand on Lysander's shoulder.

Why did I feel like the asshole?

Lysander shrugged off Willoughby's hand. "Something like that."

When the door slammed open and Juni stormed inside, Bask startled awake and tumbled off the table. Mist snorted, racing to Sleipnir and jumping like he was at the Grand National into the pocket of his blazer. Juni adjusted her feathered cap, before tapping her shoe

"Are you waiting down there to lick it?" Juni arched her brow.

Horrified, Bask scrambled to his feet. "I didn't come on it this time, so not a chance."

Magenta slid off the table, crossing her arms. "Ah, the patented start to all magic lessons: The Coming on a Shoe enchantment."

Juni studied her back, unblinkingly. "I learn something new every day as well, Crow, but I never know with the Immortals if they'll have their pants up or down."

Was it possible for someone's eyes to bulge out of their head because Lysander looked close to losing his eyeballs...?

Juni ignored Midnight and me like we were no different than the hovering candles, whose flames wavered as she passed. I'd never been used as classroom equipment before. How would it compare to being used as building, office, or agricultural equipment? And possibly I was going crazy because it wasn't like different grades of equipment were now my career choices.

"What's with the Spanish Inquisition?" Sleipnir asked, gesturing at us whipping boys.

Juni didn't even look round at Midnight and me. "It's tradition to use whipping boys to test out potions and in Divination."

"It's the hanging upside down thing that I draw the line at." I flapped my arms. "Just because I might've had a brilliant dream once about myself, a wand, and a vampire, doesn't mean that I was… Okay, I *might've* been tied up…just a little…but it wasn't in the middle of a classroom with a witch professor watching, along with other students. I did once have a nightmare though where—"

"Are you finished?" Juni inquired.

"*Ehhm*, nope, that's why you interrupted me." *Mouth, a life time's supply of strawberry dipped chocolates, if you just stop talking...* "I was telling you about this nightmare, where suddenly all my clothes disappeared—"

"Do you wish all your clothes to disappear now?"

My mouth snapped shut. Then I shook my head.

Juni sighed. "Whipping boys are secured. It saves time holding them down later."

Woah, later…?

"Hey, aren't we all reassured now?" Sleipnir growled.

When Willoughby grasped Lysander's arm, whispering to him, Juni's eyes narrowed. She spun, marching to the Princes' side of the pentacle table with a sharp *clicking* of her heels. Her eyes danced with such malicious glee that for the first time, I pitied the Princes. We Immortals had Bacchus as tutor, who scared the spikes back into me, but maybe the Princes weren't babied with treats and tucked into silken sheets, like I'd imagined?

Wait, maybe they *were* but in a whole more disturbing way.

"Why would you interrupt my lesson, Princes?" Juni demanded. "Have the Immortals been teaching you their delinquent ways?" Then she cocked her head. "Have they corrupted you into making a Dick Bet?"

Damn my prickles and call me a hamster, why had I ever lied about that when Juni had caught us?

Oh yeah, because there hadn't been another way to explain why the three of us had been standing around with our dicks out. Maybe I should've told Juni that we'd been trying out *bukkake,* only none of us had wanted to kneel and have cum splash over us because we'd all wanted in on the action?

That was the level of competitiveness that she'd respect.

"A…Dick Bet?" Willoughby flashed Bask a glance like it must've been his idea.

Bask merely fluttered his eyelashes back at him. *Flirt.*

"You don't need to be coy. I witnessed the Immortals' *explosive* contest." Sleipnir smothered his chuckle in Magenta's hair. Wow, Lysander was the same shade of red as me now. *Embarrassed twinsies.* "Guess who won?"

"The god in his own head. The mage in *my* head." Willoughby pointed at us each in turn. "And the incubus in truth."

Bask *whooped*, spinning around and wiggling his ass in a victory dance. I grinned. After watching him alone on his mattress that was separated from ours during the night, which had reminded me uncomfortably of mine in the attic, it was brilliant to see his joy.

Even if it was over his (*so not true*) dick being declared larger than mine.

Juni tipped Willoughby's chin up with her finger, and he fought not to flinch. "Excellent: you've earned a Privilege Point for the Princes. Now, you've wasted enough of my lesson. Pull down your pants, and let me judge who wins between Crown and you."

Lysander backed against the wall, clutching his pants like they'd suddenly be ripped down. "Never have I heard such an affront to my royal personage. I shall do no such thing. There's...." He gestured at Magenta. "Witches and the like in the room."

"Am I not a witch?" Juni asked, carefully.

Was it just me or had the room become much darker all of a sudden?

"You're a professor. But she's..." Lysander stared at Magenta as if for help.

"Wicked? Beautiful? Awfully good at chess?" Magenta offered.

Magenta didn't seem as helpful to fae princes as she was to everybody else. But in the unwritten code between guys against witches, I mentally slapped myself again, before diving in to save the snooty bastard. I coughed loudly to distract Juni.

"I can't feel my toes. It could be lack of circulation because the ropes are too tight or gangrene or frostbite or... Could I lose my foot? *My beautiful, beautiful foot...*" I wailed.

Midnight stared at me in amazement.

"Traditionally, whipping boys were gagged as well as bound." Juni clicked her fingers, and the ropes loosened around my ankles. Wow, that was actually better, even though it'd only been a fictional problem. I wiggled my toes. Juni circled Lysander, running her hand over his shoulders. Then she leaned closer like she intended to tuck a stray strand of his hair behind his ear, but instead, she plucked it out, and he winced.

"Hand out." She laid the emerald hair like a thin snake on his palm. "Divination needs an offering. All magic is about give and take. Like all life, magic consumes. We devour energy from each other. What are you prepared to sacrifice for magic?" She glanced at Midnight. "What will your whipping boys drink without fuss?"

"We must have become invisible." I frowned. *Being treated like equipment was definitely not one of my kinks.* "Hello, can anyone hear us? It's the ghosts of whipping boys past. We're here to haunt the prejudiced. I'd like a beer and my friend here would like…?"

"A chocolate ice cream milkshake with cherries but no extra cream," Midnight flashed his fangs as he gave a small smile, "because I'm sweet enough."

I snickered, and Midnight's eyes lit with delighted surprise like he hadn't joked with anyone for a long time. Before the Immortals, I'd had almost no one to share secret jokes with me, so I got the shy blush that now crept across his cheeks.

Juni's mouth tightened. "What drink?" She repeated like Midnight and I hadn't even spoken.

Lysander's gaze darted to mine and then away. "The rules state that they're only allowed water or juice, but it hardly would hurt to allow them this once…"

"Water it is." Juni twirled, marching back to the center of the pentacle.

Lysander sighed. Why was he disappointed? I was the one who wouldn't be getting my beer.

"Tea is merely infused water." Magenta waltzed around the table, meeting the startled Juni in front of where I hung. The scent of yew trees wound around me, as comforting as the stroke of her hand, circling my hip. "I know that it's decidedly the best thing for Divination if you're intending to add that hair."

"Do you now?" Juni's expression had gentled, however, as she studied Magenta. When they stood close together, it was impossible to miss the family resemblance between them. "How many times have you woven its magic?"

Magenta looked down. "I believe that you and I were raised differently. When you're the Blessedly Charmed who's so unique that the creation of all nature around you relies on your power even as a babe, then you're shut away and allowed only to read about magic, rather than trained and taught to freely use it. Rather a mistake, when you see how it turned out, wouldn't you say?"

Juni blinked. "I can't imagine a witch being treated like...a *mage*." I flinched at the contempt in her tone. "You're family. I don't have anyone here. We could be like sisters."

Magenta's smile was sharp, "My dear, I'm your elder by many generations."

Juni gaped for a moment, before regaining her composure. "But who's the student and who the professor?"

Magenta inclined her head. "Well played."

"Don't think that I can change the rules for you. Mother has control in this academy, and I don't even get to choose who I love."

Magenta's eyes widened, and to my shock, she clasped Juni into a hug.

Behind her, Sleipnir made gagging sounds.

At last, Magenta held Juni at arm's length. "Under no circumstances pray to Hecate to save you," she insisted, "because that bitch will screw you over."

You tell her, girl.

I'd already been strangled, branded, and had my singing trolled by Hecate. I knew there was a reason that mages prayed to the god, Pan, instead.

Juni shook herself free of Magenta, straightening her dress. "I shall remember that. Now, did you order tea?"

A Wedgewood porcelain tea pot with cups and saucers in blue and white appeared on the Immortal's side of the table. Magenta gasped, clapping her hands. *So, that was what her face looked like when she orgasmed.* I'd better remember that for the many,

many multiple times that I intended to make her look just the same.

Magenta rushed to the set, tracing her fingers along the white birds that flew around the pot. "This was my dad's," she breathed. "He'd have afternoon tea with me in the Bird Turret."

Midnight's wing wrapped around me again, and I gave into my feline need to snuggle into its warmth because I couldn't help shivering with the memory of all the times that *my dad* had sneaked my favorite lemonade to drink with me in the attic.

How could dad be gone?

Don't think about Hartley and mum's cold faces and the way that their gazes wouldn't even meet mine in the sea of black suits on Saturday.

Pan above, he was truly gone, gone, gone…

Juni paced to face Magenta across the table; she rubbed the edge of a saucer. "The service has been in the family for years. Like you, I guess."

When Magenta continued to trace the birds; her voice was dreamy and caught in the past. "I'd always follow the robins' flight — *round and round* — but they never escaped the pot. They were trapped to service, just the same as every witch." When she clasped her hands over the tea pot, Bask hissed in shock, leaping forward to pull her away, but Sleipnir held him back. *Electrocuted and burned would've been a double whammy.* My heart pounded. "You warmed the pot. I'm impressed."

"And you'll burn yourself to make a point. Consider me equally impressed." Juni calmly took Magenta's palms between hers, and her seared palms healed.

Magenta raised her eyebrow. "Does your mother know how much magic rests within you?"

"It's much safer if she doesn't." Juni's voice became sharper. "I can make things much harder for your Immortals if you tell. Now, doesn't afternoon tea usually come with…?"

"Scones," Magenta gasped, "buttered toast, cucumber sandwiches…oh, little Victorian sponge cakes!"

The food appeared, spreading out across the royal blue.

"Hey, don't imply that we can't feed our Prefect," Sleipnir grumbled.

"She's not a pet, Slippy." Bask bounced on his tiptoes. "And if it pleases you, aye it does. We crave all the afternoon tea goodness."

Bask dived on the feast of tiny sandwiches and cakes like only a starving incubus could who still made every move look both sexy and elegant. The way that he popped a cake into his mouth and then sucked the cream from his finger was sinful.

When my stomach grumbled, hungry for lunch, I

groaned. Then I realized that Midnight had as well. His breath ghosted my neck

Okay, that's what I got for being a clever foxy pants about my tasty blood.

Lysander's voice shook with anger. "My uncle sent those treats for *me*, and on my wings, he'd never wish them to reward *her*."

"Your guardian is our patron, and what he sends becomes *mine*," Juni replied. "I'll share it with whoever I please. Right now, it displeases me to share it with you. Your Food Privileges are revoked for twenty-four hours."

Lysander's face fell. "Professor…"

"Would you like to try for forty-eight?"

Magenta dropped the cucumber sandwich in her hand like it'd become infested by slugs. Was that an apologetic look that she was shooting Lysander?

Juni's expression darkened. "Start the divination spell."

"Shall I be mother?" Magenta poured two cups of steaming tea. Then she sniffed the herbal aroma with a sigh. "What a delightful blend."

"Concentrate on the liquid and the power that you wish to infuse it with," Juni instructed.

Magenta nodded. Slowly, her sparkles lit up the surface of the tea like a flaming cocktail, before sinking beneath the surface.

Lysander tilted up his chin, before marching

around the table to drop his strand of hair into one of the cups.

I stiffened. What happened next? A puff of smoke? The undead howling out Lysander's sins? Lysander's hair falling out?

Nothing.

Well, that was anticlimactic. Until, Lysander snatched the cup and turned to crouch in front of Midnight. Instantly, Midnight pulled away from me, folding his wings behind him like a soldier smartening himself up into parade position, even if he was strung up.

Lysander's expression was disturbingly gentle, as his fingers clenched around the cup. "Your duty is to help us win today by drinking this. I assure you that it won't harm you, but it will let me read the future through you. What you see is private between us two alone."

"You don't ask a whipping boy's permission," Juni snapped.

"Such wasn't my intention." Lysander's hard gaze didn't leave Midnight's. "One sought merely to make sure that he understood."

When Midnight nodded, Lysander held up the cup.

After Lysander had poisoned Bask last night in the café, would Midnight trust him today? And I hadn't had a great experience with Co-Co and its never-ending coming power either.

Just say no to potions. It could catch on as a slogan.

Yet did either of us have any choice? I mean, I had my neck on the line and Midnight had his wings.

Midnight darted out his tongue, licking with difficulty at the tea in an act of submission that was greater than anything Lysander had shown last night. When Midnight gasped in pain, Lysander laid the cup to the side with shaky hands.

Pan's hairy balls, I knew it…

Midnight thrashed wildly, and I understood at last why they bound us. His wing accidentally caught my nose, and I howled.

"You deserve this. You're a disgrace of a fae. Whoever heard of a prince who was too weak to obey or kill?" Midnight growled in a voice that terrifyingly was not his own.

Chills ran down my arms at such a commanding and cruel voice snarling from Midnight's sweet mouth at Lysander, who'd stumbled back onto his ass and looked pinned to the floor in fright at the blazing contempt in Midnight's eyes.

"Touch your whipping boy's forehead," Juni ordered.

Lysander shook his head. Who terrified him so much that he looked nothing but a pair of gleaming emerald eyes, as he tried to cover himself in his wings?

"Do you wish to lose today on cowardice? I'll cast a Shame Hex on you if I even *suspect* such a thing possible." Juni prowled closer.

Lysander's trembling hand rose to press against Midnight's forehead. Then he screamed, arching against the floor. Willoughby vaulted across the table to his side, dropping to his knees. His hair had frozen to ice, and his eyes flashed. Juni raised her hand, however, and Willoughby flew backward, crashing against the table.

"What have you done?" Magenta demanded.

"Granted Crown the power to see the future. He has enough pain in his past for me to guess that it lies ahead of him as well." Like a crow, Juni settled next to Lysander, where he lay shaking on the floor, before cradling his head on her lap. "Are you back with us?"

Lysander nodded, weakly.

"Do not fear to divine the future because we see only one path based on our past." When Juni stroked Lysander's hair away from his face, I had the sudden urge to bite off her fingers.

I blinked. Why was I so desperate to show her what it felt like to be the prey? As she continued to pet Lysander like reducing him into a shuddering wreck was a personal victory, I realized that it was because she *pretended* to be better than the other witches and that made her *worse*. She was a predator who loved the hunt. If the Princes didn't break for her, then she brought their predators alive for them.

"Can what I saw be changed?" Lysander asked.

Say yes, yes, yes…

Juni cocked her head as if in thought. "Fate is woven every day by many hands. We merely catch glimpses, which help us to see our path."

"She means *of course it can*." Magenta's gaze became flinty.

Lysander's relief was like a living thing. "Thank you."

Take that Miss Fate: your prince is thanking an Immortal.

Juni's expression hardened. "Time for my *dear sister* in the House of Crows to face *her* future."

I shook my head. "Sorry, this oracle attraction has been shut down for health and safety reasons." I cradled my bruised nose. "Look, it's damaged and not worth seeing. Come back next month, year, or how about not at all?"

"How about I close it *permanently,*" Juni demanded silkily, before muttering, "at least it'd be quieter."

I *eeped*, but before Juni could move towards me, Lysander had tugged on her sleeve. "Please, don't ask the witch to go through that. She made the potion, and it was demonstrated on me. Could that not be enough?"

Was that the first time I'd heard Lysander say please?

Juni eyed him dispassionately. "Why, if that isn't what I call *teamwork*. Yet I still have to decide the Punish and Reward Game. Any thoughts?"

"It could please you to make it a draw?" Bask said, hopefully.

Juni huffed. "Nonsense, who's been putting such thoughts into your head? Crush earned a Privilege Point for the Princes, which swings the lesson to them."

"What about Lysander losing Food Privileges?" Sleipnir demanded, and Mist snorted his agreement from his pocket.

"That's his own personal punishment, unless you wish to join him?" Juni said, frostily.

Sleipnir shoved a scone into his mouth just in case she followed through with the threat, then he did a thumbs up. "I'm good."

I shrank back, as Juni's dark gaze met mine. I scowled because when I was both one step closer to punishment at the Princes' hands *and* being killed (I was so haunting her with visions of my crooked tailed self getting funky to "Super Bad"), how much worse could things get?

"After the rudeness, refusals, and *in the witching heavens does he never hold his tongue*, of Confess this lesson, I select him as the worst behaved student."

Juni's eyes blazed with spiteful smugness. "He'll suffer in the Memory Theater. Why finally, nothing to say?"

Oww, how many times did I need to mentally slap myself before I learned?

"Now you'll wish that you'd disciplined your whipping boy," Lysander said, wearily. "At least, you shall after tonight."

I swallowed, paling. My pulse pounded. The way that Midnight twisted closer to me, cocooning me once again in the darkness of his wings only made me shake worse.

I knew what was in my past. I didn't want to face it again. What if the Memory Theater was worse than any horror?

Rebel Academy, Tuesday September 3rd

FOX

I shook, abandoned on the stage in the center of the Memory Theater. A spotlight rooted me in place like all my faults were lit up. I wrapped my arms around my middle. *They'd need a brighter light.* Then I squinted up at the tiered seats that were hidden in shadow.

The Princes sat on black seats and the Immortals on pink like it was a chessboard. I smirked. It'd be epic if the truth of this theater was that I'd been chosen to play real life Wizard's Chess with a twist: I'd love to see Lysander's expression when Magenta's magic mist swept him off the board because no way would he ever get to be King in *my* game.

Why did I have the feeling that witches wouldn't put a mage in charge of picking up litter, let alone their precious Princes?

I sighed because okay, that'd been a pleasant way to stop the terror from reducing me to as much of a pooping Rebel as Mr Fierce in front of the rest of the students. The theater was thick with the scent of burning sage. My magic prickled with the power held within this room: it was oppressive, suffocating, and *dark*.

It wanted to swallow me whole.

I shivered with unease, tipping back my head. Words swirled in and out of focus on the ceiling like they were rising to the surface of a rippling pool:

Share our pasts in order to move forward as one together.

I grimaced, closing my eyes.

More of Damelza's motivational mottoes — *brilliant*.

I'd already *shared* enough to feel like the tips of my ears would never stop burning after the Punish and Reward Game in Divination class. I'd expected something dastardly from Lysander like the Itching Powder Pants Hex.

My ass had already been squirming in anticipation.

Instead, Lysander had scrutinized me in a way that'd made my dick and balls join in the squirming. "I choose Punish."

"Shocker," Sleipnir had muttered.

"So, what's it to be?" Swinging upside down, I'd grinned crookedly. "Public execution of our social media accounts? Goodbye Instagram, farewell sweet Facebook, and so long Tinder…"

Bask had snickered.

"You possess those?" Lysander had blinked.

"If you define possess as in…do I have access to a computer, Internet, or any social media…then that'd be a *nope*. Oh look, then the punishment's already carried out. Good job."

Lysander had snorted. "Excellent try." His gaze had slid to Magenta, who'd boldly met it. "Do you not think that we should get to know each other? My order is simple: each answer the same question."

Magenta had nodded.

Lysander's smile had been sharp. "Are you a virgin?"

"Why? Are you looking for a virgin sacrifice?" Magenta had snapped.

Perhaps, he'd expected to shame us. The first answer on my tongue had been: *Of course not, I'm the legendary mage lover of the House of Jewels: The Wizard Lothario, surely you've heard of me?* But then, the spell had kicked in, and I'd been forced to tell the truth.

Lysander's eyes had widened at my shy nod. The tips of my ears had reddened.

Yet Sleipnir had stretched his arms behind his head with a cocky grin. "I'm the son of Loki. Hel's tits, no."

Bask had winked, sliding his hand down to circle his dick through his pants. His eyes had been half-lidded. "You think this much sexiness hasn't been petted?" His grin had been sly. "Don't you want to see if you could keep up?"

Lysander had flushed. Hadn't he learned yet that sometimes you *lost*, when you thought that you'd *won*?

"What an impertinent question." Magenta had tossed her hair. "My virtue is intact as befits my unmarried station, but worry not, I intend to change that soon. I have lovers now who I wish to ravish." She'd caught Lysander's gaze, and he'd shivered. I'd already been lost on the whole *ravishing* part of that. After all, I was the *legendary* mage lover, why wouldn't she want to ravish my curly-haired cuteness? *See, I could still lie to myself within the spell.* "I'm intrigued by your interest. Were you hoping to deflower us and add us to your list of conquests? Or perhaps, you lie awake at night, fretting that you're the lone virgin in this academy?"

Lysander had stormed out with his haughty nose in the air.

I'd bet my prickles and whiffling nose that despite the bluster, Lysander was as innocent as me.

Yet now, caught in the spotlight, I would have to *share* a part of myself again and this time, I wouldn't have the other Immortals backing me up. It'd been brilliant to turn the tables with them at my side, but alone on the stage, I didn't know if I had the strength to pull off the same trick.

In a flurry of feathers, Damelza appeared, and my eyes snapped open. Her silver blonde hair reflected the light, and her dress swept across the floor, as she prowled towards me.

I shuffled my feet, unable to move.

Do not poop, do not poop, do not...

With a flick of her hand, feathered straps bound each of the Rebels into their seats like the theater was a fairground ride. Wow, it'd be brilliant if it was because I'd never been to the fair. Except, I had the feeling that *I* was the ride.

"What a surprise that the criminally inclined *mage* is the first to visit my theater." Damelza's lips pinched, and my dick shriveled. "I tried to help your mother with your discipline as a child. I always knew that you'd turn out to need a firm hand, although I never guessed that my poor friend would have *two* sons with magic. I wonder if she was cursed."

My hands clenched into fists. "I missed you and your inspiring speeches. Where's the suggestion box? I have a few complaints…well, suggestions for improvement…about my induction."

Someone snickered from the theater seats. I'd bet that it was Bask.

"I'm so sorry." Damelza's eyes glittered. "Write down your complaints and hand them to Professor Bacchus."

"Really?"

"If you want to be transfigured into a footstool."

I bit my lip. "Tempting because she wears epic boots, and I have this kinky thing for them, but Pan knows that enough witches have already trodden on me in my life, so I'll pass."

Damelza fiddled with the feather at her ear, and I couldn't help the flinch because the last time that she'd touched the feather, she'd thrown it at me. *I had that effect on witches.* "Why don't you share your trauma with the rest of the class but not the kinky part because do you know what witches hate listening to the most?"

I cocked my head. "*The Wizard of Oz* soundtrack?"

Damelza's cheek twitched. "Boastful mages." *Damn my prickles, that was me screwed.* "The most delightful thing about my Memory Theater is that the Rebel doesn't need to speak. The spell will show the truth, and every student here will relive the memory alongside you."

I bit my tongue so hard that I yelped. When did I let others see the *truth*? It'd taken years of dedication to build up my walls of lies and I liked it that way, cheers.

Okay, Sleipnir and Bask had glimpsed some of the truth because of the Blood Amulet, but the secrets of their own dark pasts blasted through me in angsty rock, and they didn't pry. A guy appreciated that. But Magenta was my first kiss; she was the woman who'd brought me to life. She also didn't act like it but she was a *witch*. Would she truly want me when she saw that I was the monster of the House of Jewels?

"Shall we?" Damelza said like she was inviting me to a dance, rather than the violation of my mind. "I've never explored a mage's head before, so I'm hoping for the best but expecting the depraved worst."

All of a sudden, Louis Armstrong's gravelly voice boomed through the theater backed by the joyful flute and trumpet of "It's a Wonderful World."

My eyes widened. Damelza couldn't have picked this on purpose, right? She had a sick sense of humor because it drove me back to a spring day that I was desperate not to remember, when I'd lost all hope that I'd ever be rescued from the attic.

Damelza gripped my shoulders, spinning me to face the back wall of the theater. A kaleidoscope of images was projected onto it. They flashed like a thousand home movies that'd been ripped apart and then jaggedly sewn together from fae, vampires, and gods.

Paws save me, they must be the memories of every student who'd faced this trial.

That was it, stop this ride, I wanted to get off, and probably hurl as well. It turned out that I hated the fair.

My stomach roiled. I clutched my sweating palms tightly under my armpits. I recoiled, but Damelza held me in place.

No escape, no escape, no…

The jazz played on loop. There was no way out. There never had been. From the moment that I'd been locked away in the warded attic because my magic had come in, I'd been trapped forever.

If we lost the Rebel Cup, I'd die because of it.

Because mages were monsters.

My breath became ragged, and the images spun faster and faster.

I couldn't go back to the attic…

In my terror, I transformed into a Birman cat. I tumbled out of Magenta's hold onto the floor with a pained *yowl*. My creamy fur fluffed up and my long, crooked tail whipped back and forth in distress. A collective *aww* of cooing burst from the audience, but I was lost in my fear. I darted to the corner, cowering.

The music was even louder to my sensitive ears, and the sage burned my nose. I stared up at the giant witch who stalked towards me, before hissing. When her hand lowered towards me, and she *clucked* impatiently, my fur bristled.

Where was the treat, feathery plaything, or stroke? My furry ass was on strike, and this witch didn't even have any feline offering for me.

Damelza's eyes narrowed. "Bad kitty."

Oh, it was time to introduce her to *Master Claws*. I swiped at her, but she rolled her eyes, grabbing me by the scruff of the neck and swinging me towards the back wall.

"Unhand the cat," Magenta demanded.

"If you say so." Damelza hurled me at the wall.

My little legs kicked, and my ears flattened against my head.

Meoowww…

I landed on my *human* ass on the hard floor of the attic. *My attic*, which I'd been trapped in for a decade.

Don't freak out, poop, wet your pants, breathe, breathe, breathe…

I shook, counting down from a hundred backwards in my head to control my shock and despair. I knew that I wasn't truly back here, but it was so real. It wasn't like a memory; it was *my truth*.

I was living it again, and it turned my stomach.

I'd transformed back into a teenager, and I carded

my fingers through my unruly hair, glancing down at the plain jeans and t-shirt. They were worn because I'd only had two sets of clothes. Dad had worked hard to even get those for me, and I'd been so grateful.

I *was* grateful.

My mind became hazy, until I truly *was* my teenage self again.

Aquilo would be visiting at the weekend, and I smiled happily at the thought. I loved Aquilo like a brother. Would he find my new comedy routine funny? He needed to laugh more.

I cocked my head, as the sound of jazz wound from the garden below. Louis Armstrong's "It's a Wonderful World" lit up the dusty attic like life after a long winter. Why was someone playing music in the garden? Then I heard laughter. I leaned forward at the siren call, as for the first time in years, hope blossomed through me.

I crawled across the attic, pushing myself over my mattress and my favorite book that I always slept with because it was the first thing that dad had given to me in my captivity, and onto the window seat beneath the tiny window that looked out at the garden. No one came to this corner of the garden apart from Hartley anymore. I'd decided that it had to be mum's order to isolate me.

I covered my mouth with my hand like if I even breathed too loudly then I'd ruin something so bright in the dreariness of my life. My kitteny side purred, desperate to burst out, but I held onto my human side, aching desperately to see who was below me and *so close*.

I peeked through the window, careful not to be seen. Once, when I'd only just been locked up, a servant had caught sight of my curly hair, as I'd been looking out at the birds. When she'd reported it to mum, it'd taken dad's pleading to reduce the punishment to a whipping and not the boarding up of the window.

I'd have gone crazy without being able to see the sky. Dad had made me *swear* never to let myself be seen again. I'd been able to lie to everybody but never to dad.

Yet when I saw Hartley beneath the blossoms surrounded by presents and her friends, as music played and Glow acted the butler, all I craved was to smash the glass and call out to her.

Happy Birthday would do it. I might be a monster but I hadn't forgotten my manners.

It was a shock to remember that other people still celebrated their birthdays, and it made my chest ache that Hartley had continued to celebrate hers. Deep inside, I'd guessed that my becoming a mage and shaming my family hadn't changed anything for Hartley, but seeing it was a different ball of prickles…one that hurt.

BM — before magic — Hartley had insisted that I come to all of her parties, even though mum had said that she was spoiling me. Hartley would simply clasp my hand and yank me along like a doll. She'd rarely let me out of her sight.

AM — Hartley hadn't visited me in the attic once. I'd thought that she'd miss me as much as I missed her. My bones ached like I'd lost a limb as much as a sister.

She must lie to herself, as much as I did.

Yet now she was in *my* corner of the garden (yeah, I'd claimed it as my territory, although dad hadn't been pleased with that explanation for why I'd sprayed in cat form all over the windows). Until now, I'd only ever seen her jogging each evening around the formal gardens in the distance.

Finally, I wasn't alone. Maybe somebody would save me now?

I blinked, shuddering. *Why did that feel so familiar?*

When I studied the gang of girls in glittering party dresses around Hartley, I gasped.

Mesilande held Hartley's hand, just like Hartley had once held mine. Her red hair was caught up in silver clasps, and her dress sparkled like she'd stepped out of a fairy tale. How many times had I wanked over fantasies of her as my princess sweeping into the attic to rescue me?

Okay, a lot.

Mesilande was older than Hartley and me. She was from an ancient and powerful French coven. When I'd been young, she'd visited and stayed with us for an entire summer, and I'd developed my first ever crush. She hadn't noticed.

Oh yeah, she'd noticed.

But Mesilande hadn't been cruel like the other witches who'd have used it against me. She hadn't even become angry, when I'd told her that one day, I'd marry and protect her, which should've meant a beating because how could a non-magical male ever protect a witch? Plus, I had no right to choose who I married: I was property and breeding stock to be married off by the females of my family.

Mesilande had only laughed gently, and cupped my cheek. She'd called me her *petit knight.*

Then she'd murmured into my ear, "My mama is proposing an alliance between our Houses through our marriage. I hope that your mama accepts. You need to grow up for me, *petit knight.* I shall wait for you."

I swallowed, as I peered at Mesilande: the girl who'd promised to wait for me. Only, Pan's balls, *she'd grown up beautiful.*

I swept back my curls, rubbing at the smudges of dirt on my cheeks. I hadn't seen myself in a mirror in years, only the hazy reflection of the window. What would the elegant Parisian witch think of me if she saw me?

Hold up one prickling minute… *Why was I even thinking about being seen?*

My nails clawed into the soft wood of the window frame. My eyes burned with tears, as I watched the birthday party below, which I was close to and yet entirely separated from.

It filled *me* with happiness just to see my sister happy. Wasn't that enough? Why did I have to be so greedy? I slapped my forehead, but it didn't help because the hope had already sneaked in.

What if Hartley had held her party in that corner of the garden on purpose? She knew that I'd be able to watch from the attic and that the music would reach me. Was she trying to be kind, so that this year I could join in, rather than be isolated?

I grinned, bouncing on my knees on the window seat. I hummed "It's a Wonderful World". I didn't have much but I could steal this shared moment with my sister, Mesilande, and her friends. The sky was blue, the trees painted in multi-colors, and I could almost taste the chocolate birthday cake. Hartley looked so *contented*; I laughed because I'd hoped that she was.

What lie had they told Mesilande about me to explain my absence? Had mum told everybody that I'd died years ago or been sent away? The House of

Jewels was all about status and perfection. I knew some covens admitted to throwing their mage sons to the wolves, but the House of Jewels wouldn't want the scandal.

A dangerous fledgling hope grew in my chest, as the warm sunshine beat down, and I risked pushing myself up to watch the party. What if Hartley arranged this, so that Mesilande, who'd been one of my suitors and had whispered that she'd *wait for me,* could discover how cruelly I was being treated and rescue me?

A jolt hit me. What if all along Hartley had herself been *forced* to treat me like a monster because of mum?

My gaze darted between the two girls and then away. Wasn't I like a furry version of Rapunzel locked in the tower? I didn't have any hair to let down, but if Mesilande found out that I was still here and alive in the attic, she'd climb up and rescue me from the wicked witch (in my mind, I was brave enough to call mum that).

Only in my mind though.

My eyes gleamed, as I leaned up, resting my forehead on the window. My breath misted the glass. I trembled, flooded with adrenaline.

This was it… Just raise your hand and…

My fist fell to my side. I would be breaking a

serious rule. If they saw me, and I was wrong, then I'd lose my window.

I'd be walled up like I'd truly died.

But if I didn't, I could lose my one chance to escape. I rose my shaking fist. I might be a shimage and a disappointment of a son but I wasn't a coward.

I knelt up on the windowsill, quaking with excitement and fear. *Snails and slugs, if this worked, then I'd finally be free…*

I banged on the glass, frantically waving at the girls below. "Hey, up here, yeah, that's right. I'm up here. Hartley…*Hartley…?* Happy Birthday! I mean," then I sang, just as I always had, "Happy Birthday, sister!" Hartley froze, turning to stare up at the window. The other witches were watching me as well. They hadn't shouted back yet, but to have *anyone* looking at me was thrilling after so long alone. *I existed, and I was about to be saved.* Glow's head was ducked. I self-consciously tucked my hair behind my ear. "Mesilande, it's me: your *petit knight.* I'm trapped up here. Please, I need you to help me. Will you save me?"

Mesilande looked up, studying me with a cool smile. *She was so beautiful.* Then she arched her eyebrow and waved.

My heart leaped in my chest. I grinned, waving back.

She hadn't forgotten her promise.

Hartley's gaze met mine for a long moment. Then she whispered to Mesilande and the other witches, who all glanced up at me again, before they burst into laughter.

My grin withered and died. I flinched back, curling around myself. My cheeks flushed, and I was suddenly dizzy.

Then Hartley, Mesilande and the rest of the witches turned away and back to the party like I'd been no more than an amusing distraction. They'd known that I was locked away...*and they didn't care.*

My vision blurred with tears, and I tumbled off the window seat, retching onto the mattress. My insides felt broken. I crumpled into a ball, pulling my arms over my head, but I couldn't block out "It's a Wonderful World" and its lies.

I was a monster. No one saved the monster.

Had Hartley set me up? She'd crushed me in a way that mum had never managed because now I knew what I'd lost and that I'd never...*ever*...be saved.

I sobbed, as the world span.

All of a sudden, I tumbled onto the floor of the Memory Theater. I was still sobbing, but now I wasn't alone, a teenager, or trapped in the attic anymore. Soft arms cradled me to a woman's chest.

Woah, looked like this cat truly had become crazy.

Then I smelled the scent of ancient forests and felt

the icy touch of lips to my fevered forehead, and knew that it was Magenta holding me tightly like she was *my* knight and could save me.

I half believed that.

Had she fought herself free from the seats or had the straps lifted, since the ride was over?

When I glanced up, forcing myself to sink back into my adult body because it was disorienting as waking up from that vivid dream where you're Grand Mage and Conqueror of the Universe *now kneel before me weak covens* (okay, that *might* be one of my favorite recurring dreams), to find that you're the mage son at the mercy of your witch family. For the first minute, you're not sure which reality is real.

If they had a Dream Theater here then I was screwed.

Bask and Sleipnir crouched either side of me with their hands resting on my shoulders.

Had they seen everything…? When I studied their troubled expressions, I shuddered. *Oh yeah, they'd seen or lived through it, the same as me.*

"I suffered being trapped for many decades," Magenta murmured. "Fairy tales are a nonsense. You didn't need others to save you because *you* wished to be the knight to save others, and you did. You rescued *me* from the dark."

I caught my breath, raising my head to stare at her.

Then I wiped away my tears on the back of my hand. "Huh, maybe I *am* a legend."

Magenta smiled, kissing the tip of my nose. "You're mine."

"You think that you're the only one to be treated like the monster?" Sleipnir shifted uncomfortably. Mist circled his head in agitated laps, pawing the air. "It's the monster who's awesome enough to create their own tale."

Bask brushed the air around my foot like he was desperate for the touch, but would take even the vibrations of my magic. "I know isolation too, see, and being broken. But you're with us now, and we'll protect and love you." His eyes glittered dangerously. "Plus, if I ever meet that Mesilande bitch, I'd break my hatred of getting blood on my pretty gloves."

Magenta nodded. "They're decidedly pretty gloves. But unfortunately, *when* we catch the witch, both our pretty gloves will be shamefully stained."

Bask preened, before lowering himself closer to me. I pushed away from Magenta because I'd had enough shocks today not to want to add electric ones into the mix. The way that Bask caged me, made me feel like prey, but I'd never hungered to be caught so much in my life.

"I want to kiss you now, but seeing as I can't..." Bask's eyes glittered. "Imagine that I am and then that in my mind you haven't been a virgin since the moment we met."

Was that me whimpering? *I didn't whimper.* "Is that because of the eyefucking? I mean, I'm pretty certain that it was *me* eyefucking *you.*"

I yipped, as Sleipnir wrenched me by the curls, pulling me back towards Magenta. He held me in place for Magenta who silenced me with a kiss.

I melted into her, as her tongue twined with mine. The kiss was firm and possessive: a promise that I was no longer alone. When she drew back, I was panting.

"Soon, neither you nor I will be virgins, and it won't be in our minds," Magenta murmured, as her lips grazed my ear.

Okay, I hold my paws up, that time, I definitely whimpered.

Sleipnir traced down my spine, and I shivered. "I take it that you wish this?"

Did Mr Fierce love curling up and pretending that he was a ball that'd magically come alive...? *Yeah, he did.*

I grinned. "I knew that you were a jinni. Just don't make my wish go wrong."

"It's already gone wrong." Damelza tapped her foot next to my head, and I looked up at her, as she glowered down at me. *Whoops,* I'd forgotten that this was a lesson and not a snogging session. Maybe I could blame the trauma as a Get out of Jail Free card.

The Princes crowded behind Damelza, watching our snuggling with way too much interest. "Enough with the disgusting PDA. You survived the Memory Theater, which is more than I expected."

"Sorry to disappoint."

Damelza pulled her coat of feathers closer around her. "We all now know that you're used to that." I winced. *Wow, right for the heart.* "Here in the academy we believe in sharing both the good and the bad. Once your most private moments have been extracted, they no longer belong to you." I frowned, realizing that the kaleidoscope of images was still turning on the wall. Had my memories been added to it? Bile burned my throat. "Your past and secrets now belong to the academy, like you do."

No one could steal my past or pain, and no *witch* could. Just because they'd extracted a single moment from my life, didn't mean that they knew me, or that they owned me, any more than my mum had or the House of Jewels, no matter what any of them thought. There'd been a time when I'd have allowed myself to be married off as the dutiful son, but because I'd had magic, they'd thrown me away. So, this furry cat was claiming his own tail back.

"What about *your* secrets?" My eyes narrowed. *I was going for it...* "Gateway."

Damelza's eyes flared. "Watch your mouth, mage."

"Watch it say things like: we're training to be assassins on missions. But what are the other secrets? This whole academy trades on memories, desires, and hurts." I nodded at the feather charm behind her ear. "You can hide your lies from my power, but no one can hide secrets forever."

Magenta's smile was grim. "Your ancestors burned me because of my inconvenient truth, but witching heavens, look at this…I'm back. The past can't be buried, any more than secrets can."

Damelza gripped Magenta and me, hauling us both to our feet. "I'm the new generation of the House of Crows; you've no idea what I'm capable of. You fight for me or I *can* bury you, the past, and any secret that I wish. This academy offers you new worlds of opportunity, but I'm the Principal. I rule here, and no one has ever escaped."

CHAPTER NINETEEN

Rebel Academy, Wednesday September 4th

MAGENTA

I've never regretted the close bond to my crow familiars who kept me company for the long years that I was trapped in Hecate's Tree. When their raucous calls awoke me in the bedroom of the West Wing, before the pale sun had dawned, I did regret, however, their timing.

It was almost as frustrating as the occasion when I'd lain on the forest floor and built up the courage to *touch* myself in the way that the Rebels appeared to in the Wank Count (although, my *ladybits* were shaped differently than the twins' descriptions of their pricks, I was certain that they'd still work), and Echo and Flair had tumbled onto me, pecking at my intimates. I'd screeched, shoving away the familiars. It'd turned out that they'd thought beetles must've wriggled into my drawers.

At least, that was their excuse. *Frustrating.*

Caw, caw, caw.

I moaned, luxuriating for a final moment in the sensation of being held in my lovers' arms. The bed was warm. Sleipnir's arm was slung across my shoulder, and his pajama sleeve had ridden up. His skin lit my nerves on fire. Mist curled against his chest, snoring. Puffs of smoke blew against the sheets at each exhale. When I inched out from underneath Sleipnir, his brow furrowed.

He mumbled sleepily but didn't wake up.

On my other side, Fox appeared calm and beautiful in his sleep like he was free from the cruelties that his family had made him suffer and the fear of the academy. Last night, the way that he'd shaken as soon as us Immortals has returned through the dragon statue had terrified me because I'd recognized his despair. He'd clasped my hand like I'd fade back into a ghost if he let go.

Fox still wasn't safe here, however, even if his blond hair haloed on the pillow like he was at peace.

Wasn't this the R.I.P Academy, after all?

I smiled, stroking over one of his curls, before

kissing it. I breathed in his scent of raspberries, wishing that I could protect him…or devour him.

Perhaps, I could do both?

"*Hey, wake up, Sleeping Bosoms,*" Flair called. He hopped on the window ledge next to Echo. "*We want to talk to you, boss.*"

"*Didn't you miss us?*" Echo asked, hopefully.

I sighed, wriggling out of the covers and slipping past Bask, who'd crawled in the middle of the night to the bottom of the bed. He was meant to sleep on the mattress that'd been placed on the floor, but he'd been shaken by nightmares for the last couple of nights, and I had a sense that they were about the visiting Duchess. Obviously, in the night, he'd sought shelter from the horrors by cuddling as close as he could to the rest of us. He clutched Nile in his arms like the crocodile toy would spring to life and snap off any attackers' hands.

Did Bask not yet understand that it was *I* who'd hex anyone who sought to hurt him?

I could try for truly wicked, if I was pushed.

I tiptoed to the window, sliding onto the window seat. The braziers hadn't yet been lit, and it was cold. When I pushed open the window, the icy wind slapped my cheeks in a familiar greeting that made me grin, and I held out my arm for Echo and Flair who hopped onto it.

Witching heavens, I forgot how heavy they were.

"I missed your feathery behinds more than you know, but did we have to hold this reunion at such an unholy hour?" I grumbled.

Flair ruffled his feathers. "*The other witches are scary as fuck, boss. We don't fancy being caught and trained like…*"

"Familiars?" I arched my brow.

"*On my fangs, we're not familiars.*" Echo rubbed his head against my arm. "*We're your familiars. You'd never want us controlled like those poor dragon shifters, right?*"

I stroked Echo's beak. "I have nothing but contempt for those who rule by control. I'd free you both if—"

"*You don't love us?*" Echo gasped.

I blinked. "Excuse me?"

"*Pluck, stuff, and mount me in Crow Hall, look what your witchy muff has gone and done now!*" Flair snapped his beak with an angry clack. "*Tell him that you own him and other possessive shit, or so help me, I'll wake you up at this time every morning for the next term.*"

Ah, he knew my weakness.

I caressed Echo's wing because that made him *coo* happily, as I promised, "You're mine. I won't free you. I assure you that both your twin and you are bonded to me, and I shan't let you go."

I could hear the smile in Echo's voice. "As I've Fallen, I love you too."

The Fallen...or at least this pair, before they'd been transformed to familiars...were decidedly weird.

"Should I be worried about how you're spending your time without me?" I asked.

Flair's cackle didn't reassure me. *"Let's just say that we're exploring, unearthing secrets, and working on your behalf."*

"Consider me still worried."

"We find the time to peek in on the Princes," Echo added dreamily like that'd take the edge off my glare. *"Last night, the elf sang a song that flowed over me like a beautiful frozen river: "All is Found." I could've drowned in it."*

"Oh, and his dick looked <u>beautiful</u> too under the shower." Flair dove above my head in a victory lap. *"That's another one to me in the Wank Count."*

"Did you simply come here to boast about Willoughby's prick or...?" My tongue darted out, wetting my lower lip.

Why had Flair put that image in my head? Now that I knew the elf, I understood Echo's obsession with him. I didn't love Willoughby as I did the Immortals, but I wished that the Princes weren't divided in their own Wing. If Willoughby was lying in my arms, then I'd be able to understand why Lysander treated him as if he was as dangerous as me, called him *killer*, and manhandled him, despite the fact that he was equally royalty.

Yet also why Willoughby joked with Fox, was kind to Bask, and had helped Ambrose's son.

When Flair landed on my head, and his claws bit into my scalp, I winced. *"We came because your mage is in serious danger. I don't care a fuck about much, but I know what it'd mean to you if another mage died."*

I nodded; my throat was too tight to speak.

"We listened to the Principal and her daughter talking. You drew in the Rebel Cup on Monday and lost yesterday. Blood and bones, unless you win today, the mage dies. Your power could uproot this entire infernal academy. Unleash your witchy bitch."

I clenched my jaw. "Oh, the witchy bitch is ready. I shan't allow Fox to die for me, just like Robin did. I shall destroy this castle, rather than watch an execution on Saturday. But..." I hesitated, lifting Echo off my knee and standing. I bunched my hands in my dress. "...I love the Rebels and am even fond of the haughty Princes. I've grown attached to *life*. I wish to find a way to save us all. I'm known for death and destruction alone. Why can't I be known as more than the wicked witch?"

When I glanced up, I *eeped*.

Fox, Sleipnir, and Bask were awake, resting on

their elbows and watching me. *Why did they look so serious?*

Oh yes, to them it appeared that I was ranting about death and destruction to myself like a crazy person. Wait, had I even just pronounced my love in such an unflattering way?

"You heard that?" I asked.

They nodded at the same time.

Come on, Magenta, think...

"Be generous and merciful to her who is your slave in love." I smiled: *that'd do it.*

Behind my back, Flair *cawed* with laughter.

Fox's smile was shy. "I don't believe that you're wicked. You love me when no witch ever has."

Bask simply lay on his back, teasing up his pajamas to reveal his pale stomach. "Who wouldn't love this slinkiness?"

"It's too early in the morning for declarations of love." Sleipnir ran his hand through his mop of aquamarine hair. Mist, on the other hand, flew across the room to nuzzle against my neck with a gentle whinny. After the spell in SHP, Sleipnir couldn't hide his true emotions no matter how he tried. "You're plotting with those ghost pests again?"

"Flair says: *Tell the god to go fuck himself with Thor's hammer,*" I smirked, repeating Flair's response minus half the cursing.

"Rude." Sleipnir raised one elegant finger: "As

well as ignorant: it's called *Mjolnir*. You can tell the jerk crow that I've already hit that sweet Mjolnir's ass, or more precisely, it hit mine." Bask snickered, and I reddened. *Sweet Hecate, it was always the quiet ones.* Then Sleipnir cupped his prick through his pajamas, and I wished that I'd been able to replace those long fingers with mine. Wasn't it cruel and unusual punishment to expect a lady to resist such temptation from the gods? "Plus, brave to enter the arena of trash talk with the son of Loki. Mr Dick says: *come and suck me, and I'll show you the meaning of a chaos moment, bitch.*"

Ah, traditional banter. How I've missed it.

When Echo laughed, Flair shot him a betrayed look.

I cocked my head as if listening. "Flair says: *Why would he, when the worm doesn't look more than a mouthful?*"

Sleipnir sat up in sleepy outrage; his hair stuck out at cute angles that I longed to smooth down for him. Mist pawed the air angrily, tossing his head.

Sleipnir pointed at me. "Hey, you're making it up now."

I smiled, innocently. "Perhaps."

Bask pretended to snap Nile at me. "Naughty witch. Pet him."

"My pleasure." I stalked to the bed, crawling over Fox to straddle Sleipnir's lap.

I slipped my hand down Sleipnir's pants to fondle his prick like I'd been craving. His pupils became dilated, as his gaze met mine.

"Just a little lower," Sleipnir panted, before yelping. "On the second thoughts, that's low enough. More than a mouthful, huh?"

I leaned forward, thrilling at the silky feel of him and how quickly he'd hardened at my touch. His magic vibrated through mine; I could taste the power of every guy in the room. Yet their pleasure controlled them, as much as I craved it.

Was it pleasure or love? What was the difference?

"More than," I murmured, kissing Sleipnir's ear. He shivered. "But I'd rather that Flair didn't peck you *here*." I squeezed his prick, and he clenched his hands in the sheets. His prick, however, hardened even further. I loosened my hold, stroking it as if in apology. "I have rather high hopes for my future with Mr Dick—"

"Okay, now my balls have shriveled up and fallen off." Fox stumbled out of bed, stretching. "That's what happens when people go around talking directly to their dicks or naming them. It's as creepy as watching your partner sleep."

Wait, had Fox noticed my <u>*aww, he's sleeping so peacefully*</u> *moment earlier…?*

Bask laughed, before slinking to hover over Fox's shoulder like he was desperate to slip his arms around his neck. "Or making their partner watch *them* sleep." When we all looked at Bask, he wrapped his arms around his middle. "That was just the Duchess then?"

When my hand tightened into a fist in instinctive rage, Sleipnir howled.

"Sorry," I gasped, pulling away my offending hand and kissing across Sleipnir's furrowed forehead. "I'm still practicing my technique."

"Honestly, I'd never have known. It's okay, *Mr* Dick," he poked his tongue out at Fox, "forgives you…if he isn't broken."

I paled. "Sweet Hecate, I *broke* your boner…? Then we need to call Bacchus."

Fox and Bask were laughing (which I thought decidedly unkind of them), but they both yelled *no*.

Sleipnir's expression became grim. "On fear of the Valkyries, Professor Bacchus may be our tutor but she's not on our side. Swear you'll remember that."

I nodded.

Fox scuffed his foot against the floor; he wouldn't meet my gaze. "So, who's going to mention the white elephant in the room?" When he was greeted by silence, Fox slammed his hand against his chest, and I flinched. "*My* execution on Saturday. You weren't lying to your crows about all…that. I'd rather you didn't reign down the next apocalypse but I mean, I'd rather not die either. If that was okay."

My gaze softened. "Then we win today."

"Seriously, it's interesting how much you underestimate the Princes." Sleipnir leaped off the bed, before doubling over with a wince like he'd forgotten his injury. Then he held out his hand to me, pulling me to the wall at the back of the bedroom. Fox and Bask trailed after us. "The Membership," he announced like it was a magical spell the same as *Open Sesame*.

Ah, it *was* the same as *Open Sesame* because the wall opened, and a board that curled with the **RA** emblem and neon pink writing slotted out:

Rebel Academy Membership
RANDOMS
Confess — Whipping Boy
Curse — Whipping Boy

IMMORTALS
Crow — Prefect
Crave
Sleipnir

PRINCES
Crown — Prefect
Crush

The braziers flared with fire; their shadows flickered across the board.

"Randoms, Immortals, and Princes: R.I.P," Sleipnir said, quietly. "When we die, our names fade. This isn't simply an academy: it's a prison. The Membership is what controls our brands, wards, and the missions. It's the spell that holds the entire academy together because it was kind of written into the academy when it was created." His gaze darted to me. "I'd guess you know about that."

"Since I was a baby at the time, not really." I couldn't look away from my name because seeing it so boldly up there made the entire situation more real.

Even without the brand on my hand, I was trapped within the spell that my magic had helped to create. Oh, the cruel irony.

"Why is it divided like this? We're all Rebels. What would happen if I used my magic to *modify* the spell…?"

A slow grin spread across Sleipnir's face. "*A chaos moment.* If you broke the Membership, then the House of Crows would know, but if you moved a couple of the players around the board…? Huh, but that'd mean convincing the Princes or Midnight to join us as Immortals, and if you haven't realized yet, this entire academy is set up to keep us as rivals."

I twirled a strand of hair around my finger. "I have my ways," then I glanced between the gorgeous Immortals, "and so do you."

Bask smirked. "Who could resist such a pettable arse forever?"

"*Please pick the elf.*" Echo jumped up and down on the window ledge. "*Think of all the snowmen you could build together.*"

"How about you crows fly away now?" I arched my brow.

"*Charming,*" Flair grumbled, "*like we don't have Princes to watch in showers. Come on, brother.*"

The familiars took off in a rain of feathers, flapping out of the open window.

Fox paled. "Prisons have parole. I'll be the model prisoner. They don't execute top students, even though I'm *not* the top… Okay, I'm the *worst*…but I'll pledge to turn it around…"

Sleipnir caught Fox's hands gently between his. "There's no parole, and it kind of doesn't matter what you do because you were born a mage."

I hated that truth my entire life, but when I saw the devastation on Fox's face, I could've torn up every witch tradition and rewritten worlds.

"B-but if I try harder…?" Fox whispered.

"To not be a mage?"

"I didn't mean—"

"To not have magic?"

"Stop it." Fox tried to pull away his hands, but Sleipnir held on.

"To have been born a woman?"

"Enough, Slippy, or does it please you to be cursed forever to discover only an empty toilet roll when you need paper?"

Sleipnir took a step back, holding up his hands in surrender. "Hey, I was only trying to stop Fox from becoming like the Princes. I wouldn't wish that Fate on anyone, even a stuck-up asshole like Lysander."

Mist galloped across to Fox, landing on his shoulder. Then he nibbled on his ear as if in apology. Fox chuckled, nudging him away. Mist settled beside the warmth of the brazier instead, lowering his head to sleep again.

"Are we talking about the Fate to become pampered and top scoring students with luxury meals and quarters, as well as the best chance of winning the Rebel Cup?" Fox asked, sullenly. "Wow, save me now."

Sleipnir and Bask exchanged a glance. "Omens and runes, I swear that the only reason the Princes fight to win with such ruthlessness is that they believe the contest is about more than a trophy." Fox's startled gaze met Sleipnir's. My heartbeat raced, and my magic prickled through me. "I sort of feel sorry for their asses because they're led to believe that there *is* an escape. If they only try hard enough and prove that they *deserve* to be princes, then their kingdoms will want them back. This Rebel Cup…and everything that they suffer in the academy…is their redemption."

My guts clenched, and my throat ached. I thought of the Princes, and I shuddered at their *hope* because I understood the need for *redemption.* I didn't know what they'd done in their own kingdoms to be deposed as princes and sent here or what they were trying to make up for, but it didn't matter. I'd been responsible for Robin's death and the curse of perpetual winter. I knew about the search for atonement. I'd been lucky enough to find it in the protection of my Rebels.

"Don't you believe that rather admirable?" I said, softly.

Sleipnir raised his eyebrow. "It's dangerous, and it's also seriously cruel because *escape* is the lie. Their kingdoms won't take them back, no matter how their guardians trick them. But I guess that it's easy for them to live in the delusion." Sleipnir rested the back of his hand tenderly against Fox's cheek "I'm sorry, I just didn't want you to lie to yourself about this—"

"Like I lie about everything?" Fox stalked away from Sleipnir, curling onto the bed. He peeked at me. "And *I* find it admirable, but I'm King of Exploding Lies, as well as telling them. I'll free the Princes from their delusion, after all, I've been physician for Caligula, King George III, and Edgar Alan Poe…"

When Fox cuddled Nile like he was a whisker away from transforming into his cat form, Bask reddened with outrage, before prowling onto the bed as well. Sleipnir covered his face like he didn't dare watch.

"Don't steal Nile. He's mine." Bask grabbed Nile, cradling him like Fox had been ripping out his stuffing, rather than snuggling him.

Why had I never learned the incubus ritual that included crocodiles? Were they worshiped?

Fox scooted back. "*Woah*, snatchy. I was only planning a nice pair of crocodile shoes or possibly a handbag."

Wasn't it foolish to banter about an incubus' holy crocodile?

With a growl, Bask launched himself on Fox, who fell backward with a yelp. Bask pinned Fox with the skill of a predator: he didn't touch him, but planted his knees either side of Fox's head, pressing Nile's mouth to Fox's neck in a plushie savaging.

"*Hmm*, little help here?" Fox pleaded.

Sleipnir slipped onto the bed with a sexy indolence, resting against the headboard. He merely smiled, watching the show. Fox relaxed, when I perched next to him. He stiffened, however, when I tapped his nose.

"Apologize. My family shan't hurt each other even in play," I chided.

Fox reddened, before meeting Bask's furious gaze. "I'm sorry. Look, I have this book that dad gave me. You must've seen it in my memory last night. It's in the wardrobe with my things, and I feel about it, the same way as you do about Nile. I'll show it to you sometime, okay?"

Bask nodded, mollified. Then he held up Nile to look Fox in the eye. "Apologize to Nile."

Fox rolled his eyes. "I'm sorry for joking about the beautiful shoes that I could turn you into. Can I kiss your ugly…*sweet*…tooth and make it all better?"

Bask made Nile nod imperiously, and Fox grinned as he kissed Nile's gleaming tooth. Then Bask sat back, hugging the crocodile.

"Nile's the only thing ma ever gave me. Incubi aren't meant to own anything, see, because *they're* owned." Bask didn't look up. I edged as close as I dared to him on the bed. I craved to pull him onto my lap, and kiss his neck; his draw was mesmerizing. But Damelza's spell kept us apart, *and it was devastating*. "Bright light hurts our eyes, but here's the thing, I love the sun. I hated that my brothers and me weren't allowed out unchaperoned and had to be educated at home. I didn't wise up to the fact that ma was hiding me to try and stop the Duchess from discovering me because I was different to my brothers. I was broken long before I was bonded." Bask ducked his head, and his voice shook. "Ma caught me in the sun…basking…and she said that should be my name. She told me that I needed to be like a crocodile. Then she promised to teach me the secrets to survive in a Succubi Court, just in case… Ma trained me like a daughter, rather than a son." At last, his gaze met mine. "I'm this crocodile, and it's ruined me."

"Listen to me," I gripped the sides of Nile as hard as I wished that I could grip Bask's shoulders, "you're not ruined or broken. You're frighteningly strong, and to survive in Rebel Academy, we all need the skills that your mother taught you. Right now, do you remember the first time that I saw you lying on this bed?"

Bask's breath hitched. "I'll never forget."

"You called for me, your Ghost Immortal. I'm here now, and we're together." I finally sat back. "Undo your shirt." Bask's eyes widened, before he clumsily pushed Nile to the side. Then he undid the buttons to reveal his chest. By his ragged breathing, I could tell that the orders were feeding his pleasure, as much as his pleasure was feeding *me*. "Push down your pants." Bask slithered out of his pajama bottoms. He lay beneath me like a beautiful sacrifice. "Now touch yourself."

Bask flushed, and his gaze darted to the other Immortals. His tongue swept his plush lips; their scent of coco and almond flooded me with warmth. I was desperate to taste them.

Bask pushed open his top to circle his pink nipples, before trailing his gloved hand down his chest. He splayed his legs wider. When he teased down his inner thighs, his prick pulsed. He ran a single finger along his prick to its head.

The first time that I'd seen him like this, I'd craved him, as much as his craving for me had burned. Now, the tendrils of his longing twined with my own, sparking magic through the connection that bound all four of us Immortals. Death, pleasure, or blood: these were the Rebels who'd resurrected me. Their spirits were woven with mine.

My magic vibrated like a thousand glowing snowflakes across the snowy peaks of Bask's body.

"What do you wish?" Bask's gaze didn't leave mine.

I smiled. "The first time that you lay on this bed, imagining that you and I were lovers, what did you fantasize?" Pink crept into Bask's cheeks. *How kinky could it be?* "You please me, and it'd please me to do as *you* wish."

Bask shuddered, as both his ability to please me, and the offer of control, fed the two sides of his nature.

His eyes flared, before they dimmed again. "But you can't touch me."

Sleipnir crawled like a colorful big cat to Fox, wrenching back his head by the curls to lick a stripe down his neck. "What's the problem when you have us? We're all connected, so command away."

Bask's eyes glittered with a wicked light that made the hairs on my arms stand up at the same time as my skin tingled. My incubus might be cuddly, but he was all predator. He sprawled onto his back, as he clutched his prick more firmly.

"You wore less clothes." Bask boldly met my eye. *Challenge accepted.*

I clicked my fingers (purely for the theatrics), and my clothes melted: first my outer dress and petticoats, then my corset and drawers. I appreciated the collective gasps of admiration, as did my bosoms.

"Huh, impressive skill," Sleipnir bit his lip, "and other things."

"And useful…also to the other things." Fox grinned.

"Why are you still dressed?" Bask demanded.

Sleipnir snorted. "Sorry, Your Highness."

He tore off his pajamas with such savagery that I shivered, wishing that I'd allowed him to rip my drawers off at least, although I had a sense that it would've been rather painful for my intimates.

Fox fiddled with the buttons of his top, however, and it struck me that he'd never undressed for a lover before. Gently, Sleipnir took his hands between his, before pulling them to his sides, and undoing Fox's buttons for him. I knee walked on the bed, until I caged Fox in front of Sleipnir, kissing him as I pushed the top from his shoulders.

Fox's eyes shone, and his chest rapidly rose and fell, as Sleipnir liberated Fox's legs from his pants.

"Didn't you speak yesterday about the desire to gift your virginities? Lie down." Bask's head was twisted to watch us, as his hand sped up on his prick, and his back arched.

My pulse fluttered in my neck, as I lay amongst the satin pillows. Softness cocooned me below, whilst Sleipnir and Fox's hardness cocooned me above. I turned my head to meet Bask's gaze: this was for him. My magic lit the room, and tangled like roots through each of the Immortals, drawing us together.

I was part of the academy, and they were part of me.

"Kiss her," Bask murmured.

Fox's lips were sweet raspberries and love. They were every year that I'd yearned, and every tear that I'd cried. They were life beyond death. My second chance.

I bit hard on his bottom lip and suckled, feasting on his sweet blood. He gasped, panting.

My mage…mine, mine, mine…

Fox's curls swept my cheeks, but I didn't look away from the darkness of Bask's gaze. Sleipnir caressed his finger across my nub until it peaked, before he licked.

What was spiraling inside me like a whirlwind? Was it another moment of destruction? *The chaos moment?*

"Trust me, cherry pie." Sleipnir slipped his hands between Fox's spread legs, stroking his prick to throbbing hardness. Then he lay behind Fox, kissing between his shoulder blades, as he guided Fox's prick between my thighs. I winced but then pulled Fox closer, urging him not to stop.

Fox clasped my hands. His smile was radiant, as he thrust. Sleipnir grasped Fox's hips, rubbing his own prick between Fox's thighs in a glorious rhythm that swelled like a sea inside me.

"I love you," Bask whispered. "Just like this."

The room became as light as a magenta sun with my magic. The rays burst through my lovers at the moment that the crest of the wave hit, and I screamed; my lovers and I came together in ecstasy.

Love, pleasure, and life. At last, I'd tasted what I'd craved for so long, but it was only a glimpse that could be burned to nothing if I lost today. What would I need to unleash to protect my family, and how wicked would I become?

I'd already learned how fragile family could be. I wouldn't allow it be stolen once more by death.

CHAPTER TWENTY

Rebel Academy, Wednesday September 4th

MAGENTA

I knelt on my knees in the Bird Turret in a circle with both Immortals and Princes, before the class in Strategy. Sleipnir had told me that this class was an attempt to brainwash us Rebels into assassins (although I had no idea how a mind could be cleaned with soap). I shivered, as I glanced around at the room high above the bailey, which I'd been shut away in as much as Fox had been locked in his attic. Yet I hadn't been punished as a mage, rather adored as the Bless-edly Charmed who was too *precious* to risk in the world.

Merlin's balls to that.

Now, the room had been hollowed out. Nothing remained apart from the magical mural that'd been painted across the walls at dad's request. Byron had brought the outside into the Bird Turret, surrounding me with the nature, which my magic craved.

I twisted, ghosting my hand across the mural of Hecate's tree, which was alive again here at least; its branches rose to the roof. Lilies of the valley and foxgloves grew at its base and suffocated the room in their intoxicating aroma. Frogs hopped along the baseboards. I shuddered at the pulsing magic.

It fizzed through me, calling to me. Hecate was inside my heart, and I was inside hers. I pressed my nails hard into my palms to resist her.

I won't return to you. I'm alive now…

Fox laughed as hundreds of robins swooped overhead like a bloody cloud, and I bit my lip hard to stop myself praying to Hecate to save him today.

My goodness, old habits truly were hard to shake.

I snatched back my hand in case I was tempted to pray to the goddess, and smiled at Fox's joy. The robins had always been my favorite as a child too. Painted in the indigo roof, even though they'd been forever trapped, they'd sung their silvery songs to me. But now they were silent.

Could magic murals grieve or perhaps, after all these years, they'd become a little crazy like me?

Behind every crazy witch is someone even crazier

who made her that way. That was Number 34 in the **Principal's Motto Book**.

I could hate the mottoes, even if some of them were right.

Yet even if I and the robins were a *teensy-weensy* bit crazy, we could also be restored to our former life through love. I was certain that mother had a motto about it but I'd rather watch the way that Fox dived to his feet and ran around the circle like he was playing ring-a-ring o'roses, pretending to duck, as the robins chased him.

"Help, the birds are after me," he laughed. "My prey has turned against me. I blame global warming."

The robins twirled and dived, enjoying the game as much as he was. Lysander rolled his eyes, but Bask giggled, shifting closer to Lysander who sprawled back on his elbows.

I closed my eyes, breathing in the sweet scent of the artificial flowers. I remembered when there'd been no laughter in the Bird Turret, apart from Byron's and my own. Yet this room had been filled with other beautiful things: a brightly painted rocking horse, china dolls, and samplers embroidered with the **RA** crest. *Witching heavens, I'd hated embroidering those.*

I'd adored sitting on the window seat amongst my ranks of dolls, however, pretending to read *Jane Eyre*, as I'd sneaked glances at the Rebels below. Well, sneaked glances at one Rebel in particular: a young mage with a tumble of burnished red hair and intense emerald eyes. After all, I'd never seen a mage before (and they were meant to be as wicked as I was Blessed).

It'd made me shiver.

What did he do that was so naughty?

Byron had told me that not eating my broccoli was naughty. Perhaps, the mage had refused to eat up his greens...? I'd frowned at the bruise that'd swelled his eye and cheek. Bryon had often tried to hide bruising just like that. When Bryon would mutter that he'd been bad and had deserved it, I'd never believed it. Father had been the kindest...most fun...and *least* wicked person that I'd known. Of course, I'd barely known anyone, but compared to *mother* who'd punished Byron simply because she'd been displeased with *my* work, he'd been my hero.

I'd studied the mage in the courtyard, who'd cradled his purpled cheek. He'd been dressed as a whipping boy and hung back from the other Rebels, who'd ignored him.

Was he also my hero, rather than wicked?

I'd thrown aside my book, crawling closer to the glass and pressing my hand against it.

All of a sudden, in a spray of golden glitter, the mage transformed into a red squirrel. I gasped, clapping my hands in delight.

Why had nobody told me that mages were also

shifters?

Bubbling cauldrons, he was cute.

My fingers had clenched to snuggle him and pet his fluffy tail. He'd chattered, dancing around the hollering Rebels, who'd recoiled from him like he was a tiger, rather than snatched him up and cuddled him like he was begging for.

When Henrietta prowled from the shadows with dangerous intent, my eyes had widened. I'd known that look and it'd always ended in tears…*Byron's*.

Henrietta had clutched the squirrel by the base of the tail, swinging him into the air. The mage had let out a high-pitching whining sound like he was crying in distress and pain. His little paws had scrabbled desperately.

My eyes had smarted with tears, as I'd raised my fist to bang on the window for the first time ever.

Let him go, let him go, let him…

The magical robins had fluttered around the roof, *yeeping* in alarm. Then I'd felt a warm hand on my shoulder and had realized that I hadn't alone.

My hero had arrived. Unfortunately, Byron had also witnessed my tantrum.

I'd primly settled back onto the window seat, opening the book at a random page…*upside down*.

Did I have time to cast a Reading Upside Down Spell?

Bryon had snorted. "Good try, Magenta." He'd

plucked the book from my hand and tossed it onto the floor. His green suit had been open at the neck to reveal his peacock amulet, which he'd stroked. I could tell that had meant he was plotting something. His mouth had been tight, as he'd stared out of the window. "The boy down there is an orphan mage called Robin." His elegant fingers had brushed the amulet again. "You're lonely up here, aren't you?"

I'd warily nodded.

"What if that boy was allowed into the Bird Turret to play with you?" Bryon had straightened, *clicking* his smart heels together as if on parade.

My magic had burst from me, sparking like pink fire.

The excitement of the forbidden, mixed in with the chance to cuddle a squirrel (and rescue a Rebel from Henrietta), had me bouncing up and down on my seat.

The lack of decorum in becoming a bouncing witch would've horrified mother. I'd bounced even harder.

Bryon had raised his finger in warning. "I hate to ask it of you, but we must keep this a secret from mama, or I shall suffer."

Well, that was how to stop a witch bouncing.

My grin had slipped but it hadn't faded. "Papa, I can keep a secret. I want the mage."

Byron's icy eyes had flashed, as he'd snatched up my most loved doll and waved it in front of me.

"Pan's balls, *Robin* is not a toy. I don't suggest bringing him here, so that you can practice witch cruelty or coo over him like he's no more than this doll." My lip trembled. Byron had never spoken to me with such harshness before. *What had I done?* Bryon's expression softened, as he dropped the doll and pulled me into a hug, stroking my hair. "Calm, Magenta," he'd murmured. I'd sighed, safe in his arms. "*Hush,* now, there's no need for tears. But believe me, in here Robin shall be your *equal*. You'll share with him, and he'll choose what you play. I know that's hard to understand with what mama preaches, but let me show you a different way."

I'd nodded, nestling closer to his warmth. He'd pushed me back so that his gaze could meet mine.

"If you mistreat him, then you lose this chance," his voice had been steely. I'd quivered, tightening my arms around his waist because it'd felt like if I lost Robin, then I'd lose Byron as well. "Do you understand?"

"Robin will be my friend," I'd whispered. "I'll love him."

And I had. I'd loved him to death.

Now, watching Fox as he finally threw himself next to me, underneath the flock of painted robins, I bit back a sob because if I didn't win the contest today, then I'd have loved *this* mage to death as well.

One mistake is forgivable, but two deserves the

Revenge Hex: **88** in the **Principal's Motto Book**.

I'd hex *myself* if I let Fox down today.

When Lysander's haughty gaze met mine across the circle, and he pointed the tip of his wing at me like a golden sword, I rather thought that the fae intended to hex me himself. After what Sleipnir had shown me about the Membership, I now understood that the Rebel Cup meant as much to the princes in their own way as it did to me. Yet whatever they thought that they were proving through winning, it could never be worth Fox's life.

If I had to witch slap a few princes to prove that point, then so be it.

I inclined my head to Lysander (because manners cost nothing), and Lysander gaped at me. With a snarl, Lysander wrapped his wing around Willoughby instead, manhandling him to sit straighter in the way that I hated. Willoughby's gaze appeared hazy again like he was lost somewhere inside his own mind again.

Were all elves so inscrutable or only their beautiful princes?

At the sudden flutter of feathers, I turned to the window. When Ezekiel flew through with outstretched violet wings like the righteous angels that I'd dreamed about as a child (although none of them had such rippling muscles that warmth coiled through me, along with the desire to lick along his bronzed chest),

Tchaikovsky's "1812: Overture" burst out in all its martial glory.

Mage's balls on a stick, were even angels musical in this day and age?

I jumped, and my magic exploded from me like twinkling fireworks. They lit the shadowy room, as the rousing music swelled with bells and cannon blasts.

Sleipnir collapsed on his back with laughter, as Mist blew his own aquamarine fire to add to the light show. "Hey, look, it's the fourth of July! Do you want me to grab my guitar? I'd win this if it's a music lesson."

"Are you certain?" Willoughby arched his brow.

Sleipnir leaned forward. "Bring it on, pointy ears."

Ezekiel landed in the middle of the circle, and the music shut off. "I appreciate the enthusiasm, but this is *Strategy* class. The lesson of this music from the non-magical world is that even an Emperor can be brought down by nature. It tells the story of Napoleon marching on Russia and being defeated by their winter." His gaze darted to me, and I flushed. You curse *one* academy with perpetual winter and suddenly you're the bad guy… "Well, line up then."

He fluttered his wings impatiently, but his smile was gentle.

Fox pulled me up. I was surprised that it was Willoughby, however, who slipped his hand around

Bask's waist and helped him to stand next to him. Bask looked unsteady. The touch deprivation must be hurting him now.

How much longer before the Duchess visited?

Lysander stood next to them, and his back was so straight that I thought it wise to check whether there was a stick stuck up his behind. When I leaned to check out his unfairly tight buns, Sleipnir frowned, catching my eye. Then he waggled his eyebrows at me in amusement.

I raised a haughty eyebrow, although I allowed Mist to settle on my shoulder with a stroke of his mane because I was decidedly gracious like that.

Lysander glared at me, outraged. *Perhaps he was auditioning for the part of Napoleon.*

Ezekiel marched down the line, as if he was an officer inspecting our eccentric parade. He stopped at Sleipnir, who slouched like he was at a punk concert. Ezekiel did up Sleipnir's tie with sharp, efficient motions.

Sweet Hecate, that was the first time that I'd seen Sleipnir smartened up, and he looked *hot* in a tie. What would he look like in a suit?

I sighed. A witch could dream, surely?

I was already in my evening dress, and my own corset bit into my bosoms like they were trying to make *them* stand up for inspection. They were impressive. I pushed out my chest further.

"I did explain to you last time that you were an army?" Ezekiel sounded troubled. "That it's my job to train you as assassins to be sent on—"

"Dirty missions. We'll probably die. Teamwork." Bask pouted up at Ezekiel with his innocent face at full blast. *I defied anybody to resist that.* "Does it please you that we were listening, professor?"

Ezekiel looked like he was biting his tongue… hard. Then he crossed his arms. "I'm here to teach you to survive, and that means more than how to swing a sword or do that swirly stuff with your mist." I sniffed: *impolite.* "There's more to being royal than becoming the most powerful," his gaze swept to Willoughby who froze, "and more to war than drawing blood."

When Ezekiel's gaze swung to Lysander, the prince stiffened.

It was hard to hate the two princes, when they struggled with the same darkness as I did. Yet then my gaze fell on the pale curve of Midnight's back, as he knelt in the shadows and the robins fluttered around his shoulders to console him, it was rather easy to hate them again.

"How about more to revenge than poking fae with iron…?" Lysander drawled.

Bask examined his fingernails. "Lay off, I said that I was sorry. Do you wish that my slinky self gets on my knees?"

His innocent self wasn't kidding anyone now.

Lysander reddened. "Please don't. I wish instead that you'd remember your place. One happens to be a *true* prince, and not that travesty of a clone."

Bask winced.

Ezekiel beat his wings. "You happen to be a *deposed* prince." This time it was Lysander's turn to wince. Now *that* was a put-down worthy of a witch. "I swear that I told you to stick together as a team. Anyway, it helps for today because who's up for a little role-play?"

Sleipnir groaned. "Lightning strike me now."

Lysander glanced up at the roof hopefully. "Yes, please."

"I wasn't praying, twinkle wings." Sleipnir glared at Lysander, who didn't even have the good grace to hide his disappointment. "Couldn't we just write a twenty-thousand-word essay or take a surprise exam instead?"

Wait, those options sounded *appalling*. Why was Sleipnir sacrificing us on the academic altar?

My heart thudded hard in my chest. Fox looked as panicked as me. His hand tightened around mine.

"I've never written a *thousand-word* essay," Fox muttered, "or taken an exam that I've crammed for, and for once, that's the truth. Great Pan, I don't want to die. I'm one dead foxy, aren't I?"

"I promise that I'll protect you," I whispered; his

fingers were warm, entwined between my cold ones. "Even from an essay."

Bask's grin was wicked, as he ran his hands down his sides. "Role-play could be fun. Tell me what do you desire? Stern teacher and naughty student. I've arrived late to the lesson, and you have no option but to punish—"

"The wrong kind of role-play." Ezekiel had pinked all the way down his chest. He wrapped his wings around himself but he couldn't hide the way that his prick tented his harem trousers. Perhaps, he'd enjoy joining us for a little teacher and student get together? Although, it was possible that he'd act it out right now on Sleipnir by the way that his sparking gaze met his. "Don't frighten the others. Just because you struggle with my learning methods, doesn't mean that the rest will. I want two of you to step forward. The Prince will act out their kingdom's take on leadership. They will *role play*," Sleipnir snorted, "not their own views but the ones of those who brought them up. The Immortal facing them will counter their view with their own."

My brows furrowed. "Why?"

Ezekiel swept to the far wall, leaning against it. "How can you fight against your enemy, if you don't first understand them?" When his gaze met mine, there was an understanding that shook me. "And how do you persuade them to your side, if you don't listen first?"

Bask pushed himself forward. "Let me do this."

When Bask's knees buckled, however, and Willoughby caught him, I smiled. Bask was beautiful, mesmerizing, and as brave as any of the Rebels.

"How about you work on keeping upright, and Lysander and I make this a Prefect battle?" I cocked my eyebrow at Lysander.

Lysander's mouth tightened, and he paled. But as the rest of the Rebels formed a circle, he marched to meet me in the center with his hands held smartly behind his back.

"You'll regret this." Tremors ran through him, even though he held himself still. "This is a violation. The Fae Court should not be questioned in such a fashion."

"Have we started yet?" I asked. "Or is that just your usual arrogant ranting?"

Lysander hissed in frustration, before lowering his head and steadying his breathing. When he raised his head again, however, I gasped in shock. His eyes were cold in a way that I'd never seen before. His face looked paler and pinched. He stood even stiffer than before, and witching heavens, I hadn't thought that was possible. "Royalty have a duty to act as though above all others." I flinched in shock. It was the same cruel voice that Midnight had spoken with in Divination. "If they fail, then they bring disgrace and shame on their entire kingdom. There can be no forgiveness for such fae. Royalty must crush all rebellion before there's a chance for war. Fae must obey the hierarchy and respect it, even if that means killing."

Lysander's wings quivered, and sweat slipped down his forehead.

It was hurting him to say those things. Sweet Hecate, Lysander truly *was* a Rebel.

My eyes widened. "You don't believe any of that."

To my surprise, I was certain that he *didn't*.

Lysander raised a haughty brow. "The purpose of the exercise is that you now counter with *your* views, rather than pretend to know my illustrious thoughts."

Fox watched me intently, and I caught his eye. Well, if Lysander wished us to play it this way, then there was more than one way to skin a fae.

"What if you're given an order that you can't follow?" When Lysander flinched, I grinned. *Got you.* "It's not disgraceful to think for yourself, treat others as equals, or value life. What if the order is to kill other fae, and you *know* that it's wrong? Wouldn't it make you less of a prince simply to follow such a command blindly?"

Lysander's eyes were wild with fear, and his breathing was ragged. "One doesn't wish to play this game anymore."

"Then you forfeit the lesson to the Immortals?" Ezekiel said, casually.

At last I understood why Sleipnir had requested to be *struck by lightning*. Role-play was fiendish.

Lysander twisted to stare at Midnight, who'd hunched over, covering himself with his wings. Lysander shook his head.

Ezekiel gestured with his hand. "Your turn then."

"It's just…" Lysander took a step closer to me. He appeared lost. "… What if you lose everything by rebelling?"

My dress faded to mist, which darkened the room to fog at the memory. "I beg your pardon; did you forget already? I *died,* or is there more you'd have me lose?"

"You can lose more than your life," Willoughby said, softly.

I glanced at the elf, and then I thought of burnished red hair and intense emerald eyes and I realized that he was right.

Lysander ducked his head. "It doesn't matter. There's no way back for a fae who disobeys."

"If you've killed—"

"That's what you think of me?" Lysander snarled, and even his anger was swallowed by his hurt.

Why did I feel such guilt squirming in my gut? Perhaps, I'd better hold back with answering what was on the tip of my tongue: *ehm, of course; you're Titus' nephew.*

Unfortunately, the words must've been written across my face because Lysander stormed out of the middle of the circle, clutching Willoughby by the arm and dragging him to me.

"Why am *I* spurned, whilst you snuggle up to this other *deposed* prince?" He shook Willoughby, who didn't even try to free himself.

"Let Willoughby go, or you shall discover just how far I'm prepared to go for my new snuggle buddy," my voice was calm, yet my magic whipped around the Bird Turret.

The mural of Hecate's Tree reached out from the walls. The branches reached to snatch at the fae, curling around his wings and hoisting him into the air.

"Why?" Lysander demanded, struggling. "I thought that you were just arguing against *killers*?"

Willoughby hung his head, and his hair covered his eyes.

My magic calmed, and the mural slipped back into the wall, dropping Lysander onto his behind with a *crack* that made me wince.

Cauldrons and broomsticks, all of us in this academy were dangerous, deadly, and broken. *Who was I to judge?*

I was the wicked witch, after all.

Suddenly, there was a waterfall of crows feathers

on the far wall, and Damelza strode through with a flourish. Her hair glistened like it'd been polished, and her dress was ruffled, as if a hundred more crows had been slaughtered to give her the effect.

Adrenaline spiked through me, as my lips pinched. Henrietta had smartened herself up (and Byron and me), whenever there'd been special events with guests. I had the horrid feeling that no dangers inside the academy were as acute as those from the Rebels' own families.

When Damelza's critical gaze swept across our tense role-play with a prince on his behind, the word *killers* ringing in the air, and my own magic still thrumming in the mural, yet rested on Bask... I was certain that *knock, knock, the Duchess had arrived.*

Bask became ashen, hugging himself because *I* couldn't. I bit my lip hard. Willoughby turned to catch my eye, before standing in front of Bask like he could shield him for me.

Like he wasn't a killer.

When Sleipnir edged to join Willoughby in Bask protection duty so close that their shoulders touched, Willoughby's eyes widened as if he'd never expected that any Immortal would willingly stand at his side. Perhaps, it was more that he was startled that anyone would risk *touching* him casually...? Lysander only handled Willoughby like a guard would, pulling him from class to class.

When Fox attempted the same protection of me, my lips twitched. Shimage didn't beat centuries old Blessedly Charmed witch. Yet it was charming that he wished to be my knight.

I clasped Fox's hand, tugging him closer to my side; Mist leaped from my shoulder onto his, tossing his mane. "I love you as my equal," I whispered. "One that I'll always fight to save."

Lysander was the only Rebel to be stranded alone. He paled; his eyes were red-rimmed. He pushed himself up, standing under Damelza's inspection, as if he had an even larger stick up his behind than before.

He truly should get that looked into.

"Well, I'm shocked." Damelza's eyes glittered. "You're supposed to be learning together for excellence, professor. This isn't Warrior Training. Why's there brawling and disorder in your class?"

Ezekiel swallowed. He straightened, curling his wings around himself like he could hide.

"It's just role-play," he offered with a shaky smile. "It's not real."

"Do I need to give your wings the same treatment as Professor Ambrose's?" Damelza stalked closer.

"It was all part of the lesson," I insisted.

"Yeah, we love role-play; it's *awesome*." Sleipnir grinned, but Damelza ignored him.

Instead, she turned to Lysander. "As you know, it's one of your Guardian's orders that you don't lie to staff. So, was this lesson controlled?" I frowned, when Damelza's gaze darted between both Willoughby and me. "You should know how important it is that powers are restrained."

Like Hecate's Tree bursting out of a mural...?

Ah, sweet unrestrained magic.

Ezekiel's shoulders slumped, and his wings drooped like they were already weighted down by chains. If he was relying on Lysander's good report to avoid Damelza's punishment, then he had a mage's hope in witchy hell.

"Ezekiel's classes are tough," Lysander's voice was clipped, and he stared at the far wall, rather than meeting Damelza's eye. "He finds your weakness and then he pushes at it. The others think that he's kind and gentle. But my royal self has lived in the Fae Court, and I know how to read predators. For Ezekiel to have survived to become a teacher, he must be ruthless. He's as much a warrior with manipulation as he is with weapons. Today, he was merely attempting to teach us to face the monsters that haunt us."

Ezekiel's violet eyes opened comically large. He burrowed even further into his wings, as if he could hide from Lysander, who'd stripped him bare.

Why had Lysander saved the professor? It was strange to stare at the prince's pale face and feel a flush of pride.

To my surprise, Damelza's lips curved into a

smile, as she drew out a sky-blue sheet of paper. "I'm delighted that even a shameful Addict Angel can achieve such a report. I'll add it to your records, professor." Ezekiel nodded, mechanically. "It's perfect timing that you've been working on the monsters within, when so many of your students *are* monsters."

Even though Sleipnir didn't move, Mist stomped his feet and laid his ears back. I knew that she'd hurt Sleipnir, but it was Willoughby who dived towards her, so fast that she stumbled backward.

"My brother's letter," Willoughby demanded with such frosty violence that I shook, "give it to me."

Well, someone had just shown their regal side.

Damelza's magic slammed into Willoughby, hurling him through the air. He crashed into Sleipnir, who caught him and helped him back onto his feet.

Damelza stalked towards Willoughby, holding aloft the letter like a standard.

"It's *his* letter," Fox's voice was tight. I remembered the way that Damelza had forced him to write to Aquilo. "People who mess with other folk's post are haunted by the spirits of dead postmen. I'd hand it over now if you don't want to be haunted forever by late mail, *sorry, you were out* slips, and lost packages. I mean, it's your call."

"I'll risk it." Damelza broke the seal on the letter with a flourish.

"Let me read it later, if I must," Willoughby hissed.

"You'd make a *king* wait?" Damelza arched her brow. "Who do you think you are? Oh yes, the *would-be* king."

I studied Willoughby. Had he tried to assassinate his own brother to take the throne? Yet the way that his jaw clenched told me that I was missing something because would an assassin feel such *shame*?

"Let him read it," I said, softly. "I don't need to know what he did to be sentenced here. We're all Rebels, and that unites us. Call us monsters if you like because I'd claim that name over the bloody House of Crows."

Damelza drew in a shocked breath, before her eyes flashed pink with fury. "In your first life, you were a sheltered, naïve witch, and now, you believe yourself the wicked witch. But you've seen nothing of the true darkness in the supernatural world. I have, and maybe you wouldn't be so keen to call yourself monster, if you knew what it meant."

When she held up the letter, Willoughby let out a holler. The contents were projected in curling letters across the indigo of the roof; the robins fluttered in panic, diving away to hide.

Brother,

As much as it pains me to even think of you, I write this letter to urge you to listen to your professors, control your murderous urges, and curb your dangerous impulses.

Every day, the kingdom calls for your execution. You deserve to die. I'm certain that you believe a killer should pay for their crime. Yet you're royal, even if deposed, and so I must settle for imprisonment.

Even so, with such clamoring for your death, only good report from the Rebel Academy will save you. Do not forget why you're paying penance. If I must live with the grief of your treason, then so must you.

Your King

WILLOUGHBY DROPPED TO HIS KNEES, AS THE WORDS faded. His breathing was ragged like he was battling tears. But the Ice Prince didn't do anything as mundane as cry, surely?

"Huh, just bask in that brotherly love," Sleipnir drawled. His fists clenched. "Your king is a dick."

I crouched next to Willoughby, sparkling my magic soothingly across his skin, until he raised his head to look at me. "It wasn't hollow sentiment. I don't care what you did before, or do you judge me on being the witch whose wards trap you?"

"You should care." Willoughby's voice was raspy with suppressed tears, as he gripped me by the shoulders. His gaze met Lysander's. "Are you happy now that I've been revealed as the monster who you've always believed me to be?" He shoved me away, before stalking to the door, swinging it open. His voice was small. "Stay away from me."

"I suggest that this means the Immortals won today." My voice was unsteady, but I forced out the words like toads. "After all, the elf has forfeited by attempting to leave."

Willoughby froze, before shooting a guilty glance over his shoulder at Midnight. Yet when I studied Fox's curls and the whipping boy outfit that matched the one Robin had been made to wear, I knew that this class was Strategy, and I'd just *won*.

When the prize was Fox's life, I'd play the war game.

Damelza's grin fizzed with malicious delight, as she linked our arms like we were now best friends. I wanted to hurl.

Was there such a thing as Witch Sickness?

"Excellently played. Whatever you claim, you *are* a Crow. If only you hadn't fallen in silly love, you'd have made the most brilliant Blessedly Charmed witch. Our House would've been the envy of every coven. Well, there's no good crying over spilled magic." She waved at Ezekiel. "Today is won by the Immortals." I looked down, trying to hide my grin. *Fox wouldn't die.* Sweet Hecate, we had one more day to save him... "How exciting! The outcome to the

Rebel Cup will be decided on the final day: Torment Thursday." Then she whispered like she was promising a treat, "Torment Thursday is the most dangerous and thrilling in the contest."

My mouth tightened. "With a name like that, I'd never have guessed."

Damelza wrenched away from me, and her expression hardened. "How are you finding this second life? Is it everything that you imagined in those long years trapped as a ghost?"

My breath hitched. *Was that a threat?*

I glanced at the guys who'd saved, welcomed, and loved me. They'd helped me adapt to a world and sensations that could've been strange and frightening, transforming them into the pleasurable and exciting, instead. I'd been dead inside, but now I was alive.

I craved my lovers' pleasure, and their pleasure fed my craving. I'd never imagined that love or pleasure could feel like this, and I never wished it to end.

I smiled, softly. "I'm a Ghost Witch, and I've only just started to live."

Panic skated across Damelza's face, before a cool mask settled in its place. She fiddled with the feather behind her ear. "We shall see." *Witches' tits, that was decidedly a threat.* "But now, the Duchess from the Succubi Court is waiting in my study for Crave. It's time that she inspects you, boy, to make sure that you're pure and reformed."

Bask's eyes widened, and he shook his head. He stumbled backward, but Damelza gripped his arm.

"Please, don't," Bask begged.

I might've been naïve in my first life, but now that'd been knocked right out of me. Bask was *my* incubus. I wouldn't let the succubus who'd broken him and his bond, sending him to this academy, return to inspect and hurt him just like Willoughby's brother had with his letter. I knew now that I needed all my lovers, and it was their joint pleasure that'd brought me to life. At the start, I hadn't understood just how much that was true, but this week, the academy had taught me how close I was to each Rebel.

The lessons might be Transfiguration, Warrior Training, or Divination, but in the end, I'd learned to love.

"Why in sweet Hecate's name would you think us Immortals would let you take our lover?" I raised my brow, as Sleipnir and Fox strode either side of me, and Mist roared in agreement.

"Your second life," Damelza shrugged. "Shall I copy your mother and burn you? What if I cast the spell to trap you in Hecate's tree?"

My heartbeat thundered in my ears, and I became dizzy.

The agony of the flames... Then all alone and dark, dark, dark...

All right, I might've gone more than a little crazy.

But I couldn't go back to that twilight between veils.

Hecate, no...

Damelza gripped Bask, and he struggled to pull away from her. Yet how could I stop Damelza, when her charm controlled my powers?

At that moment, it didn't matter if I lost everything for a second time because I couldn't allow the Duchess to hurt Bask. I'd saved my mage lover from dying today, but the first Rebel whose craving had called to me, summoning me from the portrait had been the one secretly in danger all along.

I wouldn't let him suffer alone, even if it killed me.

With a burst of magic that I pulled from the air, reaching into the waves of nature, I focused on fading, thread by thread, to invisibility. Crow feathers rained down around Damelza, cocooning both Bask and her in darkness. I wrapped my own magic around hers like ivy, gritting my teeth at the lashing static.

I'd never piggybacked on another witches' magic before. Would I burn up, flaring into nothing?

Please, let me not be lost (trapped between worlds), forever...

Damelza dematerialised, dragging me along with her. Her magic pulled me too close to Bask, until I pressed against his hard chest. I bit my lip to hold back the scream, as I was electrocuted by her spell.

Then everything went dark.

TO BE CONTINUED...

Continue Magenta's adventure in **REBEL ACADEMY: CRUSH, Book Two in the WICKEDLY CHARMED series NOW**

https://rosemaryajohns.com

Crush — Book Two in the Wickedly Charmed series — is already written, so you can continue Magenta and her Rebels' adventures! The trilogy is COMPLETE and available to order.

When I attended Christ Church College, Oxford, I was always daydreaming about a hidden magical college. Rebel Academy is the result, and I hope that you love exploring the secret Oxford college. I can't wait for you to discover the battle between the Immortals and Princes in the next book with the seductive temptation of the forbidden!

You're total stars for your recommendations, word of mouth, and reviews because it's how my books reach new readers. I'm truly grateful to you. Even a single line review raises the series' visibility.

I love Rebel Academy. I hope you do too!
Thanks, you're awesome - my Rebel family :)
Rebel here, yeah?
Rosemary A Johns

Thanks for reading **CRAVE.** If you enjoyed reading this book, **please consider leaving a review on Amazon.** Your support is really important to us authors. Plus, I love hearing from my readers.

Thanks, you're awesome!

Sign up to Rosemary A Johns' Rebel Newsletter for two FREE novellas. Also, these special perks: promotions, discounts, and news of hot releases before anyone else.
Become a Rebel here today by joining Rosemary's Rebels Group on Facebook!

REBEL ANGELS

READ THE COMPLETE SERIES NOW!

The vampire's fangs shot out, and I shuddered, as he grazed them along my neck.

"I love you, Violet." Ash's pupils were blown, and his gaze was desperate. "I know that you don't want my protection." He kissed my neck; his large hands stroked up my spine. "But just once…pretend. I'm not a hero but I could be—"

"I don't need to pretend." I caressed Ash's bare chest, and his wings fluttered.

When my fingers moved towards the waistband of Ash's jeans, however, his breath hitched.

"How can you touch me?" He rested his head on my shoulder. "When you know what I am?"

"You're mine." If Lucifer killed us tonight, at least

we died claimed and together. "You're family and the Brigadier. No one can take that away."

I'd show Ash just how much I craved to touch.

I pushed open the button on his jeans, and although his breathing became harsh, he didn't stop me this time.

I slid my hand lower again…

Binge-read the addictive **REBEL ANGELS: THE COMPLETE SERIES** by the USA Today best-selling author Rosemary A Johns TODAY for FREE with Kindle Unlimited.

One-click and get this magical, dark, and sizzling hot vampire and angel Romance now!

The werewolf's lips brushed across mine, and I jolted. "May I caress you…here?"

I nodded, shuddering. He drew circles over my skin, and I heated like he was touching me inside, coiling the pleasure higher.

Lower…please, touch me lower…

When I squirmed to encourage his fingers below the fabric of my ball gown, he chuckled but only continued his maddeningly slow teasing.

"Kiss her neck, prince," the god ordered; his voice was like winding silk.

The incubus' eyes sparkled. He was feeding from the order and my pleasure.

My crimson magic burst out, whilst I experienced each of the men's pulsing, panting pleasure.

"Hold the witch's hands above her head," the god commanded. "She won't be able to stay still for what comes next…"

Escape into the world of bad, bad wolves and wicked witches in REBEL WEREWOLVES and discover Fox's mage cousin…

APPENDIX ONE: ACADEMY MEMBERSHIP

RANDOMS

Confess — Whipping Boy
Curse — Whipping Boy

IMMORTALS

Crow — Prefect
Crave
Sleipnir

PRINCES

Crown — Prefect
Crush

APPENDIX TWO: REBELS

RANDOMS

Fox, mage and shifter, Immortals' whipping boy
(Confess)
Midnight, vampire/Fallen angel and Princes' whipping
boy (Curse)

IMMORTALS

Magenta, Ghost Witch of the House of Crows,
Immortals Prefect (Crow)
Bask, incubus of the Night lineage (Crave)
Sleipnir, Norse god, son of Loki

PRINCES

Prince Lysander, Dark Unseelie Fae, Princes' Prefect
(Crown)
Prince Willoughby, Light Elf (Crush)

WITCHES

Damelza Crow, Head of the House of Crows,
Principal, Professor of Memories
Juni Crow, Damelza's daughter, Tutor of the North
Wing and the Princes, Professor of Divination and
Hunting
Bacchus, Tutor of the West Wing and the Immortals,
Professor of SHP (Spells, Hexes, and Potions)
Henrietta Crow, original Head of the House of Crows
and Magenta's mother, Principal

REBELS WHO SURVIVED AND BECAME PROFESSORS

Ezekiel, Addict Angel, Professor of Warrior Training, Dueling, and Strategy
Prince Ambrose, Seelie Fae, Professor of Shifter and Familiar Training

SUPERNATURALS

Loki, God of Mischief, Sleipnir's father
Andro, clone of Lysander
Serenity, magical Rebel Café
Mist, eight-legged horse created by Magenta, who
reflects Sleipnir's emotions

FAMILIARS

Echo and Flair, Magenta's twin crow familiars
Pet 9, Pocus, Bacchus' cat Halfling familiar

SHIFTERS

Glow, Omega werewolf, Fox's friend in the House of
Jewels
Snow, Omega werewolf in the academy, owned by
Juni Crow
Marcus, Archduke and dragon shifter
Rayn, dragon shifter

APPENDIX FIVE: WITCH COVENS AND COURTS

HOUSE OF CROWS

Magenta Crow, Blessedly/Wickedly Charmed
Henrietta Crow, Magenta's mother and Head of Rebel
Academy
Byron Crow, Magenta's father
Damelza Crow, Principal, Magenta's descendant
Juni Crow, Damezla's daughter

HOUSE OF JEWELS

Fox, mage and shifter
Hartley, Fox's sister

HOUSE OF BLOOD

Lux, Head of the Oxford Covens
Aquilo, mage, Lux's twin

SUCCUBI COURT

The Duchess, broke her bond to Bask and sent him to
academy

FAE COURTS

Prince Titus, Guardian and uncle of Prince Lysander
Prince Lysander, deposed prince
Prince Ambrose, Seelie deposed prince
Prince Ty, Ambrose's 'mongrel' son

ABOUT THE AUTHOR

ROSEMARY A JOHNS is a USA Today bestselling and award-winning fantasy author, music fanatic, and paranormal anti-hero addict. She writes sexy angels and werewolves, savage vampires, and epic battles.

Winner of the Silver Award in the National Wishing Shelf Book Awards. Finalist in the IAN Book of the Year Awards. Runner-up in the Best Fantasy Book of the Year, Reality Bites Book Awards. Honorable Mention in the Readers' Favorite Book Awards.

Shortlisted in the International Rubery Book Awards.

Rosemary is also a traditionally published short story writer. She studied history at Oxford University and ran her own theater company. She's always been a rebel...

Want to read more and stay up to date on Rosemary's newest releases? Sign up for her *VIP* Rebel Newsletter and grab two FREE novellas!

Have you read all the series in the Rebel Verse by Rosemary A Johns?

Rebel Angels
Rebel Academy
Rebel Legends
Rebel Vampires
Rebel Werewolves

Read More from Rosemary A Johns
Website: https://rosemaryajohns.com
BookBub: https://www.bookbub.com/authors/
rosemary-a-johns
Facebook: https://www.
facebook.com/RosemaryAnnJohns
Twitter: @RosemaryAJohns
Become a Rebel here today by joining Rosemary's Rebels Group on Facebook!